Birthday Shoes

Jordan had been riveted by those sexy shoes, unable to tear his eyes away from the sight of them on Janessa's slender, pretty feet.

He'd never gazed at a woman's legs and felt heat streak through him. Yet the sight of Janessa's shapely legs affected him like a lit match tossed into a pool of gasoline. He was going up in flames.

Cupid Wears Combat Boots

The cake split open, and Kayla Delaney emerged from the plaster-frosted pastry with a professional flourish.

She was clad in an oversize khaki shirt that ended in the middle of her sleekly muscled thighs. There were streaks of camouflage on her face and black leather combat boots on her feet.

"I don't know what you wished for," she said in a throaty voice, staring directly into Quinn's eyes. "But I'm what you got."

Heart and Soles

Julia Buchanan slowly turned and peered through the window of the secondhand boutique. Those shoes! Blue and green luminescent platform heels—absolutely outrageous!

"Wow," she whispered. Her heart pounded, her breathing accelerated, and her eyes were blinded by a flash of light. A tempting siren assailed her ears: Buy me, buy me, buy me!

*Don't Miss These Romantic Anthologies
from Avon Books*

Magic Slippers

BARBARA BOSWELL
CAROLE BUCK
CASSIE MILES

AVON BOOKS ◆ NEW YORK

MAGIC SLIPPERS is an original publication of Avon Books. This work, as well as each individual story, has never before appeared in print. This work is a collection of fiction. Any similarity to actual persons or events is purely coincidental.

AVON BOOKS
A division of
The Hearst Corporation
1350 Avenue of the Americas
New York, New York 10019

Copyright © 1996 by Avon Books
Birthday Shoes copyright © 1996 by Barbara Boswell
Cupid Wears Combat Boots copyright © 1996 by Carol Buckland
Heart and Soles copyright © 1996 by Kay Bergstrom

Published by arrangement with the authors
Library of Congress Catalog Card Number: 95-96096
ISBN: 0-380-78370-3

First Avon Books Printing: July 1996

AVON TRADEMARK REG. U.S. PAT. OFF. AND IN OTHER COUNTRIES, MARCA REGISTRADA, HECHO EN U.S.A.

Printed in the U.S.A.

RA 10 9 8 7 6 5 4 3 2 1

Contents

Birthday Shoes

Barbara Boswell

1

The package on the porch had the name *Janessa* printed on it.

Janessa Balint almost tripped over it as she rushed out the front door. She was running late, the bus stop was a block away, and she could already see the bus turning the corner onto Third Avenue. Janessa scooped up the package as she ran and continued her dash down the street.

Please don't let Gracie be the driver today, she prayed to no one in particular; whoever happened to be listening could handle her request. The 81C had two regular bus drivers who alternated driving the seven A.M. Ambridge to Pittsburgh route, and Gracie was the one who showed no mercy. If she saw a potential passenger racing toward the bus stop, Gracie stepped on the accelerator. She followed the transit authority rules to the letter: If a passenger was not standing at the designated bus stop at the designated moment, the bus did not stop. Henry, however, was kind. After five years, he expected

Janessa to be at the stop. If she wasn't there, he actually halted the bus and tooted the horn.

The bus pulled to a stop a minute before Janessa reached it. Had Gracie been behind the wheel, the bus would have already left Janessa standing alone in a whirl of exhaust fumes. But luck was with her. Smiling Henry was driving.

"Thank you for stopping, Henry." Janessa climbed aboard, her gratitude and relief heartfelt. "It's the best birthday present I'll get all day."

"It's your birthday today?" Henry was delighted. "Well, happy birthday to you."

Janessa slid into a seat. This was her twenty-seventh birthday, one she hadn't particularly been looking forward to. Twenty-seven! A sense of disbelief struck her as she gazed out the window at the abandoned steel mill that stood alongside the swiftly moving waters of the Ohio River. She had been taking the 81C into downtown Pittsburgh from her hometown of Ambridge, sixteen miles northwest of the city, every weekday for the past five years.

Five years. It didn't seem possible! She could remember so clearly the very first day she rode this bus; she had been twenty-two, both scared and excited about her first big job in the big city.

Janessa's lips curved. That fateful morning, she'd walked into R. F. Jordan's office just in time to hear him roar, "What idiot typed this?" Actually, that was one of his more benign comments, as she would later come to realize. She hadn't thought she would last the day in that pressure cooker of an office, let alone a whole week. And yet, somehow, she'd spent the past five years there!

"You gotta birthday present?" Shalonda, sitting in the seat behind her, leaned forward and eyed the package on Janessa's lap. Shalonda was one of the regulars on the bus. Sometimes the regulars talked among themselves when they felt awake enough for conversation.

Janessa had been so preoccupied, she'd all but forgotten the package. She looked at it again. Her name was printed on it in block letters, but there was no address or postmark. Meaning it had been hand delivered? Overnight? And by whom? The mystery vaguely piqued her interest.

"Aren't you gonna open it up?" demanded Shalonda. She was wide awake and bored this morning. The package provided a welcome distraction.

Janessa obligingly tore away the brown paper to find a rainbow-colored shoe box. The box bore no name or label, but it was imprinted with an array of dazzling colors that blended into one another on all sides of the box. She lifted the lid and stared at the pair of shoes inside.

They were black suede T-strap pumps with impossibly high, impossibly narrow heels and a thin strap to wind around the top of the ankle. The inside lining was the same dazzling rainbow shades that colored the box.

Shalonda whistled a sigh of approval. "Where'd they come from?"

Janessa lifted the shoes out of the box one by one. "My sister works at a shoe store at the mall called Feet Boutique. She must've bought them there and dropped them off at the house late last night."

Janessa examined the shoes. They were sexier than any shoes she had ever owned and undoubtedly more expensive. She worried about how much Chelsi had spent on them. Chelsi had a collection of maxed-out credit cards, but she was always ready to open another account. Janessa worried about her little sister staggering under the mountain of credit card debt she'd accrued and wished the free spending Chelsi shared her concern.

"Put them on!" urged Shalonda.

Janessa glanced down at her serviceable low heeled black leather lace ups, not at all glamorous but practical and certainly not out-of-date. She thought they went well with her new bright pink suit, an impulse buy from her last paycheck intended to counter all the boring shades of beige, oatmeal, and ecru in her closet.

Janessa eyed the shoes tentatively. "You don't think they look—well—kind of trashy? Uh, I mean, not quite the thing to wear to work?"

"Trashy?" Shalonda was aghast. "Girl, those are suede! They're too expensive to be cheap, if you get what I'm telling you?"

"I get you." Janessa grinned. "Oh well, why not? After all, it is my birthday. If this isn't the day to wear a totally inappropriate, crippling pair of shoes to work, when is?"

Except the shoes were not at all crippling. They were wonderfully comfortable, as if they'd been custom designed for her feet and had already been broken in from years of wear. There was none of that usual new shoe tightness, no cramped toes and aching arches.

Janessa strode off the elevator, still silently marveling at the exquisite feel of the new shoes on her feet. She'd walked the block from the bus stop to the office and should have been limping from the too-high-to-walk-so-far-and-so-fast shoes. Instead, they'd provided the comfort and practicality of well-made running shoes.

"Hey, Janessa!"

She turned to see Sam Zweiler, an accountant with the Edelstein & Allard accounting firm, which shared the floor with Jordan's firm, approaching her. She and Sam had started their jobs on the same day five years ago, meeting in the elevator and striking up a friendship.

"Word's out that Jordan hired a new associate," Sam chortled. "The betting books just opened as to how long this one will last. Care to place a wager?"

"I think the new associate will be fine. Mr. Jordan always hires qualified people," Janessa said tactfully.

"The same answer! I love it!" Sam hooted. "Do you realize you make that same hopeful little speech every time Jordan brings in his latest human sacrifice—ah, I mean, new associate. I could start a betting book on you!"

Janessa tried for a diplomatic smile. She was uncomfortable with the standing jokes about her boss's ever changing staff. She felt disloyal listening, though they were certainly true. R. F. Jordan, a trial and appellate product liabilities lawyer who'd made a national name for himself by defending and winning a series of lawsuits involving manufacturers and litigious plaintiffs, had also made a name for himself as the city's most demanding, impossible boss.

Jordan drove himself hard and expected his entire staff to keep up with him. "If you want to work twenty hours a day, seven days a week, and develop an ulcer within three months, work for Jordan," one of his associates had said years ago.

That particular associate was long gone, but the somewhat hyperbolic quote was repeated to this day. Though his law firm should have been expanding due to Jordan's continuing success in winning cases, he had never taken a partner. He had started the firm himself nine years ago, and no associate had ever lasted long enough to be considered. Janessa remembered one, Greg Sommers, who'd lasted slightly more than two years, a record. But then the young lawyer had announced his departure, pounding on his desk and almost shouting that he needed a life outside the office.

Jordan had been disappointed. "I thought Sommers was made of stronger stuff," he'd said glumly, shaking his head. "In another year, I planned to make him a full partner. He showed such promise, and he had a real flair for the work. What in the hell happened to the guy?"

"I think having his girlfriend get engaged to his best friend pushed him over the edge," Janessa pointed out dryly. "All that time they spent together when Greg was in the office worked against him." When Jordan gave her an uncomprehending stare, she tried another interpretation, one he might more easily understand. "Maybe it was working Christmas day two years in a row that soured him," she suggested.

"Not the Christmas thing again!" Jordan threw up his hands in exasperation and stormed out of her small office.

"Ebenezer Scrooge is alive and well and living in Pittsburgh," Janessa muttered under her breath.

"What did you say?" Jordan paused on the threshold and gave her a hard look.

"You told me never to repeat myself, remember?" she'd automatically countered, and he had strode off, scowling.

Greg Sommers was gone, and the pattern continued. Jordan hired young lawyers, usually recent law school graduates, and worked them into the ground as they tried to keep up with his frenetic, unmatchable personal energy and tireless devotion to the job. His standards were as high as his energy level, and his sharp, biting tongue did not spare anyone who fell short. Secretaries and receptionists joined the dizzying parade of young lawyers who came and left in rapid succession.

Only Jordan's investigators, two retired cops, Sully and Marhefka, stayed because their hours were their own, and they shared an enthusiasm for their work that equaled Jordan's. They were the only two employees of the R. F. Jordan firm who had more seniority than Janessa.

She had arrived five years ago as a nervous young receptionist, forced herself not to quit that same day, and slowly, day by day, had come to know the office routine and to fit Jordan's professional requirements so well that now she ran the office.

Her official position was ambiguous. Sometimes Jordan referred to her as the office manager, and she'd taken on many of those duties, but she also served as a secretary during the unfortunate times when they didn't have one. The associates called her a legal assistant because of her familiarity with Jordan's cases, though all her legal knowledge and training had been gained solely on the job. After years of night and Saturday classes, two years ago she'd finally gotten the degree in psychology from the University of Pittsburgh that she'd so desperately wanted, but being an official college graduate had brought no changes in her job description.

Whatever she was, Jordan paid her well for it. He was known for his generous salaries, which continued to lure employees, although upon leaving they inevitably said something like, "There's more to life than money."

Janessa agreed in principle, but she was not in a position to act on it. She needed the high salary Jordan paid her. Her family depended on it.

"You can't have much of a life without money," she would counter when urging a particularly promising but fleeing associate, secretary, or receptionist to stay.

She currently had high hopes for Debbie, who'd hung in as the receptionist for the past nine months, something of a record. Debbie was twenty, newly married to a parcel post delivery driver, and she dreamed of owning a house. Janessa made frequent references to that dream house during those precarious times when Debbie talked about quitting. Two current associate lawyers, Eric Ackerly and Ned Kolenda, were also becoming veterans with nearly a year's service each, and every Sunday Janessa contemplated lighting votive candles in church in hopes of their continuing tenure.

"It's supposed to hit seventy today." Sam's voice cut into Janessa's reverie. "We're actually supposed to see some sun. That's a novelty, even for April! Want to go to Gus's for some gyros and eat them in Mellon Square?"

Janessa considered it. She hadn't eaten lunch outside since last October, when the sun seemed to have taken a leave of absence from the city, and the temperatures had dropped accordingly.

"That sounds—" she began.

"Janessa, have Sully and Marhefka arrived with those videotapes yet?" The deep, sharp voice sounded behind her, and both Janessa and Sam visibly started.

"I'm on my way to the office, but I haven't been inside yet, Mr. Jordan," Janessa replied, carefully regulating her tone.

She took pains to sound calm but never apologetic, which Jordan would perceive as weak. She knew he viewed weakness with evolutionary minded contempt: Only the strong survive.

"I can see that for myself. You're standing out in the corridor gossiping." Jordan's dark brows were knitted in a scowl. He glanced at his watch and his scowl deepened. "Look at the time!"

Janessa glanced at her own watch, a reliable discount store brand. It was not quite eight-fifteen. The office didn't open officially until nine o'clock, though only Debbie and the secretaries dared to arrive at that hour, which Jordan viewed as hopelessly late. Of course, Janessa's contract specified workday hours from nine to five, but that was good for a laugh.

Sam opened his mouth as if to speak, then quickly closed it. "See you later, Janessa," he called, heading toward the Edelstein & Allard offices.

"*Mr.* Jordan?" Jordan's voice was mocking. "I haven't heard that from you in years."

"I try to keep up appearances for outsiders," Janessa said coolly. "They already think your firm is an asylum, but I like to pretend we're just a normal, everyday office with the usual protocol.''

She turned to the left and walked the short distance to the big wooden door marked with a brass plaque reading *R. F. Jordan, Attorney at Law.* Since Debbie wasn't there to buzz them in, she removed her key to unlock the door.

Jordan beat her to it, inserting his key and turning it. The action brought him directly behind her, so close that they were almost touching. Janessa felt a sudden, suffocating heat wave sweep through her. It seemed to originate from the tips of her toes, ensconced in her exquisitely comfortable new shoes, and spread upward to the roots of her hair, lingering hotly in several erogenous zones. She pushed open the door and practically raced inside.

In her haste she collided with the edge of Debbie's desk, slamming her hip into it. A reflexive gasp of pain escaped her throat.

''Are you all right?'' Jordan was behind her again.

Janessa moved quickly away, her action instinctively self-defensive. Every day when she first saw Jordan, she was slightly taken aback by how tall he was, how muscular. His hair always seemed thicker and darker than she remembered. Since he'd turned thirty-six last month, she'd noticed the first faint sprinklings of silver along his temples. His blue eyes, intent and alert and piercing under those black brows, never failed to unnerve her.

She knew from long experience that as the day wore on the odd awareness that prickled through her at her initial early morning Jordan sightings invariably lessened. He was like an allergen, Janessa had decided, and the first sight of him each day acted as a kind of allergy shot. One needed gradual but careful exposure to bolster endurance.

She walked into her small office and pulled open the pleated window shade. A stream of early morning sunlight filtered into the office, a pleasant change from the normal dreary gray that constituted a typical Pittsburgh day from fall through spring.

Safely alone in her office, she rubbed her hip, which was throbbing.

"You'll have a spectacularly colored bruise there by tonight." Jordan's deep voice seemed to fill the small room.

Janessa jumped. He was standing in the doorway, staring at her.

"You bruise easily." Jordan frowned. "I remember that time you fell off a bicycle. You had bruises from your ankles to your knees and all over your arms. God, you were a mess! I take it you've stayed away from bicycles since you haven't been black and blue and yellow and green and purple for quite some time."

Janessa remembered the accident. She'd also had bruises he hadn't seen, extending from her neck to her thighs, and her ribs had ached for weeks. "I still ride my bike," she said wryly. "I just try to keep away from cars."

"You were hit by a car?" Jordan appeared nonplussed.

She nodded, switching on her computer. She didn't like to recall that accident, which had happened nearly two years ago. A car had cruised right through a stop sign and into her. Fortunately, the driver had been going well below the speed limit, and she'd suffered only bruises and superficial cuts, though they'd certainly been painful.

"You never mentioned *how* you happened to fall off that bike, just that you did," Jordan accused. "You were hit by a car? Why, you could've been killed!"

"Well, I wasn't." Janessa guessed the notion retroactively displeased him. Replacing her would have been inconvenient.

"Did you sue? Of course not, I would've known about a suit. You never asked me for information about a personal injury attorney." He seemed miffed at the omission. "Did you consult one or—"

"I didn't consult a lawyer. I went to the hospital, was X-rayed and pronounced all right, and that was the end of it."

"It shouldn't have been. I saw those bruises. I saw how slowly and painfully you moved for days afterward. You definitely deserved pain and suffering compensation."

"Interesting you should say that," Janessa said dryly. "Because when I asked to take a few days off back then—because I was moving so 'slowly and painfully'—you said absolutely no way because we were in the middle of the Collin Candy Company trial, and my absence from the office would cause a debacle."

Jordan had the grace to look chagrined. Momentarily. "Well, it's true, your absence would have caused a debacle in the office. But you should have told me about the accident, Janessa. We could have gone up to Lewis Denny on the twelfth floor and gotten a settlement for—"

"I was fine. I am fine. I didn't want a settlement and I didn't want a lawyer. Poor old Mr. Kozalowski was distraught that he'd hit me. I don't even know why we're talking about this, Jordan. The accident happened two years ago."

"That doesn't matter, as you well know. The statute of limitations—"

"—doesn't matter to me. The incident is over, and if you keep harping on it, I'll see Lewis Denny about filing a personal injury suit against *you* for practically shoving me into Debbie's desk."

Jordan's lips twitched slightly. "That would be an interesting case, considering I was three feet behind you."

"I was only kidding, Jordan." She shifted uneasily. Jordan was staring at her with the intensity he normally reserved for trial briefs and sworn affidavits. She sought to divert him. "I don't hear anyone in the office. Are we the first ones here? I—uh—I'll go make the coffee."

"Ackerly and Kolenda are in, but the swill they make is undrinkable, almost as bad as mine." Jordan grimaced. "The new associate arrives today. Graduated from law school in December. A guy named Valerian Valstock. I'll be frank, my hopes aren't very high for this one. After what's-his-name quit last month, I needed someone right away to do research on the Winthrop appeal."

Jordan shook his head, his expression revealing both disappointment and disapproval. "The field of candidates was narrower than I've ever seen. I don't understand it. Maybe the time of year?"

Maybe your Simon Legree reputation? Janessa

thought but didn't say aloud. She cast him a covert glance, wishing he would leave. He was still standing in the doorway, blocking it. Unless he moved, she would have to pass him to get to the conference room, where the coffeepot was located.

And the thought of being near him suddenly made her dizzy.

Startled, she raised her eyes. They met Jordan's, and she immediately looked away, her heartbeat roaring in her ears. What was the matter with her today?

PMS, perhaps? Her mother and sisters claimed to suffer from the monthly affliction, but Janessa had never been affected. Unless she'd been stricken with her first symptoms today? The timing was right, and how else to explain her skittish nerves, her racing pulse, the odd lump that had formed in her throat?

She had to swallow around it. Out of the corner of her eye, she saw Jordan watching her, saw his deep blue eyes sweep assessingly down her legs and linger there. She glanced down at her new shoes and was momentarily shocked to see how outrageously provocative they were.

Janessa was suddenly, terribly appalled. She should have known not to wear those shoes to work. Chelsi had chosen them! Chelsi was nineteen years old, wore three-inch jewel-studded fake nails, and dyed her hair to match whatever holiday season it happened to be. No, Chelsi Balint was hardly a source of appropriate office wear!

Whatever had possessed her to exchange her eminently suitable shoes for these eminently unsuitable ones? Never mind that these new shoes felt as if they'd been custom designed for her, and wearing them seemed as natural as walking barefoot. As soon as Jordan left, she vowed to change back to her proper office pair.

But Jordan showed no inclination to leave. Janessa sank onto her desk chair and stared blindly at the computer screen. She tried to think of some instructions to give it, but her mind was as blank as the screen.

"Have you—" Jordan cleared his throat. "Gained weight?"

"What?" Janessa flushed as pink as her suit.

"You just look—different somehow. More—" He coughed again. "Rounded."

"Oh!" Janessa thought of the white chocolate chicken and the five caramel marshmallow chocolate eggs in the Easter basket her mother had insisted on giving her. She'd devoured the candy within days and perhaps had gained a pound or two—but that had been two weeks ago!

Surely, the results of her indulgence weren't visible! All her clothes still fit, not a thing in her wardrobe was too tight. But maybe she looked a bit hefty anyway? Janessa fumed. How typical of Jordan to bluntly declare his opinion without bothering with tact or diplomacy.

"I meant that as a compliment," Jordan said at last. There was an uncharacteristic uncertainty in his voice, as if he'd gleaned he might have committed a faux pas.

Janessa decided to assure him that he had. "Telling a woman—or anyone for that matter— that you think she's getting fat is not a compliment, Jordan."

"I didn't say that. I didn't mean that," he protested.

"Well, that's what it sounded like." Janessa glanced down at her suit jacket. Perhaps its short length was unflattering, giving the illusion of extra pounds?

"Aren't you going to make the coffee?" Jordan's voice seemed to ring in her ears.

"I have a few things to do first," she said tightly. "When I'm ready, I'll make the coffee."

He stayed there for a while longer. Though she kept her eyes glued to the computer screen, Janessa knew exactly how long he stood there, staring at her. Every nerve in her body tingled with awareness. She was so hypervigilant, she could almost feel him inhaling and exhaling.

When he finally left, she went limp as the tension drained from her. She forgot all about changing her shoes and walked to the conference room, her knees wobbly. The two associates, Kolenda and Ackerly, both around thirty, were staring gloomily at the coffeepot.

"We're out of coffee." Ackerly appeared bereft.

"How could this happen?" Kolenda moaned. "How can we get through the day without it?"

"Not to worry." Janessa smiled. "I always keep an extra supply in my office. I have enough to tide us over for this morning and I'll go shopping for more later, on my lunch—"

"—ten-minute break. Let's not delude ourselves and call it a lunch *hour*." But Ackerly was smiling now. "We're getting coffee! Janessa, you're a savior, a goddess!" he added exuberantly.

"And you look damn hot today," Kolenda chimed in. "Those are happenin' shoes, babe." He pretended to look abashed. "Uh-oh, would that be deemed sexual harassment these days?"

"Depends on who's saying it to whom." Janessa glanced down at her shoes. Her birthday shoes. She felt an anticipatory excitement, the kind she no longer associated with birthdays. Or with anything else, really. For quite some time, there'd been a decided lack of excitement and anticipation in her predictable, industrious life.

Janessa smiled. "Since it's you, Ned, I'll accept it as a compliment."

"What if it had been me?" Jordan suddenly appeared in the conference room.

Janessa, Kolenda, and Ackerly stopped smiling, stopped laughing, stopped talking at all, and stared at their boss in stunned silence.

Kolenda was the first to speak. "Er, was that a rhetorical question, sir?"

"Are you referring to the ground-breaking precedent set in *Myers v. Darroby?*" asked Ackerly, in a schoolboy-to-the-visiting-principal tone of voice.

Jordan's eyes turned to slits. "It was a joke," he growled.

2

Jordan surveyed his trio of gawking employees. They couldn't have looked more incredulous if he'd suddenly announced he was the secret love child of J. F. K. and Marilyn Monroe.

"A joke," Kolenda recovered enough to repeat. He and Ackerly managed the required laughter, strained though it was.

Janessa didn't even try. "If you'll excuse me, I'll get the coffee from my office."

Jordan stared at her. He was confused and didn't know how to deal with it. Confusion was not a natural state for him. Even more inexplicable, the source of his unacceptable, unheard of befuddlement seemed to be Janessa Balint.

Which was manifestly absurd! Jordan countered the charge with the passion of a defense attorney refuting the prosecution's opening statement.

Janessa was as familiar to him as the wallpaper in his office, as the view from his window. She'd been working for him for so long, he couldn't remember a time when she hadn't. But today, somehow, it was as if he had never seen her before—or perhaps as if he were seeing her for the first time. She looked different today, as he had tried so disastrously to tell her earlier.

He studied her more closely. Had he been

asked by the police to provide a description of her, he would have used the words *petite*, *small boned*, and *slender*. He never would have thought to add curvaceous to that list. Not until this morning.

This morning he had suddenly noticed how round and full her breasts were. And once he had noticed, he had been unable to tear his eyes away. Like a prurient adolescent, he'd stood in the doorway of her office, gaping at the way her breasts rose and fell under the soft pink suit jacket.

He'd found himself wondering what she wore underneath her jacket, which led to thoughts of her wearing nothing at all. Were her breasts the same creamy ivory as her complexion? And what about the size and shape and color of her nipples?

He wanted to see them. To touch them. To cup her breasts in his hands and feel their soft weight, to knead their rounded fullness.

Then as now, that urge sent frissons of heat rippling through him. This time, however, he restrained himself from speaking. The last time he'd almost blurted out his lascivious thoughts. To his horror, "more rounded" had actually slipped out. But Janessa had misinterpreted; she thought he'd said she was getting fat.

Jordan groaned silently. In court he was a master orator, controlled, calculating, every word chosen and measured for its impact. Out of court even his seemingly "spontaneous" outbursts were actually planned for maximum effect.

When was the last time he'd babbled like an inept fool? Not until this morning in Janessa's office, when his mind and tongue seemed to have been commandeered by some alien force.

He stepped aside to let Janessa pass. Though she usually stood a full foot shorter than his own six feet three inches, today she seemed—taller? His eyes darted to her shoes; he'd first noticed them earlier in the corridor.

Noticed? That was a paltry statement. He'd been riveted by those shoes, unable to tear his eyes away from the sight of them on her slender, pretty feet. The shoes had provided her with at least three inches of additional height and made her shapely legs even shapelier.

Once again, his thoughts rocked him. He considered himself a cerebral sort, more interested in brains than looks. Certainly, he had never gazed at a woman's legs and felt heat streak through him. Yet the sight of Janessa's legs affected him like a lit match tossed into a pool of gasoline. He felt as if he were going up in flames.

He stared at the top of her head as she passed by, near enough to feel her body heat, though they hadn't touched. He wanted to rectify that. He wanted to reach out and grab her, to pull her to him and crush her soft, curvy body against him.

The purely primal urge astonished him. He had always channeled his aggression into the courtroom, taking on plaintiffs who tried to win big money by bringing suits against the makers of products they claimed were responsible for injuries or injustices that had occurred, whether real or alleged.

But this reckless urgency that suddenly consumed him had nothing to do with the courtroom, and certainly nothing to do with products and liability judgments. This was an atavistic male urge to snatch the woman of his choice and carry her off, away from all the other men who joked and laughed and talked with her.

The light, spicy scent of her perfume filled his nostrils. Jordan felt an overpowering rush and stifled a moan. The aroma enticed him. He wanted to pull her back so he could smell it again; he wanted to bury his face against the curve of her neck and inhale until he . . .

Jordan abruptly pulled himself together. It was easier to do since Janessa had disappeared from sight.

Ackerly and Kolenda began to discuss the case they intended to bring to trial next month: A local contractor had not received a shipment of gravel, and rather than adjust his schedule, he had substituted kitty litter and mixed it to make concrete to pave the driveways in a new housing development north of the city. When the driveways began to split and crack, the home owners sued the contractor, who in turn brought suit against the kitty litter manufacturers. The kitty litter people had hired Jordan to defend them.

Jordan was looking forward to the trial. He'd spent much of the last three years doing appeals—working to overturn the trial verdicts against his clients—and had had such astonishing success that his entire practice could have been devoted to the appellate level. But appellate practice could be dry and dull, because much of it involved pointing out lapses in procedure and questionable methodology to a panel of judges. Missing were the juries and the live drama and the elements of logic and chance. Jordan thrived on the challenge of convincing a jury that the facts of a case should determine the result and not the jury's emotional reaction to the plaintiff.

Appellate work also required him to spend

much of his time on the road in the state capitals where the courts were located. Preparation for this new trial had allowed him to spend more time in his Pittsburgh office.

His eyes narrowed as Janessa reappeared carrying the emergency stash of coffee. He studied the way her thick, dark hair fell around her face, perfectly framing it. She had high cheekbones and a wide, generous mouth and she smiled often. Though not often at him.

The realization rankled. Janessa seemed to have a smile or laugh or friendly word for everybody but R. F. Jordan. Oh, she was invariably polite to him—except when she was not! She treated him differently than any other person who worked for him, said things he never would accept from anyone else. When she flashed those big dark eyes of hers at him or glanced at him from beneath her long black lashes . . .

Jordan was having difficulty swallowing. Janessa was looking at him now, her dark brown eyes—almost the shade of black coffee—alive with intelligence and challenge. He watched her approach him and suddenly felt as if he were in a free-fall, with nothing solid beneath him and nothing to steady him.

A fiery arousal tightened within him, spreading through his body, making him hard and hot. He had to sit down before his condition became apparent to Ackerly and Kolenda, or worse yet, to Janessa herself!

He couldn't imagine what her reaction would be if she knew the thoughts he was having about her—and what effect those thoughts were having on him. There was nothing sexual between him and Janessa, there never had been. He viewed her as competent and reliable and patient. He respected her, yes, but he didn't want her!

Unfortunately, his body wasn't buying his mind's declaration. Nothing sexual between them? These feelings, which seemed to have taken possession of him, were very sexual indeed.

Janessa slowed her pace to a stroll. Jordan watched the swivel of her hips as she glided by him. The bright pink suit she was wearing flattered her creamy complexion, casting her in an almost rosy glow. Funny, he had never noticed her clothes before, never actually noticed her figure either, but she had an alluring one, round, firm breasts; a narrow waist; and gently flaring hips.

Once again he found himself staring at her shoes, which accentuated her legs. Good Lord, was he developing a shoe fetish? Jordan rubbed his temples and closed his eyes. Bad move. For in his mind's eye he could see Janessa's legs, slim and bare, wrapped around him. And in his fantasy, she was wearing those eye-popping shoes.

His breath caught in his throat. It was as if he were under some kind of spell! That nonsensical thought jarred him into action. Roderick Farrell Jordan's exact, ordered mind was not given to nonsense. He had never had a nonsensical thought in his life, and he wasn't about to indulge in one now.

"Let me know the minute Sully and Marhefka arrive," he ordered, his stenorian tones echoing through the conference room. "I want to view those videotapes immediately."

"I'll buzz you the very second they set foot in the door," Janessa promised.

Jordan shot her a glance. There was definitely a mocking gleam in her eye. But instead of being annoyed, he felt challenged. And even more aroused.

Shaken to his normally impenetrable, undistractable core, Jordan fled from the conference room to the sanctuary of his own office.

Ackerly and Kolenda glanced at each other and shrugged.

"I can't believe he actually tried to make a joke," marveled Ackerly.

"I can't believe we stood here gaping like dumbfounded idiots when he did." Kolenda groaned.

"Jordan isn't exactly known for his sense of humor," Janessa attempted to console them. Though it wasn't entirely true. There had been times in the past when he had made some droll comment or picked up on one of her own. Odd, how she had never really thought of that until now. And then she recalled the joke Jordan had tried to make this morning. It had to do with sexual harassment—of her!

The very notion of sexual *anything* in relation to Jordan made her toes curl inside her new suede shoes. She felt a surge of blood to her cheeks, and every pulse point began to throb.

"Did you know we're getting a new associate today?" Janessa asked as she made the coffee, deliberately engaging the two lawyers in conversation to divert herself from her own thoughts. "Quigley's replacement."

"I saw Quigley at the City Club the other day," said Ackerly. "He looked terrific now that he's shed his Jordan house pallor and stopped drinking Maalox by the quart. He's still looking for a job but says he's never been happier."

"Quigley couldn't take the pressure," observed Kolenda. "Fighter pilots call it the right stuff; Jordan calls it the necessary stamina. Whatever, poor Quigley didn't have it."

"Necessary stamina," Janessa echoed dryly. "Number one on Jordan's list of virtues. The four cardinal virtues don't count a bit unless you possess the necessary stamina."

"Well, I don't think I do," Ackerly confided. "I'm seriously thinking of quitting. My life is starting to disintegrate under these killer working hours. My little girl doesn't even remember who I am, and I'm afraid my wife is starting not to want to remember me."

"You can't quit!" Kolenda exclaimed, sounding panicked. "That'll leave me with Jordan and a disoriented new associate. Every new associate who comes here is disoriented the first few weeks. It's kind of like being taken hostage. Ackerly, have mercy. *I'll* be the one drinking *gallons* of Maalox if you leave! And then I'll have to go too and I can't afford to, not with my car payments."

"You have to stay, Eric," seconded Janessa. "You're one of the best associates we've ever had. You and Ned are an excellent team, and I should know. I've seen plenty come and go."

"Thanks for the kind words." Ackerly smiled ruefully. "Do you mind if I put you down as a reference for my next position?"

"Sully and Marhefka just got off the elevator, Janessa." Debbie's voice came over the intercom in Janessa's office. "Will you tell him?"

Debbie always referred to their boss by pronoun and tried to keep their contact to the absolute minimum. That meant using Janessa as a go-between, but she considered that a small price to pay to keep Debbie at the receptionist's desk. Debbie was dependable and smart, and Janessa couldn't face the task of training yet another receptionist.

"Of course," Janessa reassured her and buzzed Jordan to inform him of the pair's arrival.

"Tell them I'll meet them in the conference room as soon as I can," Jordan replied tersely. "Make sure they have coffee and whatever else they want."

Though Jordan catered to no one, he came close with Sully and Marhefka. They were top-flight investigators, and their work had been the deciding factor in a number of his cases.

Well aware of their value to Jordan, Janessa led the two men into the conference room, offering coffee and whatever else they wanted. They wanted jelly doughnuts from the bakery three blocks away, and Janessa sent Debbie to fetch a dozen.

"How's that brother of yours?" Marhefka asked Janessa. He'd met her brother, Mike, a few times, when Mike had stopped by the office to go to lunch with Janessa. "Still wants to cut up brains?" He laughed at his own joke. Marhefka found Mike's ambition to become a neurosurgeon hilarious. He mentioned it whenever he saw Janessa and had a hearty laugh each time.

Janessa always smiled, though she didn't quite get the joke. Twenty-four-year-old Mike was in

his second year at Pitt Medical School and remained at the top of his class. Janessa had no
doubt he would be a brilliant neurosurgeon, and
she was helping him with his tuition and expenses.

"Mike's studying anatomy and physiology
and is working on a human corpse this semester," she told Marhefka, knowing he would rel-
ish the information.

He launched into a convoluted tale involving
the city morgue and the supply of corpses, dating back to his days on the force.

Debbie arrived with the doughnuts shortly before Jordan appeared in the conference room.

"I'm sorry to keep you guys waiting." Jordan
rarely apologized, but when he did, it was usually to Sully and Marhefka. "I was with my new
associate, and I'm already having regrets about
hiring him. I don't understand how he made
it through elementary school, let alone law
school!"

"That bad, huh?" Sully was sympathetic.

"Moronic," Jordan affirmed. "Monosyllabic.
Maybe I should have you two investigate his credentials. Judging from his performance this
morning, he must have fabricated them."

Janessa was just as certain the hapless new-
comer was merely suffering from an acute state
of Jordan-induced panic. Listening to Jordan
rattle off demands while taking in the scope of
his incredible, photographic memory and detailed knowledge of law minutiae sometimes cat-
apulted new associates into a trancelike state.

She made a mental note to visit the new associate and offer some encouraging words, and

to try to keep the less encouraging Kolenda, Ackerly, and Debbie from getting to the poor guy first.

She moved to leave the conference room.

"You'll want to stay for this, Janessa," Jordan said. He pulled back a chair at the table and held it out.

She cast him a quick glance. One might almost think he was making a request, but Jordan did not request, he ordered. She started toward another chair, expecting him to sit in the one he'd pulled out.

"Sit here." He nodded to the chair he was holding.

Janessa stopped in her tracks. *He was offering the chair to her*? Her astonishment, reflected all over her face, must have been unmistakable.

"Isn't this standard procedure?" Jordan asked, his blue eyes mocking. "I seem to recall my mother pounding a few basic rules into my head, and seating a lady was one of them."

His mention of his mother floored Janessa almost as much as his reference to herself as a "lady." She knew she was a piece of office equipment to Jordan, like a computer or a pencil. And while she knew Jordan had a mother—she'd been buying Christmas, birthday, and Mother's Day gifts for the woman for years with Jordan's credit cards—he had never brought her up in casual conversation.

What a peculiar day this was turning into! Utterly strange. As strange as Jordan and his mom's idea of holiday gift giving. Upon each occasion requiring a gift, Mrs. Jordan called Janessa from her home in Indiana with the name of a catalog and the number of the item she wanted in it, and Janessa placed the order, giving Mrs. Jordan's name and address. Presumably, the gift was delivered to Mrs. Jordan, who presumably was pleased with her own request. Mother and son did not spend holidays together; Jordan worked during them all.

Their relationship seemed impersonal to Janessa at best and cold at worst, and she sometimes wondered about the why and the how of it. It didn't take a degree in psychology to connect Jordan's avoidance of "the Christmas thing" with his lack of family ties. But when one was working during the holidays, as she so often had, irritation often triumphed over understanding.

Now she felt the strongest, strangest urge to understand. To know the private Jordan who lived inside the workaholic, peripatetic presence he'd created for himself. Until this moment, she hadn't suspected he possessed an inner self, but as she blindly stared at her smooth suede shoes, she suddenly knew he did. The insight was unexpected and unnerving. She sat down on the chair, too bemused to speak.

Jordan took the seat beside her.

Marhefka set up the tape while his partner helped himself to another jelly doughnut, his third.

"We got 'er cold with this tape, boss!" Sully exulted.

Jordan briefly outlined the details of the case. Vera Sozick, a sixty-one-year-old woman who had fallen on what her attorney claimed was the too slick, too slippery floor of a Super Save supermarket, had successfully sued not only Super Save but also the Rider Tile Company, manufacturer of the tiles on the supermarket floor. Mrs.

Sozick claimed a back injury that caused her chronic pain and was so debilitating, she was unable to return to work or even to leave her house, except for visits to her doctor. After a jury trial, both the supermarket and the tile company were found negligent and ordered to pay astonishingly high six-figure sums as compensation to poor, incapacitated Mrs. Sozick.

The Rider Tile Company had appealed the verdict, hiring R. F. Jordan to handle the case.

"While I was researching similar liability cases in other states," Jordan continued, "I found that a certain Vera Sozick had taken seven separate falls in seven separate supermarkets in seven separate states. She'd sued and collected in every case. None of the stores appealed, just as Super Save didn't." Jordan smiled a distinctly crocodilian smile. "But the eighth time she *fell*, Mrs. Sozick decided to collect twice and filed suit against the tile company for the first time."

"She broke the first commandment in negligence suits—don't get too greedy," Janessa quoted Jordan's favorite maxim.

"That's right." He grinned at her as if she were his star pupil.

Janessa was suddenly breathless. The intimacy of that shared moment caused a flame of delight to rocket through her.

"That's right," echoed Sully. "Enter me and Hef. The boss gave us orders to stick to the broad like gum on a shoe. Shouldn't be much of a job, huh? Poor old soul claimed she never left her house except to go to the doctor's for his aid in alleviating her excruciating pain."

"Wrong!" Marhefka chimed in jubilantly. He hit the lights, and the room was plunged into darkness as the videotape rolled. "Here we have the severely disabled Mrs. Sozik boarding the bus for a trip to Branson, Missouri."

A sturdy, healthy looking woman with permed champagne blond hair climbed aboard a tour bus, moving with vigorous ease. Other scenes found her displaying a powerful swing while playing miniature golf, swimming laps in the motel pool, and pushing her way to the front of the line in the countless country western theaters that lined the strip in Branson, each featuring a big-name star and promising a dazzling show. During one of the shows, Mrs. Sozick was taped volunteering to go onstage for a lively dance with the theater's star.

The tape ended.

"She looked remarkably pain-free," Janessa remarked.

"Yeah, Vera gets around real well for somebody who's incapacitated. She's on the go around the clock." Marhefka chuckled. "Sully and me had a hard time keeping up with her."

"You nailed her. Good work." Jordan stood up and shook hands with each investigator.

"Are you going to tell Mrs. Sozick and her attorney about the tape or will you take the case to court and unveil it at the trial?" Janessa asked.

"It'll depend on Rider Tile," Jordan replied. "I'll give the company president a call and lay out his options. Rider will want to contact her attorney, I'm sure. And if they take my advice, they'll also contact the police. This is a textbook case of fraud."

"Vera could end up in the slammer," agreed Marhefka. "Though I've learned that the Veras of the world are such good cons that they generally talk their way out of prison time too. She'll probably be dancing again in Branson this time next year."

"We liked Branson a lot. Caught all the shows that Vera did. Wouldn't mind another case that takes us down that way." Sully was hopeful.

"I'll keep that in mind," Jordan said dryly.

"Great! Thanks!" Sully enthused, completely missing the droll note in Jordan's tone.

Janessa didn't. The concept of Jordan choosing a time-consuming, brain-busting appellate case strictly to provide Sully and Marhefka with a free trip to Branson was nothing less than comical. When Jordan glanced at her, she was grinning.

He smiled back. Janessa's heart seemed to stop beating, then resume at triple speed.

Of course, she had always been aware of Jordan's striking good looks. She wasn't blind, and the number of women in and out of his life confirmed the opposite sex's attraction to him. But Janessa had prided herself on her own immunity to his sexual appeal. She didn't gaze into his deep blue eyes and lose her train of thought. She didn't let her eyes linger on the hard, sensual curve of his lips and wonder what his mouth would taste like. Not her!

Not until this moment.

Janessa's mouth was dry. It couldn't be happening, she thought, panic surging through her. She couldn't have suddenly developed a crush on her boss, not after five years! Immunity didn't fade; it grew stronger over the years, didn't it?

Janessa dragged her eyes away from Jordan. She clearly needed a booster shot against this attraction to him, and fast.

"Say, do you want the rest of these doughnuts?" Marhefka eyed the box longingly.

"Please, take them with you," Janessa urged.

Her mind was churning; she was desperate. She had to work fast to quell the stupid stirrings of this ridiculous infatuation! Deliberately, she conjured up Jordan's most recent offense, which was easy to do since he'd committed it such a short while ago. "Everybody around here is currently crusading against the evils of sugar, so they won't touch doughnuts. And, of course, since I'm getting fat, I don't want them around."

"Fat? You? No way, kid." Sully gave her an assessing once-over. "In fact, I'd say you ought to put on a few pounds."

"According to Jordan, I already have. He said I looked fat," Janessa said reproachfully. She savored the accompanying flash of resentment. This crush was going to be easy to crush.

"I did not say that!" Jordan felt an unfamiliar flush stain his neck and surge to his forehead.

"Well, don't listen to the guy, honey, you look terrific," Marhefka said consolingly. He turned to Jordan. "Hey, boss, have you lost it or what? Even if she'd gained three hundred pounds, you don't go around saying so!"

The two investigators filed from the conference room, the box of doughnuts tucked under Marhefka's arm. Janessa followed, engaging them in conversation, leaving Jordan behind.

He stood at the end of the corridor, watching Janessa escort the two men to the outer office door. He watched as she stopped by Debbie's desk and paused to smile and chat with the young receptionist.

Janessa was positively gifted when it came to dealing with people; the insight struck Jordan out of the blue. Oh, he'd been aware that every-body liked her, of course, but he'd always taken her patience and good-natured calm for granted. Standing here observing her, he acknowledged the worth of her gregarious, soothing warmth. He felt a wholly unexpected surge of admiration and appreciation for her. Her ability to relate to others equaled his own ability to retain details and organize facts. A classic case of the extrovert and the introvert, Jordan decided, grimacing wryly, with him in the quiet loner role.

Janessa was his opposite. People were drawn to her. She was the constant of his revolving-door office staff, the sun around whom the others orbited. She talked, laughed, and lunched with all those in her circle, including her co-workers, past and present. Except for him, of course. He wasn't her coworker, he was her boss. As such, he wasn't granted entry into her charmed circle.

His reverie was abruptly interrupted when one of the secretaries scurried by him like a mouse hoping to streak unnoticed past a preoccupied cat. Jordan frowned. Farther down the corridor, Janessa greeted the secretary with her customary expressions of interest.

When the young woman nervously showed Ja-nessa a paper—probably containing some costly, careless, and thoroughly inane error, Jordan thought grumpily—Janessa merely nodded and took the secretary and the paper into her small office.

Jordan went into his own office, willing his mind to focus on the Sozick case. Surprisingly, disturbingly, the work took far longer than it should have. His thoughts kept drifting to Janessa Balint, who seemed infinitely more compelling than the Rider Tile Company.

If he were in court, his lack of attention could result in a loss or a mistrial. That sobering admonishment shocked his brain back into robotic concentration.

3

Janessa had not wanted a birthday party and had said so many times in the weeks preceding her birthday. Unfortunately, no one in her family believed her.

"I know you said no party this year. You might think it's too much work for us, but it's no bother, darling," her grandmother said, setting the homemade chocolate sheet cake in front of Janessa. "You know this family. We just love celebrating birthdays."

Janessa flashed her brightest smile. Gram had determinedly misinterpreted her "no party" request and invited the entire clan.

"After all, you're only twenty-seven once," Great-Aunt Rita said. She made the same remark every year on everybody's birthday, altering the number to fit the specific person and age.

Janessa remembered Great-Aunt Rita telling her that she was only nine once, only sixteen once, only twenty-two once. That had been the year she'd gone to work for Jordan. . . .

The thought popped unbidden and unwelcome into Janessa's mind. Anxiety fluttered through her. What would it take to successfully expunge her boss from her brain? Today she had managed to link whatever she was doing, saying, or thinking to Jordan, a definite cause for alarm.

"I can't believe Janessa is twenty-seven," Janessa's mother, Peggy Ann, said with a wistful sigh. "When I was twenty-seven, I already had four children."

It wasn't easy to keep her brightest smile firmly in place when she wanted to groan aloud, but Janessa did it. She kept on smiling when Uncle Pete, her mom's younger brother, followed up with the remark he'd been making to her at every family gathering since she'd turned twenty.

"So when are you gonna get married, Janess?" Uncle Pete demanded jovially. "You're not getting any younger, y'know. Time to find yourself a man and settle down."

"Janessa can have any guy she wants," Cousin Gina piped up. Gina, unmarried at twenty-four, invariably came to Janessa's defense. "Why should she limit herself to one man? Stay single and have fun, Janess. I know I'm going to, for years and years."

The small dining room of Gram's house—the other side of the duplex she shared with Janessa's family—was decorated with crepe paper streamers and balloons. Multicolored cardboard letters spelling out Happy Birthday were strung across the window.

Janessa glanced around at everybody packed into the room. There were her grandmother and her mother, both widowed at young ages by the tragic deaths of their husbands in work-related accidents. Also present were her many aunts and uncles and great-aunts and great-uncles, and cousins of all ages.

The only ones missing from the festivities were her brother, Mike, who had had to stay in Pittsburgh to study for an exam, and her two younger sisters, Chelsi and Mallory. Both were working tonight, Chelsi at the Feet Boutique and Mallory at the Lady Godiva shop, where she was employed as a salesperson.

Fortunately, only a few members of the family's older generation had ever visited Lady Godiva, because along with expensive sexy lingerie, the shop also carried a variety of what was labeled erotica. "Sex toys for consenting adults," as twenty-two-year-old Mallory described her merchandise, though not to Mom or to Gram or to any of the aunts and uncles.

Janessa eyed the wrapped present marked TO JANESSA FROM MALLORY with trepidation. The shoes from Chelsi—which she was still wearing because they were so remarkably comfortable that she didn't want to take them off—had evoked a comment from every relative over the age of thirty-five. A sex toy—or even racy lingerie—from Mallory would bring down the house.

The whole family sang "Happy Birthday" and applauded and cheered when Janessa blew out all twenty-seven candles.

"There are millions of candles," little Brittany, a five-year-old cousin, exclaimed, and everybody laughed.

Janessa winced. In three short years, Gram would be putting thirty candles on her birthday cake. What a conflagration that would be!

Thoughts of that not-too-distant birthday swamped her. Would she still be unmarried, living next door with Mom and her younger sisters, taking the bus into Pittsburgh every morning to her job at Jordan's firm?

It seemed likely. Depressingly likely. How could things change? She needed the higher-than-average salary Jordan paid her; she was the major contributor to the family paycheck pool for bills and expenses.

While her mother and grandmother began to cut and distribute the cake, Janessa fought off an attack of the birthday blues. Odd how lonely one could feel, even in a roomful of well meaning relatives.

"Janessa, darling, will you take Ga a piece of cake and some ice cream?" Gram asked, handing her a dessert plate.

"Of course," Janessa agreed. She welcomed a temporary reprieve from all the gaiety.

Ga, so nicknamed by a long-grown grandchild who'd tried and failed to say "grandmother" in either English or Hungarian, was the matriarch of the family, Janessa's ninety-four-year-old great-grandmother who lived here in the duplex with her daughter, Janessa's grandmother.

Following a stroke eight years ago, Ga had reverted to speaking exclusively in her native Hungarian, and only the older members of the family, her daughter and sons, could communicate with her now. None of the later two generations had learned Hungarian, except for a few words.

Janessa carried the dessert and a cup of coffee upstairs to her great-grandmother's bedroom.

The old woman, dressed all in black, was sitting in a big upholstered armchair by the window, gazing outside at the darkening spring sky. Ga no longer cared for noise and crowds, which precluded the big traditional family parties, but she enjoyed quiet visits in her room with one or two others.

"I brought you some cake and ice cream, Ga," Janessa said a little shyly. She wished she knew Hungarian. It was awkward talking to someone who didn't understand a word you said.

Though conversation was difficult, silence was even worse, so Janessa chattered on gamely. "It's my birthday today. I'm twenty-seven, as Great-Aunt Rita is quick to point out." Janessa set up the small standing tray and placed the cup and plate on it.

Her great-grandmother was looking at her strangely. Janessa attempted to translate. "Rita, your son Lazlo's wife, your daughter-in-law." She knew the Hungarian words for son, wife, and daughter and said them, hoping that Rita and Lazlo were self-explanatory.

Ga's piercing dark eyes stared into hers, and she suddenly launched into a rapid stream of Hungarian. Her long bony fingers wrapped around Janessa's wrist with surprising strength for one so small and frail. With her other hand, she pointed to Janessa's shoes.

"Do you like them, Ga? I got them for my birthday from—"

The old woman's voice rose, becoming more impassioned. Janessa recognized the Hungarian word for birthday. Had her great-grandmother understood her? She repeated "birthday" in

Hungarian, and Ga struggled to her feet, gripping Janessa for support, her voice communicating a sense of urgency.

"I know you're trying to tell me something, Ga," Janessa said softly. "I just don't understand what it is. I remember when we used to talk. You were like a walking history book. I loved hearing all about your adventures, especially in the old country."

Her great-grandmother had been born and raised in Hungary—it had been part of the Austro-Hungarian Empire then—and had come to the United States as a young woman after the first World War, not knowing a word of English. She had married and given birth to a daughter and four sons, learning to speak and read English along with her children. It seemed so sad that such hard-won skills were now lost to her.

"My favorite stories were about the Gypsies, though they scared me when I was little." Janessa smiled in reminiscence. "I remember all your stories about the time the Gypsies camped outside your village."

She said the Hungarian word for Gypsies, and her great-grandmother nodded vigorously and began to talk faster and louder.

"I came to check on Mama," Gram said, entering the room. Her dark eyes clouded with concern. "Oh my, she is agitated, isn't she?"

"What's she saying, Gram?" Janessa asked.

Gram eased her mother back into the chair and tried to interest her in the ice cream and cake. The older woman shook her head and continued her discourse.

"She's talking about the time the Gypsies came, when she lived in that little village back in Hungary," Gram said. "They certainly made an impression on her. I've been hearing about those Gypsies all my life."

"I remember worrying about Ga's stories of the Gypsy curses," Janessa admitted. "I'd lie in bed and think about them and work myself into a strong case of the creeps."

Suddenly, the cadence of Ga's voice changed and her words, though still foreign, sounded much different from what Janessa had come to recognize as the Hungarian language.

Gram confirmed it. "She isn't speaking Hungarian anymore. I don't know what she's saying, Janessa."

"Oh, Gram, do you think she's having another stroke?" Janessa cried. "Should I call a doctor?"

But before anyone could leave the room to place an emergency call, Ga picked up her fork and sampled the chocolate cake. She gave her daughter and great-granddaughter a sudden smile and murmured, "Good, good," in Hungarian, another word Janessa knew.

"She seems fine." Gram looked relieved but puzzled. She asked her mother a few questions in Hungarian, and the older woman answered in kind. She talked between bites, finally lapsing into silence as she concentrated on eating.

"Well." Gram folded her arms and stared at Janessa. "Well, well."

"Well, what? What did she say, Gram?"

"Mama says she knows that the curse is broken, so now she can finally tell the truth. She says she is a Gypsy who has only been pretending to be a Hungarian woman named Magda Maruchek."

Janessa was confused. "But Ga's name really

is Magda Maruchek, and she is a Hungarian woman."

"Well, she just told me that she is actually a Gypsy who was cursed in a family feud, so she fled to America, changed her name, and pretended to be Hungarian." Gram seemed remarkably unperturbed by the sudden disclosure; there wasn't much that could rattle her. "Mama claims she hoped to escape the curse, but it fell upon her and her daughter and granddaughter anyway, just as predicted. Apparently, it was a three-generation type curse."

"Ga claims that you and Mom and she were cursed?" Janessa decided that her great-grandmother's Gypsy curse stories still gave her the creeps.

"Yes. According to Mama, the curse was that our men would die early, leaving their young children fatherless." Gram shrugged. "That certainly did happen. My father drowned when I was eight years old; my husband was killed in a fall in the steel mill; and my daughter's husband, your own father, died in a fire, Janessa. Three generations of fatherless young children. A string of tragic coincidences, I've always thought."

"That's exactly what they were, Gram," Janessa insisted. Tragic coincidences were bad enough, but she refused to accept that the family had been cursed. "My dad was a firefighter, which has always been a risky profession. And there were lots of accidents in the steel mills before stringent safety rules were instituted. Poor Grandpa's fall happened in the pre-safety era. As for Great-Grandfather, he went fishing, fell into the river, and drowned because he couldn't swim."

"Well, if there was a curse, Mama claims it has now ended. Oh, and she gave the Gypsy blessing to you, Janessa." Gram winked at her granddaughter. "In a Romany dialect."

"To me?" Janessa's eyes widened. "Was that the strange language you didn't understand? Gram, do you think Ga is—uh—in a fantasy world? She's talked about the Gypsies for so many years that now she thinks she is one."

"She's ninety-four, she's led a long, hard life. If she wants to be a Gypsy with certain mystical powers, then so be it," Gram said practically. "By the way, she says that the blessing began last night at midnight and it will bring luck and—"

"Come to think of it, Henry was driving the bus this morning, and if he hadn't been, I would've missed it and been late for work." Janessa chuckled. "Good thing the blessing was in effect."

"Mama says that the blessing also includes a love to last far into old age. You won't be a young widow, Janessa. You and your husband will see your grandchildren grow up."

"I'll have to be a wife first. Does Ga see any prospects on the horizon?" Janessa asked lightly.

Gram posed the question in Hungarian.

The older woman merely smiled serenely and kept on eating her dessert.

"Where's the birthday girl?" The booming masculine voice sounded throughout the small house, carrying upstairs to Ga's bedroom.

"It's Mike!" Janessa exclaimed in delight. "I didn't think he was coming. He's been so busy studying."

"He's busy but never too busy to celebrate your birthday, darling. Mikey promised he would come. Run downstairs and see him, Janessa. I'll stay up here while Mama finishes her dessert and coffee."

Janessa hurried from the bedroom. It wasn't until she was halfway down the stairs that it dawned on her that something seemed different. Very different. Not a single sound could be heard from the crowd downstairs.

Silence at a family birthday party? That had never happened before. It was as unexpected as Ga's revelation that the family had been liberated from an old-world curse.

Janessa guessed someone had suggested that Mike hide, then jump out to surprise her, and the ensuing collective silence was all part of the jovial plan. A rather flawed plan, since Mike had already announced his presence.

As she rounded the corner into the dining room, Janessa readied herself to act surprised. She would take her cue from the rest of the participants.

What she saw froze her in her tracks.

R. F. Jordan himself was standing beside Mike while the rest of the family gaped at him in astonished silence.

For a split second Janessa wondered if she were hallucinating. Had her constant thoughts of Jordan somehow conjured up his image? But if so, he was a mass hallucination, because all the relatives were staring at him too.

Jordan was most definitely here, wearing the dark gray custom tailored suit, immaculate white shirt, and eye-catching silk tie he'd worn in the office today. His corporate attire was in stunning contrast to the various sweat suits, jeans, and bright cotton T-shirts worn by the family members.

"Happy Birthday, Janessa." Blue jean–clad Mike broke the silence and stepped forward, lifting Janessa in a bear hug and swinging her around and around.

She was dizzy when he set her on her feet, though she knew the twirling wasn't solely responsible.

"Look who Mikey brought with him, Janessa." Great-Aunt Rita pointed at Jordan, as if Janessa hadn't noticed him. "Your boss," she added helpfully, in case Janessa had forgotten.

"You didn't tell us your boss was so young and handsome." Great-Aunt Dorothy smiled speculatively from Jordan to Janessa.

"Are you married, Mr. Jordan?" Uncle Pete demanded, grinning broadly.

Never had her uncle's teasing embarrassed Janessa more. And the family's speculative banter was even more mortifying than their stunned silence.

She felt her face flush as bright as the pink suit she was still wearing. She didn't dare meet Jordan's eyes, and she was still too shocked by the sight of him standing in her grandmother's dining room to think of anything to say.

"No, I'm not married," Jordan answered, feeling every eye upon him.

He looked at Janessa, who was making no attempt to disguise her extreme discomfort. He didn't blame her. He felt uneasy himself, towering over the roomful of Janessa's relatives.

"We know some Jordans," one of the older men said. "Italian family. They changed their name from Giordano. You related to them?"

"No." Jordan shook his head. "As far as I know, my name's always been Jordan. I'm not a native Pittsburgher. I—er—grew up in a small town in Indiana that was homogenous Anglo-Saxon American."

When he first moved to Pittsburgh, he had been amazed at the sheer numbers of eastern and western European ethnic groups in the area, and the strong community and church ties within each group. He was aware of the fierce pride the various nationalities took in their names and customs. Pinpointing the origins of others was a common pastime.

"Well, we're all Americans," one of the teenage cousins pointed out.

"But you're not the least bit Hungarian, Mr. Jordan?" another older man concluded, sounding disappointed.

Mike laughed. "Give the poor guy a break Great-Uncle Stephen. He was nice enough to give me a ride out here, and now you and Uncle Lazlo are grilling him on his roots. Hey, how about some of that cake, Mom? Gram's chocolate is my all-time fave."

"Of course, Mikey." His mother sprang into action, piling enormous slices of cake onto two plates, one for Mike and one for Jordan.

Great-Aunt Dorothy insisted on adding double scoops of ice cream.

"Janessa, you never got to eat your cake. Here's a piece for you too." Sharon, Uncle Pete's wife, shoved a cake plate into Janessa's hands. "Why don't you and Mr. Jordan go next door to your place and eat? It's so crowded and noisy here, with no privacy at all." Her eyes gleamed and she nudged her husband.

"Go on, go next door where you two can be alone," ordered Uncle Pete with a suggestive guffaw.

"Mr. Jordan happens to be Janessa's *boss!*" Gina exclaimed indignantly. "You're not supposed to hang out with your boss!"

Jordan looked at Janessa for a sign that she either agreed or disagreed with the bald statement. That she agreed seemed a reasonable guess, because from the expression on Janessa's face, his presence here was about as welcome as an unplanned pregnancy. Nor had it escaped his notice that she hadn't uttered a word since his arrival.

"I think we should escape from this maddening crowd," Mike spoke up, taking charge of the increasingly awkward situation. "C'mon, Janessa, Gina, Jordan. Let's go next door."

Some of the younger cousins demanded to be allowed to go too, but Gina told them "No!" in no uncertain terms. The four entered the quiet stillness of the other half of the duplex.

"Uncle Pete is such a geek," Gina complained, flopping down on the sofa beside Mike. "He didn't get married till he was almost forty because no sane woman would have him. Now all he and his nerdy female counterpart Sharon do is embarrass anybody who is still single. Imagine trying to fix someone up with her boss!" Clearly, the concept was unimaginable to Gina. "I apologize for them, Mr. Jordan," she added fervently.

"It's just Jordan, and there is no need for apologies," Jordan murmured.

He sat down on the love seat across from the sofa, the only place left in the narrow room. Janessa was already seated there, and she shrank against the side as he settled himself among the cushions.

The love seat was too small for two adults to sit comfortably without touching, especially someone the size of Jordan. Despite Janessa's efforts to keep a distance, their shoulders kept brushing and their hips were almost pressed together.

Jordan seemed oblivious to their daunting proximity. He began to demolish his enormous helping of cake and ice cream.

"How come it's just Jordan?" Gina wanted to know.

"I'm not sure. It suits me, I guess. Delicious cake," he interrupted himself to remark. "Anyway, no one has ever called me Roderick, and only my mother calls me Rod."

"Roderick. Rod." Gina frowned. "Yeah, that does sound stupid. Jordan is better."

"Another remark like that and you're going to be exiled next door with Uncle Pete and Aunt Sharon, Gina," warned Mike. He leaned forward, his eyes meeting Janessa's. "I stopped by your office tonight to catch the bus home with you, Janessa, but Jordan said you'd already left. When I told him it was your birthday, he insisted on driving me home, so I invited him in for some cake."

Janessa knew how charmingly persuasive Mike could be. On the other hand, she'd never known Jordan to be swayed by anything or anyone.

"Jordan insisted on driving you?" Janessa

pressed doubtfully. "Or did you weasel him into giving you a ride, Mikey?"

"Ah, you can still speak," Jordan said dryly. "Those are the first words I've heard from you tonight, Janessa. A *most* unusual occurrence."

"No offense, but it's a real shocker to find your boss in your grandmother's living room," Gina replied. "I would absolutely freak if my boss, Mr. Lingenfeld, showed up on my birthday."

"No offense taken." Jordan arched his dark brows. "I apologize for showing up and ruining your birthday, Janessa."

"It would take more than your presence to ruin my birthday," Janessa said lightly.

His paltry record of apologies remained intact, she decided. The sarcastic one he'd just offered didn't count. "Thank you for driving my brother all the way out here."

"It's not that far." Jordan shrugged. "Maybe sixteen, seventeen miles? And the cake was definitely worth the trip." He set the empty plate on the coffee table. "I didn't realize today was your birthday, Janessa." He cleared his throat. "Or I would have given you a card or something."

He was feeling guilty, Janessa presumed, because she gave him a card every year on his birthday. She made it a point to remember birthdays, and card shops were a favorite haunt, but she hardly expected Jordan to reciprocate. "We don't do birthdays at the office," she reminded him.

"You don't? How cheap!" Gina exclaimed. "At the bank where I work we have a cake for everyone's birthday and we all chip in to take the birthday person to lunch."

"A communal staff lunch." Janessa laughed. "Now there's an interesting concept."

She tried to imagine Jordan sitting down to dine with the staff. It would hardly qualify as a festive occasion. Conversation would be nonexistent and knowledge of the Heimlich maneuver a must.

"We'll have to try it sometime," Jordan muttered without enthusiasm. Gina's remark stung. He prided himself on paying top salaries; the suggestion that he was "cheap" rankled. Worse was his oversight of Janessa's birthday. She gave him a card every year and he'd never given her one, he realized. He felt both cheap *and* thoughtless.

"Maybe in the twenty-first century," suggested Janessa. *When I'm working somewhere else,* she thought but refrained from saying aloud.

"So how is Ga, Janess?" Mike asked. His dark eyes shone with warmth. Mike had always been one of Ga's favorites, and vice versa. "She is our ninety-four-year-old great-grandmother," he explained to Jordan. "She came almost the whole way back from a stroke a few years ago and is as mentally sharp as—"

"She wasn't so mentally sharp tonight, Mikey," Janessa cut in gently. "When Gram and I were with her earlier, Ga claimed to be a Gypsy and said the family has been living under a curse that ended last night at midnight."

Janessa declined to mention her own role in their great-grandmother's revelation. She was not about to announce that she was the recipient of a mysterious Gypsy blessing, not in front of Jordan.

"Cool!" Gina was pleased with the news. "If Ga's a Gypsy, that means we're all part Gypsy too. Remember that old record Uncle Joe used to play?" She sang a few bars of the R & B classic "I've Put a Spell on You." "Now it can be our family theme song."

Mike frowned at her. "What it really means is that Ga's mind might be failing, Gina. She might be on the verge of—of something. I'm going over to see her." He stood up and headed toward the door.

Gina glanced from him to Janessa and Jordan crammed together on the love seat. "I'm going with you, Mike." The girl jumped to her feet and followed him out the door. "I'm really worried about Ga too," she called over her shoulder.

The door banged shut behind them, leaving Janessa alone with Jordan. She knew the prudent thing would be to stand up and move to the sofa, but she didn't. She sat motionless, every nerve strung taut.

Jordan settled back against the cushions, casually draping an arm across the back. The action brought them even closer. Janessa pretended she didn't notice. Jordan certainly didn't seem to.

"Your brother Mike is a fine young man," he observed. "Smart, energetic, articulate. Too bad he's in med school. If he were a law student, he'd have a job offer waiting from me on his graduation day."

"Mike is going to be a neurosurgeon." Janessa glowed with sisterly pride. "He's always been a brilliant student. His teachers at Ambridge High still ask about him. Everybody in town is proud of Mike."

"Hard to believe he came out of the same gene pool as Cousin Gina. Did she ever work as one of our receptionists?" Jordan asked drolly. "And if not, how did I happen to miss hiring her? It seems I've hired every other airhead in western Pennsylvania for that position."

Janessa scowled. "Gina is not an airhead. She's a bit—outspoken, but she is quite bright. And in case you haven't noticed, our current receptionist Debbie is not an airhead, she is a dream."

"Uh-oh. Every time you start singing Debbie's praises, you hit me up for a raise for her. What are you, her agent or something?"

"If you'd had to train eighty-seven receptionists in the past five years, you would do whatever it takes to keep an excellent worker like Debbie in place."

"Eight-seven? That's a gross exaggeration, Janessa."

"Maybe a *slight* exaggeration," she admitted.

"I think there are at least eighty-seven people stuffed into the other half of this duplex, and that's not much of an exaggeration. Are all those people really related to you?"

"Each and every one."

"And everybody gets together often?" Jordan was truly amazed.

"Birthdays and holidays," confirmed Janessa. "Of course, I don't attend each celebration because I work such long hours. There have been times when I've been the last one to arrive at my own birthday party."

"I walked right into that one." Jordan almost smiled, but he suppressed the impulse. "Let's get back to the sheer numbers of your relatives. How do you keep them all straight?"

"Why wouldn't I keep them straight?" She eyed him oddly. "How does anyone keep their relatives straight?"

It was a rhetorical question, and she wasn't expecting an answer. Jordan, full of surprises tonight, provided one.

"I don't know. There are a dearth of Jordans, you see, just myself and my mother and a few distant cousins who don't keep in touch."

"What about your father?" Janessa dared to ask. She'd often wondered, but the opportunity to inquire had never seemed to arise. She knew Jordan's father wasn't in the picture, or she would have been placing gift orders for him from various catalogs.

Jordan stiffened. "He died when I was six years old." His voice was clipped and taut. Janessa would have thought he was impatient or annoyed had she not seen the sudden flash of pain shadow his face.

"I see," she said quietly. Her mind was percolating with thoughts and theories. She'd taken child psychology courses, and the section on traumatic loss in childhood was a field in itself, one that particularly interested her because of her own father's untimely death. She knew that the danger of a child closing off emotionally after the death of a parent was very real. The care and concern of her entire extended family had saved her and her brother and sisters from that fate.

But what about Jordan? She tried to visualize him as a confused, grief-stricken six-year-old. It was impossible; she simply couldn't imagine him vulnerable in any way.

"I only have a few dim memories of him. According to my mother, he was driving drunk the night he was killed." Jordan clearly didn't want to be perceived as vulnerable in any way. He shrugged, smiling, to assure her that self-pity was not a part of his trip down memory lane.

"My mother was furious, and rightly so, of course. He didn't have insurance, and with Mother working only part-time, we were financially strapped. Fortunately, I was in school and responsible enough to take care of myself so my mother could take a full-time job without worrying about baby-sitting fees. She went back to school at night and eventually earned her doctorate. She's now a tenured chemistry professor at Indiana University. She's as intense and absorbed by her work as I am by mine."

Janessa was outraged on behalf of the child who had not only lost his father but also had been led to believe he was lucky to be left to his own devices for hours on end. *From the ripe old age of six*!

"I see," she said again. The next time Mrs. Jordan telephoned with one of her catalog gift orders, Janessa vowed to scramble the item numbers.

"No, you don't." Jordan gave a short laugh. "I can see it in your eyes. You think my mother and I ought to decorate a Christmas tree together or do the birthday cake thing. I know our family situation is different from yours, but my mother and I are satisfied with things the way they are, Janessa. We respect each other and we see each other occasionally, when we're not too busy with work."

Which was never, because Jordan was always busy with work, and it sounded as if his mother was too. Janessa thought of her large, close family who were forever minding one another's business, offering unsolicited opinions and advice that could be maddening sometimes, yet also reassuring. She couldn't imagine Jordan's isolation, yet it explained so much about him.

"I see," she said. But Jordan was right, she didn't see at all. She couldn't fathom the emotional wasteland of his life.

She leaned forward to set her untouched cake on the coffee table. Her movements caused the tip of her shoe to touch Jordan's leg.

The effect was electrifying. Heat flashed through her from the point of contact and hit every erogenous zone in her body. She drew a ragged breath and lifted her dark, limpid eyes to his.

Their gazes collided, the impact as physical as the brief, involuntary brush of her leg against his. Janessa squirmed in the seat. She moistened her suddenly dry lips with quick darts of her tongue. Beneath her clothing, her nipples tightened into hard beads.

"I think your cousin Gina might be right about your family theme song. I feel as if I'm under some sort of spell." Jordan's voice was deep and husky.

It had a visceral effect on Janessa. A sharp bolt of desire pierced her whole body with a deep heat. Trembling, she dragged her eyes away from his.

Jordan cupped her nape with one hand while simultaneously grasping her arm with the other. He pulled her against him, his movements as smooth and agile as his verbal performances in the courtroom.

"Since I first saw you this morning, I haven't been able to think of anything but you, and I don't know what the hell to do about it," he growled. "Except this."

He lowered his head, and his mouth, hot and hard and hungry, closed over hers.

4

For a moment, panic streaked through her, and Janessa instinctively put up her hands to push him away. But then his tongue was gliding over her lower lip, and as if of its own volition, her mouth opened to him, welcoming him into the soft, moist interior.

Shaking with restless excitement, her arms slid slowly around his neck and her head tilted back under the demanding onslaught of his mouth. She heard a soft little whimper escape from the back of her throat and was helpless to stop it, as helpless as she was to stop the wild urgency that roared through her, making her cling to Jordan as their kiss deepened.

Jordan shifted, pressing her down with the weight of his body as his tongue thrust deeply into her mouth in an excruciating sexual simulation. Janessa's fingers tangled in the dark thickness of his hair and she arched against him, savoring the hard pressure of his chest against her breasts. They felt swollen and sensitive, the tips tingling and tight, and the only relief for that specific sensual ache was to rub them against him.

Her erotic, sinuous movements seemed to ignite a powder keg of sensation in him. Jordan's arms tightened possessively, his hands running over the curves of her body with long, sweeping strokes.

He smoothed his palm over her shoulder, along her rib cage, and then with a thorough slowness that was both exciting and agonizing, his fingers closed over her breast. The plump softness filled his hand and he caressed her, rubbing the cloth of her pink jacket against her, arousing her further. His thumb found the hard little pebble of her nipple and pressed it, wringing a wild cry from her.

Their mouths lifted and they stared into each other's eyes, panting and gasping for air.

And then, groaning deeply, Jordan took her lips again in a long, slow kiss that went on and on, growing hotter and wilder and ever more demanding.

His mouth was tantalizing, hypnotizing; his kisses made her weak and clingy. Janessa's mind clouded with passion, and she gave in to the hunger consuming her. She wanted to hold him, to touch him. Her need was so great that it bordered on desperation.

She slipped her hands under Jordan's suit coat and kneaded the hard muscles of his back beneath the fine cotton of his shirt. It was not enough. The material frustrated her; she wanted to feel the bare warmth of his skin.

And she wanted so much more. She wanted to wrap herself around him with nothing between them, to feel him, thick and hard and deep inside her. He was half lying on top of her and her legs parted reflexively, allowing him to lock his body against hers. The intimacy of their position revealed the burgeoning evidence of his own male need.

The insistent pressure, coupled with his hand sliding slowly under her skirt, startled Janessa out of the sensual cocoon enveloping her. She was suddenly—and most unwelcomely—hurtled back into conscious awareness of time and place.

They were in her living room, with the front door unlocked, and a host of relatives were assembled next door!

Alarmed by her stunningly uncharacteristic indiscretion, Janessa pulled her mouth away from Jordan's and pushed at his chest.

"Jordan, no!" she gasped.

He was still deep in the throes of passion, rational thought eluding him. His mouth sought hers while his hands attempted to pet her into submission. Janessa twisted her head back and forth, dodging his lips while trying to grab his wrists to restrain his hands. It was like wrestling with an octopus.

"Jordan, stop!" She dragged one of his hands away from her thigh and pulled the other from her breast. "Mike could come in at any second. Or my mom or grandmother or—or anybody else. They can't find us like this!"

Finally, slowly, Jordan let her go, straightening to sit stiffly on the edge of the love seat. Janessa watched him, her body still shivering from unslaked passion.

He seemed to be emerging from a trance. His eyes, at first glazed and unfocused, became alert and then glittered with a cool calculation that Janessa knew well. She'd seen it when he knew he had nailed his opponent's case and would emerge victorious from the proceedings.

"You're right, of course." Jordan stood up, his fingers encircling her wrist as strong and tight as a manacle. "We'll go to my place."

He pulled her to her feet with effortless ease. For a moment she swayed, weak and off balance. Jordan put his arm around her waist to steady her. "Let's go," he said gruffly, starting to the door, half walking, half dragging her with him.

"Jordan, I—we can't." Even to her own ears, her protest sounded feeble. She had to do better than that!

Janessa squared her shoulders and drew a deep, bolstering breath. "I have to go back to the party, Jordan." This time her voice was firm and clear. "Right now."

Jordan felt frustration rage through him. He'd never handled setbacks well, but this one was worse than most. He was impatient and exasperated. The last time he'd felt this way was in court, when a judge had overruled one of his most crucial objections. Except this time, along with the frustrated fury he was experiencing, his whole body was throbbing with a powerful sexual urgency.

He looked down at Janessa, whose mouth was moist and swollen and well kissed, and suddenly his mind was reeling again. He felt a thrust of need so strong and savage that it took every ounce of self-control he possessed not to scoop her up and carry her off. Away from this crowded little room and her zillions of curious relatives next door. "I want to be alone with you, Janessa."

Some small, isolated part of his mind recognized that though his need was urgently sexual, there was another component, equally strong, that was driving him. He'd never felt so connected to anyone before, and the allure of that connection was disturbingly powerful. He tried to push it aside, to focus solely on sex.

"I'm not going to beg you, Janessa," he said in a hoarse voice he scarcely recognized as his own. It occurred to him that he was actually on the verge of begging, and the realization appalled him.

"It wouldn't do you any good, even if you did," Janessa said succinctly. He pinned her with a laser-eyed stare that burst her bravado as swiftly as a prick to an overblown balloon. "I— I mean, I can't just desert my own birthday party. The entire family is there, waiting for me to open my presents." Janessa flinched. She sounded as if she was pleading with him to understand—which she most definitely was not! She was telling him what had to be done.

What if she dared to do it? teased a mischievous little voice in her head. What if she left the clan to their own devices and went off with Jordan?

We'll go to my place, he had said. To his bed, he meant.

Her insides liquified at the thought of lying naked in bed with him, of touching him, kissing him. Of feeling his hands and lips on her. Her body flushed and throbbed in a dizzying combination of anticipation and frustration.

She saw Jordan's eyes narrow. She knew he was aware that her resistance was ebbing swiftly. Jordan was superb at assessing vulnerability; he found the weak points in a case or a witness and exploited them.

Janessa decided that she would not, could not, be added to his winning scorecard. Without another word, she fled from the duplex, not daring to look back. Jordan knew where she was going. If he wanted to follow her, he would.

She told herself that she didn't expect him to. That she didn't want him to. And she was disgusted that some spark of hope allowed her to believe that maybe he would come after her.

Because, of course, he didn't.

The party was in full swing when she reentered Gram's side of the duplex. After a few dozen jokes and warnings about office romances, the subject of Jordan was mercifully dropped and Janessa went on to open her gifts.

Mallory's gift was a chaste—at least by Lady Godiva standards—white camisole. There was also a small box from Chelsi containing a three-pack of white sweat socks.

"Chelsi already gave me these shoes. I wonder why she bought me another present," Janessa murmured.

Everybody had an opinion.

"Maybe you're supposed to wear the socks with the shoes?" guessed Great-Uncle Stephen.

"After all you do for her, that girl should buy you a dozen presents," Great-Uncle Lazlo said, scowling. He did not approve of Chelsi, not her hair nor her nails, nor her style of dress and fondness for nightlife.

"Sweat socks don't count as a birthday present," Gina stated. "It's like giving somebody an iron for Valentine's Day. One simply doesn't."

"Knowing Chelsi, she probably thought she'd get by with the sweat socks and then felt guilty and came through with the shoes," said Mike.

"Those shoes . . . I don't know . . ." Great-Aunt Rita frowned. "If Janessa wasn't the one wearing them, you know what I'd say about those shoes? I'd say that a girl wearing those shoes is no lady."

"But Janessa *is* the one wearing them and she *is* a lady," Janessa's mother snapped.

"Well, Mama liked Janessa's shoes," Gram spoke up. "She said they were magic birthday shoes." Gram smiled at Janessa. "She told me so after you left her room."

Since Gram was the penultimate matriarch and had invoked Ga, the highest authority in the family, everybody promptly shut up.

The shoes were not mentioned again for the rest of the evening.

Janessa slept poorly, tossing and turning all night. Vivid erotic images of Jordan and herself, complete with sensory detail, kept appearing before her, as if her mind were a VCR that had recorded those scenes for endless replay. And then she would relive his abrupt departure and wonder and worry about what she would say when she saw him in the office the next morning.

She woke up an hour before her alarm went off and changed clothes three times before finally settling on a ribbed chemise sweater dress in a color Mallory called "stone."

Her new birthday shoes were beside her bed; she'd forgotten to put them away last night. Janessa smoothed her fingers over the suede, then impulsively slipped them on her feet. She'd never had a pair of shoes that fit so perfectly and comfortably. And the three-and-a-half-inch heels provided the extra height she'd always craved.

It was a gray, drizzly day, typical for this time of year, and she and Mike waited together at the bus stop, sharing her too-small-for-two-umbrella.

"Your boss is an interesting guy," Mike remarked. "While we were driving out here last night, he told me about some of his cases with a medical angle. I wouldn't want to be on the opposite side of the courtroom from him in a medical malpractice suit."

"Jordan seldom loses a case. The rare times that he does, everybody in the office knows to run for cover. Some keep on running and never come back," Janessa added wryly.

She half wished she had that option today. Though there was a distinct chill in the air, she felt herself growing hot. Would Jordan mention last night's burst of passion between them or act as if it had never happened? She was still trying to figure it all out. They had been talking on a level they'd never reached before; she had begun to understand him in a way she never had before; and then suddenly they'd begun doing things, feeling and needing and wanting things, they never had done before!

What was she supposed to do now? Take her cue from him, wait passively for some sign? Janessa hated being reactive; she'd been proactive long before it became a buzzword.

"When I was in Jordan's office last night, I didn't see any pictures on his desk or anything. Does he have a girlfriend, or two or three?" Mike asked ever so casually.

Janessa was not fooled. "Honestly, Mike,

you're about as subtle as Uncle Pete."

"So I'm curious, so sue me!" Mike grinned. "A little legal humor there."

"Very little," muttered Janessa.

Mike was not deterred. "I want to know what's going on, Janessa. After all, Jordan did insist on driving me to your birthday party. And I saw the way he was looking at you last night. As if he'd rather be eating you up, but he settled for the cake instead."

Janessa flushed scarlet. "You're way off base, Mikey. I've worked for Jordan for five years. We know each other too well to ever—"

"To ever what? Be attracted to each other? Fall for each other?"

"Both," Janessa said firmly. She wished she was as certain as she sounded, but sharing her confusion with her little brother was simply out of the question. She was the sane, sensible big sister, the role she'd held since their father's death. Just as Jordan had played the intensely-absorbed-in-work, no-time-for-emotions role since the loss of his father.

Suddenly, she was very nervous indeed. "I've seen how Jordan's relationships with women work. Or more accurately, don't work." She was talking more to herself than to Mike.

"Jordan meets a woman, goes out with her a few times—to dinner, to the theater, perhaps to the symphony or some kind of concert, to a baseball or football or hockey game. I know because I always make the reservations and get the tickets. At least twice he asks me to send flowers to her office—they all have offices because he only dates lawyers. I think he's working his way through the Allegheny County Bar Association.

And then boom! After about three weeks, it's over. If she calls him at the office, he leaves orders not to put through her calls."

"Three weeks," Mike repeated thoughtfully. "I can relate to that. It's time enough to get to know a girl and decide she's not worth the bother."

"Michael Stephen Balint!" Janessa shoved her brother out from under her umbrella into the drizzling rain. "That's sexist and disgusting!"

"Hey, it works both ways. Women work on the same timetable." Mike calmly stepped back under the protective shade. "Anyway, it's not Jordan's fault those women can't hold his interest."

"Jordan's real love is his work, and he ultimately resents the time away from it." She now understood why. Work was his refuge, a safe haven. He wasn't about to risk the danger of allowing himself to get close to someone, to need someone who might fail him. Or leave him. She wasn't all that different herself, she realized, startled. Unlike Jordan, she was close to her family, but she had also managed to avoid emotional intimacy with a "significant other."

Significant other? Janessa winced. She'd been reading too many pop psychology articles.

"I know where Jordan's coming from," Mike said grimly. "You go out with a woman for a few weeks and she starts making demands you either can't or don't want to meet. His situation sounds depressingly like my love life—or lack thereof." He scowled. "Why can't women realize how important a man's work is to him?"

"I can't believe you're taking his side! There is more to life than work, Mikey."

"You should listen to your own advice," retorted Mike. "When was the last time you had a date, Janess? You're always ready, willing, and available to put in all those extra hours that Jordan demands. Even on Thanksgiving and Christmas!"

"I didn't work this past Thanksgiving and Christmas. I told Jordan I wouldn't work those holidays again, and I meant it."

"Good for you! Hey, here comes the bus. And only ten minutes late."

"Oh no, Gracie is driving!" Janessa groaned. "Get ready to leap onto the bus in a single bound."

"The bus driver from hell." Mike laughed.

He wasn't laughing an hour later as they sat on the idled bus, which was blocking a lane of traffic because its front tire had gone flat.

"This is the bus *ride* from hell," he complained. "Why don't they send another bus to take us into the city? Why don't they get someone over here to change the tire?"

"You can tell he's not a regular rider on the 81C." Shalonda, sitting in front of them, smiled cynically. "We regulars know it's hopeless to gripe. It's a waste of time and energy. You might as well just stay put and shut up until they decide what to do, 'cause they're never in any hurry to make up their minds."

Janessa leaned back against the seat and closed her eyes. She was going to be late for work. The bus had broken down before, but luckily for her, Jordan hadn't been in the office those other times. He'd been out of the city doing appellate work.

He would be in the office today.

Her great-grandmother's Gypsy blessing,

promising luck, drifted to mind. Unlike the alleged curse, which had continued through three generations, the lucky blessing had obviously elapsed at midnight.

"Janessa!" Jordan stormed out of his office into the corridor running the length of the firm's suite of offices.

At the far end, Debbie sat frozen at the reception desk, as still as a mannequin. Kolenda, just coming out of the conference room with a cup of coffee, screeched to a sudden halt, sending coffee sloshing over the sides of the cup. Not a sound emanated from the offices of the secretaries and other associates.

"She still hasn't arrived?" Kolenda guessed.

"It's nine-thirty!" Jordan was infuriated. "What in the hell does she think we're running here? An office or a—a—" He broke off, unable to complete the analogy.

His sudden inarticulate lapse added to his outrage. He flew down the corridor like an angry thundercloud, staring out the glass-paneled doors into the vestibule. Nobody was getting on or off the elevators. The area between his firm and the Edelstein & Allard accounting offices was deserted.

"Maybe her bus broke down again." Debbie's voice was a mere squeak. "Any time she's been late before, it's been because of the bus."

Jordan whirled to face her. "She's been late before?"

Debbie seemed to shrink visibly before his eyes. "J-Just when her bus was late. You—You were out of town." There was no mistaking the expression on Debbie's face; she wished he were

out of town right now. Maybe even off the
planet.

"Well, that's enlightening!" Jordan's nostrils
flared. "What else goes on around here when I'm
out of town?"

"N-Nothing, Mr. Jordan, sir."

"So people do nothing when I'm not here?
Well, that figures!" The sight of Debbie cringing
in his presence stoked the flames of Jordan's temper. "You needn't sit there cowering. I'm not an
ogre, for God's sakes! Let me know the moment
Janessa gets off the elevator!" He headed back to
his office.

Valerian Valstock made the mistake of following him and asking a question. Jordan considered it the most stupid question he'd ever heard
in his entire legal career. He proceeded to tell
Valstock so. Belatedly, he apologized for his
rudeness and suggested Valstock get back to
work.

The new law school graduate emerged from
Jordan's office as pale and addled as Debbie.

Inside his office, Jordan attempted to look
through the latest copy of *U.S. Law Week*, then
closed it in frustration and began to pace the
floor. He couldn't concentrate to read, he
couldn't even sit still. He glared out the window
at the rainy sky. Everything was irritating him
today, from the lack of sun to Debbie's timidity
to Valstock's stupidity. And most of all . . . The
cause of it all . . .

He glanced at his watch. Where was Janessa?
For a split second he imagined her injured in an
accident. During one of his periods of fitful sleep
last night, he'd dreamed that he had watched a
car strike her, hurling her into the air. He had

awakened, sweating and shouting her name. A prophetic dream?

Jordan rejected the idea at once. He didn't believe in prophesies or dreams or any of that new age or old age mumbo jumbo.

No, nothing had happened to Janessa, he assured himself. He knew exactly what was going on today. She thought that the events of last night had given her carte blanche to do exactly as she pleased around here.

Jordan made an unintelligible sound, between a groan and a growl. He should have guessed this would happen. Office romances were notoriously disruptive, and although those kisses he and Janessa had shared hardly constituted a romance, the effect was the same.

She probably thought they were a couple now, that she had her boss wrapped around her little finger. She had probably slept late this morning and would sashay in around noon, expecting nothing to be said. Maybe she intended to spend the rest of the afternoon shopping!

Last night . . .

Jordan's fingers balled into fists, and he had to remind himself to breathe. He had replayed their conversation over and over in his head. He never talked about his father's death, but he'd found it surprisingly easy to confide in Janessa. He thought of her dark eyes, filled with warmth and concern as she listened to him. He'd seen her look at office staffers that way, but he never thought he could be the recipient of her sweet and undivided attention. For that brief time, he had been a member of her charmed circle; Jordan couldn't deny how much he liked being there.

His senses were suddenly filled with her. He

could taste her lips, smell her enticing feminine
scent, feel the lush curves of her body straining
against him.

He pressed his flushed forehead against the
cool windowpane. All night, those sensory memories had been replaying in his brain, over and
over again. Janessa. His body swelled with
arousal as her image appeared in his mind's eye.
He saw her flashing dark eyes, her quick smile,
her dark brows arched quizzically. He fixated on
her mouth. Those full lips. The way they'd
parted for him, welcoming his tongue inside.

The pencil he was holding snapped in two.
Shocked, Jordan glanced down at it. He'd broken
it and hadn't even realized it. Hell, he hadn't
even been aware that he'd been holding a pencil.

The incident seemed to both symbolize and
predict the catastrophe that awaited him if he
dared to indulge in an affair with Janessa Balint.
Even fantasizing about her was foolish, because
fantasies would not satisfy him. There would be
a natural progression from thought to action. If
he permitted himself to want Janessa, he would
have to have her, because he invariably got what
he wanted. He was competitive by nature, and
when he competed, he expected to win. And almost always did.

But if he won Janessa, they would both lose.
An office affair would leave a splintered mess in
its wake. Morale would plummet among the
staff. There would be a threat of litigation. And
the vital, well functioning employer-employee
relationship between them would be forever altered. As lovers, they would treat each other differently. There would be expectations and
demands. . . .

Worst of all would be the breakup. Jordan inhaled sharply. The office would be a war zone with everybody taking sides. A niggling doubt that no one would line up on his side flitted to mind, but he dismissed it as irrelevant.

What was relevant were the lessons he'd learned a long time ago: that emotional attachments inevitably led to pain and disappointment. That work was the only constant. Nothing and no one should take precedence over his work. The fact that Janessa was commanding so much of his time and thoughts was dangerous.

Jordan strode to his desk and reached for the phone. He had work to do, a law practice to run. He was not a hormonally charged adolescent driven by lust. When Janessa arrived, he would explain exactly how things were going to be between them. Perhaps he would start by delivering a lecture on the evils of being late for work.

Still holding the phone, Jordan began to plan for the encounter.

5

At ten minutes to ten, Janessa trudged into the office. Debbie gaped at her as if she were an apparition.

"Janessa, where have you been?" she cried. "He's been stomping around like a maniac asking for you! He's even scarier than usual. I have my resignation typed up, so if he fires you, I'm going too. Um, would you tell him you're here? He demanded to know the second you set foot in the building."

Janessa ran a hand through her damp hair. Her clothes were damp too. She'd expected her new shoes to be ruined, but they'd remained immune to water damage and still looked brand-new. It was almost magical.

She could certainly use a little magic this morning. And what a long, wet, utterly maddening morning it had been—and it wasn't even ten o'clock! Eventually, the transit authority czars had acknowledged that the 81C could not complete its run with a flat tire, but by the time a repair crew had been dispatched, the drizzling rain had escalated to a teeming downpour. The 81C passengers had had to stand on the boulevard in the deluge while the crew struggled to put the new tire in place. Janessa's umbrella, like everybody else's, had become waterlogged, dripping moisture rather than repelling it.

Now she had to explain it all to Jordan.

"I'll go see him now," Janessa said, sighing wearily.

"Oh, Janessa, please be careful!" Debbie wailed.

Janessa grimaced. Debbie was acting as if she were about to enter a cell housing Hannibal Lecter.

Janessa dimly recalled that she had been dreading her first encounter with Jordan this morning, but the bus ordeal had replaced her nervous tension with a pervasive exasperation.

Debbie was overreacting, Janessa decided testily. So what if she was a bit late? Flat tires happened; bureaucratic snafus within the transit authority were legendary. Jordan would understand.

Wouldn't he?

She entered his office. "Good morning, Jordan. You wouldn't believe what—"

"You're right, I won't believe whatever excuse you've cooked up for being late, so don't waste your breath."

Janessa gulped. The iciness in his voice was blood congealing.

Jordan rose to his feet, his slow, deliberate movements subtly threatening. A courtroom trick, Janessa knew. Nevertheless, it was effective. She backed up a little.

"The bus—" she began, but Jordan cut her off again.

"I said I don't want to hear it, Janessa. I expect everybody to be at work on time, and I have no intention of making allowances for you."

Janessa knew she had a choice. She could either be intimidated and meekly choke out an apology—which he would throw back in her face—or she could match his bellicose behavior with her own.

Spending nearly three chilly, rainy hours in the company of the exquisitely obnoxious Gracie and her fellow disgruntled passengers undoubtedly influenced her decision. If Jordan was spoiling for a fight, Janessa was ready to give him one.

She drew herself to her full height, which, thanks to her shoes, was three and a half inches taller than usual. "I didn't ask you to make allowances for me, Mr. Jordan! I have a valid excuse for being late, but if you want a written note from the transit authority, I'll make sure you're provided with one."

Jordan's dark brows narrowed and his skin flushed a dull red as anger flooded him. "Who the hell do you think you're talking to, lady? In case you've forgotten, I happen to be your boss—"

"As if I could forget!" Janessa cut in. "You've always made it clear that it's *your* office and everybody here had better do things *your* way the second *you* say so, because *you're* the big boss. Well, there are other words that more accurately describe you, Mr. Jordan. Slave driver. And I am not your slave!"

She paused to catch her breath. Jordan's face was grim, and the bitter hardness of his stare unnerved her. Janessa conceded that perhaps she'd gone too far.

Jordan said nothing, and his silence was chilling. As he meant it to be. Janessa had often heard him describe how effective a well-timed silence in the courtroom could be. But knowing that he was using that very tactic right now did not alter its effectiveness.

She had to restrain herself from rushing to fill the intimidating silence with a nervous apology. Jordan would verbally annihilate her if she fell into that trap.

They glowered at each other.

Finally, Jordan spoke, enunciating each word with icy precision. "Your attitude and your behavior are completely unacceptable, Miss Balint. I refuse to tolerate such rudeness and defiance."

Miss Balint? Janessa flinched at the contemptuous formality. He had never called her that; she'd been Janessa since the moment they'd met.

Furthermore, he sounded like a judge handing down a life sentence with no parole. And what was her crime? Commuting on a crummy old bus with lousy tires and then daring to respond in kind to his bad mood! A capital crime, indeed!

Janessa was offended all over again. "Well, *I* refuse to be scolded like an irresponsible child. And I also refuse to be bullied and subjected to your unreasonable tirades."

"You also refuse to arrive at the office on time and you refuse to treat me with the respect that an employer has every right to expect from an employee." His voice, harsh and acerbic, sliced through her. "But you certainly don't refuse to accept the very generous salary I pay you, Miss Balint."

"What's that supposed to mean? I earn every penny of my paycheck ten times over!"

"Not when you waltz into the office at whatever hour suits you. Not when you—"

"I know what you're trying to do." Janessa felt sick and shaky with anger and some other undefinable emotion she didn't want to examine.

Suddenly, it was clear to her. Jordan had decided that their passionate interlude last night was a complication he did not care to deal with, and so he was consigning her to oblivion, as he always did when a woman proved to be an annoying inconvenience.

He had kissed her a few times last night and—how had Mike phrased it?—decided she was not worth the bother. If she hadn't been late this morning, he would have found some other excuse to provoke this confrontation. He wanted her gone and would seize any reason to get rid of her.

Well, she was not going to stand quietly by and let him sack her! Janessa's pride surged swiftly and fiercely to the fore.

"I'll spare you the trouble of firing me, because I quit, Mr. Jordan," she heard herself say in a voice ringing with triumph. She'd beaten him to the punch and there was a thrill of satisfaction in that. "I'll clear my desk and leave immediately."

She turned and stalked out of the office.

Jordan stared blindly after her. He could remember feeling this way only once before, on the football field during his high school playing days, when a 200-pound behemoth had rammed into him, knocking him to the ground. He'd landed on his back, striking his head, and had lain there on the grass, his skull aching, too winded to breathe or speak.

She had quit! Her announcement was still ringing in his ears. He was floored. He prided himself on keeping one step ahead of the opposing side to avoid any last-minute surprises, but Janessa had outwitted him superbly.

Black rage boiled up inside him. He had been expecting repercussions from last night, but Janessa had pulled out all the stops.

It was second nature to him to hypothesize the opposition's motives and objectives, and he did that now, mentally outlining Janessa's agenda. He saw it all with horrifying clarity....

After last night's confidences and mind-shattering kisses, Janessa figured he would be in thrall to her and she could do whatever she

pleased. She could come in late, she could scold
him like a harridan, announce she was quitting,
and then expect him to run after her and beg her
to stay. *She thought he was that desperate for her.*

And here he stood, on the verge of doing exactly what she expected him to do!

The conniving, manipulative little witch!

Jordan dropped down onto his chair, propping
his elbows on the desk and grasping his throbbing head in his hands. He was actually shaking
from the force of his anger. He yanked open his
desk drawer and shook several antacids into his
hand.

He chewed vigorously, his teeth gnashing the
tablets into miniscule pieces.

The encounter had not gone at all as he had
planned.

Now she'd done it!

Janessa's momentary triumph faded before
she'd even left Jordan's office. She had quit her
job and egregiously offended her boss. She knew
Jordan too well to entertain any delusions that
he would forgive the nasty scene. As for a reference for a future job, it would probably be
more prudent to tell potential employers that
she'd spent the last five years in prison than to
rely on a good recommendation from Roderick
Farrell Jordan.

She was still so infuriated that the pain remained on the periphery. But she knew it was
there, aching deep down inside her, waiting to
torment her when the sharp edge of her anger
blurred.

Tears burned her eyes, but she fought to keep
them from falling. Whenever she thought of

never coming to this office again, of never seeing Jordan again; when she thought of the way he'd tricked her into resigning because he had kissed her and decided she wasn't worth bothering with . . .

She blocked those thoughts by concentrating on counting to twenty in Hungarian. Maybe Ga would teach her to count higher. She would certainly have lots of time to learn!

Panic seized her, and as awful as it was, it was preferable to the hollow ache inside her.

She certainly had plenty of reasons to panic. By quitting she had forfeited her unemployment benefits; if she'd waited for Jordan to fire her, at least she would have had those! She thought of the household bills that would not be met without a chunk of her salary, and her insides churned like a centrifuge.

Debbie walked into her office, tears running down her cheek. "Janessa, I heard you're leaving. Oh, what am I going to do? Danny and I need my paycheck, but I can't work here if you're gone. I can't deal with him without you."

Kolenda, Ackerly, and Valstock solemnly filed in next.

"So it's true?" Ackerly looked at Debbie weeping all over Janessa and frowned. "Well, that cinches it for me. I'm getting out. There will be mass chaos around here while Jordan tries to replace you, and I'm not up to it. There's more to life than money."

"How did everybody find out?" Janessa asked. She and Jordan had raised their voices in anger, but they certainly hadn't screamed the place down.

Valstock looked embarrassed. "That secretary

Lisa and I listened outside the door. She said we needed to have a handle on the situation. Lisa is already typing up her résumé, and if things are going to be as bad around here as everybody is predicting, I think I'd better ask her to type mine too."

"Quitting is not a smart move," Janessa murmured. "Think of your unemployment benefits—I didn't think of mine."

"Well, I can't wait around to be fired. I'm going to spare myself that scene." Debbie shuddered.

"I think it's a damn shame." Kolenda was frowning. "Janessa, I have some contacts at some other law—"

"What is this? A cabal or a wake?"

All heads turned at the sound of Jordan's booming voice. He was standing in the doorway, surveying the group crowded into Janessa's small office.

"There is no reason for either." He walked into the office. Debbie jumped out of his path, taking refuge behind Ackerly. "Janessa, I refuse to accept your resignation."

Janessa stared at him in bewilderment. She must be mistaken. Was Jordan offering her job back?

"If you'll excuse us?" Jordan's request sounded like a direct command. Which, of course, it was.

Debbie and the lawyers vacated the premises immediately. Jordan closed the door behind them, then leaned against it, staring broodingly at Janessa, who stood behind her desk as still and mute as a statue.

Jordan cleared his throat. "Why do you take

the bus to work? Don't you have a car? Why don't you drive?"

Whatever she had been expecting him to say, it wasn't that. "You sound like Marie Antoinette wondering why the peasants don't eat cake if they're so hungry," she said dryly.

"I saw where you live. It's working class, not peasant conditions."

"Ah, tactful as always." Janessa rolled her eyes. A strange elation kindled inside her. They were back on their old familiar footing; it was as if their terrible spat—and her impulsive declaration—had never occurred.

"I'll try to explain it to you, Jordan. You see, we working class proles who have clawed our way up from peasant origins have to rely on public transportation because it costs plenty to park a car all day long in the city—provided there are enough parking spaces, which there aren't. And yes, I do have a car," she added.

"And car payments, I assume?" Jordan asked coolly.

She nodded, glancing out the window. It was raining even harder than before.

"Not to mention the financial assistance you provide to your family."

Janessa cast him a quick, questioning glance. Jordan met her eyes, holding her gaze as if by some invisible force.

"Your brother Mike is very talkative," Jordan explained. "During the drive to Ambridge last night, he told me that you help support your mother and sisters and always have. He said you also help with his expenses."

Jordan paused for maximum effect. "Your little temper tantrum would have been disastrous to you and your family had I decided to accept your foolish, impulsive resignation, Janessa. Luckily for you, I decided that calmer heads should prevail."

Janessa watched the sardonic curve of his lips and her color deepened. She was trapped, and Jordan knew it. She knew his thought patterns so well, she could almost see the strategy he'd mapped out in his mind. Once his anger had cooled, the always pragmatic Jordan had realized that her absence would create a greater inconvenience for him than her presence would. So he was going to do her the big favor of allowing her to continue as his slave. However, there would be certain conditions. . . .

"However, there are certain conditions," Jordan said, and Janessa had to suppress the bubble of cynical laughter that welled inside her.

"What's so funny?" he demanded. "You tried to hide it, but I caught a clear glimpse of that mocking little smile of yours."

"You're mistaken. What do I have to smile about?" Janessa tilted her head quizzically, making her dark eyes wide and round. "I'm actually very contrite and grateful for your generosity. Your calmer head has saved me and my entire family from disaster."

"You've said all the right words," Jordan growled, "but nobody knows better than me that tone and expression convey far more meaning than what is actually said. It's called subtext, and you're a champion at it."

"I'm afraid you've misunderstood, Mr. Jordan," Janessa said silkily, proving that she was indeed a champion in the art of subtext.

However, at this particular moment, her own

behavior was confusing her. She knew she should be down on her knees, figuratively speaking, thanking Jordan for this second chance, because quitting her job so impulsively had been the most stupid thing she had ever done. Yet, she was taunting him—oh, she knew very well that she was—and she couldn't seem to make herself stop.

"I'm simply waiting for you to apprise me of those certain conditions you mentioned. Sir," she added for good measure.

He stared at her, his blue eyes glittering. "Are you?"

"Although I can probably guess what they are."

"Can you?" he asked in a strangled tone. His face was flushed and his hands were clenched at his sides. He was clearly struggling for control, and knowing Jordan, he would win the struggle.

Some perverse impulse—she seemed to be brimming with impulses today—challenged her to make him lose that steely control. It would be sweet revenge to see him ranting and raving.

She strolled around her desk and leaned against it, folding her arms in front of her. She languidly crossed one ankle over the other, her movements slow and deliberate. Glancing down, she caught sight of her sexy black shoes and grew even bolder.

"Condition number one—I must never be late again. If the 81C should ever have another flat or a breakdown, I should get off the bus and hitchhike into town."

"Janessa—"

"But, of course, you don't believe I was late because of the bus. You think I deliberately overslept and then pinned the blame on the bus. Ha! Well, maybe I did."

Jordan stared compulsively at her legs, at her slender ankles. Those shoes she was wearing . . . He tried to drag his eyes away. This sudden preoccupation with her shoes was worrisome.

"Don't be flippant, Janessa," he said hoarsely. "I know you didn't plan to be late. I happen to know the bus had a flat tire that took hours to fix, because I called the transit authority and they confirmed it."

"And do you feel guilty—not to mention foolish—for ripping into me like a demented megalomaniac?" Janessa's tone and smile were as sweet and artificial as aspartame. "If you don't, you should." Enmity and challenge shone in her eyes.

"Don't, Janessa," Jordan gritted through his teeth.

"Don't what?" she snapped.

"Provoke me. I know exactly what you're trying to do, and it won't work."

"Which brings us to condition number two." Janessa tossed her dark hair. As if mesmerized, Jordan watched it tumble over her shoulders. Tension quivered between them.

"I am supposed to forget that you kissed me last night. You didn't mean to, your system was on overload from all the sugar in my grandmother's cake. It's the classic Twinkie defense. If it worked in a murder case, why not apply it to a case of impulsive passion? Poor Jordan. You're terrified that now I'll make all sorts of presumptions on the basis of last night and try to take unfair advantage here at the office."

Janessa actually laughed at the startled expression on his face. He was clearly incredulous, maybe even a little spooked, that she'd accurately nailed that point.

"No, I'm not clairvoyant," she assured him. "*You're* transparent. And don't worry, I won't be chasing you around the office hoping for a repeat performance of last night. I don't *want* a repeat performance."

"Don't you?" Jordan drawled. He began to cross the office, his movements so slow and subtle that she was scarcely aware of his progress.

"No! Last night was quite enough, thank you very much. Of course, I'm sure you don't believe me. After all, you think I'm a liar. You didn't believe my bus story until it was verified for you." Just the thought of him daring to cross-examine the transit authority, hoping to catch her in a lie, made her burn.

"Well, I don't want you to touch me, Jordan. Since your ego is the size of the Third World, you'll probably demand verification of that, but—Oh!" She broke off with a gasp. He was standing directly in front of her, towering above her.

"I don't need verification of anything. I told you I know what you're doing, Janessa. You're trying to make me shut you up. Well, it worked," he added huskily.

His hands closed on her shoulders and he yanked her against him, clamping his mouth over hers.

It was no leisurely, preliminary kiss. Instantly, his tongue probed deeply, intimately, forcing her mouth to open wider. Janessa didn't even think to protest. The sense of inevitability and rightness that suffused her when he took her in his arms usurped any anger.

She moaned and wrapped her arms around his neck, feverishly kissing him back. It was as if the intervening hours since they had last kissed didn't exist, as if they were picking up where they'd left off last night.

They were in the midst of a flaming passion that grew swiftly and fiercely. They were both swept back into the heat of an emotionally intimate connection so natural and strong, it seemed to be destined.

Janessa's right hand caressed the back of his neck, feeling the short bristly hairs at his nape, while her left hand glided over his back to his midriff and the flat plane of his belly. An unfed sensual hunger drove her, a yearning that she couldn't control. The need to touch him, to be close to him, was too powerful to resist.

He buried his mouth against the curve of her neck, his lips burning on her sensitive skin. Pushing her back against the desk, he slowly sank on top of her, so they were both reclining on the desk top. His arms gathered her closer as he took her mouth again.

A tiny whimper escaped from her throat when he used his muscular thigh to separate her legs and settled himself in the notch of her feminine heat. His throbbing male urgency spurred an answering need deep within her.

The rampant sexuality of their positions incited them both. Janessa arched against Jordan, clinging to him, moaning as he cupped her breasts with his hands. He fondled them, drawing his thumbs over her tightly drawn nipples.

They thrust against the lacy material of her bra and the ribbed sweater dress.

"I want to see you," Jordan whispered, lowering his mouth to her breast. "To taste you." He nuzzled her, becoming increasingly frustrated by the clothes that served as barriers between them.

"Oh, Jordan, I've never felt like this before." Janessa gasped, clinging to him. "I-I feel as if I'm going out of my mind."

"Good," he growled. "Because my mind is already gone."

They looked at each other and laughed together in a sweet shared moment.

And then the almost unbearable excitement claimed them again, sweeping them back into the whirling vortex of passion.

His hands slid over her, around her, and found the zipper in back that ran the length of her dress. He grasped the tab and began to tug, so intent on his mission that he didn't even notice the sudden, earsplitting ring of the telephone.

It rang twice, three times. Janessa tensed and tried to sit up. Jordan was still busy with her zipper; he'd pulled it the whole way down its track.

"Jordan." She pushed at his chest. "Jordan, my phone is ringing."

"Someone will pick it up," Jordan murmured. He was oblivious to everything but the sensual hunger raging inside him. He succeeded in slipping the dress over her shoulders, and his eyes flared at the rounded swell of her breasts beneath her pale blue satin slip.

"Janessa?" Debbie's voice sounded nervously over the intercom. "Janessa, I answered your phone because you didn't, and you always answer your phone." Her voice rose shrilly. "Janessa, I know you're in there. Please answer me, if you can. Is—Is everything all right? Should I call for help?"

Groaning, Jordan dropped his hands and stepped back. "Call for help?" he repeated incredulously.

"Debbie watches all the tabloid TV shows," Janessa explained breathlessly. "To her, an angry boss and an unanswered phone add up to an atrocious crime. She's probably already rehearsing for her interview on 'Hard Copy.' I'd better take that call immediately."

Still half lying on the desk top, Janessa twisted to grab her phone with one hand while trying to hold up the bodice of her dress with the other.

"I'm here, Debbie. Everything is all right."

"When you didn't answer your phone, I thought maybe—" Debbie began, but Janessa quickly cut her off.

"Please put the call through, Deb."

She knew Jordan was watching her, though she couldn't bring herself to meet his eyes. The image of the two of them, writhing with abandon on her desk top, made her whole body flush with a disconcerting mix of passion and embarrassment.

Hopefully, Valstock and Lisa were not standing outside with their ears pressed to the door!

"Janessa, it's me!" Her sister Mallory's voice came over the line. "Janessa, I'm so scared!" Her voice wavered and then broke into sobs. "You won't believe what happened at the store this morning. We were robbed!"

6

"It's—very kind of you to take me to see Mallory." Janessa stole an uncertain glance at Jordan.

They were in the front seat of his car, a stately pearl gray Lexus, driving in congested, stop-and-start traffic to the suburban strip mall where the Lady Godiva shop was located.

As far as Janessa knew, this was unprecedented—the first time Jordan had ever left the office during weekday working hours for a reason not directly related to a case. The staff had watched in awestruck silence as the pair departed.

"You needn't sound so astonished," Jordan said gruffly. "I am capable of kind impulses and occasionally I actually succumb to them. Your sister needs you, and I think we both agree that you've taken enough buses for one day."

Janessa made no reply. Once again the brief conversation with her younger sister replayed in her mind, and she tried to tamp down the fear that threatened to swamp her.

Mallory had been hysterical, and the police officer at the scene had taken over the call. He told Janessa that her sister was practically incoherent with fright and was unable to provide any infor-

mation about the crime except that a man armed
with a gun had entered the Lady Godiva Shop
and forced her to empty the cash register. It
would be useful if Janessa could come to the
store to be with her sister; the girl was badly in
need of emotional support.

Janessa sensed there was more that the officer
didn't want to reveal over the telephone, and her
imagination ran wild with possibilities, all of
them bad. Her thoughts had been so filled with
fear for Mallory that she'd scarcely noticed Jordan had straightened her dress and carefully
pulled up the zipper.

"I couldn't help but overhear. The officer pro-
jected his voice loud enough to be heard in the
next county," Jordan had muttered tersely.
"Comb your hair and fix your lipstick, and I'll
drive you to wherever your sister works."

At the time, Janessa had been too distracted to
object.

Only now, sitting next to Jordan in the car, did
she reflect on the intimacy of that scene: she held
her compact mirror as she reapplied the lipstick
his kisses had rubbed off and brushed her hair
that his fingers had tousled, while Jordan
watched closely, his eyes never leaving her.

"What kind of store is this Lady Godiva
place?" Jordan's voice cut into her reverie.

Janessa jumped, startled.

"Relax, Janessa. You're strung tighter than a
high wire."

And so was he, Jordan conceded grimly. Their
interrupted erotic romp on the desk top had left
him restless, tense, and on edge.

He should be in the gym, working out on the
rowing machine or the Stair Master, to sublimate
the force of his sexual energy. Sitting next to Ja-

nessa, so sexy and achingly gorgeous, instead
served to intensify that drive—a drive that was
already too potent for his peace of mind.

When had she become so alluring? Had she
always been this fascinating, and if so, why
hadn't he noticed until yesterday?

It all had begun then, he realized in a flash of
perception. He had taken one look at Janessa,
standing by the elevator with her accountant
friend, and he hadn't been the same since. He
wanted to be around her constantly. He couldn't
stop looking at her or thinking about her.

He'd jumped at the chance to drive her brother
to her birthday party last night, because it meant
the chance to see her again, and he was suddenly, insatiably curious about her life outside
the office. He'd seen her surrounded by her family, and then, when they were alone, they had
unexpectedly connected emotionally and physically. And now he wanted even more.

Jordan went down the list of symptoms as if
he were charting the progress of a disease.

Or a spell.

His practical, logical nature made him immediately discard black magic as a cause. He might
feel bewitched and beguiled, but he didn't believe in magic. No, this case was basic and elementary. Janessa's beauty and warmth and
charm had been there all along, and he had suddenly taken notice.

The mystery to him was how he had managed
to keep his hands off her for five long years,
when now it took every ounce of willpower he
possessed to keep from reaching over to touch
her.

What would she do if he laid his hand on her

knee and then slid it under her skirt, following the silky length of her thigh until he—

"Lady Godiva is a women's lingerie shop," Janessa said, answering his question.

Her words filtered through the hot red haze of Jordan's fantasy. "Lingerie," he repeated. He nearly groaned aloud. He needed no further stimuli; his senses were already on overload.

He trailed into the store after Janessa, trying to keep his eyes averted from the racks of lacy brassieres, matching panties, and garter belts in every color of the rainbow. There were also eye-popping garments he couldn't identify made of silky, sensuous materials, mostly in shades of red and black.

"Oh, Janessa!" Mallory, a tall, pretty brunette, rushed toward them and threw her arms around Janessa. "I'm so glad you're here!"

A young police officer stood nearby watching the sisters embrace. Jordan walked over and introduced himself. "What can we do to help, Officer?"

"Bringing Mallory's sister over was a big help," the policeman said. "That creep didn't only rob the place, he terrorized the poor girl."

"Oh, no!" Janessa's eyes filled with tears. "Mallory, did he—hurt you?"

"Not physically." Mallory shuddered. "But he went around making disgusting remarks and—and fondling stuff. It was so gross, Janessa. And scary too."

"Being held at gunpoint by a profane psycho is very traumatizing," the policeman agreed, his voice warm with sympathy. "I can give you the phone number of a crime victims support group, Mallory. I've heard they can be helpful."

"*You've* been so helpful, Tom," Mallory said

softly. "I'm so lucky you were the one to answer my call. You've been so wonderful and patient and understanding."

Officer Tom flushed with pleasure. Janessa and Jordan caught each other's eyes.

"Mallory, do you feel calm enough to give the officer a description of the robber now?" Janessa interjected.

Mallory nodded. "But I feel a little light-headed. Could I sit down?"

The policeman gallantly swept a chair under her and Mallory sank down on it. He squatted on his haunches in front of her. "Just breathe deeply and take your time, Mallory. You're completely safe now," he said soothingly.

Mallory nodded again. The questioning began. It was an intense one-on-one session that did not require outside parties. Janessa and Jordan drifted to the other side of the store.

"Am I imagining things or are they flirting with each other while filling out the crime report?" Jordan murmured under his breath.

"Knowing Mallory, she'll end up dating him. She's had guys falling at her feet since she turned thirteen."

"She's an attractive woman," Jordan conceded. "But she lacks your—" He cleared his throat. "Charisma or something."

"I thought you were going to say 'my brains,'" Janessa said dryly. "In our family, I'm considered the smart sister, and Mallory and Chelsi are the beautiful sisters. At least until Chelsi shaved off half her head and got a nose ring."

"Beauty is in the eyes of the beholder," Jordan said drolly.

Janessa choked back a laugh. Under the circumstances, laughter struck her as unseemly. She concentrated instead on Mallory's lucky escape from danger and murmured a silent prayer of thanks to their father, grandfather, and great-grandfather. She considered them an ethereal triumvirate who took a personal interest in family matters and helped out when they could. Protecting Mallory from a psycho gunman in Lady Godiva must have been one of their more interesting challenges.

"What are these things?" One rack of provocative garments had captured Jordan's attention and he stared incredulously, not daring to touch. "Do women really wear them?"

"They're called bustiers," Janessa informed him. "And yes, some women wear them. They used to be considered underwear, but now they're worn as outerwear too. Mallory and Chelsi wear them in the summer with jeans shorts."

Jordan's brows arched. "May I assume that you don't go parading around in such a costume?"

"Good heavens, you sound as disapproving as Great-Uncle Lazlo," Janessa said lightly.

"A neat dodge, but you haven't answered my question." Jordan was in full cross-examining mode.

"And I'm not going to," Janessa replied, wandering to the opposite end of the store. The answer was no, but while bustiers and ripped jeans shorts weren't her style, she didn't care for the condemning note in Jordan's voice. If he was expecting prudish assent from her, he wasn't going to get it.

Jordan stared at Janessa, who was absently

browsing through the racks of teddies—he knew what *they* were—and visualized her wearing one in his bedroom. Briefly. Until he removed it.

His loins throbbed with a stabbing pleasure that bordered on pain. It was becoming increasingly difficult to stand straight. Rather desperately, he glanced around for another chair, but Mallory was sitting on the only one, her policeman-hero hovering over her.

In sheer self-defense, Jordan walked gingerly into the smaller adjoining room. There was no lingerie in here. On the shelves and countertops were a variety of items that Jordan hesitated to label. Into what category did a game called Dirty Dice: Enjoy Throws of Ecstasy fall? And then there were the velvet cat-o'-nines in various colors and the flavored edible body creams.

His eyes widened, and he backed into a pyramid display of bottles of Wildfire Body Lotion, nearly knocking it over. ONE OF OUR BEST SELLERS, the sign boasted.

Jordan didn't doubt it. But his body was in no need of a special lotion to set it afire. There was already a blazing urgency roaring within him. Inspired exclusively by Janessa.

He couldn't go on this way! He wouldn't! It was time he took control of this unpredictable, inexplicable, totally unwelcome obsession with Janessa Balint.

He strode purposefully back to her.

"So when I called my boss to tell him about the robbery," a woeful Mallory was telling Officer Tom, "I said I didn't feel safe and I wanted to close the store and go home for the rest of the day. And he said if I did, not to bother coming back to work 'cause I'm fired. What am I going to do, Tom? I'm too nervous to stay here today."

"Quit, Mallory," advised Janessa. "I've never been crazy about you working at this place. It's too isolated, way down at the far end of the mall, and I don't think you should risk being around here, in case that creep does come back."

"But I don't want to quit or be fired!" Mallory wailed. "I need my job!"

"Maybe Chelsi could get you in at the Feet Boutique," Janessa suggested. "They always seem to have an opening. In fact, the turnover rate there seems to be one of the few that exceeds the turnover in Jordan's office."

"I object," Jordan exclaimed. "There can be no comparison between my firm and a place called the Feet Boutique."

Janessa overruled the objection by ignoring him. "Mallory, you don't have to continue working here. We can manage while you take the time to look around for another job."

"But I love working here!" cried Mallory. "You meet the most interesting people!"

Jordan exhaled impatiently. "Let me see if I have the facts straight, Mallory. You want to go home today, but you don't mind coming back here to work tomorrow, even if that nut is still on the loose?"

Mallory nodded, sniffling.

"We'll beef up the security patrols," Officer Tom promised. "I will personally make certain that the mall, especially this end of it, is under close surveillance. If that creep comes back, I promise we'll nab him, Mallory."

"I know you will, Tom," Mallory purred.

Janessa felt a little of her anxiety lift. It seemed that Mallory was going to have her very own private police protection.

"Get me your boss on the phone, Mallory," Jordan commanded in his officer-of-the-court voice, and Mallory instantly responded by dialing the number. She moved more efficiently than a number of secretaries he'd employed, Jordan observed. Perhaps when they had another opening in the office . . .

Janessa, Mallory, and Officer Tom listened as Jordan informed the shop owner that Mallory was leaving for the day on the advice of the police officer in charge of the investigation, and that if her job was in jeopardy, her attorney, R. F. Jordan, would immediately file suit against the shop owner as well as the company that owned and managed the entire mall.

He finished by rattling off a string of numbers—ordinances, perhaps? Janessa didn't know, but only R. F. Jordan could make numerals sound so coldly ominous that one quaked at the sound of them.

Jordan hung up moments later. "Your boss said to close the shop, go home, and take it easy for the rest of the day," he told Mallory. "Take off tomorrow if you feel the need, and of course, there is no question that your job is secure. Your boss is grateful that you are unharmed and appreciates your courageous behavior in the face of personal danger."

"Wow!" breathed Mallory. "He sure didn't say that to me. You must've scared him to death. You kinda scared me, you sounded so godawful *mean!*"

"It's a talent of mine." Jordan shrugged. "Just ask Debbie, eh, Janessa?"

"Debbie does find you assertive," Janessa said diplomatically.

"I'll drive you home, Mallory," Officer Tom volunteered. "It's almost my lunch break anyway. Maybe we could stop and get a bite to eat along the way."

"Oh, Tom, that's so sweet of you!" Mallory sighed, gazing worshipfully at him. "I'd just love to!"

"We have to head back to the office, Janessa." Jordan glanced at his watch. "I have a working lunch with a colleague in half an hour." He stalked briskly outside to his car.

Janessa gave Mallory a good-bye hug, then started for the door.

"Janessa!" Mallory's voice halted her. "Those shoes you're wearing are so cool! So sexy! So unlike you! Where'd you get them?"

"Didn't Chelsi tell you?" Janessa smiled. "She bought them for me for my birthday."

"Chelsi bought you sweat socks," Mallory countered flatly. "I know because I lectured her about it. I told her sweat socks are an ultralame birthday gift, but she bought them anyway, with her employee discount. She can be so cheap, except when it comes to herself and then she spends, spends, spends!"

"But then who gave me these shoes?" Janessa was flummoxed. "They were in a box on the porch with my name on them."

"Was there a card attached? Did you ask Chelsi if she gave them to you?"

"I haven't seen Chelsi in a couple of days,"

Janessa admitted. Sometimes their youngest sister stayed with friends for several days, depending on her party schedule. "And there wasn't a card attached to the box. I just assumed they were from Chelsi because they're shoes and—"

"The Feet Boutique doesn't sell anything that expensive and classy." Mallory studied Janessa's shoes with a critical eye. "Their stuff is cheap junk that stains your feet and disintegrates in water."

Considering how well her shoes had survived this morning's torrent of rain seemingly eliminated them from originating at the Feet Boutique. "But then where did they come from?" asked Janessa.

"Looks like you have a mystery on your hands," Officer Tom suggested cheerfully. "One that involves giving instead of stealing. A refreshing change."

Jordan stuck his head in the door. "Janessa, we're already running late," he called impatiently. "Let's go. Right now!"

"He reminds me of my drill instructor in the marines," the young cop said rather admiringly. "A real motivating, can-do kind of guy. Not the sort who tolerates screwups, though."

"That's Jordan," agreed Janessa. "But he has a warmer side," she felt compelled to add.

He also possessed a passionate side she had personally experienced, and a considerate side he'd exercised today on Mallory's behalf. He had a sense of humor, he could feel pain, he was much more than the invulnerable lawman-of-steel image he liked to project. Funny how Jordan had gone from one-dimensional to multi-faceted in twenty-four hours. Or was it simply her perception of him that had changed?

"Can I borrow those shoes sometime, Janessa?" Mallory couldn't take her eyes off them. "You're about a size smaller, but maybe I could jam my feet into them. Of course, I'd feel like one of Cinderella's stepsisters." She frowned, not caring for that particular role.

"You'd better get moving before the Drill Instructor busts you to private, Janessa," kidded Tom.

Janessa heeded his advice. She did not want to presume on Jordan's newly revealed yet mostly untested "warm side." Calling a quick good-bye, she hurried outside.

Jordan was preoccupied and quiet on the drive back to the office. He merely grunted when Janessa thanked him profusely for driving her to Lady Godiva and for his intervention with Mallory's boss.

"I don't remember anything about your working lunch today," she ventured after another long silence.

Her memory lapse was disconcerting to her because she knew his daily schedule as well as she knew her own home telephone number.

"I don't remember who the colleague is, where you're to meet him, or what business you'll be conducting," she admitted uneasily.

"That's because the working lunch is fictitious. I plan to send out for a burger and eat at my desk."

"I see. You made up that meeting to hurry us out of Lady Godiva." Janessa was surprised she hadn't realized that immediately.

"There was no reason for us to hang around

there," Jordan said curtly. "I had visions of your sister and her admiring officer friend arranging a double lunch date for the four of us."

"What an appalling waste of your valuable time that would've been!" Janessa was flippant, and more than a little hurt, though she was loath to admit it, even to herself. Certainly, she would never admit it to Jordan.

But she didn't have to. "I can see that it's beginning already," Jordan said grimly. "I was hoping we could avoid a showdown, but we're obviously headed for one."

"What do you mean, a showdown? This is Pittsburgh, not the O.K. Corral."

"Janessa, avoidance of the issue will only complicate things further." He sounded like a judge scolding a recalcitrant witness. "We are in a problematic situation and we have to deal with it. I am your boss and you are—" Jordan paused.

He couldn't immediately articulate her job title. She performed too many different functions to list just one. Office manager. Legal assistant. Confidential secretary. Receptionist when need be. Smoother of troubled office waters. Trustworthy gofer. Indispensable girl Friday.

His heart seemed to leap into his throat. There was no denying it. He'd become extremely dependent upon her around the office. And it would be so easy to become emotionally dependent on her too. Remembering how he'd basked in the warmth of her attention last night released a pang of yearning in him. Recalling how he'd nearly become unglued in the Lady Godiva shop by simply watching her unleashed a wave of panic.

For the first time in his life, his precise thought

processes were going haywire. Adding insult to injury, the cause was a woman. It seemed a devilish irony. In the past, he'd always scorned men who lost their heads over women, considering them hapless chumps.

Well, he would not be one of them. R. F. Jordan could separate business from pleasure, work from personal life. He would prove it right now.

"This can't go on!" he blurted out. "Office romances are a prescription for disaster and I refuse to become embroiled in one. If we have an affair, we can't continue to work together, Janessa. It's as simple as that."

Janessa's jaw dropped. "I don't remember asking you to have an affair with me."

She tried to keep her voice light and breezy. To display the hurt welling within her and the ferocious swell of anger that accompanied the pain would be to give too much away. She would not give Jordan that power over her, let alone bolster his already gargantuan ego by confirming how very much she cared about him.

"The way I see it, we have two choices." Jordan was already outlining the strategies, just as he might present options to a client. "I can fire you on grounds that will enable you to collect your unemployment benefits—something like 'office downsizing' would be perfect—and provide an excellent reference, and we can allow the attraction between us to develop into a fullblown affair. Conversely, we can agree to put an end to all the gazing and groping and return to the smooth working relationship we've developed over the past years."

Janessa stared at him. He was completely serious. He apparently believed that compartmentalizing one's thoughts and feelings was not only possible but preferable. As if one could turn off desire at will. Janessa studied his hard, implacable profile and decided that if anyone could do so, it would be Jordan.

Put an end to all the gazing and groping, he'd said with a callous frankness that set her teeth on edge. He'd reduced their passion to that!

"You certainly have a talent for putting things into perspective," Janessa said, holding on to her temper, though just barely. If Jordan could be cool, well then, she would be the human equivalent of dry ice! "How shall I ever choose between those two irresistible offers? Well, I'd better weigh the options. First, unemployment benefits, a good reference, and an affair with you."

She tilted her head and pretended to be seriously considering it. "I would probably have to take care of all those inconvenient courtship details. After all, you don't know how because you've never done it. That's always been my job. So I'd have to make the dinner and theater reservations and send myself flowers at least twice. And after three weeks our affair would be over, because your relationships never last longer than that. Hopefully, you'd have someone in place in the office to intercept my calls, in case I was stupid or desperate enough to phone you."

"You're not being fair, Janessa," Jordan protested. "You—You've taken everything out of context."

His face was flushed and his voice was strained. He couldn't deny that Janessa did all those things during his brief courtships. But to hear her state it so baldly shook him. It made him sound so shallow and cold and uncaring. *He wasn't!*

"You don't understand," he murmured. "I'm a very busy man who values efficiency and sees no reason to waste time on a relationship that is going nowhere."

It was exactly like Mike had said! Just enough time to get to know the woman and decide she wasn't worth the bother. Janessa burned. Well, Jordan wasn't going to get that chance, not with her.

"I understand completely, Jordan. Which brings me to option number two," Janessa continued smoothly. "Putting an end to all the gazing and groping and returning to our smooth working relationship that we've developed over the years. That's my choice, Jordan. I'd rather keep my job than have a three-week fling with you."

Silence reigned for the remainder of the drive. Neither spoke on the elevator and both retreated to their respective offices without a single glance in the other's direction.

Later that afternoon, during her lunch break, Janessa walked to Kaufmann's department store and headed straight for the shoes. Mallory had insisted that her new black shoes were not a present from Chelsi. So who had placed them on the doorstep—with her name on the package?

The idea of an anonymous gift struck her as odd, maybe even spooky. Suddenly she didn't want anything more to do with her black suede shoes.

Janessa bought a pair of sensible brown pumps that were perfectly appropriate for office wear. Her feet felt pinched and constricted by the time she'd walked back to the office. By the end of the day she was hobbling to the bus stop. Though her mystery shoes were tucked inside the Kaufmann's bag, Janessa did not remove her crippling brown pumps in favor of them.

When she got home, she put the mystery shoes back in the rainbow box she'd saved and placed it high on her closet shelf. Though she couldn't bring herself to discard them, she wouldn't wear those shoes anymore.

She might want to wear them, but there were many things one might want to do but couldn't, Janessa reminded herself sternly. Many things one might want to have that were bad for you.

She shocked herself by bursting into tears.

7

Four weeks passed. Rainy, chilly April turned into rainy, chilly May, though the TV forecasters kept insisting that sunny spring weather was on its way to the tri-state area—eventually.

There was a chill of a different kind reigning in the firm of R. F. Jordan.

Jordan was scrupulously polite to Debbie and the secretaries. "He hasn't yelled in a whole month. It's like a miracle!" they marveled. But his demeanor toward Janessa was icy. Communication between them was almost nonexistent.

He avoided her whenever possible. When dealing with her on an office-related matter was unavoidable, he sent a message via one of the associates or secretaries or arranged a meeting in the conference room, taking care to never, ever be alone with her. There was always someone else on hand, even if that person's presence was superfluous to the issue being discussed.

As the days turned into weeks and Jordan continued to remain coldly remote, Janessa knew that he meant the distance between them to be permanent. Though he had insisted that she choose between her job and an affair with him, it seemed that he resented her choice. She'd guessed that his ego might be a bit dented at first, but his prolonged unfriendly and aloof behavior surprised her, saddened her too.

She missed the ease of their earlier relationship. They'd had a camaraderie that had been deepening into intimacy. All traces of it were gone now, effectively abolished during that car ride back to the office from the Lady Godiva shop.

At first, she'd expected their working relationship would soon revert to its usual form, but it was clear that wasn't going to happen. Jordan's curtness toward her was unrelenting and cut her to the quick. On good days he treated her as if she were a stranger. On bad days he acted as if she were a stranger to whom he'd taken an instant dislike.

She was hurting, Janessa admitted. Maintaining a cheerful, normal facade at work sapped her energy, and when she left the office each day, she was overcome with a dull weariness that nothing could ease. She had a hard time falling asleep each night, and when she finally did, she inevitably awakened too early and lay lonely and brooding until dawn's light streaked the sky.

Every day it grew harder to be around Jordan,
knowing that the emotional distance between
them could be measured in light-years. When
she thought of another year, another month,
even another week of it, she felt like crying.

She wished he would fire her so she could get
on with her life, but she guessed that he was
hanging tough, waiting for her to break first and
quit. They were at an impasse, and she saw no
way out.

One late May evening, when the rain had
stopped and the temperature miraculously
reached a balmy near-seventy degrees, Janessa
took her great-grandmother for a walk. Their
pace was very slow, and Ga's frailty did not permit her to go any farther than from the front
porch to the sidewalk and back. But the flowers
were in bloom and the birds were chirping, and
the old woman's face was alight with pleasure.

Janessa wished she could derive so much en-
joyment from such a simple outing.

"Ga, remember that Gypsy blessing you told
me about on my birthday?"

She held her great-grandmother's arm as they
headed slowly toward the maple tree at the edge
of the small front yard. "Well, it's not that I believe in either magic blessings or curses, but it
seems to me that if there really was a blessing,
it's turned out to be a total dud."

She drew a deep breath. "You won't believe
what's happened, Ga. I'm in love with my boss
and, of course, he doesn't love me. There, I finally admitted it! The whole situation is such a
cliché, it's embarrassing."

Janessa heaved a dejected sigh. "Who would

have thought it would happen to me? I'm supposed to be so sane and mature and responsible. There is a twist, though. Jordan actually offered to have an affair with me—translated, that's a three-week fling—but he said I'd have to choose between him and my job. Well, it's been four weeks since he made that offer. Do you realize that if I'd chosen the fling, it would be over by now? At least I'm still employed."

Her great-grandmother said a few words in Hungarian. Janessa thought one of them might be "bird." Or was it "shoe"? Her grasp of the language was really weak.

Although there was a definite communication gap between them, Janessa decided it was better that way. It felt good to finally talk about her dilemma, but she didn't want to disillusion the rest of the family, who venerated her alleged common sense. Not even Chelsi, who was not known for her good judgment, had ever made the idiotic blunder of falling in love with her boss. And their cousin Gina would be absolutely appalled!

Ga made the perfect confidante. Not asking questions, not offering advice, not understanding a word she was saying.

"I know I did the right thing, Ga. I made the only choice I could make. No woman in her right mind would give up a well paying job, including good health insurance benefits, when she has bills to pay and a family who depends on her."

Her great-grandmother patted her hand, perhaps reacting to her gloomy tone and expression.

"It's terribly prosaic and not at all romantic, but that's the way it is for the women in this family," Janessa continued sadly. "Except for

Mallory, I suppose. What are the odds of getting robbed and then falling in love with the investigating officer in the case? But it happened to Mal. She and Tom are madly in love. Oh, and by the way, the creep who robbed her got caught last week when he pulled an armed robbery at a gas station."

"Shoes," Ga said in clear and unmistakable English. "Birthday shoes."

"Ga, you said birthday shoes!" Janessa exclaimed in astonished delight. Was her great-grandmother regaining her English language skills? "What about the birthday shoes?"

Ga lapsed back into Hungarian.

"She'll say an English word now and then," Gram said later when Janessa told her about Ga's unexpected mention of the birthday shoes. "Very rarely and never in context. It's just a lost sound floating around in her head, I guess."

Janessa was disappointed. She could have sworn her great-grandmother was trying to communicate with her.

The next morning, on a whim, she delved into her closet and removed the shoes that had turned up on the porch on her birthday. They looked as beautiful as she remembered, and she couldn't resist the urge to wear them again. Her ominous feelings of anxiety concerning their unknown origins suddenly seemed silly. Janessa slipped the shoes on and was struck anew by how marvelous they felt as she walked around her bedroom.

The weatherman had promised a warm, clear day and Janessa decided to believe him. She chose a black pleated skirt and a black-and-white striped blazer, both in soft silk crepe. The shoes provided an effective finishing touch.

When it was Henry instead of the relentless Gracie who rolled the bus to a stop—Henry had been on sick leave for the last month—Janessa felt more cheerful.

But in the office, her spirits plummeted once more when Jordan walked by her without offering even a perfunctory hello or casting a glance in her direction.

Janessa berated herself for her foolish disappointment. Why had she hoped, even for a moment, that Jordan would stop ostracizing her? Because it was sunny outside instead of raining? Because Henry had replaced the toxic Gracie? Because she was wearing the mystery shoes after her great-grandmother had uttered "birthday shoes" in English?

"Janessa, Mr. Robert Vickers is here to see you," Debbie's voice sounded over the intercom. Though Janessa didn't know who Mr. Robert Vickers was, she could tell by the awed respect in Debbie's tone that the visitor had impressed the young receptionist.

"Mr. Vickers doesn't have an appointment, but he says it's very important that he speak with you," Debbie continued in her most professional tone.

Janessa smiled. It appeared that Mr. Vickers had clearly won over Debbie; she was doing her very best to impress *him*.

Janessa agreed to see him at once. She had nothing pressing on her schedule.

After spending a few moments in the company of the elegant, impeccably attired man who entered her office, she knew why Debbie had been bowled over by him. The man radiated money, class, and power, yet displayed a smooth, self-deprecating warmth and charm.

Mr. Vickers introduced himself to Janessa and handed her his card, which identified him as the hiring attorney for Mellot, Reed, Ingersoll, and Lockhart, the oldest, largest, and most prestigious law firm in the city, with branch offices all over the country.

"I'll come straight to the point, Miss Balint," Vickers said. He was still smiling, but his eyes glittered with determination.

Janessa recognized that glow. Jordan had it in his eyes when he was adamant about winning. It meant that the glitterer had no intention of giving up until he'd achieved his goal.

"There are several attorneys at Mellot Reed"— Vickers used the shortened form of the firm's name—"who came to us from Jordan. Working here was a *tough* but excellent training ground for them." He gave her a meaningful look.

Janessa managed a polite, uncertain smile.

"Miss Balint, these attorneys are unanimous in singing your praises. For years, I've heard about your invaluable office skills and your deft handling of personnel problems. In short, you're exactly the kind of person we want working at Mellot Reed, but we were unable to extend a job offer to you until now. Our current office manager is retiring, and we would like you to take the position."

Janessa stared. She was being recruited for a job at the city's largest, most prestigious law firm? Not only that, but the hiring attorney himself had made the trip, unsolicited, to offer her the job! She knew enough about law firms and hiring etiquette to realize how very unorthodox the situation was.

"I-I truly don't know what to say, Mr. Vickers," she managed, nearly too astonished to speak.

Vickers smiled. "I know I've caught you by surprise, Miss Balint. We both know that by coming here, I've circumvented the usual hiring process, but that should tell you how very much we want you at Mellot Reed. I am here to make you an offer you can't refuse."

Janessa gulped.

Vickers laughed. "I do not mean that as a threat, of course, but as an inducement that you will not want to resist."

He quoted a salary well beyond her current one. Included was a better health plan and a two-week paid vacation, compared to the one week she had now and dared not take all at once. She took her five days off here and there when Jordan was out of town. Her absence from the office when he was around was not permitted.

"Our offices are closed on holidays, and though our attorneys have the option to come in, *you* would not be expected to work on weekends," Vickers said, his eyes gleaming. "In fact, we would forbid it!"

Janessa was fully aware that the refugees from Jordan's office had suggested throwing in that incentive. Forbidden to work on weekends and holidays! What a concept!

"Finally, you would have a leased parking place issued to you in the garage attached to our building." Vickers smiled triumphantly, having delivered his coup de grace.

"Take your time. Think it over," he continued smoothly. "I hope that within one week you'll give us the answer that we at Mellot, Reed, Ingersoll, and Lockhart are hoping to hear. We very much want you on our team, Miss Balint."

He shook her hand and left, beseeching her to call if she had any questions. He acted as if she'd done him a wonderful favor by merely allowing him into her office and listening to his offer.

Janessa stood in the narrow corridor, dazed. She'd been offered a dream job, and she knew it.

Lisa and Valstock slipped out of the conference room and joined her in the hallway. Janessa eyed them warily. Those two had forged a conspicuous alliance during the past month.

"Janessa, we couldn't help but overhear," Lisa exclaimed.

Janessa suspected Debbie had tipped them off about Robert Vickers's appearance, and they'd made certain that they couldn't help but overhear by pressing their ears to the door. Or perhaps they'd moved on to using a stethoscope for better acoustics.

"Imagine Robert Vickers coming here in person to hire you!" Valstock was awestruck. "My God, it's as good as winning the lottery!"

Ackerly and Kolenda joined them. News traveled fast in the firm of R. F. Jordan.

"Congratulations, Janessa, you deserve it." Ackerly gave her a quick hug.

"I've kept in contact with Pederson and Wilk over at Mellot Reed," Kolenda said. "They asked me to let them know when you seemed ready to leave and I said now. After all, Jordan's been treating you like a—"

"What's going on?" The door to Jordan's office

opened, and he appeared on the threshold.

"Robert Vickers from Mellot, Reed, Ingersoll, and Lockhart just left," Valstock announced baldly.

"Vickers?" Jordan scowled. "That pirate? Who is he trying to lure away this time?" He glowered at Ackerly and Kolenda. "You might as well be honest. If you don't want to work here, then—"

"Vickers isn't interested in us, Jordan," Kolenda said. "He came to see Janessa."

"He offered her a leased parking place and a two-week vacation!" Lisa squealed. "It's like a dream come true!"

Jordan blanched. "Robert Vickers came here to offer Janessa a position at Mellot Reed?"

"It's a Cinderella story for every woman who's ever been unappreciated in an office." Lisa sighed happily.

"Does that make Robert Vickers the fairy godfather or the charming prince?" Valstock asked, and he and Lisa giggled.

Until they noticed Jordan glaring at them. "Doesn't anyone have anything to do around here?" His voice was low and terse, which was even more alarming than his usual roar.

Everybody scattered to their offices. Janessa had turned back to hers when Jordan's voice stopped her cold.

"I want to see you in my office immediately, Janessa." Without waiting for her, he walked into his office and sat down behind his desk.

Out in the hall Janessa attempted to gather her scattered wits. Too much was happening too quickly. Too many people were talking at her, blocking the sound of her own thoughts.

"You don't have to do what he says, Janessa."

It was Debbie speaking. She'd crept from her post to Janessa's side to offer moral support. "Mr. Vickers told me how much they want you at Mellot Reed. You can start there tomorrow if you want, so if Jordan tries to give you a hard time, just tell him to—to take this job and shove it!"

Janessa managed a wan smile. "It'll be okay, Debbie. Just don't let anyone listen at the door, okay?"

"Okay. I never thought it was right, but Lisa and Valstock like to play spy."

"It's an unprofessional habit they're going to have to break," Janessa said, knowing she would be quoted. Debbie nodded vigorously.

Janessa entered Jordan's office and closed the door.

"You wanted to see me?" she asked quietly. It occurred to her that this was the first time she'd been alone with Jordan since their fateful drive back from Lady Godiva.

"I didn't realize you'd been job hunting." His voice was sharp, his statement an accusation. He didn't look at her. Instead, he seemed fascinated by his pen, a sleek, ultraexpensive Mont Blanc.

"I haven't been job hunting. Mr. Vickers's visit was a complete surprise, as was his job offer."

"What did he offer?" Jordan asked brusquely, and Janessa quoted the terms.

"That's ridiculous!" he snapped. "Not only are they overpaying you, no one in that particular job description has leased parking. They're setting a stupid, costly precedent that they'll regret. Before long, they'll have to sack you to restore the proper financial status quo."

Janessa stared at him wide eyed. The ice that had encased him for the past month had cracked. His voice wasn't cold and curt, it was fiery with anger.

She watched him throw his pen onto the desk and contrasted that spontaneous gesture with his robotic movements of the past four weeks. Was the real Jordan finally back?

He rose to his feet and walked around the desk, glaring at her.

Janessa didn't even try to suppress the smile that curved her mouth. She was undoubtedly, certifiably insane to be glad that he was glowering and sniping at her, but it was such a relief to see the old Jordan that she couldn't help it.

"Well, if they try to fire me because they don't like paying what they offered me, will you take my case when I hit them with an unfair labor practice suit?" She folded her arms in front of her chest and met his blazing blue eyes.

"You know damn well I only handle product liability cases. You can take your unfair labor practice suit and—"

"—shove it?" Janessa asked politely.

"If this is a scheme to get a substantial raise and an extra week of vacation and a leased parking place out of me, it's not going to work, Janessa."

"It's not a scheme. You can call Robert Vickers yourself and verify his offer to me. Shall I get him for you?" She picked up his phone.

"Put that down," growled Jordan.

She complied. "So you believe me? You don't think the whole office is in on a conspiracy to get me a—"

"Why would you want to work at Mellot Reed?" Jordan cut in, trying another tack. Janessa recognized the maneuver.

"As opposed to working here? Let me count the ways. One, I—"

"Did you apply for a job there because I told you that you had to choose between an affair with me and your job here? You said you chose your job, but now you've changed your mind and you—"

"I told you I did not apply for that job!"

The blunt, tactless Jordan she thought she preferred to the silent, remote Jordan was fast losing his charm. They were both infuriating. "As for me changing my mind and choosing a predictable, temporary fling with you, I can only say— ha! You wish! I'll never be that desperate!"

"Won't you?" He started advancing toward her and Janessa automatically backed away from him. "I think you are desperate, Janessa. I think our—estrangement has been driving you crazy. Crazy enough to cook up this new job offer."

Janessa's back hit the wall and she glanced quickly around her. It was too late to make a run for the door. Jordan was directly in front of her, putting a hand on either side of her head, effectively blocking off all paths of escape.

"I don't know what you mean." She held her head high. "What estrangement are you talking about?" she asked coolly.

His body leaned into hers, pressing her against the wall, letting the warmth of his hard frame suffuse her. His face was just inches from hers, and when Janessa looked at his hard, strong mouth, she trembled.

"That's better," he whispered. He touched his

lips to hers, brushing them lightly across her mouth.

"No." Her voice was husky but firm. She laid her hands against his chest and pushed.

Jordan didn't budge. "Are you saying no, you won't make dinner and theater reservations or send yourself flowers or buy tickets for the requisite musical and sporting events using my credit card?"

His lips feathered hers, and he adjusted the hard arousal of his body against her soft curves. They seemed to be a perfect fit.

"Well, you won't have to, Janessa. I intend to handle all those details myself."

"And how long will this courtship last?" She twisted her head, trying to avoid his seeking lips. "The usual three weeks?"

"In case you haven't noticed, it's been four weeks since I—er—issued my ultimatum. If I were operating on that timetable, whatever interest I had in you should have ended a week ago. Instead, I—"

He paused to take a deep breath. "I've driven myself crazy this past month. I can hardly concentrate because all I can think about is you. That's never happened before. There's never been a person who mattered more to me than my work."

"And I do?" she whispered, knowing how difficult that admission was for him to make. Wanting to hear him make it again.

Jordan stared deeply into her eyes and said nothing at all.

"You didn't seem driven to distraction this past month," she felt compelled to point out. "From what I could tell, it was business as usual, except I was a pest you wished wasn't around."

"Business as usual? That's rich!" Jordan laughed without mirth. Suddenly, a torrent of words seemed to burst from him. "Thank God Ackerly and Kolenda have stayed on top of things, because I've been useless. Even that Valstock character has done more than I have this past month. As for wishing you weren't around, I wanted you around constantly, Janessa. I'd sit here in my office and think of all the things I wanted to talk about with you. I'd lie awake at night and imagine making love to you. But you've been as cold as the iceberg that sank the *Titanic*. As a matter of fact, you've sunk me! I've never felt so low in my entire life. You won't look at me, you don't talk to me, you never smile at me. You don't even want to be friends anymore."

Janessa's heart seemed to miss a beat. "Do you want to be friends, Jordan?"

"I want more than friendship and you know it. I love you, Janessa," he said, placing staccato kisses over her cheeks, her throat, and her lips. "I think I've loved you for years, but I was too thick headed—or too deep in denial—to realize it."

She felt a sweet, fierce thrust of hope and desire. "You don't have to embellish your case, Jordan. We're not in court."

"Honey, this is more important than any argument I've made in a courtroom and I am *not* embellishing. It wasn't until you lit into me about my insultingly predictable three-week relationships, and told me you'd rather have your job than me, that I realized the truth. That I loved you—and that you despised me. Worse yet, you had every right to hate me. You saw me as a shallow, slave-driving cad. And by making you choose between me and your job . . ."

His voice trailed off. "I guess that just confirmed every negative belief you had about me. This past month has been hell, Janessa. I wanted to reach out to you, but I couldn't. I kept waiting for you to—come to me first."

"Because you love to win," Janessa murmured. "But I couldn't have made the first move, Jordan. You set up a lose-lose situation for me."

Her dark eyes suddenly filled with tears. One of them trickled down her cheek. "And guess what? I don't like to lose either. We both have awfully strong defenses and we've been using them against each other."

"I know," Jordan said huskily. "Don't cry, baby."

"I'm not crying."

Another tear fell and he wiped them both away with his thumbs. "Don't hate me, Janessa. Give me a chance to try to win your love."

"I don't hate you, Jordan." She threaded her fingers through his hair and smiled wryly at him. "And you know it. You wouldn't attempt a tell-all confession and a mea culpa speech unless you knew what response you would get."

She knew him so well. Because she'd loved him so well and so long?

Jordan smiled at her. "And what response am I going to get?" He nibbled at her lips. "You know I demand certified confirmation, which means hearing the verdict spoken aloud."

"The verdict is that I love you." She slid her arms around his neck. "And I think I've loved you for years too, but I was too thick headed or too deep in denial to realize it. It's the only explanation. Otherwise, I'd have left this *gulag* of an office years ago—and I certainly wouldn't have worked all those weekends and holidays! On a subconscious level, I must have wanted to be near you."

"You must have." Jordan looked incredibly happy, his expression joyful and boyish and carefree. Janessa had never seen him smile such a smile, not even when he'd won his most important appellate case.

"It all started on my birthday," she mused. "You came to my party and kissed me, and nothing's been the same since."

"I remember that party so well because I usually hate parties, but I was hell-bent on getting to yours. Mike had no choice but to accept my offer of a ride that night. I half believed it when your cousin mentioned that Gypsy spell. I was definitely under your spell, sweetheart. Still am and always will be."

"My great-grandmother said the shoes I was wearing were magic birthday shoes." Janessa glanced down at her feet. "I'm wearing them now." She was struck by one of the strangest thoughts she'd ever had. Suppose the shoes really were magic, causing Jordan and herself to recognize the love they'd felt—would always feel.

"Do you think—" she began.

"I think we're made for each other," Jordan said in the same forceful tone of heartfelt conviction that convinced juries to see things his way.

"I think so too." Janessa stood on her tiptoes and angled her mouth to his, gently brushing their lips together. One of his hands came up to cup her nape and the other fastened on her waist, pulling her even closer. His mouth took hers in a deep, slow kiss.

The kiss was magical, a promise and a commitment filled with passion and love.

It was a kiss that went on and on until both were flushed and breathless and hotly, urgently aroused. Finally, Jordan moved away from her, though he took her hand, as if unable to break physical contact with her.

"We're leaving for the day," he announced, his voice husky and thick. "I want you too much to chance an episode of *deskus interruptus* here in the office. We're going to my apartment."

"I've never been there," Janessa said dreamily, allowing him to lead her out of his office.

She thought she saw Lisa and Valstock lurking behind the conference room door, but she was too bemused and too aroused and far too happy to care if the office spies were gathering data.

"You can decide if you want to live there after we're married," Jordan announced as they walked past the receptionist's desk.

He didn't lower his voice, and Debbie overheard him. The telephone receiver she'd been holding slipped from her fingers as she gaped at the departing couple.

"We're getting married?" Janessa stared at him with unconcealed amazement.

"As soon as you pick the date," Jordan said. "You don't think I'm going to let you get away from me, do you?"

"You don't have to marry me to keep me from accepting that dream job at Mellot Reed, Jordan," she said, her dark eyes teasing.

"I'm going to make certain your dream job is being my wife," he growled. "I'll match any office terms that pirate from Mellot Reed offered. Plus, I'm adding marriage without a pre-nup to sweeten the deal. And when we go home at the end of each day together, I'll offer you benefits that'll keep you so satisfied, you won't ever want to leave me."

They entered the elevator and stood side by side, very proper and conventional, amidst their fellow passengers. Janessa nudged his foot with hers and they caught each other's eye, exchanging secret smiles. It wasn't until they were safely ensconced in Jordan's car that they abandoned propriety and fell into each other's arms, kissing wildly.

Jordan's apartment was located in a high rise in Mount Washington, a neighborhood set above the city with a spectacular view of the three rivers flowing in the valley below. But today, neither Janessa nor Jordan were interested in the scenery. They had eyes only for each other.

There was no first time awkwardness between them. It was as if they'd been sharing a love and a life for years. They kissed and laughed their way to the bedroom, shedding bits of clothing, pausing for a caress that simply couldn't wait.

He slipped her shoes off her feet while Janessa watched him dreamily. It was odd how very aware she was of him removing her shoes when she'd been too dazed to remember when or where he'd taken off her bra. But right now, her thoughts were very clear. And they were all of Jordan, and the long and happy marriage they would share.

When Jordan lay on the bed beside Janessa, he

gazed down at her, his blue eyes flaring with passion—and with love. "We're going to spend the rest of our lives together, Janessa."

She knew that tone well; he used it when he decided to take a case. It meant absolute, irrevocable commitment to the cause, whatever the outcome. For better or for worse. It was true for them before they'd even taken the vows.

"Oh yes, Jordan," she breathed, clinging to him, her body shivering with need, her love for him filling her heart and her soul as his body filled hers.

They both sighed as their bodies joined, ending the long, lonely, and utterly frustrating time apart. They were meant to be together. And to stay together. They pledged their love as the passionate fires flared to flashpoint, thrusting them higher and higher into a sublime dimension of physical pleasure and spiritual union that neither had experienced before.

But they would experience it time and time again during their long, happy life together.

Epilogue

One year later

"I'll tell Janessa that you're here, Chelsi," Debbie said to the girl with the spiked aqua hair who shifted impatiently from foot to foot in front of the reception desk.

"She's not expecting me. I was in town, so I thought I'd surprise her," Chelsi said.

Debbie buzzed Janessa's office. "I never saw anyone with twelve earrings in one ear. Didn't it hurt?"

"Nah!" Chelsi shrugged. "I have a real high tolerance for pain. I didn't make a sound when I got any of my tattoos either."

Janessa came out of the office and hugged her little sister. "Chelsi, what a surprise!" she exclaimed. Seeing Chelsi was always a surprise. The last time she'd seen her sister, Chelsi's hair had been magenta and cut in geometric angles only a mathematician could fully appreciate.

"You're looking fat, Janess!" Chelsi said jovially. "Of course, being six months pregnant will do that to you. And in another three months, you'll be so big you—"

"I think Janessa looks beautiful, and Jordan does too," Debbie inserted loyally.

Janessa threw her an appreciative smile and ushered her youngest sister into her office.

"How is that rich, handsome brother-in-law of mine?" Chelsi asked cheerfully. "And no, I'm not here to hit you up for some cash. This time."

"Jordan's fine. He's in court today. Since he's made Ackerly and Kolenda full partners, his work schedule is much easier. He wants to have plenty of time to spend with the baby."

"And you'll be a mostly stay-at-home mom who handles office business from your home computer. Cool!" Chelsi sat in Janessa's chair and swirled around. "That's the kind of setup I want whenever I get married. Which brings me to the point of my visit."

"You're getting married?" Janessa's heart almost stopped. If there was anyone less ready to be a wife, it was her baby sister.

"Not even!" shrieked Chelsi. "Mallory's the next one, six months from now. Six more months of listening to her plan her wedding ... Talk about boring! And I can't believe we'll have to wear those dweebish pastel bridesmaid gowns. Gina is having a fit. She says she looks putrid in pink and she's right. Thank God you and Jordan were considerate enough to get married without all the *Bride's* magazine insanity."

Chelsi paused long enough to take a quick breath. "Anyway, while Mallory and I were talking about dyed wedding shoes, we remembered those black shoes of yours—you know the sexy ones you thought I bought for your birthday when I really got you sweat socks?"

"I don't know what happened to those shoes." Janessa frowned, puzzled. "I thought I'd moved all my stuff into Jordan's apartment after our

'wedding, but I couldn't find those shoes anywhere. Mom looked too and said they weren't
home. Then Gram thought she saw Ga with
them, but she must have been mistaken. How
would Ga get my shoes? Why would she want
them?"

Janessa felt her baby stirring within her and
laid her hand against her swollen abdomen, a
soft smile curving her lips.

"Maybe Ga did swipe your shoes 'cause she's
sick of wearing those orthopedic oxfords Gram
always buys for her," joked Chelsi. "Rats, I
wanted to borrow those shoes. I thought they
were so cool! And we wear the same size—it just
kills Mallory that her feet are bigger than ours."

The sisters shared a laugh, and Janessa offered
to take Chelsi to lunch.

The package on the porch had the name *Laura*
printed on it.

Laura Novotny almost tripped over it as she
rushed out the front door. She was running late,
and she scooped up the package as she ran, continuing her dash toward her car, which was
parked in front of the row house she shared with
her two Siamese cats, Chopstick and Chan.

She tossed the package into the front seat and
steered the vehicle into the street. Today was her
twenty-ninth birthday, one she'd been dreading.
She was one year away from turning thirty, yet
her life hadn't changed a bit since she was
twenty-one, when as a brand-new nursing school
graduate, she'd begun working the graveyard
shift at the local hospital emergency room. . . .

Barbara Boswell

—✦—

I was born and raised in the Pittsburgh area with my two sisters and left to attend college in Washington, D.C., where I met my husband, Bill. I practiced as a nurse while he was in law school in Charlottesville, Virginia, where Susan, the first of our three daughters, was born. Our second daughter, Sarah, was born in Mississippi, and our youngest, Christy, in Germany, where we were stationed with the United States Air Force. Bill and I have been married twenty-six years and have lived in a house along the Ohio River north of Pittsburgh for the past eighteen years. I love cats (we have five) and I love writing stories about families. No family is complete without humor—in fact, it's a necessary survival trait in my experience—so I always try to mix a fair amount of it into my writing. I particularly enjoyed writing this story for *Magic Slippers* because injecting that note of otherworldliness into the story was a first for me. I hope you enjoyed reading it as much as I enjoyed writing it.

Barbara Boswell

Cupid Wears
Combat Boots

Carole Buck

Prologue

The combat boots—size seven, black leather, standard military issue—arrived on the first Friday in June, three days before the woman who was destined to wear them appeared on the scene.

Quinn Harris was attending to what he privately thought of as the "clerk and jerk" part of his responsibilities as CEO of Alpha Camp, the survival training school he'd founded a little more than three years ago, when the shoe box containing the footwear was deposited on his desk by a retired noncom named Lester Baines. A recipient of the Medal of Honor, Lester had served under Quinn's father, the late General Stephen Sterling Harris, as well as under Quinn himself.

"Thought you might want to take care of these personally, Boss."

" 'These' being what?" Quinn asked, scrawling his signature at the bottom of a thanks-but-no-thanks response to an inquiry from a Los An-

geles–based leisure industry mogul who thought
Alpha Camp had "major franchise potential"
and wanted to discuss the possibility of starting
a chain of survival training schools.

"The boots you ordered for your movie star."

Quinn stiffened, his mind abruptly conjuring
up the image of a singularly provocative female.
She had a piquantly sexy face, dominated by ex-
pressive hazel eyes and framed by chestnut curls.
Her body was all creamy skin and come-hither
curves.

"Kayla Delaney isn't *my* movie star," he disputed, lifting his gaze to meet Lester's as he
clamped down on an unsettlingly familiar surge
of desire. The first time he'd experienced it had
been about five years ago—a scant four months
after the accident that had killed his wife and
critically injured their seven-year-old daughter,
Stephanie Lynn. He'd been slumped in front of
the television, clicking the remote control from
channel to channel, numbly searching for distraction. An actress he couldn't recall having
seen before had suddenly materialized on the
screen. Within seconds his blood had been humming, his body hardening. He'd sat, riveted,
through the remaining forty-five minutes of a
made-for-TV flick titled "Shady Lady." It wasn't
until the credits rolled that he'd discovered the
name of the woman who'd so aroused him—
Kayla Delaney. "I've never met her."

"But you're sure goin' to. And once you do,
you'll be dealin' with her, one-on-one, for six
straight weeks."

"I'll be whipping the lady into shape so she
can make audiences believe she's capable of
blowing away a bunch of bad guys."

"Even so—"

"She's coming to Alpha for basic training," Quinn stressed, wondering uneasily whether Lester had picked up on his susceptibility to Kayla Delaney. "You were a platoon sergeant once. Did you establish warm, fuzzy relationships with any of your recruits?"

The retired noncom seemed taken aback by this question. "Got a letter from one a few years back," he eventually conceded.

"Oh?" Quinn lifted his brows inquiringly.

"Damned fool was runnin' for Congress. Wanted me to vote for him."

"I take it you didn't."

"Hell, no! Figured there's enough idiot politicians in Washington without electin' some ex-grunt who couldn't dial 911 unless he called information to get the number first." Lester snorted contemptuously. "Not that it mattered. He won in a landslide."

"That's democracy for you."

"Ain't it just." The older man eyed Quinn for a second or two, then reverted to his initial theme. "About the boots—"

"I'll take care of them, Sergeant Major."

"*And* your movie star?"

Once again Quinn's mind filled with the image of a lushly alluring female. He did his damnedest to blank it out.

"Yeah," he agreed tersely, disciplining his expression into neutrality. "I'll take care of her, too."

1

As a fourteen-year veteran of the movie industry, Kayla Delaney had had a lot of experience with predawn makeup and wardrobe calls. Still, she didn't consider herself a "morning person."

Which isn't to imply that she hadn't meant to get up in time for the five A.M. meeting that was supposed to mark the start of the intensive, six-week training program her agent—Irwin "Would I lie to you?" Ortiz—swore was crucial to her becoming (at long, long last) an overnight sensation. She had.

To this end, she'd politely requested a four-fifteen A.M. wake-up call from the front desk of the small motel that was going to be her home base for the next forty-one days. She'd also carefully set the radio–alarm clock in her modestly furnished room to go off at half past the hour, just in case.

It wasn't her fault that the night manager of the Last Chance Motor Lodge had neglected to ring her at the prearranged time. And while she was willing to take responsibility for her semiconscious decision to swat off the alarm in order to cop a few more minutes of rest, she hadn't *deliberately* gone back to sleep. She'd simply succumbed to exhaustion.

To put it bluntly, the two months immediately preceding her arrival at the Last Chance had been a bitch. She'd been driven to the brink of burnout by the process that had finally resulted in her landing the lead in a project that, without a single foot of film having been shot, was being touted as *the* hottest action flick of the year.

That she'd been nobody's first (or second, or third, or fourth) choice to play the character industry wags were referring to as "Mad Maxine" went without saying. After nearly a decade and a half in Hollywood, Kayla Delaney was long past the "fresh face" stage. This was a decided disadvantage in an industry that thrived on the exploitation of new talent. Also working against her was her age. At thirty-five, she was considered too old (by show biz standards) for the "babe" roles that had made up the bulk of her career.

And then there was the issue of her talent. She wasn't a bad actress by any means. She'd even netted an Emmy nomination for her work in a TV movie a few years back. Still, she was no Meryl Streep, and she knew it.

The powers that be had demanded that she audition eight times and screen-test twice before they'd decided she was "perfect" for the part. Kayla had survived this frequently humiliating ordeal by fantasizing about how Mad Maxine would react to being similarly jerked around. She was inclined to think that doing so had lent a persuasive gloss of reality to her line readings.

"*Moving Target* will do for you what *Basic In-*

stinct did for Sharon Stone," her agent had predicted the day she'd signed her contract. He'd practically been salivating over the prospect of collecting his ten percent of her future earnings.

"As long as nobody's expecting me to take off my panties before I uncross my legs on screen," she'd murmured as she inked her name on the dotted line. She'd been shaking inside, riven by a combination of excitement and dread. Mad Maxine was a make-or-break part for her. If she blew this chance, she'd be lucky to get work pitching products on late-night infomercials!

"Not to worry," Irwin had said, shifting effortlessly from profit shark to soother-of-the-star mode. "You've got an ironclad 'no nudity' clause."

Which didn't mean the producers wouldn't pressure her to flash some flesh, Kayla had reminded herself a tad cynically. Especially given the money they were spending to buff up her far-from-flabby body.

That she'd be expected to get herself into top physical condition for *Moving Target* had been obvious to her from the start. What she hadn't anticipated was that she'd find herself contractually obligated to undergo a month and a half of rigorous military-style training at a "survival camp" in northern California prior to the start of filming.

It was this obligation that had landed her in Room 216 of the Last Chance Motor Lodge. While Kayla was fully prepared to do what needed to be done to transform herself into the lean, mean fighting machine her bosses envisioned, she'd balked at the idea of bunking in the camp's barracks with a bunch of strangers.

Since she was to be instructed one-on-one rather than as part of a group, the studio had conceded the point and agreed to pick up the tab for her "special" accommodations.

The man who'd been hired to be her personal trainer was the owner of the survival camp, an ex–Special Forces officer named Quinn Harris. She'd been told—ordered, really—to meet him in the Last Chance's lobby at the uncivilized hour of five A.M. on the second Monday in June.

It was Quinn Harris who'd invaded her dreams as she surrendered to slumber after shutting off the shrilling alarm. Or so she assumed. She hadn't actually met the guy yet. Still, she'd heard enough about him from *Moving Target*'s director—who'd attended Alpha Camp for two weeks the previous year and described it as the most "elemental" experience of his life—to form a vivid mental image of the man.

She was running through what looked like the bombed-out ruins of Beverly Hills' famed Rodeo Drive clutching an Academy Award in one hand and a machine gun in the other. Chasing after her was a huge, sun-bronzed hulk clad in nothing but a green beret, a pair of cartridge-crammed bandoliers, and khaki-colored BVDs.

Harris the Hulk was wearing boots, too. Big, black ones. Perfect for kicking people when they were down, then grinding them into the dirt.

Kayla, who was shoeless in her dream, could feel the ground shake beneath her bare soles each time her pursuer slammed his foot down.

Thud. Thud. THU—

She came awake with a start, her fingers fisting, her throat constricting, her brain fixating on a terrible truth. The thudding she was hearing wasn't a phantom sound effect generated by her subconscious. It was real.

Someone was pounding on the door of her motel room!

Kayla levered herself into a sitting position. The digital readout on the the bedside alarm clock snagged her attention. Five fifty-eight, it said.

She groaned.

Thud. Thud.

"*Delaney!*" The voice coming through the door was low but pitched to carry. It was also male. Very, very male. "*Are you alive in there?*"

Kayla swallowed hard, her stomach roiling. "Yes," she managed to call out. "Just—uh—just hang on. I'm coming."

No response.

Kayla kicked free of the tangled bedsheets, then swung her legs over the side of the mattress and stood up. She padded across the room, forking her fingers through her long, sleep-tousled hair. She'd messed up, no doubt about it. But maybe she could explain—

"*Delaney?*"

Well, maybe not. The individual on the other side of the door didn't sound inclined to take prisoners, much less listen to excuses.

Kayla squared her slim shoulders and stiffened her spine. Then she reached for the door's chain lock. A split second before touching it she pulled back, appalled by what she'd been about to do. Had she lost her mind? The man standing outside her motel room was a stranger! She had no proof he was Quinn Harris. She hadn't even asked who he was, for heaven's sake! She should be phoning the front desk to report a potential celebrity stalker, not opening the door to him!

"Wh-who—" she stopped, grimacing at the wimpiness of her tone. Taking a deep breath, she tried again. "Would you please identify yourself?"

Better, she thought. But Mad Maxine would have omitted the *please*.

There was a brief silence. Eventually the stranger outside her motel room reeled off a name, a former military rank, and a serial number followed by a succinct summation of his current "mission." It was a very persuasive recitation.

Bracing herself for the worst, Kayla undid the chain lock and opened the door.

And then she stared. Just . . . stared.

Kayla Delaney had been exposed to a lot of extremely attractive men during the course of her career. In point of fact, she'd worked with several actors who were prettier than she was, and she wasn't exactly a dog. But never in her life had she been confronted by a male as compelling as Quinn Harris.

He stood an inch or so over six feet. If there was a superfluous ounce of fat on his body, it didn't show. Broad of shoulder and narrow of hip, he radiated the coiled-spring physical power of a jungle cat.

She figured him to be several years her senior, probably pushing forty pretty hard. It was difficult to tell for sure. One thing was certain: Quinn Harris was fully, unflinchingly adult. At a time when many men were victims of the Peter Pan syndrome, she suspected this was one male who'd started turning his back on boyish things as soon as his voice broke. Maybe before.

Quinn's dark hair was cropped close to his well-shaped skull. While the style was similar to the buzz cut currently affected by a number of Hollywood's macho sex symbols, Kayla would have bet money that his adoption of it had nothing to do with a desire to follow the latest fashion trend.

His eyes were midnight blue. She thought she'd seen something like shock detonate in their intense azure depths as she'd opened the door, but she couldn't say for sure. Whatever the flash of feeling had been, it had vanished in a heartbeat behind a starkly impenetrable, steadily unreadable gaze.

His other facial features didn't add up to matinee idol handsomeness by any means. His aquiline nose canted slightly to the right, having obviously been broken at least once. The sensuality of his mouth seemed to war with the ascetic shape of his forehead and sharply angled cheekbones. An age-whitened scar bisected the bottom of his stubbornly squared chin.

This is never going to work, Kayla thought, stunned by the urgency of her response to the man who, in a very real sense, held her professional future in his hands. *There's no way—*

"Which part of the message didn't you understand, Delaney?"

She blinked. "Excuse . . . me?"

"The message you got when you checked in yesterday. The one telling you to meet me in the lobby this morning. Which part didn't you understand?"

"I understood—"

"Ah." Quinn smiled sardonically. "My mistake. You understood the message but you decided to blow it—and me—off."

"No!"

"Then why have I been twiddling my thumbs downstairs for nearly an hour? Do you have a problem telling time, Delaney? The message specified rendezvous at oh five hundred. That's five A.M. That's when the big hand is on the twelve—"

"*I overslept!*" Attraction gave way to animosity. Who did this khaki clad jerk think he was? The Great Santini? Rambo? General Norman Schwarzkopf?

Dark brows lifted derisively. "You overslept?"

"Yes! I turned off the alarm when it rang at four-fifteen—that's when the big hand is on the three and the little hand is on the four, by the way—and I went back to sleep! I didn't mean to, but I did." She glared at him. "What are you going to do about it? Toss me into the brig? Give me a dishonorable discharge from your camp? Flog me?"

"Stockade."

"H-huh?" Kayla stammered after a moment, her surge of temper receding into bewilderment.

"We army types toss people into the stockade, not the brig."

"Oh." She made a vague gesture. "I . . . uh . . . fine. Whatever."

There was an awkward pause. Kayla glanced away. Her awareness of Quinn Harris' masculine appeal reasserted itself with unnerving potency. She shifted from one foot to the other, suddenly wishing she'd taken the time to don a robe before

she answered the door. While the oversize cotton
T-shirts she wore to bed covered all the essentials
and then some, the cling of the wash-softened
fabric against her naked skin made her feel very,
very vulnerable.

She fought down an urge to cross her arms in
front of her chest. Such a gesture would reveal
too much about her turbulent state of mind. As
far as she could tell, her companion was indif-
ferent to her on a sexual level. The last thing she
wanted was for him to suspect that her response
to him was anything but equally ho-hum.

"Delaney?"

Kayla brought her gaze back to meet Quinn's.
Something in his expression made her pulse stut-
ter. *Get a grip*! she commanded herself.

"Look, Major Harris," she said after a few seconds. "I'm sorry I kept you waiting this morning. I don't want you to get the wrong idea about
me. I'm not a Beverly Hills bitch. I'm not some
valley airhead. I'm serious about the work we're
supposed to do. It's important—*extremely* important—that I be ready when *Moving Target* starts
shooting at the end of July. So, please. Believe
me. The next time you tell me to meet you somewhere at oh five hundred, I'll be there."

There was another pause. Not quite as unsettling for Kayla as the previous one, but difficult
enough. Whether her words had touched a chord
in the man standing before her, she had no idea.
She hoped her apology hadn't sounded desperate. There were a lot of people who got off on
making others grovel, of course. But some inexplicable instinct told her that for all his bullying
tactics, Quinn Harris wasn't one of them.

"Okay," he eventually said.

"Okay?" Was this some kind of trick? "That's . . . all?"

"You were expecting a good conduct medal?"

Kayla's temper flared anew. "No," she snapped. "Of course not."

"Then what?"

"Then"—she battled to regain her cool—"nothing."

A glint of amusement appeared in Quinn's eyes. "You're sure?"

"Positive."

"Glad to hear it."

Kayla bit back a retort, reminding herself what was at stake. Infuriating though he might be, she couldn't afford to alienate this man. Drawing herself up to her full five-foot-eight height, she said, "Give me fifteen minutes to pull myself together."

"Make it ten."

A sense of triumph rippled through her. *Got-cha*, she thought smugly. *I can be ready in five.*

"Okay, Major," she acquiesced aloud, keeping her expression demure.

"You can drop the rank, Delaney. Just call me 'sir.' "

Kayla allowed herself a few seconds to imagine Mad Maxine's response to this arrogant directive. "Whatever you say . . . *sir*," she finally replied. "I'll meet you in the lobby in ten minutes."

Quinn's lips started to curve upward. Slowly. Sexily. The resultant smile stole her breath and sent shivers skittering through her nervous system. After a moment he glanced down the length of her body, then brought his gaze back up to her face. For one lunatic instant, Kayla feared her knees might buckle.

"Dress for dirt," her trainer-to-be advised.

2

Quinn glanced left, watching as Kayla bent forward from the waist. Experience told him she was trying to ease the discomfort of the green nylon army rucksack she was wearing. He figured the thirty-five pounds of gear he'd personally loaded into the so-called Alice pack must be weighing pretty heavily on her after a lengthy road march plus a two-mile trek through rough terrain.

Yet she hadn't complained once. What's more, she'd kept up with the pace he'd set without a lot of huffing and puffing.

Sure, there'd been an *I'll show you* subtext to Kayla's stoicism. He'd offered her the option of resting several times, but he had been flatly rejected. She'd given the distinct impression that she'd drop dead of exhaustion before she admitted she needed a break.

As for her assenting to their current stop . . . well, he hadn't given her much choice in the matter. After informing her that he was going to take a load off and chow down, he'd ordered her to do the same. She'd bridled at his deliberately dictatorial tone and cocked her chin at him. She'd then snapped out one of the most insubordinate "Yes, sirs" he'd ever heard.

Much as he believed in the importance of maintaining good discipline, Quinn had to admit that this show of feistiness had amused him. At the same time, he couldn't help but admire the lady's spirit.

Admiration was *not* an emotion he'd anticipated feeling in connection with Kayla Delaney. At least not before she'd opened her motel room door to him. The first instant of eye contact had affected him like a karate kick to the solar plexus. He was still reeling from the impact—and its implications.

He'd known there'd be a testosterone-fueled rush of attraction. How could there not be? But hard on the heels of the initial surge of lust had come a flood of emotions for which he had not been prepared.

On-screen, Kayla Delaney exuded a very obvious sexuality. Her allure in person was a subtler thing—sunshine and wildflowers rather than musk at midnight. She had freckles on her nose, for heaven's sake! And while no one was ever going to mistake her for a boy, her "real life" figure appeared less aggressively va-va-va-voom than the one she showed off on celluloid.

There was something ... *vulnerable* ... about her.

Quinn hadn't expected that. No way. No how.

"You can take off the wart if you want," he said abruptly, shrugging out of his own Alice pack and dropping it on the ground.

Kayla straightened with a grunt, giving him a wary look. "Excuse me?"

"The backpack," he clarified, reminding himself of the need to stay focused on the business at hand. "Some guys call it 'the big green wart.'"

"Oh." Kayla began struggling clumsily out of her pack's nylon straps.

"Want a hand?"

"Absolutely not."

"Suit yourself." Squatting, Quinn opened his rucksack and studied its contents. He briefly contemplated several foil-wrapped items, then shoved them aside and rooted around until he located two rectangular packets sheathed in thick brown plastic. He extracted them and tossed one to Kayla.

"What's this?" she asked, sitting down on the ground. She handled the packet gingerly, as though she feared it might explode in her face.

"Lunch."

"As in"—there was a sudden growl from her stomach—"food?"

"What you have in your grubby hands, Delaney, is a MRE."

"Say again?"

"A MRE. A Meal Ready to Eat. The army developed them to replace C rations." Quinn watched as Kayla opened her packet and peered inside. "There's a rumor MRE is really an acronym for meals rejected by everyone. I think yours is spaghetti and meatballs."

She flushed as her stomach rumbled again. "Oh . . . yum."

"Sorry. The quartermaster was out of lobster." Although some attendees insisted on eating nothing but MREs during their stay at Alpha, the vast majority dined very well in the camp's mess hall. The foil-wrapped items Quinn had shunted aside a few minutes ago were a "real food" lunch for two he'd had made up before he'd headed over to the Last Chance Motor Lodge. He'd hauled out the MREs on impulse, curious to see Kayla's reaction to them.

"What's your MRE?"

He checked. "Barbecue pork with rice. Want to trade?"

"I'll stick with the pasta, thank you."

The *pasta*? Well, Quinn supposed military-style spaghetti and meatballs did, technically speaking, fall into that particular food category. But in terms of taste and texture . . .

Put it this way. Chef Boyardee had nothing to worry about.

They ate without speaking for several minutes, serenaded by birdcalls and soothed by the rustle of breeze-stirred leaves. Quinn found himself wondering at the seeming heartiness of Kayla's appetite. At first he thought it was another example of her determination to show him that she could—literally—take anything he cared to dish out. Then he recalled the scene back at the motor lodge and realized the truth.

"Didn't have time to grab breakfast, hmm?" he needled.

The question netted him a nasty look but no verbal comeback. As Kayla returned her attention to her meal, she licked a drop of tomato sauce from the right corner of her mouth. The sinuous curl of her pink tongue sent a shaft of heat arrowing straight to Quinn's groin.

He shifted involuntarily, swallowing hard. A partially chewed mouthful of ersatz barbecue threatened to clog his windpipe. He nearly choked.

"Problem, *sir*?" Her tone suggested she'd be

more than willing to take a stab at performing an emergency tracheotomy if there was.

"I'm fine." He cleared his throat. "How's your, uh, pasta?"

"It could use some oregano. How's your pork?"

"I've tasted worse."

There was a brief pause.

"I'd *heard* the Green Berets had some strange eating habits, you know," Kayla commented after a moment. "When you said we were stopping to chow down, I figured you were going to produce a live chicken and order me to bite its head off."

"Nah." Quinn forked up the remainder of his pork barbecue. "That's not until the third week of training."

"Oh, good. Something to look forward to."

It was now mid-afternoon, and they were about a quarter mile from Alpha's main buildings. Quinn had called another halt. Kayla removed her rucksack and collapsed against the trunk of a tree.

"Do . . . all . . . your campers . . . have to do this . . . this?" she asked, panting.

"Do what?" Quinn dropped down beside his own discarded Alice pack. "Go on the nature walk?"

"The . . . *nature walk*?"

"Staff nickname."

"Staff, as in a bunch of ex–Green Berets?"

"Not exclusively. We've got some ex–Army Rangers, too. Plus a dozen or so former Navy SEALs and a few marine recon experts who come in for certain courses. We even had three retired S.A.S. guys—that's Special Air Service, they're Brits—on staff last year."

"I stand corrected." Kayla wiped the back of her right hand against her forehead, leaving a smear of dirt behind. It balanced the smudge on her chin. "But . . . to get back to my question. Is this 'nature walk' a regular part of the Alpha program or is it something you dreamed up especially for me?"

"Getting paranoid, Delaney?"

"Just being realistic . . . sir. You've already admitted to forcing me to eat an MRE when you had a gourmet-style picnic stashed away in your rucksack."

Quinn chuckled. "I shared in the end, didn't I? *And* I gave you first choice on the sandwiches."

Kayla pulled a face, grumbling under her breath as she plucked at the front of the mudspattered sweatshirt she was wearing. The plain black garment had obviously seen better days. Quinn wondered about that. Most of the show biz types who came to Alpha turned up in brand-new, top-of-the-line wilderness gear. One guy actually claimed his camouflage jacket had been tailored by Giorgio Armani!

Maybe Kayla was trying to deglamorize herself in preparation for her new role, he speculated. Lord knew, her choice of sleepwear was utilitarian in the extreme. Which wasn't to say he hadn't been jolted by the sight of that white cotton sleep shirt she'd had on this morning. Because he had been. He'd been rocked right down to his socks!

It was strange. He'd seen Kayla Delaney sporting lace and leather in the movies and decked out in sheer nighties in his imagination. Yet his response to those visuals was nothing compared to what he'd felt when she opened the door to her motel room clad in nothing but that sleep-rumpled, sexily oversize—

"What about the walk?"

Quinn shifted uncomfortably, grateful for the loose fit of his fatigue-style khakis. What the hell was going on with him? He was harder than a flagpole! Was this what he was going to have to contend with for the next six weeks? His anatomy snapping to attention every few minutes?

"Everybody takes the walk," he said. "One way or another."

"Meaning?"

"Meaning that . . ."—he shifted again—". . . well, a lot of our students are like the guy who's going to direct your movie. What's his name? Jack?"

"Zack," Kayla supplied dryly. "Zachary T. Reynolds."

"Oh, right." Interesting, he thought, trying to shut his mind to the throbbing rod of flesh between his thighs. *Moving Target*'s leading lady didn't sound as though she was enamored of the man who was supposed to make her a star. "Anyway. A lot of our students are like him. Overachievers who're searching for 'meaning' in their lives or new ways of testing themselves. We put them through the same hump-through-the-woods drill you did. It's a fast way to flush out the quitters."

"I . . . see."

"We also do a week-long course exclusively for families," Quinn went on, warming to his subject. "For them, the nature walk's about sticking together and working as a team. And then there are the programs we run for cancer survivors and people with disabilities. Their nature walks may seem like aimless rambles compared with the others, but every step represents a personal achievement."

He paused, thinking of his daughter. The tragedy that had killed her mother had also shattered a dozen of her young bones. There'd been a period when he feared she would be permanently crippled. She was fine now, thank God. Fully recovered and ready to take on whatever life sent her way.

Maybe a little *too* ready, as far as he was concerned. Stephanie Lynn—"Stevie"—was Quinn's greatest pride, his purest joy. She was also the source of his deepest insecurities. Less than five months from her thirteenth birthday, Stevie was on the threshold of adolescence. The ramifications of her inevitable maturation scared the living daylights out of him.

Him. A man whose military decorations included a Distinguished Service Cross, Silver Star, and a Purple Heart.

The thing was, he'd been *trained* for combat. But when it came to guiding his daughter along the path from girl to young woman . . .

"I didn't realize," Kayla murmured.

Recalled from his uneasy reflections, Quinn scrambled to pick up the thread of their conversation. After a moment he asked, "Didn't realize what?"

"What your camp's really about." Kayla offered him a ruefully apologetic smile. "I thought Alpha was basically a high-priced playground where people like Zack Reynolds could come and live out their commando fantasies."

Quinn found himself returning her smile before he registered he was doing so. His anxieties about Stevie retreated, at least temporarily.

"There are times when that's *exactly* what it is," he conceded frankly. "Still, fulfilling commando fantasies is very profitable. It helps underwrite some of the other programs the camp offers."

"Is that why you agreed to train me?"

The question—and the direct look that accompanied it—caught Quinn off guard. His reasons for taking this job were something he preferred not to examine too closely. "Partly," he answered carefully.

"Just . . . partly?"

He adjusted his position again and glanced away. What was he supposed to tell her? That she'd been the star of his sexual daydreams for years? That he'd accepted her studio's obscenely lucrative job offer more for the opportunity to meet her in the flesh than for the money?

The Kayla Delaney he'd thought he knew from the movies might have gotten a kick from eliciting such confessions, he reflected. But not the Kayla Delaney he'd encountered that morning at the Last Chance Motor Lodge. And certainly not the Kayla Delaney with whom he'd spent the past nine hours.

"Quinn?"

He brought his gaze back to hers, thinking fast. "What can I say?" He deliberately infused his tone with a hint of sucking-up-to-the-celebrity unctuousness. "I'm a big admirer of your work."

Kayla looked surprised. And something else Quinn couldn't quite put a name to. Then, abruptly, she started to laugh. "Oh, *sure* you are."

"I am." He inflected the words a tad too insistently, making what essentially was the truth sound like a lie. "Really."

"Uh-huh."

"You don't believe me?"

"Not much, no."

Quinn gestured, indicating he didn't know what he could do to persuade her of his sincerity. His new trainee's attitude intrigued him. Most of the show biz people who came to Alpha seemed to take it as a given that he and the rest of the camp's staff were intimately familiar with, and unfailingly enthusiastic about, every facet of their careers. They accepted the most extravagant of compliments as no less than their due. Whereas Kayla . . .

"You don't have to stroke my ego," she said, derailing his train of thought. "I know why I'm out here in the woods with you. If the only reason you're out here with me is financial, that's okay. I'd just like to find out where I stand. Especially after what happened this morning."

Quinn stayed silent for a few moments, trying to reconcile the woman sitting a few feet from him with the woman he'd watched on-screen. Finally he said, "The prospect of getting a hefty five-figure check for six weeks' work made accepting this training gig pretty easy. But the prospect of working with you wasn't exactly a turnoff, either. Because, whether you believe it or not, I *am* a fan. Plus"—he smiled crookedly— "I was definitely up for an excuse to get out from behind my desk."

Kayla furrowed her brow. "Why should you

need an excuse? I thought you owned Alpha Camp. Aren't you in charge?''

"I'm at the top of the chain of command." Quinn decided to defer an explanation that this wasn't necessarily the same thing as being *in charge*. Kayla had little chance of understanding how Alpha worked—assuming she really cared—until she became acquainted with Lester Baines. "That means I get stuck shuffling papers and signing checks."

"Not your favorite activities, hmm?"

"I'm a field guy, not a REMF."

"A REMF?"

"Rear Echelon Mother—uh—" Quinn broke off abruptly, genuinely embarrassed. It wasn't that he believed his listener was unfamiliar with the word he'd been about to say. If memory served, he'd heard her use it at least once or twice in a movie. Still, one tenet of the code of conduct instilled in him by his late father was that a gentleman did not swear in mixed company.

"I see," Kayla commented blandly, swatting a stray strand of hair off her perspiration-sheened forehead. "How long were you a 'field guy' in the army?"

Grateful for her smooth shift of conversational gears, Quinn took a moment to settle himself then answered, "I put in nearly thirteen years. I was discharged in April of ninety-one."

"That was just a few months after Operation Desert Storm, right?"

"Yeah," he affirmed, slightly surprised by the accuracy of her memory.

"Did you . . . like . . . it?" The inquiry was hesitant, as though Kayla feared she might be moving into touchy territory. "Military life, I mean."

He expelled a breath, knowing from experience that it was difficult to explain his feelings about his former profession to a civilian. "I was an army brat," he eventually replied. "My father retired with two stars."

"He was a general?"

"Yeah." A sense of loss suffused him. "He died about seven years back."

"And your mother?"

"She died when I was a kid." He'd been five. He'd tried desperately not to cry when he'd been told, fearing such a reaction would be derided as babyish. It had been his father—his tough, tested-in-combat father—who'd shown him that there was nothing unmanly about shedding tears.

"Any brothers or sisters?"

Quinn shook his head, uncertain why he was being so forthcoming. "What about you, Delaney?" he asked, turning the tables. "Any siblings?"

"No." The answer held a strong note of regret. "Your parents?"

Kayla's eyes slid away from his. "They're both gone," she responded, her voice tight. "My mother died nine years ago this September. My father passed away about six months later. They were all the family I had."

A silence fell between them. Overhead, a pair of birds swooped and sang. Quinn heard people yelling and cheering some distance away. He figured the clamor was coming from the camp's obstacle course, off to the west.

"Why did you leave the army?" Kayla suddenly asked.

Quinn supposed he should have anticipated this question, but he hadn't. His gut knotting, he forced himself to meet his trainee's gaze once again. "I didn't have a choice."

"You mean, you . . . *had* . . . to get out?"

"I mean, my wife was killed when a drunk driver smashed into her car," he replied, his tone as flat and final as a cemetery slab. "Our daughter Stevie—Stephanie Lynn—was with her. She was badly injured. I couldn't give her the time she needed and maintain my career, so I resigned my commission."

Kayla blinked, her throat working. "I'm sorry."

Quinn steeled himself against the compassion in her lovely hazel eyes—against the inexplicable sense of connection he'd felt from the moment she'd opened her motel door to him. Dammit! Why couldn't Kayla Delaney have turned out to be the phony baloney show biz sexpot he'd expected? Why did she have to be so . . . so . . . *real*?

"Yeah," he finally responded. "So am I."

It didn't seem to Kayla there was a lot to be said after that. Or maybe there was too much, and she didn't know how to begin expressing it. Whatever the case, she and Quinn completed their "nature walk" in near silence.

They finished up at the exercise field in the center of the camp. At one end of the grassy quadrangle, some three dozen "campers" were being put through their physical paces by a pair of strappingly built instructors who clearly believed that sweating and getting screamed at were good for the soul. At the opposite end, a mismatched trio—a powerfully muscled black man with a shaved head, a whipcord-lean white guy with a blond ponytail, and a wiry Latino with a Zapata-style mustache—were demonstrating hand-to-hand combat techniques for another group.

No one seemed to pay the slightest heed to Kayla. She found this a little weird. Although she didn't expect to cause a major celebrity sighting stir—she wasn't Demi Moore or Julia Roberts, for heaven's sake!—she was accustomed to attracting a certain degree of attention when she appeared in public.

Of course, she'd never appeared in public with her hair scraped back into a haphazard braid, wearing no makeup and filthy sweats. . . .

"The firing range is that way," Quinn said, gesturing west as they moved toward a large, stone and timber building on the north side of the quadrangle. "And the obstacle course. I'll run you through that tomorrow morning. We'll hold off on starting your weapons orientation until we get your conditioning program settled. Movie bang-bang is basically faking, anyway."

"Fine by me." While Kayla believed she was mentally prepared for the physical part of her regimen, the shooting stuff made her nervous. She'd never *touched* a gun, much less pulled the trigger on one.

"You have a problem with firearms, Delaney?"

She checked herself in mid-stride. Her companion stopped, too. She turned to face him, ratcheting her chin up a notch. "If I do," she answered evenly, "I'll get over it."

Something flickered in the depths of Quinn's dark blue eyes. Exactly what it signified, Kayla couldn't say. She only knew it touched off a quicksilver tremor of response inside her.

She wanted this man's approval, she realized with a jolt. Not the way she wanted the approval of producers or directors or audiences, though. That approbation was based essentially on her ability to pretend to be someone else. What she wanted from Quinn Harris was an appreciation of . . . of . . . *her.*

Whoever "her" was. There were moments— more in the last year or so than there used to be—when Kayla wasn't certain she knew.

"I'm sure you will," Quinn said after what seemed like a very long pause.

They started walking again.

"What's that?" Kayla pointed toward a large, one-story structure with solar panels on its roof. Her reasons for asking were twofold. First, she figured it behooved her to get to know her way around the camp as quickly as possible. Second, she thought it was a good idea to remind herself (and Quinn!) that theirs was supposed to be a *professional* relationship.

"The mess hall." The answer was crisp, as though he'd picked up on her intention to steer them onto an impersonal track. "We also use it for lectures. The towers you see in back are for climbing and rappeling practice. Those"—Quinn indicated a row of buildings set along the south side of the quadrangle—"are the barracks. We can billet up to eighty at a time. There are special pits for unarmed combat practice behind them. And this"—he came to a stop in front of the stone and timber building—"is Alpha HQ."

As he spoke, the building's double-screened door swung open and an older man dressed in faultlessly pressed fatigues stepped out. His crewcut hair was gunmetal gray, his face was weather-beaten, and his brown eyes held a time-tempered wisdom. His precise age was difficult to pinpoint. He could have been anywhere from fifty to seventy.

Big, he wasn't. But he radiated an aura of bull-dog toughness that transcended size. He also stood as though he had a steel pole for a spine.

Looking at him, Kayla suddenly recalled how Quinn had sidestepped the issue when she'd voiced her assumption that, as owner of Alpha Camp, he must be "in charge" of who did what. Instinct told her she was about to be introduced to the reason for his refusal to assert a claim of absolute authority.

"Delaney, this is Sergeant Major Lester Baines, U.S. Army, retired," Quinn said. "Sergeant Major, Kayla Delaney."

"Pleasure, ma'am."

"Glad to meet you, sir." Kayla wasn't sure where the honorific came from. It just seemed appropriate to use a respectful form of address.

The older man smiled. "No need to 'sir' me, Miz Delaney. That's for officers."

"So . . . you aren't . . . ? I mean . . . you—you weren't . . . ?"

Lester Baines' smile expanded into a snaggle-toothed grin. "No, ma'am," he responded. "I worked for a living when I was in the army."

"He won the Congressional Medal of Honor?" Kayla echoed with a touch of awe about ninety minutes later as Quinn drove her back to the Last Chance. They would have been off sooner, but Lester Baines had maneuvered her into the HQ building by suggesting that she might like to use the "facilities." She had. And once she'd relieved herself—and seized the opportunity to wash up—he'd taken her on a tour, then offered her a cup of coffee.

The tour—which had included an encounter with Mike Matsui, the camp's medic, who styled himself "The Wizard of Gauze"—had been both informative and entertaining. The coffee had been scalding hot and heavily sugared.

"During his third tour in 'Nam," Quinn replied. "It's nothing he'll talk about, but I thought you might be interested."

"Oh, absolutely. Lester Baines is an amazing character."

"Definitely one of a kind."

Kayla shifted, wincing inwardly as her stressed-out muscles protested at the movement. "He obviously dotes on your daughter."

"It's a mutual admiration society. Stevie loves to hear his stories about my days as a clueless second lieutenant."

"There was a time when you didn't know everything?" The teasing remark just slipped out. It startled her. Having long ago realized that the men who controlled the entertainment business generally did not like smart-mouthed women, she'd learned to think twice about what she said to whom. She frequently ended up saying nothing at all. But with Quinn . . .

Her companion chuckled, the husky sound feathering through her nervous system. "I learned fast, Delaney."

"I'm sure." She changed position again. "I hope I have a chance to meet Stevie while I'm up here."

The statement garnered her an assessing

glance. Kayla sustained the scrutiny steadily. She'd meant what she said.

"I can practically guarantee you'll run into her," Quinn responded, returning his gaze to the road. "Lester and his wife live next door to us. Ruthanne keeps an eye on Stevie when school's in session. During the summer, Stevie tends to hang out at Alpha. She pitched in last year during one of our family courses. And she sometimes plays victim for Mike Matsui when he's doing first aid demonstrations."

"Really?" Kayla was surprised. "After what you said about her being so badly injured, I'd think that would be the last thing she'd want to do."

"I wasn't sure it was a good idea at first," Quinn admitted, bringing the car to a halt as he pulled up in front of the motor lodge. "But I've come to the conclusion that pretending to be hurt is Stevie's way of working through some issues left over from the time when she really was. She held a whole lot in back then. Little Miss Stoic, the nurses called her. When she does her thing with Mike, she's all moans and groans and an occasional bloodcurdling scream." He smiled briefly. "She'll probably ask you for acting tips."

"I'll be glad to share what I know," Kayla promised, unhooking her seat belt. She swung open the car door and got out.

She felt Quinn's eyes tracking her as she walked in front of the vehicle and headed for the Last Chance's lobby. She kept her chin up, her shoulders squared, and her spine straight. She told herself she could slump into an exhausted heap once she was out of his sight.

"Delaney!"

Her heart skipped a beat. She pivoted around. Quinn had rolled down the driver's side window. There was something about his expression. . . .

"Yes?" she asked warily.

"I'll meet you on the quad at Alpha tomorrow at nine A.M."

"At *nine*?" Her voice spiked. "What happened to oh five hundred?"

"If you want to haul your derriere out of bed at the crack of dawn, feel free. I plan to sleep in."

She moved closer to the car. "Then this morning's little rendezvous was—what? Your idea of a joke?"

"More like a small exercise in psy-ops."

"I beg your pardon?"

"Psychological operations. It's a Green Beret speciality."

"In other words, you were messing with my head."

"I prefer to think of it as establishing who's going to be running the show for the next six weeks."

Kayla considered this for a few moments. Then, dulcetly, she advised, "I think you'd better think again . . . *sir*."

Quinn Harris smiled at her, much as he'd done that morning when he'd stood on the threshold of her motel room. Her body began to throb with impulses she was too weary—and, she fervently hoped, too wise—to act on.

"Call me Quinn, Delaney," he said.

Kayla took a steadying breath. Psy-ops, huh? Well, two could play at that. Forget Special Forces expertise. She'd survived fourteen years in Hollywood, the head-messing capital of the universe!

Tilting her chin, she summoned up the most sizzling look in her repertoire and countered, "Call me Kayla, Quinn."

3

Kayla Delaney learned a number of valuable lessons before lunch the following day. Chief among them was that running an obstacle course offered her endless opportunities to fall on her face. Her sole comfort as she availed herself of these opportunities was that there was only one witness to her klutziness.

"*Ooomph,*" she exclaimed, the air rushing out of her lungs as she hit the ground on the far side of the vertical wall climb.

Temporarily stunned by the force of her tumble, Kayla stayed where she was. Out of the corner of her eye, she saw Quinn hunker down beside her sprawled body. While she was clad in a sweat suit similar to the one she'd worn the day before, he'd traded his fatigues for a pair of khaki shorts and an olive-drab tank top. His muscles rippled sleekly beneath his sun-bronzed skin as he squatted.

After a moment he asked, "What's the problem, Kayla?"

"No problem," she lied through gritted teeth,

pushing herself into a kneeling position. She hurt from head to toe and had bruises on top of bruises. She was also sweating in places she hadn't realized were capable of producing perspiration. "I simply succumbed to an irresistible urge to worship the ground you walk on."

Quinn grinned briefly, his gaze flickering over her. "I have that effect on a lot of trainees."

"I'll just bet." Kayla mentally replayed her fall, trying to figure out what she'd done wrong. "I can't seem to get my brain and body in sync."

"I'm not sure you've got them in the same time zone at the moment."

She grimaced but didn't dispute the assessment.

"Do you want to call it quits?"

"*Excuse me*?" Her voice rose on a mixture of indignation and disbelief.

"Just for today." His clarification was quick and clearly intended to mollify. "You went full throttle on the nature walk yesterday and you've been pushing hard all morning. Why don't you give it a rest?"

"No way." She shook her head, her sweat-sodden braid slapping against her nape. "I'm going to get 'round this obstacle course."

Quinn remained silent for a few seconds, obviously torn between approval of her determination and concern for her well-being. Eventually he acquiesced, saying, "It's your call." He rose in a seamless, smooth-as-silk movement. "But keep in mind this is only the second day of a six-week program."

"How could I forget?" Kayla retorted, clambering to her feet with more speed than sense. A wave of wooziness washed over her. Gritting her teeth, she steadied herself, then took a tentative step forward. Then another. And then—

A sudden stumble threatened to send her nose-diving into the dirt once again. Reacting with a speed that would have been intimidating under other circumstances, Quinn caught and steadied her. Then he swung her up into his arms and cradled her against his broad chest.

"*Quinn!*" she gasped, the musk-male scent of his skin filling her nostrils. The warmth of his body penetrated the fabric of her sweat suit. She felt herself flush. "What are you doing?"

His hold on her tightened. So did his expression. "Succumbing to an irresistible urge to sweep you off your feet."

She had the sexiest toes he'd ever seen.

Inappropriate though it undoubtedly was, this was Quinn Harris' first thought after he'd removed Kayla's shoes and the white cotton socks she wore inside them. While the lady didn't precisely cooperate in the procedure, she at least refrained from kicking him.

He couldn't explain his reaction. He wasn't exactly a connoisseur of feminine podiatric allure. Was it the shape of her toes that was turning him on? The shell pink polish on their tips?

Then again, maybe he'd simply lost his grip on sanity during the five or six minutes it had taken him to carry Kayla from the obstacle course to Alpha's HQ building. He'd known the moment he picked her up that he was making a mistake. How big a mistake had become embarrassingly obvious once he'd started to move.

"I'm all right, Quinn," Kayla insisted for the dozenth or so time. They were in his office. She was perched on the edge of a chair. He was kneeling in front of her. "There's nothing wrong with my feet. Neither of my ankles is broken, twisted, or sprained. Will you please stop making such a fuss?"

Quinn sat back on his heels, silently acknowledging that he was probably overreacting. He'd checked carefully and found no sign of injury.

His gaze drifted toward the shoes he'd taken off. They were good, sturdy cross trainers, he noted. Not a premium brand, but not bargain basement footwear, either. He vaguely recalled that the brown hiking shoes Kayla had had on yesterday had been manufactured by the same—

Whoa. Back up. Cross trainers? *Brown hiking shoes*?

"Why aren't you wearing combat boots, Delaney?" he demanded.

Kayla blinked several times, plainly thrown by the question. After a moment she replied, "Aside from the fact that I don't have any, you mean?"

"Don't *have* any?" He flashed back on her failure to show up at the appointed hour the previous morning. And on the quasi insubordination of some of her subsequent behavior. For all that she'd pledged to cooperate in her training, it was obvious to him that Kayla Delaney had a mind of her own. Which was fine by him. He admired independent thinking. But if his new trainee had decided she was going to make some kind of stand against regulation footwear, it was time for her to revise her agenda. "Everybody who attends Alpha is issued combat boots. I ordered a pair in your size the same day your studio confirmed you were going to—"

Quinn stopped, abruptly realizing that he had

no idea where those boots were. He remembered their delivery, of course. He *also* recalled that his daughter had shown up before he'd decided where to stash them.

Last Friday had been the final day of the school year, and Stevie had arrived at Alpha in a very strange mood. She'd moped around, muttering and making a nuisance of herself. When one of the staff instructors had breezed in and greeted her with a casual "Lookin' good, Stevie," she'd reacted as though she'd been smacked across the face with a dead fish.

Although her behavior in recent months had been problematic on occasion, this had been way outside the norm. Quinn had tried to ascertain what was wrong. After several minutes of crankily insisting that everything was (big sigh) *okay*, his daughter had suddenly burst out with a litany of complaints about her appearance. Although she hadn't flat-out said so, she'd given the distinct impression that she blamed him for the situation.

He'd been unnerved for a couple of reasons. First, he knew he was abysmally ignorant about female fashion. Second, it seemed to him that there was only one logical explanation why, after years of indifference, his daughter was suddenly worrying about the stylishness of her clothes and haircut.

Oh God, paternal instinct had yelled. *She's got some boy after her.*

Trying to keep his anxieties in check and respond to his daughter's needs, he'd offered to take Stevie shopping the following afternoon. She—the same girl who'd once declared him to be the strongest, smartest daddy in the whole wide world—had seemed appalled by the idea. She'd been only slightly more receptive to his subsequent suggestion that perhaps Ruthanne Baines could help her pick out some new items for her wardrobe.

Kayla Delaney's combat boots had gotten shunted aside during the course of this discussion. He thought he'd left them on his desk when he'd departed for the day, but he couldn't be—

The sound of a feminine voice uttering his name with a questioning inflection and the feel of a foot nudging against his chest yanked Quinn back into the present. "Wh-what?" he stammered, looking up.

"Are you all right?" Kayla asked, gazing down at him.

He got momentarily sidetracked by the luminous temptation of her wide set eyes. While shades of gray and green dominated her pupils, they contained flecks of gold and amethyst, too. Odd. He'd never noticed that when he'd watched her movies. And given the number of times he'd seen some of them . . .

"Quinn?" Kayla's voice had dropped a note or two and acquired a hint of throatiness. There was a new tinge of color in her cheeks as well.

"Uh—" *Cool it, hotshot!* he ordered himself. *No fraternization with the trainees!* "I'm just—"

"Got some Ace bandages and an ice pack, boss," Lester Baines announced, making a quicktime entrance into the small, wood-paneled office.

Saved by the sergeant major, Quinn thought wryly. It wasn't the first time, of course. Although who was being saved from whom—or what—was a bit unclear in this instance.

"Thanks, Lester." He stood up, schooling his expression into blandness. "But it looks as though we won't be needing them."

"I appreciate your concern, Sergeant Major," Kayla said.

"Can't be too careful with your feet," Lester declared with the unshakable conviction of a veteran infantryman. "If there's a problem—"

"There is," Quinn picked up. "But it's not with her feet. It's with what she's been wearing on them."

The older man seemed puzzled for a moment, then started to grin. "Finally remembered those combat boots you said you were gonna personally take care of, huh?"

"Now, wait a minute—"

"You know where they are, Sergeant Major?" Quinn asked, overriding Kayla's protest.

"I think I can lay my hands on 'em."

"Well, then—"

The front door of the HQ building opened with a slam. This was followed by the sound of someone dashing down the hallway. The precipitousness of the entrance and the lightness of the footfall revealed to Quinn who the "someone" was long before his preteen daughter skidded to a halt in the doorway of his office.

"Tex was at the top of the rappeling tower and he said he saw you carrying the movie star across the quad," Stevie reported breathlessly, her bright blue eyes darting back and forth. "What happened? Did she get hurt? The Wiz had to go into town, but I'm pretty sure one of the trainees in José's group is some kind of a doctor. A vet, maybe. Where is she? Is she okay?"

Midway through this verbal outpouring, Quinn realized that Kayla was hidden from Stevie's view behind him and Lester. As the last question tumbled from his daughter's lips, he stepped aside. He was curious to see what she'd make of the "movie star"—and vice versa.

Stevie's jaw dropped. She flushed hotly and sent Quinn an accusatory glare. Although it had not been his intention to embarrass her, he obviously had. Dammit, he thought, cursing his unwitting insensitivity. He should have realized. . . .

"Hello, there," Kayla said, getting to her feet. Her voice was warm. So was the smile that illuminated her fair-skinned face. He saw his daughter's discomfort melt away like snow before spring sunshine. "You must be Stevie Harris. I'm Kayla Delaney. You have no idea how thrilled I am to see another female around this place!"

"So, you've never met Keanu Reeves?" Stevie asked disappointedly about twenty minutes later as she escorted Kayla (who was now properly shod in combat boots) over to the mess hall for lunch.

"Who's Kee-noo Reeves?" Quinn heard Lester Baines mutter on his left. The two of them were walking a few paces behind Stevie and Kayla.

"The young guy in that movie about the bomb on the bus," he answered.

"Sorry, no," Kayla said. "But as I mentioned, I admire his work."

"You do know Brad Pitt, though, right?"

"A little bit. We've talked at a couple of parties. And yes. He's definitely as attractive in person as he is on the screen."

"Wow. And you actually *tried out* for a movie with Tom Cruise?"

"He the kid who did that fighter jock picture?" Lester wanted to know. "*Top* something?"

"*Gun*," Quinn quietly supplied, watching the interaction between Kayla and Stevie with an odd combination of emotions. Although his daughter seldom hung back when it came to making new acquaintances, he'd never seen her open up to a stranger this quickly. He supposed the glamour of Kayla's profession had a lot to do with it. And yet . . .

"Yes," Kayla confirmed with a musical laugh. "I actually tried out for a movie with Tom Cruise. It was quite a few years ago. He got the part, I didn't."

"Wow," Stevie said again as they reached the mess hall. "I mean, I'm sorry you didn't get the part. I'll bet you would have been really good in it, whatever it was. My dad has some of your mov—"

"Allow me, ladies," Quinn cut in swiftly, striding forward and yanking open the door. His pulse had kicked into overdrive when he'd realized what his artless daughter was on the verge of revealing. While it was okay for Kayla Delaney to know that he was familiar with her movies, he had no desire for her to discover that he had quite a few of them at home on videotape.

"*Ladies*?" Stevie giggled merrily as she marched by him.

Kayla nailed him with a quick sideward glance as she followed his daughter inside. Instinct told

him she was remembering the tone he'd taken
the day before when he'd described himself as a
big admirer of her work.

"C'mon, Lester," he said, ushering the older
man ahead of him.

The mess hall was filled nearly to capacity and
was very noisy. Yet within five seconds of Kayla's entrance, the place went absolutely still and
silent. Well, *almost* absolutely silent. There was a
loud clatter from the back of the room as some
guy apparently lost his grip and dropped a lunch
tray.

Who was responsible for what happened next,
Quinn never found out. But someone took it into
his head to shove back his chair and stand up.
A moment or two later, *everybody* was jumping
to attention.

"Geez," he heard Stevie observe in an awestruck whisper. "This is better than when General Schwarzkopf came to dinner last summer!"

Quinn looked at Kayla. Although he knew she
had to be accustomed to public attention, she
was plainly taken aback by this reaction. He
could hardly blame her, given that the same people who were now staring at her had totally ignored her yesterday afternoon as she'd walked
through the quad.

This cold shoulder treatment had been the un-
intended result of his having passed the word
that he expected everyone affiliated with Alpha
to respect Kayla Delaney's privacy. He'd tried to
revise his edict at this morning's staff meeting,
explaining that respecting the lady's privacy
didn't mean behaving as though she were invisible.

"Just show her proper military courtesy," he'd summed up to his staff.

It seemed he needed to refine his instructions a wee bit more. . . .

Suddenly Kayla stiffened her spine and lifted her chin in a movement Quinn was beginning to know very well. For one unsettling instant, he thought she was going to snap off a salute to the waiting throng.

"As you were, gentlemen," she ordered crisply. "Carry on."

Amazingly everybody did.

They fit perfectly, Kayla marveled, wiggling her toes. Nothing had ever felt so comfortable on her feet. She'd run five miles in them this morning without a single pinch. They'd been equally accommodating during two-plus hours of calisthenics.

It was now late Monday afternoon. While nearly a week had passed since she'd first tucked her tootsies into the black, lace-up-the-front leather boots presented to her by Quinn Harris and Lester Baines, she still couldn't treat them as just another pair of shoes. There was something . . . empowering . . . about them. They seemed to compel her to stand tall. To hang tough. To be (in the words of the army recruiting commercial) all that she could be.

Funny thing, Kayla mused as she limbered up for what was to be her first session in one of the unarmed combat "pits" behind barracks row. She'd always been dubious about the shoes-as-destiny theory of life propounded by some of her female acquaintances in Los Angeles. Even as a little girl, she'd found the story of Cinderella and the glass slipper hard to swallow. Yet when she considered the sense of confidence that seemed to infuse her each time she pulled on her new combat boots, she felt this skepticism easing.

Take that stunt she'd pulled in the mess hall, for instance. While she'd hardly survived fourteen years in show biz by being a shrinking violet, she knew—absolutely, positively *knew*—she wouldn't have had the nerve to toss out a line like "As you were" had she not been wearing the proper military footwear. Why, even now . . .

"Feeling feisty, Delaney?"

Controlling a start of surprise at this inquiry, Kayla pivoted to confront its source. Quinn stood a few feet away. He was clad in the shorts and tank top combo she'd started to think of as his "stripped for action" outfit. He was smiling. Something about the shape of his smile—or maybe it was the look in his intensely blue eyes—suggested hungry cats and hapless canaries.

"Feisty and then some," she stated boldly. "I'm ready to kick some butt."

"Any particular butt in mind?"

"Whatever's available."

Quinn chuckled. "I think those combat boots are going to your head," he commented, moving forward. Three lithe steps brought him within touching distance of her.

"Could be . . . sir," Kayla concurred, her pulse quickening. One thing the combat boots had *not* done was lessen her vulnerability to her instructor. Quite the contrary. Her attraction to him was getting stronger. What's more, she was becoming increasingly certain that the attraction wasn't as one-sided as she'd believed during their initial meeting.

How she felt about all this, she was trying to sort out. She was not given to indulging in short-term flings. While many of her show biz colleagues behaved as though sex were simply nature's way of saying hello—or, more practically, an effective method of sealing a deal—she'd never done so. She'd had a few affairs over the years. But with each of them, erotic consummation had been preceeded by genuine emotional connection.

Her agent had indicated on more than one occasion that her refusal to put out had cost her, career-wise. She didn't doubt it. But it simply was not in her nature to barter with her body.

There was a brief silence. Quinn's eyes narrowed, his expression growing thoughtful.

"Okay," he finally said, hooking his thumbs into the waistband of his snug fitting shorts. "I gather they're going to bring in some martial arts champion to choreograph the hand-to-hand sequences for your film. What I'm going to teach you while you're here at Alpha is the basic moves. I'll also show you how to take a hit or a fall and not get hurt."

"Sounds good to me." Kayla smiled crookedly. "Especially the part about not getting hurt."

"Well, I can't promise there won't be any bumps and bruises. But I'll try to avoid doing any real damage."

"I'd appreciate that."

"Have you had any training in self-defense?"

Kayla shook her head. "I've thought about taking lessons. I realize L.A. isn't the safest place in the world. I *do* carry a little can of pepper spray in my purse."

"Not exactly the best place for it to be if you ever get into trouble," Quinn pointed out trenchantly. "But leaving that aside . . . according to what I've read of the script, your character has a thing for kicking bad guys in the *cojones*."

"Mad Maxine does seem inclined to go for the groin."

"Who?"

"The woman I play in *Moving Target*."

"I thought her name was Dinah."

"It is. But some studio smart aleck tagged her 'Mad Maxine'—you know, a reference to the part Mel Gibson played a few years back?—and it stuck."

"I see. Well, a knee to the nuts may work fine for Mad Maxine. But just so you know, it isn't necessarily the best move in a real life assault situation."

"It isn't?"

"No. Number one, it's predictable. Better to do something unexpected. Number two, it tends to leave you off balance. If you don't connect, you're likely to go down and go down hard. And three"—Quinn paused, his mobile mouth twisting—"getting it in the family jewels isn't fun. But it's not usually fatal. A determined assailant can push through the pain."

"What would you recommend instead?" Kayla was genuinely interested. "In a real life assault situation, I mean."

"First of all, don't fight if you don't have to." The advice was quick and unequivocal. "Run like hell and scream bloody murder if you can. If you can't . . . well, say you get grabbed from behind. Smash down on the guy's instep with your heel, then go for his solar plexus with your elbow. Put your whole body into it. If you're facing the attacker and you've got something sturdy on your feet, you might think about a toe slam to the ankle. Or better yet, to the kneecap. If you get lucky, you'll cripple the guy for life. And these"—Quinn held up his hands, fingers clenched, thumbs extended upward—"can be very handy in close-up combat. Go for the eyes."

Kayla controlled a wince, slightly unnerved by this dispassionate recitation.

"I'll give you a shot at trying that kind of stuff before you go back to L.A.," Quinn promised, adjusting his stance. "But first, the basics."

"I think I can handle tha—AAAH!"

Thud.

Kayla landed flat on her back on the ground. She lay there, staring up at the cloudless blue sky and trying to determine exactly how she'd gotten from standing to supine in the space of, oh, maybe half a second.

"You okay?" Quinn inquired, bending over her.

She propped herself up on her elbows. "Compared to what?"

Her "attacker" laughed, his even teeth showing white against his tanned skin. Then he extended his hand. After a brief hesitation, Kayla reached up and took it. The press of his hard palm triggered a jitter of excitement within her. The curl of his long fingers around her wrist escalated the response.

A moment later she was back on her feet. It seemed to Kayla that Quinn retained possession of her hand longer than was strictly necessary.

Then again, perhaps she was projecting. Perhaps *she'd* been the one who'd held on for an extra, illicit instant.

"Not bad for your first fall," Quinn declared, taking a step back. His expression was unreadable. "You went right with it."

"I didn't have much choice."

"You could have tensed up. Tried to fight gravity. That's what a lot of people do and that's how some of them get hurt. You relaxed."

"Are you trying to tell me that 'go with the flow' is some kind of martial arts concept?"

Quinn seemed slightly startled by this question. Then he smiled and said, "In a sense. Now, let me explain what I did, why I did it, and how you could have countered it."

Kayla had taken ballet lessons when she was a girl. In an odd way, Quinn's method of teaching the "basics" of unarmed combat reminded her of them. His emphasis was on balance, position, and timing. Only occasionally did he do something to remind her that the maneuvers he was demonstrating with such fluid masculine grace could be used to maim or kill.

Although he plainly took care to keep his promise not to inflict any "real damage," he wasn't easy on her. If she made a mistake or lost focus, he took her down without compunction.

Somewhere around the tenth time he did this, a group of campers jogged by under the supervision of the bald-headed black man Kayla had seen on the quadrangle her first afternoon at Alpha. They'd been introduced in the mess hall several days ago. His name was Nathaniel "Tex" Fournier, and he was a former Army Ranger.

Several of the runners shouted encouragement

as they passed by. Tex called out, too, offering advice about how she could turn the tables on Quinn.

Kayla staggered to her feet and waved at her well-wishers. She was gulping for air and sweating like the proverbial pig, but she felt weirdly exhilarated.

"How are you holding up?" Quinn asked, wiping his forehead with the back of his hand. A faint sheen of perspiration was the only indication he'd spent the past hour doing anything more strenuous than ambling in a park.

"I think I've pretty well gotten the knack of landing on my derriere."

"You'd like to try something more challenging, hmm?"

"Well . . ."

Quinn assessed her without speaking for several moments. Kayla returned his gaze steadily, psyching herself into what she'd come to consider her woman-as-warrior mind-set. She centered her body almost without thinking, distributing her weight evenly over her booted feet.

"All right," Quinn agreed, a provocative glint entering his eyes. "I'll teach you a judo shoulder throw. First, we face off. . . ."

Kayla practiced the moves he showed her over and over. Finally she felt as though she'd mastered them. But before she had a chance to assert this, Quinn preempted her with a gruff, "Okay, Delaney. This is for real."

He came at her fast. There was no time to get ready. No time to review what she was supposed to do. She had to react . . . *right then.*

Grabbing Quinn's right forearm with her left

hand, Kayla pulled forward, forcing him to over-balance. She stepped into him with her right foot, pivoting her body so her right shoulder slammed into the general vicinity of his right armpit. She bent her knees slightly, tugging down with her left arm, then heaving up with her entire body. After that, it was all a matter of momentum.

"All RIGHT!" she crowed, fervently wishing there'd been someone around to see her triumph. Giddy with adrenaline, she pumped her fists in the air and performed a little victory dance. So what if gloating wasn't nice? She'd done it! She'd actually tossed Quinn Harris right on his—

And then she realized that her vanquished assailant wasn't moving. *Hadn't* moved, in fact, since he'd landed on the ground. She stopped dancing.

"Quinn?" she asked tentatively, edging toward the spot where he lay sprawled in ominous, eyes-closed stillness.

No answer.

A sense of dread crept over her. She repeated his name.

Nothing. Not even a twitch.

Oh God, she thought, appalled. *I've killed him.*

Trembling, Kayla knelt down next to Quinn. She extended her right hand, intending to feel for a pulse. *Please*, she prayed. *Oh, please*—

In the space of a single, panicked heartbeat, Kayla was gripped, flipped, and pinned on her back with a tautly muscled forearm pressed lightly against her windpipe.

"*Wha*—?" she croaked, staring up into Quinn's lean, compelling face.

"Delaney, Delaney, Delaney," he murmured

on a reproving sigh. "Mad Maxine would be very disappointed in you."

Kayla had to struggle to draw breath. The problem wasn't the arm across her throat. It was anger. Pure, unadulterated anger. "You *tricked* me!"

"Uh-huh," Quinn confirmed without a hint of remorse. "When it comes to self-defense, you worry about Number One—not the other guy."

Goaded far beyond the boundaries of good sense, she tried to hit him. He parried the blow effortlessly. "Let go!" she demanded, struggling.

"Calm down first."

"You're not in charge of me!"

"Maybe not." The concession was accompanied by a grunt and a shift of position. "But I'm on top right now, so I make the rules."

And then it happened. One moment Kayla was glaring up at the man with homicide in her heart; the next moment her gaze had fused with his and fury was giving way to something infinitely more dangerous.

The flame of desire had been kindled within her the first time she'd seen Quinn Harris, but she'd managed to keep it banked and under control. Now it flared up like a wildfire, making her burn.

Quinn was burning, too. She could see it in the febrile brilliance of his midnight blue eyes. Hear it in the harsh rhythm of his breathing. Feel it— oh, Lord, could she feel it!—in the tension of his powerful body.

"Kayla," he whispered hoarsely, caressing up her torso to cup the underside of her right breast. The curve of his palm was possessive. The

warmth of his fingers seemed to sear directly through her sweatshirt and bra.

"*Yes*," she whispered in return, her voice husky.

Quinn lowered his head, bringing his mouth within an inch of hers. She felt the fan of his breath. Her eyelids fluttered down.

The first few moments of contact were light. Not so much tentative as testing. Tantalizing. Quinn seemed to be sampling the taste of her. She shuddered as he delicately licked the middle of her bottom lip. She shuddered again, whimpering involuntarily, as he raked the same sensitized spot with the faintly serrated edge of his front teeth.

The pressure of his mouth became more demanding. She opened to him, inviting the slick velvet sweep of his tongue. She stroked his back as he deepened the kiss, relishing the ripple and release of his muscles.

More, she thought greedily, dizzily aware of the burgeoning thrust of Quinn's potent masculinity. Much . . . more.

Suddenly he stiffened. Seemed to try to pull back. Her initial assumption was that his resistance was some kind of tease—a bit of sexual psy-ops, as it were. This assumption was shattered when two syllables penetrated her pleasure-hazed brain.

"*Yo, boss!*"

Comprehension didn't dawn. It clouted Kayla right between the eyes like a sledgehammer.

She was lying on the ground making out with a man she'd known for a week and a day, while a Congressional Medal of Honor winner looked on!

"Quinn!" she hissed, trying to wriggle free. "Get off!"

He levered himself up a few inches. "Fight me."

"*What?*"

"This is unarmed combat, Delaney," her partner in ill-considered passion growled, eyes blazing. "Let the sergeant major see you give me your best shot."

Kayla did what she had to. She followed orders.

4

"**I**s it embarrassing to kiss a guy you hardly know in front of somebody else?"

Kayla nearly choked on a chunk of cucumber from the salad she'd ordered for lunch. "Excuse m-me?" she finally managed, regarding Quinn Harris' twelve-and-a-half-year-old daughter with dismay. Was it possible? Was Stevie aware of what had happened five days ago behind the barracks back at Alpha Camp?

And if she was, who had told her? Her father? Or Lester Baines?

"Like when you're making a movie," the girl blithely clarified, taking a slurping drink of the chocolate milk shake she'd chosen to accompany her bacon cheeseburger and fries. "You sometimes have to do a love scene on the very first day, right? With some actor you've just met. And there's all these crew guys around, watching. Is it, like *totally* humiliating?"

Kayla practically swooned with relief. "No," she responded after a few moments. "Not totally."

"But kind of."

"Definitely, kind of."

"Is it ever . . . romantic? I mean, like, if the actor's really cute and nice?"

Kayla sighed and set down her fork. She was reluctant to destroy the girl's illusions about show business, but she felt she had to put a few basic facts on the table.

"Some love scenes are easier than others, Stevie," she said carefully. "But romantic? No. I think real romance requires privacy. And a movie set is anything but private. Plus, you have to think about practical things when you're doing a screen kiss. Like which way you should turn your head. Or how you're going to keep from bumping noses. Or what you'll do if you run out of breath and start gasping."

Stevie dragged a fry through a pool of catsup and popped it into her mouth. "I worry about that stuff in real life."

"You . . . do?" *Dear Lord*, Kayla thought with a sudden surge of protectiveness. *She isn't even thirteen!*

"It's not that I'm *doing* anything," Stevie added, scrunching up her face. It was difficult to tell whether she regretted this situation or was grateful for it. "I just . . . well, you know. Try to imagine it. Being with a guy, I mean. So, like, if it ever happens, I won't act like a complete geek."

"That sounds very smart of you," Kayla responded. "And it *will* happen, Stevie. So don't try to . . . rush."

There was a pause. Praying she'd said the right things in the right way, Kayla picked up her fork and went back to eating her salad. Her companion scarfed down several more fries and took another gulp of milk shake.

"Sergeant Major told me what you did to Dad, you know," Stevie eventually volunteered.

Kayla's heart lurched. She glanced around, fervently hoping that none of their fellow diners were given to eavesdropping. "What I did to your father?"

"On Monday. In the combat pit."

"Oh."

"He said it was *really* funny." The girl snickered, her sky-colored eyes fizzing with unfilial glee. "Sergeant Major said Dad couldn't stand up straight for at least five minutes afterward and that he was crouched over like the Hunchback of Notre Dame, holding his—"

"*Stevie,*" Kayla interrupted a bit desperately, setting down her eating utensil once again. She supposed she should be glad that Lester Baines had been so thoroughly deceived by Quinn's hit-me-with-your-best-shot ploy. But it was difficult, burdened as she was by the memory of what had gone before. "Please. I feel badly about what happened between your father and me. I'd just as soon not have to relive it over lunch."

Stevie blinked. "I—I'm sorry," she stammered. "I didn't know my talking about it would upset you, too."

"I'm not upset. It's just that—" Kayla stopped, the implications of the final word of Stevie's last sentence suddenly registering with her. " 'Too?' What do you mean . . . too?"

Stevie flushed to the roots of her dark, pixie-cut hair. "Dad's even touchier about what happened than you are. I mean, I mentioned it *once*—like, I was making a joke, you know?—and he told me to put a sock in it! He used his young-lady-if-you-were-in-the-military-you'd-be-a-candidate-for-a-court-martial voice, too."

"I think I've heard that tone once or twice myself in recent days," Kayla murmured ruefully. Quinn had been the epitome of spit-and-polish professionalism since Monday's hand-to-hand encounter. Realizing she couldn't match his by-the-numbers aloofness, she'd reverted to the *I'll-show-you* attitude that had gotten her through her first day of training. They were managing for the moment, but she knew some kind of reckoning was coming.

"You're sure you're not mad at me?"

"Positive."

"Good." Stevie beamed. "And just in case you might be worried that Dad blames you or something, he doesn't. I overheard him tell Sergeant Major that he took full responsibility."

"You . . . did?"

"Uh-huh. Which makes sense. I mean, Dad was in charge of the lesson. If you accidentally goofed up and kneed him in the—uh—well, *you know*, he has to take the blame because he didn't make certain you did everything right."

"I see." Kayla didn't know whether this explanation made her feel better or worse. Worse, probably. The idea that Quinn would declare the fault to have been entirely his . . .

"I know you!"

The source of this assertion (or was it an accusation?) was a chubby man with a very bad hairpiece who'd materialized beside the booth in which they were sitting. He was pointing at Kayla.

"I beg your pardon?" she responded cautiously. Although she felt it was important to be pleasant to fans, she was always conscious that there were some very strange—even dangerous—people around.

"No!" the man exclaimed, shaking his head so violently his toupee slipped to one side. "Don't tell me! *Don't tell me!* I know you. I've seen *all* your movies! Every single one! You're—uh—uh—uh—"

"Kayla Delaney," Stevie finally whispered.

The man gave her a disdainful glare. "No, she's not," he disputed, then turned his beady gaze on Kayla. "No, you're not."

"Yes," she informed him. "I am."

The man seemed stunned. Finally he drew himself up and huffed, "Well, in that case—*never mind!*"

And with that plainly meant-to-crush comment, he lumbered away.

Ah, the glamour of celebrity, Kayla thought. Then she frowned, startled by the depth of her sarcasm. There'd been a time when being recognized *had* been glamorous. But in the last few years, coping with the consequences of being in the movies had become more and more like ... well, *work*. And not terribly satisfying work, if truth be told.

Would the situation improve after she played Mad Maxine? she wondered. Would her attitude?

She wanted to answer yes. Absolutely. No doubt about it. But something prevented her from doing so. She couldn't lie to herself. She couldn't pretend that there wasn't a possibility that starring in *Moving Target* would make things worse.

"Does that happen to you a lot, Kayla?"

Stevie's obvious shock at what she'd just witnessed resonated with Kayla in a disconcerting way. "Fortunately, no," she said after a moment, summoning up a light laugh. "But just in case this restaurant is a weirdo magnet, what do you say we make our escape and so some shopping?"

Buying clothing didn't rank very high on Kayla's list of preferred activities. Although her career demanded that she keep a few cutting edge outfits in her closet, she had no passion for trendy fashion. She was inclined toward classically simple attire and tended to purchase in multiples when she found an item she liked.

This current crawl through a mall about forty minutes away from Alpha Camp had been prompted by necessity. The workout gear she'd brought with her from L.A. simply wasn't sturdy enough to withstand the wear and tear of her training. She needed some really durable garments.

Kayla had intended to go shopping alone. Because she was scheduled for half-day sessions on the weekends, she'd decided that Saturday afternoon would be the perfect time to take care of her errands.

Stevie had turned up just as she was cooling down after a grueling series of calisthenics. Having felt an affinity for the girl from the moment they'd met, Kayla had been genuinely glad to see her. She'd also appreciated having someone to act as a buffer between her and Quinn.

Why she'd mentioned her shopping plans, Kayla wasn't sure. But the instant she had, she'd seen a yearning expression enter Stevie's eyes. Almost before she'd realized what she was doing, she asked the preteen if she'd like to come along. Stevie had immediately turned to her father with an oh-please-oh-please-say-it's-okay appeal. Although plainly reluctant to do so, Quinn had granted her the permission she was seeking.

"Do you see anything you like, Stevie?" Kayla asked as they culled through the offerings at a shop that specialized in athletic attire.

The girl's response was the verbal equivalent of a shrug.

"I'm getting awfully tired of being the only one trying stuff on, you know."

"Why? You look good in *everything*."

The unspoken corollary to this assertion—that she, Stephanie Lynn Harris, looked good in nothing—came through loud and clear.

Kayla assessed her young companion covertly. Quinn's daughter was tall for her age, which undoubtedly was a problem. She was also skinny as a soda straw, despite a voracious appetite. What's more, her features—a feminized version of her father's, in many ways—were a far cry from cookie-cutter cuteness.

That Stevie would blossom into a strikingly attractive woman, Kayla was absolutely certain. She also knew there was no point in saying so. An almost adolescent girl suffering from appearance anxiety was not likely to be comforted by the notion that she would "grow into" her looks.

"What about this?" she asked, spying an appealing looking outfit and pulling it from the rack. "I'll bet it would be terrific with your coloring."

Stevie hunched her shoulders. "Nah. I don't think so."

They moved on to another shop a few minutes later. Kayla's feet were starting to ache. She wished she'd worn her combat boots instead of sandals.

"Kayla?" Stevie asked as they paused to examine a display of T-shirts.

"Mmm?"

"Did you have lots of boyfriends when you were growing up?"

Uh-oh.

"I had a few," Kayla answered honestly. "But none when I was your age."

Stevie chewed on her lower lip for several seconds, then leaned in and whispered, "Did you have . . . breasts . . . when you were my age?"

Kayla resisted the urge to laugh at this sotto voce inquiry. She flashed on an image of Quinn Harris struggling to explain the vagaries of female physical development to his daughter and felt an unexpected rush of sympathy.

"Actually, I was flat as a pancake when I was your age," she admitted.

Stevie's gaze flicked to her chest, then back up to her face. "Have you had, like . . . um . . . you know. Uh, implants or anything?"

It was not an untoward question, Kayla reflected. Cosmetic surgery was a fact of life in her profession. She sometimes felt as though she were the only person in Hollywood who hadn't submitted to the knife!

"Nope," she replied. "I'm all natural. And incidentally, I was flat as a pancake through my sophomore year of high school. I didn't need a bra until I was sixteen."

Stevie took a few moments to digest this information before confiding, "This girl named Brittany joined my class near the end of the year. She wears a bra. And makeup. And she has this really wiggly walk."

"Ah." A juvenile Jezebel. She knew the type.

"All the boys think she's a complete babe."

Kayla rolled her eyes and drawled, "Men are *so-o-o-o* superficial."

Stevie seemed stunned by this blanket condemnation of the opposite sex, then started to laugh. "Yeah," she concurred feelingly. "They are sometimes. Totally superficial."

There was a pause.

"All the boys, huh?" Kayla finally asked, probing delicately.

Quinn's daughter flushed. "Well, there is this *one* boy," she confessed. "Michael. We hung around together most of the year and I thought we were, like, friends . . . you know?"

"And then Miss Bra-Wearing Brittany showed up a couple months ago and he started acting like a fool?"

"Yeah." An emphatic nod. "Exactly."

Kayla patted the girl's narrow shoulder. "I understand what you're going through, Stevie. Really. I do. I wish I could give you some no-fail trick for making things go back to the way they were between you and Michael. But if there is one, nobody's clued me in about it. The best I can say is that if your old buddy prefers Brittany to you, it's his loss. Because you're something very special."

Stevie regarded her warily, plainly torn between a desire to believe the compliment and a fear she was being fobbed off with a psychological lollipop. Finally she asked, " 'Special' isn't a nice way of saying *weird*, is it?"

Kayla shook her head. "Absolutely not!"

"Well . . ."

"Trust me."

They spent a few more minutes browsing through the T-shirts, then headed to another shop. "Stevie?" Kayla ventured as they strolled.

"Yeah?"

"Do you talk to your father about the things we've been discussing?"

Stevie stopped dead in her tracks, her eyes widening with shock. "You mean, like, about Brittany? And boys? And . . . having *breasts*?"

"Well, uh—" Actually that's exactly what she'd meant.

"Of course not! He'd *never* understand!"

"But you two seem so close." Although she'd noticed some tension between father and daughter, Kayla had also felt the unconditional affection and abiding trust that bonded them. Quinn and Stevie's relationship reminded her of how much she'd lost when her parents had died. Of how essentially solitary her existence had become as she'd moved into her thirties.

"Oh, we are!" Stevie rushed to assert. "My dad is the *best*. If you knew some of the things he's done for me—like, after the car crash that killed my mom? I was hurt, really bad. Without him . . ." The girl stopped speaking, temporarily overcome by emotion. Recovering, she went on. "The thing is, I'm starting to grow up. But I don't think he's handling it really well, you know? Sometimes he acts like he wishes I'd stay a baby. And sometimes . . . sometimes it's almost like he wishes I was a *boy*!"

"I don't think that's true," Kayla protested. "Your dad loves you, Stevie. Why, the very first day I met him, he talked about how terrific you are. If he's been acting weird . . . well, a lot of fathers seem to have problems coping with the concept that their little girls aren't going to be little girls forever."

"I guess." Quinn's daughter sighed heavily. "I mean, I know Dad *tries*. It's just that—well, like, a couple of weeks ago he wanted to take me clothes shopping! Can you imagine, Kayla? He probably would have made me get dresses with pink ruffles and rosebuds. I would have looked *gross*!"

"I doubt that," Kayla responded dryly. "Still, you probably have a point. Most men have no clothes sense at all." She paused, mulling over a sudden idea. After a few moments she said, "I tell you what. Why don't you pick out a few really cool outfits? You can take them home and show them to your father. Clue him in on your style. It'd be my treat."

"*Seriously*?"

"Seriously."

"Well"—Stevie wrinkled her nose—"I *did* see some cute stuff when we were in the Gap before lunch."

"Like that stone-washed denim skirt?"

"Yeah."

"And what about the red jumper with the black trim?"

"Oh, that was neat! Only . . . I'm not sure they had it in my size."

"C'mon." Kayla beckoned, feeling quite pleased with herself. "Let's go find out."

5

Where are they? Quinn wondered, pacing back and forth across the worn but still beautiful Oriental rug that covered much of the hardwood floor in his living room. The rug, like the excellent pieces of antique furniture that were scattered throughout the modest-sized home in which he and Stevie lived, and the land on which Alpha Camp had been built, was an inheritance from his father.

Although he'd been tempered by the hardships of war, General Stephen Sterling Harris had had a keen appreciation of the "finer" things in life. The scion of a wealthy California family who'd married a woman from a similarly gilt-edged background, he'd also had the financial wherewithal to indulge his expensive tastes.

Quinn was grateful for his father's material legacies, of course. But had he been left nothing but his memories of the man, he would have counted himself richly blessed.

He glanced at his wristwatch. It proclaimed

the time to be six twenty-one. He looked at the clock sitting on the stone and mortar mantel of the living room's fireplace. It said six twenty-four.

Dammit, he thought, clenching and unclenching his hands. *They should have been back long before this! The mall isn't that far away. What if—*

The sound of a car engine snapped this line of thinking. Quinn crossed to a window in four swift strides. Yanking back the drapes, he peered outside. The sedan Kayla had rented for the duration of her training at Alpha was just pulling into the driveway at the side of the house.

Quinn took a moment to whisper a brief prayer of thanks for his daughter's safe return. That out of the way, he started to get angry.

"Keep your cool," he muttered as he took up a strategic position near the front door. "Just stay frosty."

This was easier said than done, unfortunately. The mere thought of Kayla Delaney made him hotter than hell.

He never should have let Stevie go shopping with her, he berated himself. Never mind that his daughter had looked at him with the most pathetically pleading expression in her repertoire when the issue had arisen. He should have said *no*.

He should have said *no* to the urge that had seized him five days ago, too. Playing possum after Kayla had thrown him had been stupid enough. But kissing her? *Had he been out of his mind?*

Probably. And his current mental state wasn't exactly—

The front door swung open and Stevie bounded into the house carrying a large shopping bag. She was beaming.

Her expression cut Quinn to the heart. It wasn't that he didn't want his daughter to be happy. He did. Desperately. Yet he bitterly resented the fact that the credit for her present ebullience belonged not to him but to the woman who followed gracefully in her wake.

"Dad!" Stevie exclaimed, pirouetting around the foyer. "You have to see the clothes we bought! Kayla has the best taste in the *world*!"

"Stevie," Kayla demurred. She then turned toward Quinn and said, "I realize we were gone a long time. I hope you haven't been—"

"It's Miss Delaney, Stevie," he interrupted, biting off each word.

Stevie halted in mid-twirl. "H-Huh?"

"She's 'Miss Delaney' to you." Quinn focused on his daughter, fervently hoping that he could keep his awareness of Kayla at a manageable level if he didn't look at her. The brief instant of eye contact when she'd started to apologize had nearly undone him. Even now he could feel the effects of it humming through his nervous system like an electric current.

"But I've been calling her Kayla since we met! Don't you remember? She said—"

"I don't care. I'm your father, and I say you're going to call her *Miss Delaney* from here on out."

Quinn realized that he was behaving like an ass, but he couldn't seem to stop himself. He was goaded toward even greater idiocy when he saw Stevie glance at Kayla as though seeking her guidance. All of a sudden it was two against one and he was very definitely the odd man out. It hurt.

"I understand your point, Quinn," Kayla began. "But it really isn't—"

"If you understand my point," he snarled, forgetting his decision about avoiding eye contact and glaring at her, *"why don't you stay out of this*?"

Kayla went rigid. Her cheeks got very pink, then very pale.

Quinn sucked in a ragged breath, appalled by his lack of control. He shifted his gaze back to his daughter. She was clutching her shopping bag to her flat chest and staring at him with horrified eyes.

"I'd like to speak to Miss Delaney alone, Stevie," he said after a moment.

"Why?"

"That's none of your business."

"If you're going to talk about me, it is."

"Stevie—"

"What about my new clothes?"

"We'll discuss them later."

"Suppose I want to discuss them *right now*?"

"What you want and what you're going to get are two very different things, Stephanie Lynn." Quinn swept his arm out, pointing in the direction of her bedroom. "Stop arguing and go."

Stevie's expression turned mutinous. She opened her mouth, clearly intending to dispute his command. But before she had a chance to speak, Kayla drew her attention by uttering her name in a softly chiding tone.

Oh God, Quinn thought as he watched another exchange of exclusively female-to-female looks.

"All right," his daughter acquiesced after a few seconds of nonverbal communication with her new mentor. "I'll go. Thanks for taking me shopping, Ka—Miss Delaney. Everything you bought me is wonderful."

"It was my pleasure, Stevie."

"G'night."

"Good night."

Stephanie Lynn Harris made her exit, nose in the air, behaving for all the world as though her father didn't exist.

That Kayla would have a few choice words to say once his daughter got out of earshot, Quinn pretty much expected. What he had not anticipated was that she would round on him like a battle-ready Valkyrie.

"*What* is your problem?" she demanded. "I can understand you being upset that we were gone so long. I should have called. I'm very sorry I didn't. But even so—to treat Stevie the way you just did? To behave like some dictatorial, finger-pointing jerk? My God, Quinn! Are you *trying* to alienate—"

"Excuse me," he cut in furiously. "How I deal with my daughter is my business. I don't need advice from a childless would-be movie star!"

Kayla flinched but didn't back off. "Oh, *really*?"

"Yes, really!" he retorted, ruthlessly squelching a pang of regret for the cruelty of his previous words. He was in the right in this situation, and he knew it. Stevie was *his* child! "And I don't need you buying my daughter clothes, either! I'm perfectly capable of supplying her with a wardrobe."

"Oh, I'm sure you are." The words dripped

disdain. "But are you capable of making her happy about having to wear any of it?"

The question struck Quinn on the raw, as he had no doubt it had been meant to do. "What the hell is that supposed to mean?"

"You're such an expert, figure it out for yourself." Kayla glared at him. "And you might keep in mind that your daughter is a twelve-going-on-thirteen-year-old girl. Not a baby. Not a boy. And not—repeat, *not*—some enlistee you can bully into shouting 'Sir, yes, sir!' every time you snap out an order."

With that, she turned away. Quinn grabbed her by the forearm and forced her back to face him. "I want to know what you meant by that crack about making Stevie happy," he growled, fighting an urge to shake the answer out of her.

Kayla jerked free of his grasp, her expression warning him against trying to touch her again. Somewhere in the back of his mind, Quinn noted that she'd assumed a classic defensive posture as she pulled away from him. If he hadn't been so angry, he probably would have applauded the evidence of how thoroughly she'd absorbed her initial lessons in the martial arts.

"To borrow your words of a few minutes ago," she said acidly, "what you want and what you're going to get are two very different things!"

"*Dammit*—"

"You can swear 'til you're blue in the face. I'm out of here."

Again Kayla spun away. This time Quinn made no effort to stop her. If truth be told, he was a little afraid of what he might do if he laid hands on her a second time. She got within a few steps of the front door when she checked herself and pivoted back around.

"One last thing," she spat out. "How dare you tell Lester Baines that what happened Monday was all your fault? I wanted that kiss just as much as you did. Maybe *more*, considering how long it's been since I've had a man touch me without script directions! So if there's any blame to be accepted—any responsibility to be claimed—half of it's mine!"

Quinn closed his eyes. Blood thundered in his ears. Snatches of the diatribe he'd just heard—especially the line about her having wanted Monday's aborted kiss as much as he had—reverberated through his brain.

Punctuating the cacophony was the sound of Kayla slamming the door on her way out.

She slammed the door on her way in, too, when she arrived back at Room 216 of the Last Chance Motor Lodge a short time later. She then proceeded to stomp around, cursing Quinn Harris. And herself. And the effect he had on her. If she'd been wearing her combat boots, she probably would have considered kicking a wall.

Her fury began to abate after about ten minutes. As it did, a small voice from deep within her—her conscience, perhaps?—began to suggest that maybe, just maybe, she'd been a tad unfair. Had it *really* been necessary for her to denounce Stevie's father as a "dictatorial, finger-pointing jerk"?

Of course, Quinn had verbally counterpunched by describing her as a "childless would-be movie star." Now *that* had hurt. It had hurt because it was the truth. Not the whole truth, but a significant chunk.

Kayla sighed. She'd found herself taking stock of herself in recent days. She wasn't certain why. Maybe it had something to do with the "stand tall" impulse she seemed to experience whenever she put on her combat boots. Whatever the cause, she'd begun to look inward in a serious way in the past week or so. She'd had a rather mixed reaction to what she'd seen thus far.

Worn out as she'd been when she arrived to begin her training at Alpha, she still felt pretty good about herself. And why not? While her love life wasn't what she'd like, she had scads of acquaintances and more than a few true-blue friends back in L.A. Her health was excellent; her finances, in reasonably good shape.

As for the professional side of the ledger . . . well, she had plenty to be upbeat about there. Nerve-racking though it might be, her semi-stalled acting career was on the verge of shifting into high gear. What's more, *she* was the one responsible for the impending change in her show biz status. The role in *Moving Target* hadn't been presented to her on a silver platter. She'd had to fight for it.

The problem was, her Tinseltown prize seemed to be losing some of its luster. While the prospect of playing Mad Maxine still excited her, there was a part of her that wondered whether doing so would prove as satisfying as befriending young Stevie Harris. That same part also questioned whether hearing Zack Reynolds or some other director gushingly tell her she was "Terrific, babe, just terrific" would mean as much as catching a gleam of approval lurking in the depths of Quinn Harris' dark blue—

Knock. Knock. Knock.

She froze, her gaze slewing toward the sound. "Kayla?"

It was Quinn. His voice was threaded with uncertainty. Kayla couldn't help recalling the way he'd sounded the last time he invoked her name through her motel room door.

"Kayla, please. Open up."

She clenched her hands and called, "Why should I?"

There was a long pause.

"Because I need to talk with you," Quinn responded at last.

The obvious retort—that his "need" meant nothing to her—trembled on the tip of Kayla's tongue. She swallowed it unsaid.

She crossed slowly to the door and undid the locks with unsteady fingers. She was going to have to face Quinn eventually, she told herself. It might as well be now, on what was nominally her turf. Besides. *He'd* come to *her.* That gave her the upper hand.

At least, it was supposed to.

"I'm here to apologize," Quinn said as soon as she opened the door.

Kayla lifted her chin, suspicious of this no-excuses approach. "Oh?"

"I acted like an idiot."

"If that was acting, you deserve an Academy Award."

Quinn spread his hands, palms up, signaling that he didn't intend to argue the point. "The truth is," he said quietly, "I was jealous."

"Jealous?" She stared at him, confused. "Of *what*?"

"Of the look I saw on my daughter's face when she walked in the door with you this evening."

"I don't . . . understand."

"A few weeks ago, I offered to take Stevie shopping for new clothes. She reacted as though I'd suggested we go out and bludgeon bunny rabbits for their fur. Today she got a similar invitation from you and she couldn't wait to go."

Kayla caught her breath. Lord, why hadn't she *realized*?

"Quinn, I'm sorry," she said. "I was so caught up in making friends with Stevie, it never occurred to me you might feel—uh—uh—"

"Threatened?"

Kayla frowned at the word. She found it difficult to believe that Quinn Harris could feel threatened by *anything*. He seemed so strong. So sure of himself and his place in the world. Still, there was no denying that his earlier behavior had been that of a man in the grip of a very powerful emotion. And childless though she might be, she could imagine few emotions more potent than a parent's fear of being rejected for another by a beloved child.

"It's been just the two of us for nearly five years," Quinn confided. "Even when her mother was alive, Stevie was pretty much a daddy's girl. And after the accident . . ."

"She told me how much you did for her."

"I would have done *anything* for her back then." His voice resonated with emotion. "And I'd do anything for her now. Only I don't—I mean, I'm not—"

"You aren't sure what's supposed to be on the agenda?"

Quinn sighed and shook his head. "There are times when I feel like I've been dropped into a mine field without a map. One misstep and"— he sketched an explosion with his hands—"ka-BOOM."

"Well, you're not alone. Your daughter's feeling a little confused about what she's meant to be doing, too."

"She told you that?"

Kayla hesitated, wary of betraying Stevie's innocent secrets. "Not in so many words."

"If she's got some kind of problem—"

"She doesn't."

"Then why has she been acting like she does?"

How could such an intelligent man be so obtuse? Kayla wondered. Then she asked, "Does the word 'puberty' mean anything to you?"

Quinn blanched. "Are you saying Stevie's started her—"

"No!" She grimaced, torn between compassion and exasperation. "I'm saying she realizes she's facing some major changes in her life. Stevie has a lot on her mind right now, Quinn." She looked him squarely in the eyes. "Including you."

"Me?"

"She's worried about your coping with her, uh, impending maturation."

Quinn looked blank. Then, amazingly, he started to chuckle. The chuckle became a laugh. Soon he was roaring. His unbridled humor was contagious. Though she struggled not to do so, Kayla began laughing as well.

Their shared hilarity lasted for a long, long time.

"Oh, m-man," he finally gasped, wiping his eyes. "And here I thought I was being so cool about her growing up."

"*Cool*?" Kayla hooted, sagging against the door frame. "Not even close."

A few seconds ticked by. Kayla looked at Quinn, then looked away. A moment or so later she looked at him again. This time, their gazes caught and clung. The air seemed to thicken and pulse.

"So . . . you think Stevie's basically okay?" Quinn asked, his voice not quite steady.

Kayla braced herself against the resurgence of what she knew was a dangerous attraction. "Are you soliciting my opinion as a childless would-be movie star?"

"I'm sorry." His eyes darkened. "I had no right to say that to you."

"Why not? It's true."

"Even so . . ."

Quinn reached out then and stroked the arm he'd snagged when she'd turned away from him less than an hour before. Kayla quivered at his gentle touch. Her body started to simmer.

"I think Stevie's basically terrific," she said a bit breathlessly, striving for control. "And speaking as someone who was once a twelve-year-old girl . . . I also think she's got a basically terrific father."

Quinn's faintly calloused fingertips feathered over the sensitive flesh of her inner elbow. "Really?"

Although the temptation to close her eyes and luxuriate in the seductiveness of his caress was very strong, Kayla resisted it. She reminded herself that she'd never surrendered to the lure of an on-location fling.

"Yes, really," she replied, forcing herself to ease back a few inches.

It was a subtle rejection as rejections went, and one which, in all honesty, she wasn't sure she meant. But Quinn picked up on it immediately and withdrew his hand. His expression was impossible to read.

"Do I take it you accept my apology?" he asked after a fractional pause.

Half of her was desperately relieved at how swiftly he'd backed off. Half of her was deeply resentful of it. All of her was tingling from the residual effects of his tantalizing touch. "If . . . you accept mine."

"Deal."

Kayla scraped together a steadying breath and infused a little Mad Maxine steel into her spine. "Of course, accepting your apology doesn't mean I won't try to boot your butt during unarmed combat practice on Monday."

Quinn's mouth quirked. "I'd be disappointed if it did."

They stood silently for several seconds. Eventually Quinn cleared his throat and said, "Well, I guess I'd better be getting home."

"Your daughter's probably wondering where you are."

"I think Stevie's got a pretty good idea of my location."

Kayla felt her cheeks grow warm. "Is she—I mean, did you leave her?"

"Lester Baines dropped by after you left. She's probably enlisting him in a plot against her finger-pointing jerk of a dad at this very instant."

Her flush intensified. "I didn't mean that, Quinn."

"Yes, you did."

"Well, even if I *did*, I shouldn't have said it."

"I've been called much worse, Kayla. Besides. You apologized."

"And you . . . accepted."

"Exactly. Although I do reserve the right to resolve any lingering bad feelings next time we go hand to hand."

A small laugh bubbled up in Kayla's throat. "I'll pack painkillers."

"Try body armor." The retort was accompanied by a blatant, down-up perusal. Every hormone in her body seemed to jump to attention in response. "Tomorrow on the quad. Oh eight hundred. Full gear."

Kayla inclined her head, no longer trusting her voice. Quinn turned away. She started to retreat into her motel room. She stopped as he suddenly pivoted back, her heart missing a beat as their gazes reconnected.

"What would you say to the idea of having dinner with me some night this week?" Quinn's tone was mild. The look in his eyes was anything but.

"I'd say . . . I've *had* dinner with you," Kayla parried. "Several times. In the mess hall." She hadn't intended to take her meals at the camp. It had just worked out that way. The leaping-to-attention incident aside, she'd found the mess a very convivial place. Rather like a studio commissary.

"I had something less communal in mind."

"You mean"—she shifted her stance, swallowing—"just the two of us?"

Dark brows lifted with a hint of challenge. "Unless you feel the need for a chaperon."

She definitely felt the need for something and that unnerved her. "Isn't there some rule against . . . fraternization?"

Quinn obliterated most of the distance between them with a single step. For one dizzying moment, Kayla thought he was going to kiss her again. Instead, he lifted his right hand and brushed the tip of his index finger against her lips. She shivered, the sensual simmer within her threatening to become an overtly sexual boil.

"Forget the military code of conduct," he murmured in a low, dark, velvet voice. "It's a simple question, Delaney. *Will you have dinner with me?*"

Her answer was inevitable. Unequivocal. And, Kayla suspected, very unwise.

"Yes, sir," she said, gazing up into Quinn's eyes. "I will."

6

I wanted that kiss just as much as you did. Maybe more, considering how long it's been since I've had a man touch me without script directions!

She couldn't have meant it, Quinn told himself four nights later as he tracked Kayla's return from the ladies' room of the restaurant he'd selected for their "noncommunal" dinner. Unless people in Hollywood were even more perverse than gossip mongers claimed, it was inconceivable to him that Kayla Delaney could be hurting for masculine attention. Why, at this very moment, he could see two . . . no, *three* male diners ogling her as she made her way back to him! There was a waiter who seemed pretty damned interested, too.

He stood up as Kayla reached their table. She acknowledged the courtesy with a nod, reseating herself opposite him.

"You're frowning," she commented, brushing back a stray tendril of red-brown hair. She was sporting a casually upswept coiffure that seemed to be in imminent danger of tumbling down around her shoulders. It was a very provocative style. "Is there a problem?"

He took a deep drink of the draft beer he'd ordered when they'd first sat down. The outfit she had on rated pretty high on the provocation scale, too, in his opinion. No matter that the cream cotton top was loose fitting. No matter that the hemline of the matching skirt modestly covered her knees. To look at those garments was to think about the supple body beneath them. And to think about that body was to—

"Quinn?"

"No problem." He set down his mug. "I was just thinking that you clean up very nicely." It wasn't exactly a lie. An overnight rainfall had turned parts of the Alpha landscape into mud. Kayla had been filthy by the time she'd headed back to her motel to change after their training session.

"Why, May-juh Harris." Kayla faked a Dixie drawl. "Such . . . *gallantry*."

He grinned. "I'm not saying muck doesn't become you, you understand."

"Oh, Ah *do* understand. And Ah'm on the verge of swoonin'—"

The return of their waitress brought an abrupt halt to this banter. The young woman served their entrées—steak for him, grilled fish for Kayla—with dispatch, then inquired whether they wanted anything else. After receiving a politely negative response, she moved off. A minute or so of silence followed.

"Stevie's been telling me about her big trip to Washington in August," Kayla eventually reported, squeezing a lemon wedge over her fish. "She's very excited about seeing her grandparents again."

"Betsy's folks are crazy about her." Quinn sliced into his steak. He was feeling unusually carnivorous this evening. "She's their only grandchild."

"Your . . . wife . . . had no brothers or sisters?"

He glanced across the table. "There's no need to tiptoe around the subject, Kayla. I don't have a problem talking about Betsy. I'll admit it was difficult right after she was killed. It hurt to just say her name. But I wanted to keep her memory fresh for Stevie, so I learned to put aside the pain and refer to her whenever an opportunity arose. My father did that with me after my mother died. I grew up feeling as though I'd known her because he was so open about who she'd been and what she'd been like."

"Your father sounds like a remarkable man."

"He was tough as nails in a lot of ways, but he had a tender streak."

"He must have been very cultivated, too. All those wonderful antiques Stevie showed me . . ."

One Sunday each month, Quinn invited members of the Alpha staff who weren't working or otherwise occupied to have supper at his home. Wives, kids, and girlfriends were also welcome.

At his daughter's insistence—"You have to do something nice to make up for how mean you were to Kayla," she'd declared over breakfast—he'd asked Kayla to come to this past weekend's get-together. She'd hesitated at first, then accepted. Although there'd been a brief period of awkwardness after her arrival, her self-deprecating charm had carried the day.

"My father did a tour in Japan early in his career," Quinn recalled. "He became intrigued by the samurai. They were masters at making war. But they also wrote poetry, arranged flowers, and devoted themselves to rituals like the tea ceremony. My father said it seemed strange to him at first. Then he realized that their appreciation of peaceful pleasures gave them a special incentive to give their all on the battlefield in the defense of civilization."

"Was your father the reason you went into the army?"

Quinn took a bite of his steak, considering. "He was part of it. But I was drawn to the discipline, too. And the camaraderie. Plus—well, it may sound corny, but I wanted to serve my country."

"Did he encourage you?"

"Not at first. I planned to try for a slot at West Point, but he said I needed to get a good taste of civilian life before I made up my mind to commit to the military. I ended up at Georgetown. Did an internship with the State Department. I thought about joining the Foreign Service. But when push came to shove, I realized that what I really wanted to be was a soldier. From then on, my father backed me all the way."

"Was your wife from a military family, too?"

"Lord, no. Her father was a banker. I met Betsy at a party in D.C. a couple months after I finished Ranger training. She was a freshman at Foxcroft. We got married about a year later. Three days after we came home from our honeymoon, I was sent to El Salvador."

"Good God." Kayla bobbled her fork, nearly dropping it.

"It was rough on Betsy. She didn't understand the world she was marrying into. There were parts of my work I couldn't share with her. I was also gone a lot." An enduring sense of guilt gripped him. After several painful seconds of silence, he confessed, "I was in the Persian Gulf when she was killed. Things were—well, let's just say I wasn't easy to get in touch with. I . . . missed . . . her funeral. And I wasn't there for Stevie during the first twenty-four hours after she regained consciousness."

"Oh, Quinn."

He instinctively shied from the sympathy in Kayla's whispered invocation of his name. What was it about her that made him offer up truths he'd revealed to no one else? he wondered uneasily. He'd never spoken about the stresses his career had placed on his marriage. Yet here he was, on the verge of spilling his guts to a woman he'd known less than three weeks!

"Let's talk about something more pleasant," he said abruptly, spearing another piece of rare meat. "Like you. Do you come from a show biz family?"

A peculiar expression flickered across Kayla's

face, but she acquiesced to his ham-handed change of conversational direction. "Hardly," she responded with a wry laugh. "My dad was an auto mechanic. My mom did temp work on occasion, but she was basically a full-time home-maker."

"So what happened? Did you step out on stage during a grade school play and realize you'd found your calling?"

"Actually, I'm what you might describe as an 'accidental' actress."

"A . . . what?"

Kayla traced the rim of her glass with the tip of one finger. "It happened during my junior year of college. I was studying for a degree in education."

"You wanted to be a teacher?" The notion startled him. Then he began to think about the warm rapport she'd established with Stevie. About the spunk and the smarts she'd shown in her training. Suddenly he found it very easy to picture Kayla Delaney taking control of a classroom full of kids.

Hazel eyes met blue ones for a moment and Quinn knew his skepticism had not gone unnoticed. He wanted to apologize, but Kayla didn't give him a chance. "My family was having serious financial problems," she went on evenly. "It looked as though I was going to be forced to drop out. Then I heard about this beauty pageant that offered scholarship money as prizes."

"So you entered, won, and got discovered?"

"Not exactly. I was only second runner-up. But one of the judges was a producer. He offered me a screen test. Before I really figured out what was happening, I was making my movie debut."

"And you've been acting ever since."

"I wouldn't call what I did in that first film *acting*," she returned dryly. "But the director was satisfied. He even cast me in his next picture. The rest, as my agent, Irwin Ortiz, would say, is cinematic history."

There was something slightly off about Kayla's comments, Quinn mused. Unfortunately he couldn't get a fix on exactly what that "something" was. She obviously cared about what she did. He still vividly recalled the intensity with which she'd told him how important it was for her to be ready for the start of shooting on *Moving Target*. Still, to listen to her talk . . .

"This new role is a departure for you, isn't it?" He wondered whether what he was sensing might be insecurity about tackling an unfamiliar kind of character. "You've never played anyone like Mad Maxine."

"It's . . . a challenge." There was a hint of evasion in her tone.

He leaned forward slightly. "Because of all the training?"

"That's part of it. I mean . . . well, *Moving Target* is a big deal for me, Quinn. I've never been above the title in a big budget picture before."

"Lots of pressure, huh?"

"Lots of *everything*." Kayla sighed, shaking her head. "I can't tell you how many actresses were approached about playing Mad Maxine before I was. Even after I got my hands on a copy of the script, I had to battle my way through about a dozen studio minions before I was given a chance to read."

"Why did they make it so difficult for you?"

"Oh, it wasn't personal." She pulled a droll

face. "Which isn't to say it didn't *feel* personal at times. Still, I understood the resistance wasn't really because of me, Kayla Delaney. It was because of my ... uh ... situation."

"Which was?"

"I've been around a long time, and filmmakers like new talent. I've never made an action movie. Plus, I'm not exactly a spring chicken."

Quinn almost laughed at the absurdity of this last statement. Almost, but not quite. His impulse toward humor died when he realized that her words had not been meant as a joke.

"You're not exactly an old hen, either, Kayla," he pointed out.

She gave him an off center smile. Something about the curving of her lips reminded him of the exasperation he frequently felt when he listened to civilians try to explain how the military "really" operated.

"I work in an industry where actors over fifty are considered prime stud material," she replied simply. "Thirtysomething actresses are advised to think about collagen injections and character roles. Now, I'm not saying it's impossible for female performers to transcend age. And I don't deny that Hollywood seems pretty hot on boy toys lately. But even so ..."

Her voice trailed off into eloquent silence. Quinn nodded slowly, understanding her point yet loath to accept it. "Did you ever consider bailing out?" he asked after a few seconds. "Maybe ... going back and getting your degree? Following through on your plan to become a teacher?"

"Ever heard the joke about the man who cleaned up after the elephants in the circus?"

He furrowed his brow, puzzled. "I don't think so."

"There's this old guy whose job is to follow after the elephants and scoop up their poop. He hates it. Complains all the time. Finally someone asks him why he doesn't quit. He clutches his chest, horrified. 'What?' he cries. 'You want me to give up *show business*?' "

"I . . . see." And in an odd way, he thought he did.

"Which isn't to say I equate my career as an actress with pushing a broom behind a bunch of pachyderms." Her caveat was accompanied by a quick, not entirely convincing laugh. "It's just that . . . well . . ."

"The entertainment industry can be addictive despite the crap?" The assessment came out sounding harsher than Quinn had intended. It was the result, he supposed, of the residual anger he felt about the treatment Kayla had described in connection with her casting as Mad Maxine.

"It does get into your blood. But to go back to your original question—yes. There *have* been moments when I've considered bailing out of the biz. I suppose some people might think I've been hedging my bets, just in case. I've taken courses on and off over the years, and I'm actually within sight of having enough credits for a BA. I also volunteer with a tutorial program in South Central L.A. whenever I'm not tied up on a project." She paused, her expression growing reflective. "How doing *Moving Target* is going to affect things is anybody's guess."

"From what you said earlier, it sounds like it could change your life."

A complex and contradictory series of emotions flashed through Kayla's changeable gray-green eyes. "In some ways," she said quietly, "it already has."

"Here we are," Quinn announced about ninety minutes later as they reached her motel room door. Despite her protests that there was no need to do so, he'd insisted on escorting her from the car.

"Here we are," she echoed, turning to face him. A whiff of citrus-spice cologne tantalized her nostrils. Her breath snagged at the top of her throat.

Quinn had been almost as dirty as she when they'd finished today's training schedule. In her opinion, he'd cleaned up "very nicely" and then some! Clad in snug-fitting jeans, a white T-shirt, and a dark linen sports jacket, he could have passed fashion muster at any of L.A.'s ultra-trendy nightspots. Yet, as appealing as she found his easy male elegance, there was a part of her that would have preferred seeing him in a sweaty tank top and shorts or mud-stained fatigues.

"I'm glad you came this evening, Kayla," he told her after a few seconds.

"I'm glad I did, too. Thank you for asking me."

There was a pause. It was merely awkward at first, but it became increasingly tense as it went on. And on. And on.

"There's something I've been wondering about."

The look in Quinn's intense azure eyes sent a

streaking heat racing through her veins. Kayla felt her pulse accelerate. "Yes?"

"It has to do with a . . . comment . . . you made when you brought Stevie home from shopping on Saturday."

"O-oh?" Her voice cracked mid-syllable.

"Mmm." His gaze flicked downward to her lips then returned to her eyes. "Exactly how long has it been since you were kissed for real?"

Kayla felt herself flush. "I was angry when I said that."

"So you were exaggerating by implication?"

She considered lying but found she couldn't. "I know the kind of image I project on-screen," she finally replied. "But in real life, I'm not very . . . social."

"By choice, I'm sure."

The tang of Quinn's cologne tantalized her nose again. Beneath the subtle fragrance was the more primitive scent of warm male flesh. Was it her imagination, or had he moved closer to her in the last few moments?

"I get asked out," she conceded carefully. "But it's been awhile since there was anyone who, uh, well, uh—"

"Piqued your interest?"

"Something like that, yes."

Quinn waited a beat or two, then lifted his right hand and traced the curve of her left cheek. Slowly. Oh, so slowly. Kayla's lungs emptied on an involuntary exhalation as he stroked beneath her jaw. She began to tremble.

"I guess the men in L.A. haven't figured out what turns you on," he murmured.

"And you . . . h-have?" she challenged unsteadily, her heart pounding.

Quinn slid his hand back to cup her nape. His eyes blazed sapphire beneath partially lowered lids. "I sure as hell hope so."

Their second embrace was infinitely more complicated than their first. From the start, Quinn made assumptions about the level of sexual intimacy between them, which somewhere in the back of her mind Kayla knew she should be contesting. The trouble was, she didn't want to. Because as ill-advised as she understood it was, she'd been making assumptions as well.

She kissed him back. Hotly. Hungrily.

Quinn spoke her name on a shattered breath as he ravished her lips with teeth and tongue. He stroked his hands down her back, his palms curving against her bottom. She shifted her hips, instinctively seeking the ineffable mating of soft to hard, female to male. He groaned deep in his throat, his fingers pressing against her flesh. A searing thrill raced up her spine.

Kayla lifted her arms, circling Quinn's neck. His short cropped hair teased her fingertips. Angling her head, she offered him more intimate access to her mouth. He took it as though it was his right to do so.

How long they kissed, Kayla never knew. Time temporarily lost all meaning for her. Perhaps it speeded up to match the wild rush of her pulse. Perhaps it slowed—even stopped—to permit her to savor each sensation she was experiencing to the fullest. It didn't much matter.

There was no hesitation, no holding back, until the mind-blowing moment when she felt his fingers begin to knead the burgeoning nipple of her right breast. Her *bare* right breast. Without her realizing what he was doing, Quinn had slipped

his hand under her top and undone the front of
her bra.

Her body was saying "yes." Yet as the ramifications of the liberty he'd taken registered, Kayla's brain started yelling *NO!*

He sensed it. Somehow, some way, Quinn
Harris divined her inner turmoil and began to
ease back, lifting his lips from hers and with-
drawing his hand from beneath her top.

"What's wrong?" he asked, his voice low and
taut.

Kayla stared up at him. She could see the
strain of denial in the dark brilliance of his eyes
and the hot-blooded flush along his cheekbones.

"Too f-fast," she stammered. "I'm not . . . I'm
not *ready* . . . for this, Quinn."

He searched her face intently for several seconds then asked, "Are you saying you don't
have any protection?"

Protec—?

Oh, Lord. She hadn't even thought about birth
control! Which she should have, because she
didn't have any with her. Her diaphragm was
back in her apartment in L.A., probably shriveled
up from lack of use. And since she didn't keep
a "just in case" supply of condoms . . .

Kayla stiffened, suddenly recalling Quinn's
earlier assertion that the men she knew in L.A.
hadn't figured out what turned her on. She also
remembered the preemptory way he'd initiated
their second kiss.

*Had he insisted on walking her to her motel room
door because he'd figured this was his chance to score
with her sexually?*

"Do *you* have protection with you?" she demanded, lifting her chin.

For a moment she thought he was going to become angry. Then, surprisingly, his expression eased. He looked . . . rueful.

"No," he answered. "I don't. Although I'll admit to fantasizing about situations in which I'd want to make sure everything was safe for both of us."

Kayla glanced away, coloring at the reference to fantasizing. She'd indulged in a few sexual daydreams about her and Quinn, too.

"Kayla?" His tone was gentle. Almost tender. So was the touch of his fingers, urging her face back toward his. She didn't resist.

"There's a philosophy a lot of people in the movie industry seem to subscribe to," she said, meeting his compelling eyes once again. "It boils down to the notion that anything they do on location—away from home—doesn't count. I don't believe that. I think every action has consequences. Making love has never been a no-strings thing for me. I need *time* to decide if it's the right thing to do."

"Time is something we don't have a lot of, Kayla."

"I realize that. And that's another problem with this . . . this . . . whatever it is between us. The notion of getting involved with someone *knowing* there's a clock ticking is very scary to me."

"But you're not ruling out the possibility?" The look in his eyes promised he'd accept her answer, whatever it was. All he wanted was the truth.

Kayla's pulse fluttered. A honeyed warmth filled her veins. "No," she admitted after a few seconds, feeling herself flush again. "I'm not. I'm

... attracted ... to you, Quinn. But I can't just— I mean, I don't want—"

He silenced her by pressing a finger lightly against her lips. She felt the contact clear down to the soles of her feet. "I understand," he said. "You need time. I want you, Kayla. I want you very much. But if you have doubts—well, let's say I share your belief that actions have consequences. And some of my behavior to the contrary, lovemaking isn't a no-strings thing for me, either."

There was a moment of silence. Then Quinn lowered his hand and took a step back. It was all Kayla could do not to reach out for him.

"I'll see you tomorrow," he told her softly, his eyes gazing deeply into hers.

"Tomorrow," she concurred, dipping her head.

As it turned out, Kayla didn't have to wait until the following day. She "saw" Quinn Harris again that night ... in her dreams.

7

To say that the next sixty-odd hours were trying ones for former Special Forces major Quinn Harris was a bit like describing the Battle of Little Big Horn as a bad hair day for General Custer. Fueled by quick caresses, covert kisses, and a lot of X-rated imagining, his hunger for Kayla Delaney deepened and grew more intense.

Still, he told himself over and over that restraint was vital. Desire deferred was not—please heaven!—necessarily desire denied.

He didn't want a wham-bam-thank-you-ma'am romp with "his" movie star. At least, not anymore. Honesty forced him to admit that he'd spun a few hot and horny scenarios after he'd accepted the job of preparing Kayla for *Moving Target*. But the notion that she might be in the market for a casual fling had died the moment he'd met her. He'd known, with a certainty that had penetrated every cell of his being, that she wasn't—

"Kayla not with you, boss?"

Quinn started, nearly dropping the mug of coffee he had no memory of having poured. Steadying himself, he turned to face Lester Baines. The older man stood just inside his office door. He was holding a large padded envelope. It bore the logo of a well-known courier service.

"Sorry, Sergeant Major," Quinn apologized gruffly, setting his coffee mug down on his desk. "I didn't catch what you said."

"I was wonderin' whether Kayla was still around." If the retired noncom sensed anything odd, he gave no sign of it. But Quinn knew from experience that this seemingly oblivious demeanor could be deceptive. Lester Baines missed very little.

"Uh, no. No, she's not." He began massaging the nape of his neck. "She went back to the motel after we finished today's training session."

Back to the motel . . .

Back to Room 216 . . .

The realization that he'd just been spoken to again jolted Quinn back into the present. "Wh-

what?" he stammered, lowering his hand from his neck.

"I said, the trainin' seems to be goin' pretty good," Lester answered mildly, moving forward. "With Kayla, I mean."

"Yeah," Quinn affirmed after an awkward moment. "It is."

"Heard she's turned out to be a real fine shot, too."

Quinn smiled crookedly. Kayla had proven to be unusually gifted with a handgun. Her last session at the camp's firing range had attracted a small but appreciative audience of Alpha staffers. With the exception of one shot—which had either been a fluky miss or a wickedly effective reminder that the character she was training to play had a penchant for going for the groin— she'd performed impressively.

"She spent her first couple of days missing the target because she'd flinch just before she pulled the trigger," he replied. "But once she got over that . . . yeah. She's hitting center mass, dead on, nearly every time."

There was a pause. Quinn picked up his mug again and took a sip. The coffee was cold. He set the mug back down, fiddling with its handle. Eventually he asked, "Why did you want to know whether she was still around?"

Lester held up the padded envelope. "This came for her. Marked 'Personal' and 'Urgent.' It's from some guy in Los Angeles named Irving Ortiz."

Quinn's heart lurched at the word "personal." It returned to a more normal rhythm when he heard the name of the packet's sender.

"*Irwin* Ortiz," he corrected. "That's Kayla's agent."

The older man glanced at the label as though confirming this information, then said, "Could be important. Think somebody should take it over to her motel?"

For the first time since the start of this conversation, Quinn looked Lester Baines squarely in the eyes. Any hope he'd had that his feelings for Kayla Delaney had gone unremarked died right then. Lester *knew*.

"Look, Lester," he began carefully, "I don't want you to get any ideas. . . ."

"Ideas is for officers, boss. I just follow orders."

Quinn knew better than to challenge this "I'm only a humble subordinate" pose. He also realized that he couldn't deny his attraction to Kayla. He opted instead to argue the pitfalls of getting involved with her.

"Kayla Delaney's a movie star. Or she will be, after *Moving Target*."

"Seems to me you knew what she was before she showed up."

"No." He shook his head. "I *didn't* know. I thought I did, but I was wrong."

"You like her better in real life than on-screen, huh?"

Quinn expelled a breath on a long, hissing sigh. "Yeah," he said. "I do."

As did his daughter. That was another factor he knew he had to take into consideration. Stevie had formed a very close relationship with Kayla. Just the other day, she'd said something about wishing Kayla could stay at Alpha "forever."

There'd been an odd little edge to her voice as she'd spoken. He'd gotten the unnerving impression that she expected him to take steps to make sure she got what she wanted.

"So?" It was a challenge.

"So . . . a lot of things." Quinn clenched his hands, frustration coursing through him. "Not the least of them being that she'll be gone in three weeks."

"Operation Desert Storm lasted . . . what? Four days and change?"

He opened his mouth to make the obvious retort: *He didn't want to make war on Kayla Delaney, dammit, he wanted to make love with her!* Then some instinct for self-preservation kicked in and he snapped his mouth shut again. It didn't really matter. One glance at Lester's face told him that the older man had divined exactly what he'd been about to say.

"No guts, no glory," the recipient of the Congressional Medal of Honor counseled quietly, extending the envelope. "You want to be the one who makes this urgent, personal delivery to Kayla or not?"

Quinn took the packet.

"Ruthie and I were plannin' to take in a movie tonight," Lester went on. "She's got somethin' picked out starrin' that young Kee-noo Reeves guy. Seems she's a big fan, don't ask me why. Anyway, I asked Stevie if she wanted to come along, and she was real eager. We figure to grab supper somewhere along the line. You'd be welcome, too, unless you've got somethin' better to do. . . ."

*   *   *

Kayla stared into the mirror that hung above the sink in the bathroom of her motel room. Should she or shouldn't she? she demanded of her reflection. And if she did . . . what would happen?

Dangerous questions. And within a nanosecond of formulating the last one, her infinitely obliging imagination started producing a series of outrageously erotic answers. Her breathing pattern altered radically. Her body began to quiver. Her nipples stiffened against the nubby surface of the towel she'd wrapped around herself when she stepped out of the shower.

Gripping the sides of the sink, Kayla struggled for control. She'd never thought of herself as an especially sensual woman. Yet there'd been moments since her arrival at the Last Chance Motor Lodge—like now, like Wednesday night, like that afternoon in the combat pit, like the first time she'd clapped eyes on her trainer-to-be—when she'd felt as though she were in *heat!*

And it was getting worse. Well, no. Perhaps "worse" wasn't quite the right word. But her desire for Quinn was definitely becoming more and more difficult to resist. Her body had been shrieking with frustration when she'd returned to the motel after today's training session. She'd sought to quell the clamor for completion with a cold shower. It had worked . . . as long as she'd kept the water running.

Heaving a restless sigh, Kayla glanced around for her hairbrush. She spotted it sitting amid a haphazard collection of grooming supplies on the back of the commode. As she reached out, her hand knocked against something.

"Oh, *no!*" she cried as two bottles toppled to the floor and shattered. She started to retreat but froze as a piece of glass jabbed into her left heel.

Swearing under her breath, Kayla lifted her foot so she could extract the offending shard. It hadn't gone in very deeply, so there was only a tiny bit of blood. She staunched the small cut with a piece of tissue, then tiptoed out of the bathroom.

She didn't even consider ringing the motel's front desk and asking for help. She'd made the mess, it was her responsibility to clean it up.

After shedding the towel, Kayla donned one of her cotton sleep shirts. She then scrounged up an elasticized band and used it to fasten her hair away from her face. Finally she slipped on her black leather combat boots.

At precisely the same instant, someone rapped on her motel room door.

"Kayla?" he called through the door.

"Quinn?" She sounded uneasy. Suspicious, even. Given their previous encounters in this particular location, Quinn couldn't blame her.

"Yeah." His fingers tightening on the envelope he'd taken from Lester Baines. "I've got something for you. It's from your agent. It's marked urgent."

There was a pause. Then, "Uh . . . okay. I'm coming."

Quinn rocked back on his heels, conscious of a sudden speedup in his pulse. His mouth went dry as he heard the rasp of the safety chain being undone. His palms grew damp as he saw the knob turn.

The door swung open. Kayla stood before him, lips slightly parted, cheeks faintly flushed. She was clad in what looked like the same tantalizingly oversize T-shirt she'd had on the first time they'd met. The budding thrust of her nipples was arousingly evident beneath the soft white fabric.

His gaze slid lower. And lower still. Kayla shifted as though he'd touched her. The garment she was wearing rippled softly, seeming to catch and cling at the juncture of her thighs.

His breath clogged in his throat. His heart was hammering. He could feel the elemental throbbing of his blood from the tips of his toes to the top of his skull. He wanted her so much. . . .

"*Kayla,*" he somehow managed to whisper. "*Please.*"

"*Yes,*" she responded huskily, her wide set eyes shimmering with heat.

He dropped the packet from Irwin Ortiz.

A moment later, Kayla was in his arms.

"Are you . . . sure?" Quinn demanded in an emotion-roughened voice as he half dragged, half carried her across the threshold of her motel room. "Please. Kayla. Tell me you're sure."

Kayla lifted her arms and twined them about his neck, pressing her body against his. She was trembling with excitement. She sensed the same anticipatory force vibrating through Quinn. It thrilled her in ways words couldn't begin to express.

"I'm sure," she affirmed, inhaling his scent, absorbing his heat. "I'm . . . very . . . sure."

She was. Completely. Unconditionally. The doubts she'd had were gone, swept away as though they'd never existed. The temporariness of the situation be damned. *This is what she wanted with every fiber of her being.*

And unlike before, she was fully prepared to act upon her desires.

"I have protection," she volunteered boldly as she heard the motel door slam, isolating them from the rest of the world. She'd bought a box of condoms at the local pharmacy the day before. Not because she'd been certain that she and Quinn were going to end up in bed together. She hadn't been. She'd made the made the purchase because it had been the responsible thing to do, given the potency of their physical attraction. It was better to be ready for an intimacy that never occurred than to find herself in a situation where she would be tempted into playing sexual roulette with her future.

"Me, too," Quinn responded with a ragged laugh, nuzzling a path down the line of her jaw. "I raided the stash in the camp dispensary before I came over. Just . . . in case."

A split second later, he captured her mouth with his own. She surrendered with a greedy sigh, welcoming the questing thrust of his tongue.

"Good," he groaned against her lips. His kiss was fevered. Almost fierce. Kayla's blood sang in reckless response. "You taste so . . . *damned* . . . good."

"So do you," she whispered, fumbling with the buttons of his khaki shirt as they staggered in the general direction of her bed. Frustrated by the clumsiness of her fingers, she abandoned the polite approach after a few frantic seconds and simply tore the garment open. Her palms sought the hair-whorled contours of his tautly-muscled chest.

With hands no steadier than her own, Quinn tugged up the hem of the her white cotton T-shirt. She shuddered violently as he caressed her naked skin, her breath jamming at the top of her throat in response to the jolting shock of pleasure his expert touch evoked.

She peeled his shirt back and down, somehow managing to strip it off him. A moment later he pulled her T-shirt over her head. The elastic band that had been restraining her hair snapped, releasing a tangled cascade of chestnut-colored curls.

Bodies fused, they moved a few steps closer to their destination. Kayla whimpered as she felt the scrape of Quinn's teeth against her neck. The whimper became a mewing cry as he began to lavish a series of erotic, open-mouthed kisses over her shoulders. His hands continued to stroke her newly bared flesh, igniting sweet, searing fires of need.

Operating purely on instinct, she undid the waistband of his pants and eased it downward. She desperately wanted him as naked as she was.

Yes, she thought, her body suffusing with the most elemental of urges. *Oh, yes.*

A moment later, they bumped into the bed. Seconds after that, they tumbled down on top of it. Kayla felt the mattress sag slightly under their combined weight, the springs creaking in protest.

"B-boots," she stammered breathlessly, her

sensation-dazed brain suddenly latching on to what seemed to be a very salient fact. "I'm still wearing my combat—"

Quinn levered himself up a few inches, fighting his way free of his pants. His gaze met hers for a sizzling instant. Her heart skipped a beat. Her breathing pattern snarled. She temporarily lost the ability to speak. Then he flashed the wickedest grin she'd ever seen in her life and her entire nervous system went into sensory overload.

"Keep them on," he ordered with a dark, almost devilish laugh.

She did.

There was nowhere Quinn did not touch. Few places he did not taste. Kayla gave herself over to his intoxicating love play, then turned the tables and indulged her own adventurous urges.

Inch by inch, she discovered him. She licked along the hard ridge of his collarbone. Kissed her way down his hair-whorled chest. Charted the shallow indentation of his navel. When he groaned his pleasure at her sensual attentions, she felt a glorious surge of feminine excitement.

After a time, Quinn caught her arms and drew her upward. He claimed her mouth in a long, lingering kiss. She melted against him, her body suffusing with an exquisite flood of response.

He teased her nipples with his thumbs, coaxing them to pucker and peak. "Tell me what . . . you like . . ." he commanded hoarsely.

"*That*," she told him on a half-suffocated cry. Her blood surged, wild and wanton. Turning her head, she pressed an ardent kiss against the base of his corded throat. His perspiration-sheened skin tasted faintly of salt. She could feel the untrammeled jump of his pulse against her lips.

The fever rose. Higher. Hotter. Their mouths locked in an insatiable kiss. Tongues intertwined, presaging an even more intimate coupling.

And then the moment arrived. A host of sensations, each one more urgent than the next, compelled them irresistibly toward the ultimate release.

"*Kayla . . .*" Quinn's breathing was harsh. His need, rampantly obvious. A shudder wracked his powerful body, testifying to the stress of self-discipline.

"*Yes . . .*" Her desire for assuagement was no less acute than his.

He shifted, moving up and over, then thrusting deep inside her. The rush of pleasure provoked by the gliding, sliding plunge into the secret core of her was indescribable in its intensity. Kayla clung to Quinn's broad shoulders, arching up in convulsive response. He withdrew slightly, then thrust again, seeming to penetrate to the very mouth of her womb. She stroked downward with her hands, pressing against the base of his spine.

What happened next was ecstasy. Emphatic. Absolute. Beyond anything Kayla had ever experienced. And the most glorious part of the incendiary rapture was that she knew, with total certainty, that it was mutual.

"Kayla?"

"Mmm?"

"Are you . . . all right?"

"*All right?*" She gave a throaty laugh, stretching languidly. "If I were any more 'all right,' you'd be picking me up in pieces, Quinn."

"Ah." There'd been a hint of anxiety in his voice a moment before. Now there was only satisfaction. Uniquely *masculine* satisfaction. A woman inclined to find fault with the opposite sex—which Kayla was not, as a general rule— might even characterize his response as smug.

"Of course"—she levered herself up on one elbow so she could gaze down at his face—"I *am* a little curious about this footwear fetish of yours."

Quinn furrowed his brow. "Footwear fetish? What are you—*oh*." He flushed. Then he chuckled. "The combat boots."

"Uh-huh."

"I'm not quite sure how to explain that."

"You're not?" Kayla wondered fleetingly where her boots were. They were definitely not on her feet any longer.

"It was an . . . impulse." Quinn reached up and brushed a lock of hair behind her left ear, his fingertips feathering sensually against the sensitive outer rim and lobe. "There was something about the combination of those boots and that big, white cotton T-shirt that just . . . well . . ."

"Made you want to snap to attention and salute?"

He chuckled again. "You might say that."

"There *is* something special about those boots," she commented reflectively, sketching a whimsical design on his chest. She teased the taut bud of his right nipple with the edge of one nail. Quinn caught his breath, stiffening in instantaneous response. A heady sense of power rippled through her. "Just out of curiosity . . . are there any other potential 'impulses' I should file away for future reference?''

The implications of what she'd said didn't occur to her until after she'd uttered it. Quinn trapped her hand with one of his own. Their gazes fused.

''You think we have a future?'' His tone was quiet but intense.

Kayla felt her heart skip a beat. Maybe two. While she tried not to turn away from the tough stuff in life, she'd never exactly run out to confront it, either.

''I think we have three weeks, Quinn,'' she finally answered.

8

''So?'' Teddy bear brown eyes peered anxiously from behind thick lenses. ''What do you think?''

''I think a CD-ROM based on Alpha Camp is a great idea, Ronald,'' Kayla answered sincerely. While the technical aspects of the lengthy pitch she'd just listened to eluded her, she knew a marketable concept when she heard one.

She also knew she wanted to disengage herself from this protracted conversation and get back to Quinn, but she was having difficulty finding a graceful way of doing so. Ronald Nutley, who described himself as one of the highest-paid for-

mer hackers in Silicon Valley, was not the kind
of man who picked up on the usual social cues.

It was now the middle of her fourth week at
Alpha. The camp was having a Fourth of July
cookout. Earlier in the day, several instructors—
including Quinn—had performed a precision
parachute jump onto the quadrangle. Kayla had
found the display both thrilling and terrifying.

The current crop of campers—all computer industry employees whose multibillionaire boss
was underwriting their attendance at Alpha's
two-week survival course as a means of increas-
ing their "team" spirit—had had similarly mixed
reactions to the airborne show. While most had
been fascinated by the aerodynamic principles
involved, a half dozen or so had proclaimed the
descent *totally cool* and clamored for information
about how they could start skydiving. Several
others had passed out cold, allowing the Wizard
of Gauze the opportunity to deliver an im-
promptu lecture on coping with unconscious-
ness.

"It'd be really educational, Kayla," Ronald assured her. "We'll start with training exercises.
Going through an obstacle course, for example.
Doing hand-to-hand combat. And we'll include
stuff from the lectures we're having, too. Prepar-
edness and planning. First aid. Differentiating
between edible plants and the ones that can kill
you. I'm trying to get the Wiz—you know, Mike
Matsui?—to be real detailed about exactly *how*
you'd die if you ate, say, *Amanita virosa* or *Inocybe
patouillardii*. The payoff will be a series of inter-
active scenarios. Like—your plane crashes on a
remote mountain in the middle of the winter.
What do you do to survive?"

"I think I'd begin by finding out how many of my traveling companions were vegetarians," Quinn said blandly, coming up behind Kayla.

She turned, deeply pleased to see him but slightly appalled by the implications of his comment. He gave her a roguish smile, his gaze flickering over her with subtle suggestiveness. Her body started to tingle.

"Vegetarians?" Ronald echoed. "But why would—oh. *Oh!*" A remarkable series of emotions flickered across his pudgy face. "That could be *amazing*," he finally declared, staring at Quinn with something akin to awe. "Of course, we'd have to be careful. With all the heat about cyberporn, we wouldn't want to get accused of advocating cannibalism, too. But still—"

"You know, Ronald, you really should talk to Lester Baines about this," Quinn interrupted.

The computer programmer blanched. "The s-sergeant major? M-me?"

"He's an expert on eating men alive."

"Uh—I, uh—"

"I think he's over by the grill. Don't worry about deserting Ms. Delaney. I'll look after her."

"Okay." Ronald nodded several times, clearly unable to resist the command beneath Quinn's casual tone. "I—I'll go see h-him. Thanks."

"That was a terrible thing to do," Kayla chided as he trudged away.

Quinn lifted his brows. "And I thought you wanted to be rescued."

They began strolling west toward a cluster of Alpha instructors. Quinn made no attempt to touch her. Kayla understood why. He had made it plain that he believed public displays of affection would be bad for camp discipline. He'd expressed concern about his daughter's response, too.

"Lester won't bite," he commented after a few moments.

"Oh, come on! He was calling this group 'tent pegs' before they showed up." The term, Kayla gathered, was Lester's assessment of the only military role people like Ronald Nutley were suited to play.

"True," Quinn conceded with a grin. "But he's mellowed considerably since one of the 'tent pegs' promised to help him program his new VCR."

She had to laugh. Then, growing serious, she asked, "What's your reaction to Ronald's CD-ROM idea?"

"I like it better than the franchise proposal I got a few weeks back."

"Franchise proposal?"

"The CEO of an L.A.-based leisure industry conglomerate thinks survivalism is the next big vacation trend. Don't ask me why. I gather it has something to do with getting back to basics and the end of the millennium. In any case, he approached me about the possibility of starting a chain of Alpha Camps."

"With you in charge?"

"Mmm."

Recalling a fragment of the conversation they'd had during her nature walk, Kayla said, "*That* would certainly keep you behind a desk."

Quinn grimaced. "Tell me about it."

They reached the group they'd been heading toward. There was a lively discussion going on.

"Okay, okay," Peter Wiseman—the blond-haired hunk Kayla had spotted doing a hand-to-hand demonstration with Tex Fournier on her first day at Alpha—was saying. "I can see keeping the martial arts classes if we emphasize philosophy as much as fighting. But we'd definitely have to blow off the weapons training. There's no *way* I'm putting a loaded Browning in some street punk's hand!"

Tex laughed sardonically. "Considering most of 'em are used to MAC-10s and Glocks, what'd be the point?" He turned, flashing a smile of greeting at Kayla. "Yo, Miz Movie Star."

Kayla had been surprised by how quickly she'd begun to feel at ease around Alpha's plainspoken, *mucho* macho instructors. She'd eventually realized that they reminded her of the movie tech guys she'd worked with over the years. Although Irwin Ortiz had once suggested that it was a tad declassé, she tended to gravitate toward members of the crew rather than her fellow performers during the making of a film. They began to seem almost like family to her. The separation at the end of a production was often an emotional wrench.

"Yo, Tex," she responded, bestowing a quick smile on everyone present. "What are you talking about? Running a course for the Bloods and Crips?"

"Close." This came from José Reyes, the mustachioed Latino who'd been the third member of the unarmed combat trio. "Some big bucks foundation has been talking to Quinn about doing a pilot program for what the social workers call 'at-risk youths.'"

"Really?" Kayla glanced at Quinn, her interest genuinely piqued.

"Yeah," he affirmed. "Sort of an Outward Bound for potential gangbangers."

She frowned slightly. "Boys?"

"Sure, boys," Peter said.

"What about girls?"

"*Girls?*"

"Yes, girls." Kayla glanced from man to man. "Young women. Females. I do volunteer work with kids in South Central L.A. Not all the 'at-risk youths' are of the masculine persuasion. I've met dozens of girls who'd benefit from the kind of discipline you instill up here. Going through a program like Alpha would do wonderful things for their self-esteem. And it wouldn't hurt them to learn a little self-defense, either."

"Females have—uh—special needs," said a scholarly looking former Special Forces officer who, Kayla had learned, had been an explosives expert.

"Howie, what would you know about a woman's special needs?" Tex jibed.

"About as much as you, man," Peter cracked. "Which probably explains why your latest girlfriend was looking so scraggly last time I saw her."

"Hey, if Leeza was looking scraggly, it's because I've been keeping her—"

"Guys," Quinn said. His voice was quiet, his tone calm, but he shut down the bawdy banter completely.

At first, Kayla didn't understand why he'd interrupted. Then she realized that he'd done so because of her. She wasn't certain how to react. The idea that a man felt the need to protect her not-so-delicate sensibilities seemed strange. Not necessarily unpleasant or offensive, but definitely . . . strange.

"You've got a point, Kayla," José conceded after a few seconds. "But Howie's right, too. Girls would be tough to handle."

"Get some ex-military women to help," she suggested. She looked at Quinn again, her mind racing. "You hire contract instructors, don't you? Former Navy SEALs? Retired members of the S.A.S.? Why not recruit some *female* veterans?"

Quinn regarded her thoughtfully, one corner of his mouth quirking upward. "That's not a bad idea," he finally responded. "Not a bad idea at all."

"Hey, maybe you could come back, Kayla," Peter proposed.

"M-me?" She was stunned by the idea.

There was a murmur of agreement from several of the other staffers.

"Yeah," José picked up. "I mean, if you've been working with this kind of girl . . ."

"'Course, you might not be the best role model on the shooting range," Tex added slyly, provoking a chorus of groans.

Kayla flushed and pulled a face. "You're never going to let me forget that little episode, are you?"

"Watching a guy get shot in the crotch kind of sticks in a man's brain, Kayla."

"It was a paper target, Tex!"

"Don't matter," someone else declared. "It's the principle."

"I didn't do it on purpose."

"*That's* what makes us nervous," Quinn teased.

"What makes you nervous, Dad?" Stevie asked, materializing at her father's side. Kayla was pleased to note that she was wearing one of the brightly colored tops they'd purchased on their shopping expedition.

"Nothing, honey," Tex responded smoothly, winking at her. "Your daddy's the original Mr. Cool."

"We were talking about Kayla coming back to do a guest star gig as an instructor," Peter added.

Stevie's sky-colored eyes widened. "Really?" A delighted smile blossomed on her face. "That'd be *awesome!*"

Quinn said nothing.

Neither did Kayla.

The following Monday, a team from *Celeb*—one of the country's hottest "personality" magazines—came to Alpha Camp to do a story on Kayla's transformation into Mad Maxine. Although Quinn had agreed to cooperate with the PR endeavor, part of him felt as though he were aiding and abetting enemy forces. It was selfish, he knew, but he didn't want Kayla, whom he cared for so deeply, to be reminded of the life that was awaiting her once she left him.

He didn't want to be reminded of it, either.

Being the focus of the attentions of a top photographer *and* a famous-in-her-own-right show biz interviewer must be heady stuff for someone who'd essentially been told she was over the hill, Quinn reflected with a pang. And the entourage dispatched by the producers of *Moving Target*—a hairdresser, a makeup artist, a wardrobe consultant, and a superslick "handler" whose job seemed to be to suck up to the press while stick-

ing catchy quotes in Kayla's mouth—had to be
a big ego boost, too.

"Pretty neat, huh, Dad?" Stevie asked in an
excited undertone, sidling up to him as the magazine's photographer directed Kayla into a dy-
namic pose on the obstacle course. Each time the
man seemed on the verge of being satisfied,
someone from the studio support team leapt in
to fluff his subject's ponytail, regloss her lips, or
apply an artful smudge of dirt to her workout
gear.

"Mmm," Quinn replied noncommittally,
watching Kayla shift from position to position,
offering the photographer a seamless assortment
of angles and expressions to shoot. While the intensity of her concentration was palpable, she
seemed perfectly at ease in front of the camera.
This is my world, her demeanor said. *I know exactly what I'm doing.*

"I wonder what it's like, having all those people fussing over you," Stevie mused aloud. "I bet
some of it would get kind of old after awhile.
But a lot of it—well, like, when Kayla was getting her makeup fixed after they took those pictures of you and her doing hand to hand, she
said something about being thirsty. At least three
people jumped up to get her a drink. And when
she told them all she wanted was a glass of water, they offered her about five different kinds of
bottled stuff—with bubbles, without bubbles, flavored with lime, colored with raspberries, im-
ported from France, on and on." Stevie snickered
mischievously. "Must have been a nice change
after weeks of being ordered around by you.
Like getting promoted from private to princess."

Quinn carefully disciplined his expression. He

was uncertain how much Stevie knew about the true nature of his relationship with Kayla. She'd never raised the issue. While he was loath to keep secrets from his only child, he'd decided that in this instance, if she didn't ask, he wasn't going to tell.

"Has Kayla complained to you?" he said after a moment, his stomach tightening. He'd been tough on "his" movie star; there was no doubt about that. But he'd thought . . .

"Complained?" Stevie stared at him as though he'd just sprouted a second nose. She shook her head in vehement denial. "Of course not! Kayla's not into whining. She let the makeup guy pluck her eyebrows for about twenty minutes and didn't flinch once! Of course, she *did* get a little cranky when the wardrobe lady said she shouldn't wear her combat boots for the photographs. Kayla told her no boots, no pictures, and the lady backed off. But besides not whining— well, she's *glad* you've made her train so hard, Dad. She wants to be totally ready for her movie."

Quinn remained silent. As his gaze strayed toward the ongoing photo shoot, his memory replayed the pledge Kayla had made during their initial face to face.

Look, Major Harris, she'd said. *I'm serious about the work we're supposed to do. It's important—extremely important—that I be ready when* Moving Target *starts shooting at the end of July. So, please. Believe me. The next time you tell me to meet you somewhere at oh five hundred, I'll be there.*

"Dad?"

Quinn stiffened, then looked back at his daughter. "What, honey?"

"Can we visit Kayla in Hollywood?"

"Has she invited . . . us?" His breath snagged in his throat as he tried to decide what pronoun to use.

"Not right out," Stevie admitted, wrinkling her nose and squirming a bit. "But I *know* she'd like us to come see her."

"Stevie—"

"Aren't you going to want to see Kayla after she goes back home?" The inquiry was blunt.

"It's not a question of wanting," Quinn replied, feeling as though he was marching into emotional quicksand. "Kayla will be incredibly busy once she gets back to L.A. Making *Moving Target* is going to take up nearly all her time. Plus, she'll probably be doing interviews and—"

"Okay, people!" the photographer called imperiously. "That's it for this setup. On to the shooting range!"

"Major Harris?" It was the magazine interviewer, a trendily dressed brunette whose obviously surgically enhanced breasts made Quinn think of Howitzer shells. She stepped in close, giving Stevie a saccharine-sweet smile as she basically elbowed her aside. "I was wondering if you could give me a few minutes. I'm *dying* to know more about your military career. . . ."

"So, what did you think of Ms. Dennis?" Kayla asked many hours later, propping herself up on one elbow and gazing down at her bed partner. The shift of position made the soft, secret parts of her body throb. She was sore in a few places, but it wasn't the kind of soreness she minded. She and Quinn had had few opportunities for physical intimacy during the past sev-

eral days. They'd been able to snatch this
evening in her motel room because Stevie was
attending a pajama party being held to celebrate
the birthday of José Reyes' eldest daughter.

"Who?" Quinn asked vaguely, lifting a hand
to stroke her face. His fingers moved gently
along the curve of her cheek.

Kayla trembled in response to his practiced,
provocative touch. No matter that he'd taken her
to ecstasy and beyond twice already tonight. She
wanted him again. Desire rippled heatedly
through her system, momentarily depriving her
of the power of speech.

Quinn's mouth quirked, indicating that he was
aware of the effect he was having on her, and
enjoying it. "Kayla?" he prompted after a second
or two.

"Dodie Dennis," she finally managed to reply.
"The writer from *Celeb*. I saw you talking with
her. It seemed very . . . intense."

"Oh, her." He snorted. "She's a gun groupie."

"A *gun* groupie?"

"Yeah. There's a certain kind of woman who
gets turned on by men who handle loaded weapons for a living. They chase after cops a lot.
SWAT guys, especially."

"And members of the Special Forces?"

"Mmm."

"So . . . you didn't find her attractive?" Kayla
knew there were better ways to spend the lim-
ited time they had together than asking jealous
questions, but she couldn't seem to stop herself.
The sight of Dodie Dennis snuggling up to
Quinn had affected her at a very visceral level.

"Leaving aside her rudeness to Stevie, no. Not
particularly."

"Oh." She shifted again, hooking a lock of hair behind one ear. "A lot of men do. Find her attractive. She's got a very—uh—"

"Aggressive chest?"

Kayla flushed, an involuntary laugh bubbling up in her throat. "Well . . ."

Quinn regarded her for several seconds. The humor that had shone in his eyes when he'd characterized Dodie's upper body faded. It was replaced by an expression that made Kayla's pulse quicken and her already ruffled breathing pattern unravel even further. And this was *before* he looked down at her naked breasts.

"Delaney, Delaney, Delaney," he murmured in a husky voice, raising his ardent gaze to her face. "There are men who like quantity and men who like quality. You want to know my reaction whenever Ms. Dennis heaved those ballistic bazooms of hers at me? It was all I could do to keep myself from yelling 'Incoming' and ducking for cover."

"I . . . see."

"I hope you do, sweetheart."

She trembled at the endearment. Although Quinn was a very skilled and tender lover, he seldom resorted to "romantic" language. He was a man who felt actions spoke louder than words.

They kissed then, their mouths meeting in a slow, sweet caress. She parted her lips. The kiss deepened. Their breath mingled. Their tongues intertwined in languid courtship. She made a soft sound of pleasure. . . .

"Mmm," Quinn breathed when he finally lifted his mouth from hers.

"Mmm-hmmm," she concurred.

There was a pause. She nestled close to him,

relishing the leashed power of his warm nude body. His right arm curved around her waist.

"That was quite a performance you put on today," he finally commented.

"You liked my movie star act, hmm?"

"It was very . . . persuasive."

Kayla blinked, uncertain how to interpret Quinn's tone. "I guess I *did* get a little carried away with all the attention," she admitted after a moment or two. "I'm afraid I was a bit of a bitch to the woman from wardrobe."

"Stevie said you put your foot down on the issue of your combat boots."

"Oh." Kayla found herself wondering what else Stevie might have said. "Well . . . I felt it was important. It may sound silly, but those boots mean a lot to me. I plan to wear them in *Moving Target*. I think they'll help me stay true to character."

"You're really looking forward to playing Mad Maxine, aren't you?"

She hesitated, thinking about the corners of her soul she'd peered into since arriving at Alpha Camp. About the self-doubts she'd experienced.

She had to be honest with herself. A lot of what had gone on today with the *Celeb* photo shoot had struck her as phony and frivolous. She'd asked herself, "What am I doing?" more than a few times. Still, there had been a part of her that had gotten off on being the star of the show. She'd waited for it. She'd worked for it. *She deserved it!*

"It's the biggest break I've ever had," she finally said.

* * *

Four days later, Kayla sat in the bathroom of her motel room shining her combat boots. Lester Baines had given her extensive advice about the proper care of military footwear, and she was determined to do things absolutely right.

She sighed, spreading black polish on the toe of her left boot with a clean cloth as she wondered how things were going back at Alpha. The "tent pegs" were winding up their two-week stay with a special nighttime survival exercise. One of the instructors who'd been scheduled to help coordinate the program had been called away on a family emergency. Quinn was filling in for him.

Another chance to get out from behind his desk, Kayla thought with a crooked smile.

She knew he relished the opportunity. But Lord, she wished he were—

The phone rang in the other room. Kayla dropped everything and ran.

"Hello?"

"Kayla?"

"Irwin." She slumped down on the bed, chastising herself for being foolish. What had she expected? That Quinn was going to call her from the field? "Hi."

"'Irwin . . . hi'?" her agent mimicked. "That's *all*? You want to send me back into therapy?"

"Sorry." She swatted a stray lock of hair away from her face. "I'm just a little tired."

"Well, maybe it'll pep you up to hear that the contact sheets from the *Celeb* photo shoot are making the rounds. You wouldn't believe the buzz. The studio is plotzing with excitement and that shmuck Zack Reynolds is acting like he personally discovered you. No. Worse. He's acting like he gave birth to you! But why not? The pictures are beyond terrific. You look sensational, babe. Like a gorgeous, sexy Amazon. Which, I gotta tell you, is gonna mean extra pressure to show some—"

"*No*," she cut in fiercely. "Absolutely not!"

"Okay! Okay! God. Forget I mentioned it."

"I'm serious, Irwin. I'm not dropping my top, and I won't approve a body double. I've got an ironclad no-nudity clause, remember? If Zack Reynolds or the studio execs have a problem with that, they can kiss my combat boots!"

There was a stunned silence on the other end of the line. Kayla drew a shaky breath, feeling a bit stunned herself.

"Geez, Kayla," her agent finally said. "How do you *really* feel?"

"Sorry," she apologized again.

"Given your current mood, I'm almost afraid to ask this, but I guess I don't have much choice. Have you had a chance to read the script revisions I had couriered up?"

Kayla sighed. The revisions had been in the packet Quinn had brought to her motel room two weeks ago. It had taken her awhile to get to them.

"Yes, I've gone through them," she said, massaging her left temple.

"And?"

"Who's this secondary female character, Naomi, who's suddenly appeared in the story?"

"Zack had a brainstorm for a subplot about Mad Maxine mentoring a younger woman. Kind of a surrogate daughter, you know? Along the lines of what Sigourney Weaver did in *Aliens*. He figured it would be a way of capitalizing on your . . . uh . . . maturity."

"My *maturity*?" Her voice rose. "What does Zack see me as? Yoda?"

"Huh?"

"Yoda! The ancient Jedi master in the *Star Wars* movies! Short. Wizened. Played by a Muppet!"

"Oh. Yeah. I mean, no. *No*. Of course not. Like I said, everybody associated with the picture is *nuts* about you! Those *Celeb* photos have them drooling to get started."

Kayla expelled a short, sharp breath. "Have they cast Naomi yet?"

"An actress named Amber Greeley. She's new. Zack found her."

"Is that 'found' as in picked up and became intimately acquainted with, by any chance?"

"They're . . . dating."

"What's she like?" As if she couldn't guess.

"Blond, busty, and a couple tacos shy of a combination plate in the brains department."

"She's landed the second lead in a major studio picture, Irwin! How stupid can she be?"

Her agent clicked his tongue. "It seems to me that we've had some discussions about the career benefits of being friendly to the right people."

They had, of course. And Amber Greeley's "overnight" success notwithstanding, Kayla wasn't about to change her mind on the subject.

Still. It was so *galling.* . . .

"Kayla?" Irwin probed in a walking-on-eggshells tone.

"What would happen if I didn't do *Moving*

Target?" she suddenly asked. She wasn't certain where the question had come from. It seemed to have erupted out of her.

"Because of Zack's bimbo?" Irwin sounded horrified. "Kayla. Baby. Please. The chickie is nothing. You'll blow her off the screen, I *promise* you."

"Forget Amber." Now that the possibility had been raised, Kayla felt compelled to pursue it. Not that she was seriously contemplating tossing away the chance she'd been waiting for her entire career. "Just tell me—"

"You're not back on your teaching kick, are you?"

She flinched at his tone but persevered. "Answer the question, Irwin. *What would happen if I dropped out of this picture?"*

"Voluntarily, you mean?"

"Yes."

"After I suffered a massive heart attack and died, cursing your name?"

"That bad, huh?"

There was yet another pause. Finally Irwin exhaled on a long, gusty sigh. Kayla knew by the sound that he'd run through all the alternatives and resigned himself to telling the truth. This was unusual. While her agent seldom flat-out lied, he tended to view unconditional honesty with the same enthusiasm that vampires supposedly regarded garlic and crosses.

"If you bail on this project," he said quietly, "you're toast in Tinseltown."

"Suppose I told you I'm not sure I'd care?"

Irwin gave a humorless laugh. "I'd say it's a damned good thing you're coming back to L.A. a week from Sunday."

They talked for a minute or so more, then Kayla murmured an excuse about having work to get back to and bid Irwin good-bye. Her hand was shaking as she hung up the phone.

When she returned to polishing her combat boots a few moments later, she discovered that there was one facet of footwear care Lester Baines had neglected.

He hadn't told her how to remove tearstains from black leather.

9

"*P*ssst! Kayla!"

Checking herself in mid-stride, Kayla pivoted toward the door to Mike Matsui's dispensary. Stevie was peering out, beckoning to her.

"I need to talk to you!" the girl said in a stage whisper.

Kayla glanced back toward Quinn's office, wondering what was going on. There'd been a message waiting for her at the Last Chance's front desk when she'd come downstairs this morning. It had said that Quinn was postponing their training session until noon because he needed some sleep after baby-sitting Ronald Nutley and the other computer nerds all night.

She'd been disappointed. Deeply disappointed. After her conversation with Irwin Ortiz, her desire to be with Quinn had become acute.

It wasn't that she expected him to soothe the emotional tumult she'd experienced in the wake of her telephone conversation with Irwin Ortiz. She recognized that her dilemma was hers alone, and that she was the only one who could resolve it. Still . . .

"What's up?" she asked, approaching Stevie.

Quinn's daughter ushered her into the Wizard of Gauze's office and shut the door.

"Stevie, is something wrong?" Kayla was beginning to get concerned.

The girl shook her head. "Nuh-uh. Everything's fine. Last night's exercise went great, considering."

"Considering?"

"Considering what weenies some of the computer guys are. Don't get me wrong. They all seem really nice. And I know they're total brains. I mean, you wouldn't *believe* the stuff they told me about scamming the phone company and hacking into encrypted data files."

"*Stevie—*"

"I'm not going to use any of it!" She giggled merrily, clearly enjoying the effect she'd created. "It's just cool to know."

Kayla drew a steadying breath, briefly chastising herself for *ever* having found fault with Quinn's performance as a parent. "Let's get back to last night's exercise," she suggested, trying to keep her tone mild. "You say everything went all right?"

"Yeah. No casualties. A couple of guys wandered off and got lost for a while, but somebody found them. Another couple peed in poison ivy. I heard the Wiz is *really* pissed at *them*. But basically, things went okay."

"And your father?" Kayla hoped the sudden rush of warmth she felt in her cheeks didn't show.

"He's okay, too. He's in his office with Pete and Tex. I asked them to distract him for a few minutes so I could talk to you privately."

"Talk to me about what?"

"Well, next Thursday is Dad's birthday—"

"It is?"

"Uh-huh. There's going to be a surprise party in the mess hall that night after dinner." Stevie grimaced. "Well, maybe not a *surprise* surprise. I'm sure Dad will figure out what's going on ahead of time. He always does. But he'll pretend he's clueless to be a good sport. *Anyway.* A bunch of the guys are getting him funny presents, and me and Sergeant Major are going to do a skit about his career. And I was thinking that maybe you could do something, too."

Kayla's heart lurched. "Do . . . something?"

"Yeah." Stevie nodded, gazing up at her in supplication. "Like sing. Or dance. *Please*, Kayla? It'd be so great. And it would totally *stun* my dad."

Kayla ended up saying yes, of course. But not because of the pleading expression in Stevie's big blue eyes. What she found irresistible was the notion of "stunning" Quinn Harris.

She also had a good buddy back in L.A.—Jeffrey van Sant of Beverly Hills, formerly Jack Sanders of Bayonne, New Jersey—she knew she could rely on for help.

Br-r-r-ing. Br-r-r-ing.

"Lifestyles, Unlimited."

"Hi, this is Kayla Delaney—"

"Oh, hello, Ms. Delaney! Are you back in L.A.?"

"Not quite yet. Is Jeffrey available?"

"You bet. He just got in from a site survey for a wedding."

"Anyone I know?"

"Someone *everyone* knows, but I can't tell you her name. The tabloids are tapping our phones again. Hold on . . ."

Click. Click.

"Jeffrey?"

"Kayla! Sweetie! Oh, God. You have no idea how wonderful it is to talk to a *sane* person. Actually, you don't even have to speak. Just let me listen to you breathe rationally. I've had it up to my receding hairline with hyperventilation."

"Difficult client?"

"Difficult, I can handle. We're talking completely wacko. And dumb. I mean, if stupid was snow, this woman would be a blizzard. But never mind that. A friend of a friend of a friend gave me a sneak peak at the photos that are going into *Celeb*. You look absolutely fabulous."

"Thanks, Jeffrey."

"What's the dish on the gorgeous ex–Green Beret hunk who's been training you? I just *love* a man out of uniform."

"He's the reason I'm calling. His birthday is coming up—"

"And you want me to plan a party!"

"Not exactly. I need a cake."

"A *cake*? Sorry, sweetie. I don't do Betty Crocker."

"Not that kind of cake. I need something I can . . . uh . . . pop out of."

"*Kayla Delaney*! You little *slut*!"

"It's not what you think."

"It's not?"

"No. Definitely not."

"Oh, rats. I was hoping you'd finally kicked off your goody two shoes."

"I'm into combat boots these days, actually."

"Really? That sounds potentially kinky. I don't suppose—"

"The *cake*, Jeffrey. Can you help me out?"

"Of course, I can help you out. You're my favorite ex–upstairs neighbor in the world. You're also the woman who encouraged me to follow my dream of trying to impose a modicum of good taste on this tacky, tacky town. I *owe* you. When do you need this *faux gâteau*?"

"By Thursday afternoon at the latest."

"No *way*."

"There has to be."

"All right. All right. Let me think. Mmmm. How would you feel about leaping out of something that's slightly used?"

"Used?"

"Yes. An acquaintance of mine runs an, ah, *adult* message service—"

"Not the strip-o-gram people."

"Don't be a prude, sweetie."

"I don't want anything X-rated, Jeffrey. There's going to be a twelve-year-old girl at this party. *And* a Congressional Medal of Honor winner."

"Not to worry. I'll rent an angel cake."

Although he feigned astonishment quite convincingly, the shouts of "Surprise!" that greeted Quinn Harris when he walked into the Alpha mess hall on the evening of his thirty-ninth birthday were not unexpected. Nor were the gag gifts

given him by members of his staff. Even the
comic dialogue performed by his daughter and
Lester Baines—a spoof of his military career involving characters named "Private Problem,"
"Major Difficulty," and "General Disaster"—
was something he'd anticipated. But when José
Reyes and Mike Matsui rolled out a huge white
cake surmounted by an electric torch . . .

He blushed like a boy.

"Make a wish and blow out the candle!" somebody hollered. The suggestion was endorsed by
a great deal of laughter and applause.

He glanced around, his gaze lingering briefly
on his daughter's beaming face. Stevie nodded,
clearly urging him to do as he'd been told.

He stepped forward, a bit uncertain about how
one "blew out" a flame-shaped bulb. After a moment he took a deep breath, leaned in, then exhaled with a noisy *whoosh*.

The candle clicked off.

The cake split open.

The crowd went wild as Kayla Delaney
emerged from the plaster-frosted pastry with a
professional flourish.

Her hair was loose, tumbling over her shoulders in wild, chestnut-colored waves. She was
clad in an oversize khaki shirt that ended in the
middle of her sleekly muscled thighs and was
cinched at her slender waist with a webbed belt.
There were streaks of camouflage on her face and
black leather combat boots on her feet. She
looked gorgeous.

"I don't know what you wished for, sir," she said
in a throaty voice, staring directly into his eyes.
"But I'm what you got."

That's when Quinn Harris received his birthday surprise.

That's when he realized he'd fallen in love with a woman who would be leaving him in less than seventy-two hours.

He fought it. For the better part of a day and a half, Quinn struggled with his emotions, reminding himself over and over that he'd initiated his affair with Kayla knowing—*knowing!*—it couldn't last. But as the clock ticked inexorably toward her departure for L.A., he found it harder and harder not to express what was in his heart. Finally what had been increasingly difficult became impossible. . . .

"Don't go," he said.

Kayla paused in the act of tying her boots, looking up at him with a bewitching smile and luminous eyes. They were in her motel room at the Last Chance. He'd knocked on her door about ninety minutes ago, ostensibly to escort her to Alpha for her final training session. They'd ended up making love.

Fast, feverish love.

Slow, sweet love.

"There's a five-mile run on my schedule," she responded huskily. "And one last trip around the obstacle course. I've *got* to go."

"I don't mean don't go right now. I mean don't go . . . period."

In the space of a single heartbeat, Kayla lost most of the color in her face. "What?" she whispered.

"Stay here. With me. With me and Stevie."

Quinn's pulse was pounding. His palms were starting to sweat. The fear he'd felt in combat was nothing compared with this. "Marry me, Kayla."

"*M-Marry you*?" Her eyes were huge. She was trembling.

Quinn took a step forward, closing most of the distance between them. But something stopped him from reaching out, from trying to touch.

"Yes," he affirmed, his throat tight.

"You . . . want me to give up *Moving Target* and become your wife?"

His stomach knotted. He realized what he was asking. But there was no other way. He knew from painful personal experience the toll long separations took on a marriage. Long separations would be inevitable if Kayla accepted his proposal and went on making movies. And if playing Mad Maxine impacted her career as it seemed destined to do . . .

He'd gotten a preview of her pending celebrity during the magazine photo shoot. He hadn't begrudged her the attention. How could he? But he didn't want to contend with spotlights, flashbulbs, and public scrutiny on a regular basis, either. And he certainly didn't want to become *Mr*. Kayla Delaney.

"I want you to stay here," he answered. "I . . . love you, Kayla. I love you with all my heart."

"Oh, God." Tears welled up in her gray-green eyes. She blinked them back. "And I . . . l-love . . . you, Quinn. So much. So m-much."

He waited for the *but*. He could hear it coming. Finally he got tired of waiting and supplied the caveat himself: "But not enough to forget about playing Mad Maxine."

Kayla flinched as though she'd been struck. "That's not fair."

"Forget fair. *Is it the truth?*"

"It's not either-or!" Her voice rose.

"I think it is," he countered, clenching his hands. "I love you, sweetheart. I love you and I want to marry you. I want us to make a life together. But if you're going to be running off to God knows where—"

"I *told* you what I went through to get this part! I *told* you how much *Moving Target* means to me!"

"I guess I was hoping the last three weeks had persuaded you to change your priorities."

There was an awful pause. Finally Kayla shook her head. "I . . . can't."

That night in the mess hall, there was a "hail and farewell" ceremony in Kayla's honor. How she got through it without breaking down, she never knew.

The worst moment came when the man whose proposal she'd rejected—but to whom she knew she'd given her heart—called her up before everyone and presented her with a small velvet-covered jeweler's box.

"Wh-what—?" she stammered, accepting the gift with trembling fingers. For one insane instant she wondered whether Quinn might be trying to pressure her into accepting his suit by renewing it before a group of people—including his daughter—for whom she'd come to care very, very much.

"Open it and see," he said without inflection.

She stared into Quinn's lean, compelling face for several seconds, feeling a little sick. He gazed back at her, his expression impossible to read. Finally she looked back down at the box. Taking a deep breath, she did as she'd been bidden.

"Oh." Tears shimmered across her field of vision. "Oh . . . Quinn."

"We decided you deserved a memento of your Alpha experience," she heard him explain. His voice seemed to reach her across a great distance. "And since we don't give out medals for performance above and beyond the call of duty here, we thought this might be a good alternative."

Nestled inside the satin-lined box was a small gold pendant attached to a delicate gold chain.

The exquisitely detailed pendant was shaped like a pair of combat boots.

Kayla Delaney boarded a plane back to L.A. early the next morning. She did so with the teary sound of Stevie's good-bye echoing in her ears and the bittersweet taste of Quinn's farewell kiss lingering on her lips.

Around her throat she wore her new gold pendant.

Her trusty combat boots, spit shined to a lacquerlike gloss by Lester Baines, were tucked away in her luggage.

10

*K*nock. *Knock. Knock.*

"Five minutes, Ms. Delaney," a deferential male voice called through the door of the lushly appointed mobile home that had been designated as Kayla's private domain during the making of *Moving Target*.

"Thanks," she called back, closing the script she'd been reading and setting it aside. She wondered wryly whether this "five minutes" would last as long as the previous one. It had stretched on for, oh, maybe an hour.

To say that her new picture was not getting off to a swift start was to understate the case. She'd been ready to go to work since seven A.M., but Zack Reynolds had yet to shoot a single frame of film!

"Day one, and we're already a week behind schedule," she'd heard a gaffer grumble when she strolled around the set after lunch, trying to get a feel for what was (and wasn't) happening. "What kind of sense does that make?"

"The same kind of sense it makes when a picture grosses three hundred million and the studio claims it's still running in the red," someone had retorted with a cynical chuckle. "That's show biz."

265

She glanced toward the trailer's elaborate entertainment center, one of many "star perks" Irwin had taken it upon himself to negotiate for her. The digital clock on the front of the state-of-the-art VCR proclaimed it was half past three in the afternoon.

Half past three. Mmm. If she were back at Alpha . . .

Stop it! Kayla told herself fiercely, getting to her feet. *You made your choice. Learn to live with it.*

Easy to say. Hard to do. If the eight days since her return to Hollywood had taught her nothing, they'd taught her that.

She'd been welcomed back to Tinseltown with air kisses, admiring comments about her Mad Maxine physique, and an apparently endless stream of invitations to "do" breakfast, lunch, dinner, or drinks. After fourteen years in the industry, she was suddenly the flavor of the month.

It felt funny. Not funny good or funny bad. Funny . . . weird. As though it were happening to someone else.

Sighing, Kayla crossed to the vanity table at the other end of the trailer. The tickle of the plush carpet against her soles reminded her that wardrobe had not yet returned her combat boots. Some eager-beaver gofer had spirited them away hours before, explaining that the costume designer had decided they required scuffing up for the sake of "character integrity."

Switching on the lights that rimmed the large mirror above the vanity, Kayla assessed her reflection. She grimaced slightly at what she saw. She hadn't been sleeping well since her return, and there were smudgy shadows beneath her eyes that no amount of concealer cream could mask.

Fortunately the weary look would serve to her advantage for the time being. The first scenes scheduled to be shot were ones that would come late in the film, when Mad Maxine was at the peak of her action heroine form physically but deeply conflicted about what she'd been driven to do. The kvetching of her personal makeup artist (another first-time perk she owed to her agent's status-conscious negotiating) notwithstanding, a hint of haggardness would enhance her on-screen impact.

Kayla sighed again, her gaze straying toward a flower arrangement on the left side of the vanity. There'd been a number of "good luck" offerings waiting in her trailer when she'd arrived this morning, including a huge bouquet of long-stemmed roses from her agent, an exotically elegant spray of orchids from Jeffrey van Sant, and a gargantuan fruit basket from her "admirers" at Alpha Camp. But the gift that had brought her to the brink of tears was the small nosegay she was looking at now.

Go with the flow, the card that had accompanied it read. *Love, Quinn and Stevie.*

Her right hand crept up to the base of her throat, brushing against her combat boot pendant. Although she knew the necklace would have to be removed before she went before the cameras, she intended to keep it on until the last possible moment.

Oh, Quinn, she thought sadly. *It didn't have to be either-or. We could have found a way—*

Knock. Knock. Knock.

"We're ready for you now, Ms. Delaney."

Kayla stiffened, a flock of butterflies suddenly hatching in the pit of her stomach. She inhaled on a short, sharp breath, her fingers closing around the pendant.

Her *boots*! She still didn't have her *boots*!

"Ms. Delaney?"

"Coming," she called, releasing the pendant and lowering her hand. "And would you please remind wardrobe that Mad Maxine can't kick butt if she doesn't have her combat boots?"

The individual on the other side of the door responded by saying something she couldn't quite catch but which sounded reassuring.

She gave her reflection one last glance, then flicked off the makeup mirror lights. *It's show time*, she told herself.

She crossed to the door and opened it. She stepped outside.

"*Wha*—?" she gasped as she tripped over something and started to pitch forward.

Nearly six weeks before, Kayla Delaney had stepped and stumbled on an obstacle course. She'd been saved from taking an ignominious nosedive into the dirt by a man she'd come to love more than any other. But there was no one—nothing—to save her now.

Go with the flow, something deep inside her advised.

Kayla did. Which was just fine until she slammed into the concrete at the bottom of steps.

She heard a sickening *crack*.

A shaft of searing pain pierced her left arm.

"Oh . . ." she moaned, bile rising in her throat. Then she fainted.

Quinn rubbed the back of his neck, studying the prospectus spread before him. He hoped—vainly, he suspected—that loosening the knotted muscles in his nape might ease the tension in another part of his anatomy.

Eight days had passed since he'd kissed Kayla Delaney good-bye and put her on a plane back to Los Angeles. Eight days. It felt like eight weeks. Eight months. Eight goddamned *years*. He ached for her, both physically and psychologically. He felt as though a part of him had been torn away.

He'd been a fool, he told himself. An arrogant, pigheaded fool. How could he have demanded that she choose between him and her career? He didn't even have ignorance as an excuse. He'd presented his options—his "either-or" as Kayla had called it—with full knowledge of the kind of sacrifice he was asking.

He still believed that husbands and wives who spent long periods apart placed their relationship at risk. Although absence might very well make the heart grow fonder, it undercut the day-to-day intimacy that seemed to him to be the foundation of a strong marriage.

But "togetherness" wasn't supposed to be the responsibility of just one partner. Yet that had been the tack he'd taken when he'd proposed to Kayla. He'd put the burden entirely on her.

And she'd almost accepted it. He'd seen in the agonized expression in her eyes—heard in the anguished tone of her voice—how close she'd come to giving up her nearly realized dream of movie stardom for him.

Not for herself. Not for them and their future. For *him*.

Thank God she hadn't. As badly hurt as he'd been by Kayla's rejection, he'd come to realize that she'd done the right thing. He'd also come to hope that the farewells they'd said didn't have to be final. There was something he could do—

"Daddy! Daddy!" Stevie suddenly called from the front of the house. Her voice was shrill. "Come here!"

Alarmed as much by Stevie's reversion to the childish "Daddy" as by her overwrought tone, Quinn leapt to his feet. He dashed out of his small home office and raced down the hall to the family room. He found his daughter standing in front of the television set, staring at an automobile advertisement.

"Stevie, what the—"

She turned from the TV. Her face was pale, her eyes huge and more than a little accusatory. The look of accusation was nothing new. Although she'd not come right out and said so, Quinn knew his daughter blamed him for Kayla's departure from their lives. His efforts to explain the situation had been inadequate at best. He'd finally been driven to telling Stevie that she'd understand when she got older. This, predictably, had gone over like the proverbial lead balloon.

"I think something's happened to Kayla," Stevie said tightly.

Quinn went cold, assailed by a series of horrible possibilities. *"What?"*

"I turned on this show business news program to see if there was anything about the first day of shooting on *Moving Target*. Right before they went to a commercial, the lady on the show said they had the story of a tough break next—and then they put up a picture of Kayla!"

The car commercial came to an end. Another ad, this one touting a breath freshening toothpaste, began. It was followed by a promo for a weekend documentary, which was followed by a plug for a new talk show. Then there was a public service announcement about the importance of recycling. By the time that concluded, Quinn was ready to put his foot through the TV set.

Finally the face of the show biz program's perkily blond hostess reappeared on the screen. Only she looked a tad less perky than usual.

"Some bad luck today for actress Kayla Delaney," she intoned. "After surviving six weeks of grueling, Green Beret–style training to get ready for her starring role in the new action flick *Moving Target*, she's now on the casualty list." A still photo of Kayla clutching her arm in obvious anguish popped up on the screen. Quinn took an involuntary step forward. "Witnesses report Kayla took a serious tumble as she was leaving her on-location trailer this afternoon and fractured her left arm. She's been forced to withdraw from the film. Director Zack Reynolds says he's deeply disappointed by the turn of events, but he adds that *Moving Target* will go forward."

The photo of Kayla dissolved out. The perky blonde appeared on the screen again, this time in a two-shot with her dapperly dressed cohost.

The cohost shook his head, his expression suitably sympathetic. "As you said, a real tough break for Kayla Delaney. Any details on what caused her fall? I mean, could we be talking . . . lawsuit?"

"No word on that," the blonde responded. "As for the cause of the accident—well, it sounds like a PR gimmick, but sources on the scene *swear* she was tripped up by a pair of combat boots!"

*　　*　　*

Irwin Ortiz looked like Woody Allen but
dressed like the cinematic stereotype of a Co-
lombian drug kingpin. He was a man of many
moods. On the morning after Kayla's accident,
his mood was morose in the extreme.

"It's all my fault," he asserted mournfully,
wringing his hands.

Kayla shook her head at this patently ridiculous statement as she settled into a wheelchair.
No matter that she was perfectly capable of ex-
iting the hospital under her own power. The producers of *Moving Target* had insisted that she be
rolled out of the place, just as they'd insisted she
remain under medical observation overnight.
Concern about her condition, they claimed. Desperation to avoid a multimillion dollar lawsuit
for negligence was probably more accurate.

"How did you come to *that* conclusion, Irwin?" she asked, shifting her cast-encased left
arm very gingerly. Somewhere in the back of her
mind she wondered why she wasn't feeling as
unhappy as her agent looked. Maybe it was the
painkillers she'd been given, but she was suffused with a sense of peace she hadn't known in
. . . in . . . *years.*

She'd had a horrible night, there was no dis-
puting that. The loss of the professional opportunity for which she'd rejected Quinn's proposal
of marriage had shattered her. She'd wept until
she could weep no more, finally falling into a
restless slumber filled with dreams about what
would have, could have, and should have been.

By all rights, she should have awoken this
morning depressed and drained. Instead she'd
greeted the new day with an odd combination of
equanimity and expectation.

Her agent heaved a gusty sigh. "If I hadn't told you that you couldn't bail out of *Moving Target*—"

"Hold it right there," Kayla interrupted, holding up her right hand like a traffic cop. "You didn't *tell* me I could or couldn't do anything. You gave me your best professional counsel. *I* decided to honor my contract just like *I* fell over my pair of combat boots."

"Which nobody's admitted to leaving on the steps of your trailer."

"Does it really matter who did it? They were there. I tripped over them, broke my arm, and got dropped from the picture. Stuff happens, Irwin. Sometimes you can fight it. Sometimes you've got to go with the flow."

Her agent stared at her, his jaw slack, the expression in his eyes somewhere between utterly appalled and absolutely astonished.

"You're not upset," he finally said, plainly having trouble grasping the concept. "You've lost a part you battled tooth and nail to get, a part you worked your ass off to prepare for—and you're genuinely not upset. *What the hell is wrong with you?*"

Kayla hesitated, her mind flashing back on something Quinn had said right before she'd told him she couldn't marry him under the conditions he'd set.

I guess I was hoping the last three weeks had persuaded you to change your priorities, he'd declared.

"Kayla?" her agent prompted, looking a bit alarmed.

She smiled at him. "Let's just say I've decided that there are more important things in life than being a movie star."

*   *   *

She repeated a variation on this assertion a short while later to the reporters who'd gathered in the lobby of the hospital to cover the aftermath of her tumble from cinematic grace. They seemed as bewildered by her words as Irwin had been.

"You mean, you're *quitting* show business?" one of them asked.

"I'm going on to other things," she replied. "Or maybe I should say, I'm going back to them. Before I got into the movies, I wanted to be a teacher. I'm within a few credits of earning my degree. I've been volunteering as a literacy tutor in—"

"But what if someone came up with an absolutely terrific offer?" a stringer from one of the tabloid TV shows pressed. "The role of a lifetime with a seven-figure fee. Are you telling us you'd turn it down?"

Kayla fingered her combat boot pendant for several seconds, then cocked her chin. "I don't know," she said truthfully. "I'd like to think I'm the kind of person who's always going to be open to new proposals—"

"What about a revised version of an old one?" a resonant male voice suddenly inquired in a low but carrying tone.

Kayla turned around. Standing several yards away was Quinn Harris. The expression on his compelling, sun-burnished face stole her breath away.

She spoke his name on a shattered gasp of happiness, knowing her heart must be in her eyes.

A moment later, she was in his arms. Cameras clicked like adrenalized crickets. TV videographers cursed each other as they elbowed for line of sight advantage. Reporters shouted questions, demanding to know who, what, where, when, why, and how.

"Oh," she dimly heard Irwin Ortiz say as Quinn literally swept her off her feet. "*Now* I understand."

They were granted refuge from the media horde by a Valkyriesque nurse named Peggy Butler, who snagged Quinn's attention by yelling "Yo, soldier!" then guided them to an empty administrative office. Kayla later learned that Ms. Butler was a military veteran who'd known General Stephen Sterling Harris before he'd gotten either of his stars. Kayla also discovered that Ms. Butler had safeguarded their privacy by standing guard outside the door of the office she'd escorted them to. Even the British contingent from the celebrity press—normally unstoppable in pursuit of a story—had been cowed by her.

Much of what Kayla and Quinn said to each other in the immediate aftermath of their reconciliation wasn't terribly coherent. It was lovers' verbal shorthand, punctuated with kisses and caresses.

Eventually Quinn got around to trying to explain the reasons behind the me-or-your-career condition he'd placed on his initial marriage proposal. He then astounded her by declaring that if she wanted to go on making movies, he had a way to minimize the separations it would cause.

"*You'd sell Alpha and move to L.A.?*" she echoed in disbelief when he paused to draw breath.

He nodded, his midnight blue eyes solemn. "I told you about the leisure industry mogul who's interested in starting a chain of survival camps. Well, it seems my first turndown only whetted his appetite. He bumped up his offer substantially when I went back and indicated I might be willing to rethink the idea."

Kayla swallowed hard several times, understanding the implications of what Quinn was offering to do. "You . . . you'd turn yourself into a—uh—RUMF for m-me?" she asked in a shaky voice.

"REMF," he corrected with a soul stirring smile. "And yes, I would. But it wouldn't be just for you, Kayla. It would be for *us.*"

"You love what you do now. I don't want you to give that up."

"But your career—"

"I meant what I told the reporters. I'm bowing out of the biz. I'm not saying I couldn't be tempted back on a temporary basis some time in the future, but my professional goal right now is to become a teacher. And if you're still contemplating the idea of running an Alpha program for 'at-risk' kids—"

"It's just about a done deal. A week for boys. A week for girls."

"Oh, Quinn . . ."

They kissed again, breath merging, tongues mating. Quinn caressed Kayla with lavish strokes. His touch was intensely passionate, yet infinitely protective of her injured arm. She responded to his ardor without inhibition.

Finally he eased back a bit and reached into the pocket of the sports jacket he was wearing. He brought out a small velvet-covered box much like the one that had contained her combat boot pendant.

"Marry me, Kayla," he said huskily, snapping the box open and holding it out. "Please. Marry me."

"Oh, Quinn," she gasped, taking in the subtle ice-and-fire of small rose-cut diamonds and intricate white gold filigree. "It's *beautiful*."

"My mother wore it. And my father's mother before her."

Kayla looked up at him. "I'll cherish it the way they must have," she pledged. "Will you . . . will you put it on?"

It was easier said than done, given the shakiness of his hands and the cast-hampered condition of her left ring finger. But the heirloom jewel was finally slid into its proper place.

"I have a confession to make about your movies, Kayla," Quinn said softly, charting the curve of her cheek.

She smiled. "You lied about having seen them."

"No."

"You lied about having *liked* them."

"No again. The truth is, I saw you in a TV movie titled 'Shady Lady' a few years ago and I, well, I got turned on. And I stayed turned on. The main reason I agreed to train you for *Moving Target* was that I wanted to meet you for real."

She felt her smile fade. "Was I"—she moistened her lips—"what you expected?"

"You were more, sweetheart. Much, much more."

Kayla Delaney and Quinn Harris were joined in holy matrimony in a small but joyous ceremony in the Alpha Camp mess hall seven weeks later. The event was overseen by Jeffrey van Sant of Lifestyles, Unlimited, who was tactfully dissuaded from hiring a marching band or ordering a twenty-one-gun salute.

Standing by the groom was his best man, retired Sergeant Major Lester Baines.

Attending the bride—who broke with tradition and gave herself away—was Miss Stephanie Lynn Harris. Many of those present commented on the girl's radiantly happy demeanor. Her new stepmother suspected it had something to do with the fact that a certain young man had apparently wised up to the shallowness of the charms of a bimbette-in-training named Brittany. She refrained from mentioning this suspicion to Stevie's father, figuring he had enough on his mind.

A wonderful time was had by all, including Irwin Ortiz. He kept the guests in stitches with an only-in-Hollywood saga of how a lean, mean, feminist-oriented action film named *Moving Target* was being turned into a bloated melodrama about an ex-novice nun turned ninja stripper. Industry wits were already calling it *Molting Turkey*.

Save for a delicate gold pendant worn by the new Mrs. Quinn Harris, there were no combat boots involved in the nuptial ceremonies. But there was a whole slew of them tied to the bumper of the limousine that carried her and her husband off to their honeymoon.

Carol Buckland

——

CAROL BUCKLAND is the award winning author of more than two dozen short contemporary romances written under the name Carole Buck. The recipient of *Romantic Times'* Love and Laughter award and a Georgia Romance Writers' Maggie, she's had a number of novels on the WaldenBooks' romance best-seller list.

In "real life" Carol is a veteran broadcast journalist. She's currently a senior news writer for CNN in Atlanta. A member of the political coverage unit, she also does on-air film reviews for the network. Job-related travels have taken her to Moscow, Madrid, Malta, Tokyo, and numerous U.S. cities.

In her spare time, Carol bakes cookies and collects frogs. She feeds the former to her newsroom colleagues. Contrary to the scurrilous rumors spread by anonymous sources, she does *not* kiss the latter.

Heart and Soles

Cassie Miles

1

Julia Buchanan froze in her tracks. A weird sensation prickled the hairs at the back of her neck. Despite the blazing August sun, goosebumps quivered on her forearms, and she almost dropped the hangers that held her dry cleaning.

Slowly, she turned and peered through the window of a ratty little secondhand boutique on Denver's Colfax Avenue. Those shoes! Absolutely outrageous! Those blue and green luminescent platform heels looked as if they could strut right out of the display window all by themselves.

"Wow," she whispered.

This might be love at first sight. Her heart pounded, her breathing accelerated, and her hazel eyes were blinded by a brilliant flash of light. A tempting siren song assailed her ears: Buy me, buy me, buy me.

No! Absolutely not! No way would she let herself purchase those shoes. Platform heels were impractical. The color was absurd. Those were the kind of crazy shoes that a wild, impetuous woman would buy. *And that's not me.*

Julia Buchanan worked hard to be neat and tidy and practical to the nth degree. That was her identity. That was her fate.

She stepped back from the window and saw her own reflection in the glass. Unimaginative straight brown hair fell almost to her shoulders. Her features were perfectly symmetrical. Her short-sleeved suit jacket was beige. The blouse was cream. *A vanilla milk shake*, she thought. *I look like a vanilla milk shake. An efficient, responsible, twenty-eight-year-old milk shake.*

Still . . . She glanced back at the exotic shoes.

Spencer would have loved them.

Spencer? Her body stiffened at the thought of him. The worst thing she could possibly do was to start remembering Spencer. He was long gone from her life. In her book, Spencer Kendall, the history professor, was . . . history.

She hadn't seen him in more than four months. Exactly 131 days ago. Not that she was counting.

"Good-bye, shoes."

Determinedly, Julia marched away from the storefront and over to her gray Honda Civic, parked around the corner. She unlocked the car door, hung her dry cleaning in the back, and climbed inside. The interior was an oven. The gray leatherette seat seared through her blouse and jacket. The steering wheel was hotter than a branding iron.

She turned the key in the ignition, knowing that she needed to go to a mall and find a sensible, comfortable pair of black leather pumps. But Cheesman Park was only a few blocks away, and the cool, verdant shadows of tall oaks and elms beckoned to her.

Cheesman Park was where she and Spencer had met last year, on October 31st.

Almost a year ago, on the eve of Halloween, Julia had been certain that some particularly irritating hobgoblins had cursed her for one day.

First thing in the morning, her car wouldn't start.

When she went to take the bus to work, she only had a twenty dollar bill in her purse. No exact change.

After scrounging her penny stash, she found bus fare. Four dimes, four nickels, and forty pennies.

She was late for work at Morton Accounting Services. Julia had hoped to slide into her cubicle unnoticed, but that wasn't the way her luck was running.

"Miz Buchanan," said a teasing voice, "late-comers are docked in pay, you know."

"That's not funny, Karen." But Julia grinned at Karen Gallegos, who occupied the adjoining cubicle. "Especially since I'm taking off at noon. Can you do me a favor? My car's on the fritz. I need a ride at lunchtime."

"This is going to cost you," Karen threatened. "A burrito to go from El Caliente."

"You've got it."

After a morning of correcting the payroll records for an advertising firm whose deductions had apparently been figured by a chimpanzee with an abacus, Julia was thrilled when the hands on her wristwatch struck high noon.

She flung herself into the passenger seat of Karen's late-model station wagon and sighed. "Thank goodness it's Friday."

"And Halloween," Karen said. "What are you doing to celebrate?"

"Maybe I'll read a horror novel. And you?"

"First I'll take the kids trick-or-treating. Then, at about midnight, I'll put on my sexiest vampire outfit and seduce my husband."

"Kinky," Julia said.

She directed Karen to a print shop on East Sixth Avenue, where she picked up 150 résumés.

"A hundred and fifty?" Karen questioned. "Don't you think that's a bit much?"

"I really want to find another job."

"Well, you know what I think. You and I should open our own little accounting firm. Gallegos and Buchanan."

"Buchanan and Gallegos," Julia automatically corrected. "And you know I'm not that brave."

"But you're brilliant and I'm brilliant. And we've both slaved for Morton for over three years. Come on, Julia. Take a chance. What have you got to lose?"

"Oh . . . everything."

It was easy for Karen to suggest self-employment. If they failed, Karen had an adoring husband to fall back on. Julia had only herself, and she didn't dare risk her savings to start a business.

Julia opened the lid of the stationery box and studied her crisply printed résumé. Her credentials were impressive. Graduated cum laude. Completed her CPA degree in record time. She was fluent in virtually all the computer languages and systems. "I look pretty darn good on paper," she confided to Karen. "I'd hire me."

Disinterested, Karen scanned the single page. "Very nice. But I thought you graduated in eighty-eight."

"I did." Julia stared at the printed résumé, then at her original. Apparently, the Halloween demons were still at work. "Oh no, I wrote eighty-six. It was my mistake."

"This is a sign," Karen said. "You should forget this job search and open up shop with me."

"I can fix this." With her black pen, Julia carefully changed the six to an eight. "There. All better."

"I'm telling you, Julia. It's an omen."

"A simple mistake," she said matter-of-factly.

After picking up two El Caliente burritos to go, Julia asked Karen to drop her off at Cheesman Park, which was near the office building where she had her two o'clock appointment.

"Good luck," Karen said grudgingly. "If you change your mind, I'm ready when you are to start up Gallegos and Buchanan, Incorporated."

With an hour until her appointment, Julia crunched through the carpet of leaves and settled on a park bench near the swing sets. It was a golden Indian summer day in Colorado, when the temperature was pleasantly cool, the skies were blue, and the air smelled tangy like apples.

Setting her burrito and soda pop on the bench beside her, she opened her briefcase and took out the box full of résumés. Might as well change them while she was sitting here. With her black pen, she carefully made the correction.

A six to an eight. A six to an eight.

Carefully, she took a bite of burrito. A six . . .

But the hobgoblins weren't done with her yet.

A wet, black nose poked her kneecap, and Julia jumped.

The nose was attached to a handsome white dog that was trailing a blue leash. He looked at her with bright eyes, seeming to grin.

"Hello, boy. You're a Samoyed, aren't you? Sammy?" She patted the top of his head. His fur was soft as ermine. This dog was definitely not a neglected mongrel. She eyed the leash. "I'll bet somebody's looking for you, aren't they?"

A huge pink tongue lolled from his mouth, and he slurped at her hand.

"No!" Julia said firmly. She shouldn't have encouraged the beast. She was, after all, on the way to a job interview, and she didn't want white dog hairs on the wool navy blue suit she wore beneath her trench coat.

But the dog was now her friend, so familiar that he apparently felt no qualms about sharing her lunch. Her burrito—paper wrapper and all—disappeared into the furry white jaws.

"Stop it, Sammy. What do you think you're doing?"

Obviously, he was eating her lunch.

"Hey!" came a loud shout. "Hey, lady! Hang on to that dog!"

She peered along the path that circled Cheesman Park and saw a man racing toward her. He was tall and lean, wearing Levi's and a corduroy sports jacket. His thick, dark blond, sun-streaked hair reminded her of Robert Redford's.

"The dog," he yelled. "Hang on to the dog."

Belatedly, Julia reached for the leash just as Sammy leapt backward. He thrashed the burrito wrapper in his mouth and bounced in a circle, dragging the leash.

"Here, Sammy." Julia made a grab and missed. Then she lunged. Her trench coat flapped around her. The box containing her résumés overturned, and the heavy bond paper spilled to the ground like autumn leaves.

The sensible side of her personality warned her that nabbing a wayward Samoyed was not her problem. She ought to gather up her résumés and pull herself together before her appointment.

But Julia was acting on instinct. On her feet, she charged toward the dog. He danced away, wagged his tail, and yipped. She stomped on the end of the bright blue leash, then picked it up and held on tight. "Gotcha!"

Before she knew what had happened, the dog darted right, then left, then around her legs. Holding his leash was like being tethered to a whirling dervish. Julia lost her balance. She went down on one knee. But she still had the leash in her hand, and she held it up triumphantly to the tall blond man.

"Thanks," he said, slightly out of breath. "I've been chasing this puppy for the better part of an hour."

Though she could have scolded him for not taking proper care of his animal, her words stuck in her throat as she looked up into the bluest eyes she had ever seen.

When he took her hand and helped her to her feet, his lingering gaze seemed to penetrate her skin, warming her. And she had the strangest sensation in the pit of her stomach. It was almost as if she was coming face-to-face with her destiny. Karen would have called this reaction a sign, an omen. But Julia was far more inclined to believe she had a touch of indigestion.

"I'm Spencer Kendall," he said.

"Julia Buchanan."

"That's not my dog."

"Then why—"

A young boy, about eight years old, raced up and joined them. With his red hair and freckles, he looked like a Norman Rockwell painting of the all-American kid. He flung his skinny arms around the Samoyed's neck.

"Bad dog," he said. "You gotta stop chasing those squirrels."

"A boy and his dog," Julia said under her breath.

"It doesn't get much cuter," said Spencer. "I think we're witnessing a Kodak moment."

Unfortunately, cuteness wasn't going to help her find a new job. Julia bent down and started picking up her résumés. Some were dusty from the leaves. Some were damp from resting on the earth. Some were destroyed.

Spencer helped, gathering up the sheets of heavy white bond paper. He glanced at one. "A girl and her résumé?"

"And it doesn't get much more desperate than that." She weeded out the demolished résumés and stacked the others.

"You're an accountant." He read from the résumé. "And you're currently employed at Morton. That's one of the biggest accounting firms in Denver."

"But my little cubicle is ten feet by twelve feet."

"Claustrophobic?"

"Very. I have a job interview at a smaller place with bigger potential." She checked her wristwatch. "In thirty-nine minutes."

The kid came over and thanked them while his dog sat obediently beside him.

"Are you going to be all right?" Julia asked. "Can you get home from here?"

"Sure. Thanks again." He pivoted and strolled away from them as if he had not a care in the world.

Julia shook her head. "There goes a terminally adorable little boy."

"It was nice of you to help," Spencer said. "More than nice, actually. You were kind of amazing—the way you grabbed the leash and held on."

"Aw, shucks, it was nothing."

"Let me buy you a new pair of pantyhose."

If that was a pickup line, it was the strangest approach she'd ever heard. Most guys asked if they could buy you a drink. Or if they could show you their etchings. "Pantyhose? Why?"

His warm blue-eyed gaze slid down her body and came to rest at her knees.

Julia glanced down the length of her beige trench coat, which was now smeared with mud. When she'd fallen on one knee, she'd torn her nylons. This wasn't just a run. From the knee down, her pantyhose were shredded. "I can't go to a job interview like this."

"Probably not," he agreed.

Julia sighed. Maybe Karen was right. Maybe the universe was telling her that she shouldn't even try for this job.

"My car's right over here," Spencer said. "I could get you some new pantyhose and drop you off at the interview."

Without a functioning vehicle of her own, Julia didn't have much choice. "Let's go."

With her good résumés salvaged and stashed in her briefcase, she fell into step beside Spencer. "How did you get involved with chasing that boy's dog?"

"It seemed like the right thing to do." He shrugged. "I was on my way to someplace else, and I realized that this was an incredible, beautiful day. Since it usually snows on Halloween in Denver, I figured this was a gift, and I ought to take a walk in the nearest park."

"So you're having a good day?"

"An excellent day. And you?"

"It could be better." This was turning into the day from hell. A busted car, late for work, a mistake on her résumé, tearing the knee out of her pantyhose. But Julia found herself grinning up at him. If there had been rain clouds overhead, meeting Spencer might have been her silver lining.

They came to the sidewalk on Ninth Avenue, and Spencer frowned.

"What's wrong?" she asked.

"I could have sworn I left the car here."

Alarmed, Julia asked, "You don't think it was stolen, do you?"

"More than likely I misplaced it."

Her eyes narrowed. Misplaced his car? "Does that happen often?"

He pointed to the north. "Let's try Tenth."

Julia glanced at her watch. Twenty-eight minutes until her appointment. "Maybe I should just postpone this meeting."

"I won't let you down," he promised. "I'll get you there on time."

His reassurance felt strangely comforting. "Why?" she asked. "Why should you care? I mean, apart from the fact that you're the kind of guy who helps a kid when he's lost his dog, why should you be worried about me?"

"I like you." He pointed. "There's the car."

It was a faded blue Volkswagen bug. Vintage would have been a kind description, and Julia was disposed to be kind. She liked Spencer, too.

He opened the passenger door for her, ran around to the driver's side, and slid behind the wheel. "Okay, Julia. Where do we get panty-hose?"

"There's a drugstore over on Ninth."

He negotiated the circuitous one-way streets with admirable speed and parked at the curb. "You've got to come with me to pick them out. I don't know about sizes or colors."

Inside the drugstore, she selected pantyhose. Spencer paid for them. Quickly, they were back in his car. There were nine minutes until her two o'clock appointment.

"Where's your meeting?" he asked.

She gave him the address.

He fired up the Volkswagen. "Go ahead and change, Julia. I won't look."

She bunched up her trench coat. In the narrow bucket seat, she wriggled free from her shredded pantyhose. This was nuts! She ought to be taking deep breaths, mentally preparing herself for an effective interview. She whipped out the tan pantyhose from their package and slipped them over her toe.

Spencer stopped for a red light, and she glanced up into his warm blue eyes. "You're looking!" she accused.

"I lied," he cheerfully admitted.

"You bum!"

"You've got great legs, Julia." He slammed the car into first gear and sped away from the light.

Trying to keep her skirt down, she pulled the waistband of the pantyhose up. There was no possible way to accomplish this feat without displaying the entire length of her legs.

"Stop watching, Spencer."

"I won't peek."

"Are you lying again?"

"Yes."

He parked in front of the four-story office building where she had her appointment. Julia checked her wristwatch. One minute and thirty seconds to go.

"Thank you very much, Spencer." She turned to him. Though she should have been annoyed by his blatant ogling, she felt gratified that he liked her legs, that he couldn't keep his eyes off her. "I hope we'll meet again. Someday."

He caught hold of her right shoulder and turned her toward him. His blue eyes riveted to hers, and she felt herself being drawn toward him—not totally against her will.

This was so unlike her. Julia wasn't the sort of woman who kissed men she'd known for less than an hour. She tried to be careful in her relationships, to build a foundation, to plan each step.

Her lips parted, inviting him, welcoming him.

His mouth pressed firmly against hers. This was not a tentative kiss. He was claiming her with a fierce, hard, arousing passion.

And she was ready to submit. Her willpower drained as an electric surge of pure, sensual, unadulterated excitement raced through her body. She was on fire. Instantaneously combustible.

And yet it was as if they had known each other for years, as if they had been lovers forever.

The sweep hand on her wristwatch ticked away the seconds, and she didn't care. Time was irrelevant.

Breathless, she broke away from him and sank back in the bucket seat. She could feel his gaze possessing her.

"I got you here on time," he said.

"The hell with this job interview." She turned and confronted him directly, eyeball to eyeball. "I'm going to start my own accounting firm with Karen."

"Good for you, Julia."

"Buchanan and Gallegos," she said. "My name first. It's alphabetical, after all."

He nodded. "Come with me tonight. To a Halloween party."

She thought of Karen, seducing her husband in a vampire costume. Could Julia possibly indulge herself in a similar fantasy? *No, certainly not. Not in any way.* It wouldn't be right to move so fast. She barely knew Spencer.

"Please," he said. "I have a two-person costume, and I need somebody to be the other half."

"What kind of two-person costume?" she asked suspiciously. "You're not inviting me to be the back end of a horse, are you?"

"I'd never ask you to hide inside a horse costume. That would be a waste of a beautiful and exciting woman."

Exciting, eh? "I'll go. What are we going to be?"

2

"Siamese twins?"

Julia stared at the tent-sized sweatshirt he stretched out on the back of his sofa. There were two neck holes at the top.

"Siamese twins," Spencer said. "We both get inside the sweatshirt and stick our heads out the holes and—"

"It'll never work. You're at least six inches taller than I am. We don't match."

"You could wear very high heels," he suggested.

Julia rolled her eyes. "I don't think so, Spencer."

She was, in fact, beginning to rethink her entire afternoon. She'd blown off her job interview and made the snap decision to start her own accounting business with Karen as a partner. Was that realistic? Even though she'd been considering that possibility, such drastic action had not seemed possible until this afternoon—not until right after Spencer kissed her.

And that was a great kiss, one that she would always remember. If she kept a diary, she would have written pages about that kiss. But it hadn't been logical or practical. And it wasn't like her. When had she forgotten her take-things-one-step-at-a-time philosophy of life?

When? It was the first moment she'd laid eyes on him. When she'd looked up from her résumé and seen this tall blond man running toward her, her life had been somehow transformed. Almost like magic.

No, not magic. Julia didn't believe in fairy tales and mystical charms.

The simple explanation was that Spencer had brought a new energy. He'd charged into her existence, throwing her careful plans into utter disarray. Really, she should have been upset. Really? Then why couldn't she stop smiling?

She glanced around the first floor living room of his rambling old brick house, which was not far from the governor's mansion. The furniture was heavy, big, and masculine. There was not a doily, a mirror, or a flower in sight. But the hardwood floors were swept clean. The only clutter was a stack of newspapers by the door and today's *Denver Post* spread out on the dining room table. "You have a cleaning person," she guessed.

"Once a week, whether or not I want her, my aunt Ginny comes over, tidies up, leaves me cookies, and tells me I really ought to be getting married so she won't have to do this anymore."

"There's an antiquated concept," Julia said. "Getting married so you'll have a housekeeper."

"Ginny's an old-fashioned lady."

Tentatively making herself at home, Julia sat in a rocking chair near the red brick fireplace. "Tell me about yourself, Spencer. What do you do for a living?"

He held up the extra-large sweatshirt. "I'm not a costume designer."

"I guessed that."

"I'm a history professor at Wellington Women's College. I was born in Glenwood Springs, and I've lived in Colorado for most of my life." He cocked his head to one side and stared with one of those intense blue-eyed gazes that cut through her defenses and touched her soul. "Is that respectable enough for you?"

"I wasn't questioning your intentions."

"Sure you were. And I don't blame you. We haven't been formally introduced. I didn't come to you with references. We just ran into each other in the park. Then I grabbed you. And I kissed you." He tossed aside the sweatshirt. "You don't strike me as the kind of woman who blows off an afternoon and comes home with a stranger."

"I don't? Why not?"

"The little navy blue suit. The white blouse. Trench coat."

"Well, you're right," she said. "I've never done anything like this before."

He sat on the sofa near her rocking chair and propped his feet on the wood coffee table. "If you're uncomfortable, I can take you home."

She didn't want to leave. She wasn't in the least tiny bit afraid of Spencer. But there was a wariness in the back of her mind, a sense of being off balance and out of control.

"I don't know, Spencer. You make me feel . . ." She searched for a word. "You make me feel spontaneous. And that's not natural for an accountant. I try to plan, to think ahead. I don't like surprises."

"Like being kissed when you don't expect it?"

"Oh no, I liked that," she admitted without hesitation. "I liked it a lot."

"Then it's decided. You'll stay." He squinted

at her. "I think you'll be good at being spontaneous. Wearing bright colors. Crimson. Purple and green. Maybe a miniskirt?"

"Don't hold your breath."

"But, Julia, you've got great legs."

Her gaze rested lightly on him. He really was a charming, handsome man with blond hair that begged to be tousled. His legs were long. His shoulders broad. He was as sexy as the day was long, and she didn't know how he could teach at a women's college without being propositioned ten times a day.

Without thinking of appearances, Julia ran her tongue across her lower lip. She remembered the taste of his mouth on hers and wished he would kiss her again.

"Are you hungry?" he asked.

She nodded. Sammy the Samoyed had eaten her lunch, and she hadn't had a bite since breakfast. Maybe lack of food accounted for the unusual sensations that tingled below the surface of her skin. "I'm starved."

His kitchen was another surprise. Instead of the typical bachelor microwave and a couple of pans, he had a well-equipped workspace with a butcher block island and gleaming copper-bottom pots hanging from an overhead rack.

"You like to cook," she deduced.

"I'm no James Beard, but I do okay. And you're in luck." He held a wicker basket toward her. "Help yourself."

What marvelous treats was he offering?

"Candy," she said with some disappointment. "Hershey's bars and Milky Ways?"

"Hey, it's Halloween."

Julia selected a miniature Hershey bar with almonds. Expecting him to be a gourmet chef was a little too much perfection to ask for in one man.

She despised cooking, probably because food preparation and cleanup had been her assigned chore from the time she was thirteen years old. Mom had expected dinner to be on the table when she came home from work at six, and Julia had learned how to whip up burgers and thaw frozen pizza in record time. Though her younger brother and sister were content with fast food, Julia could still hear the frustrated tone in her mother's voice. Burgers, again.

Spencer dug into the double-wide refrigerator and took out a glass bowl covered with foil. He turned to her. "How about chicken salad and a toasted bagel?"

"Great," she said enthusiastically.

Julia perched on a stool at the counter and watched as he tossed the mysterious ingredients. "What's in there?"

"Chicken breast, apple, dates, raisins. A little bit of chopped chutney. All I really need is mayonnaise."

Awestruck, Julia observed as he cracked an egg one-handed into the blender and added some spices. Powdered mustard and cayenne were among them. Then he slowly poured in a measured amount of oil. "Extra virgin olive oil," he said.

"Can I help?" she asked.

"It's easier if I do it myself."

He moved with admirable efficiency. Stirring and tossing and slicing and toasting. When he placed the plate in front of her, she was thoroughly enchanted.

The first bite was delicious. The second was

even better. Julia dabbed at her lips with a paper napkin. "Where did you learn how to do this?"

"Self-taught survival skills. As long as I've got to eat, it might as well taste good."

"It's more than that," she said. "I mean, I have to eat, too. But the closest I come to gourmet is picking up deli food."

All fed and feeling cozy, she followed him back into the front room.

"Now, let's try on this sweatshirt." He slipped into his side first and held out the arm for her. "Go underneath and wiggle in here."

"Okay, but it's not going to work. You're too tall."

As soon as she ducked under the sweatshirt material, Julia knew she was making a huge mistake. She tried to keep a distance between them, but there wasn't enough maneuvering room. Her fingers groped at his firm torso. She couldn't help rubbing against him. Her face pressed against his chest as she fumbled for the arm opposite his. She inhaled his warmth, an intoxicating scent.

Finally, her arm plunged through the sleeve. Her head emerged from the neck hole.

Spencer bent his knees to put his head at the same level. Inside the sweatshirt, he wrapped his arm around her. "There's a full-length mirror in the hallway upstairs. We should go take a look."

"Up the stairs?" Her voice sounded strangled. Being this close to him was having a devastating effect on her.

"We'll coordinate our walking," he said. "Ready? Left leg. Right. Left . . ."

On the stairs, she almost fell, and he caught her. Their lips were only inches apart. The glow from his eyes was fiery hot, and Julia felt herself melting.

He guided her the rest of the way until they stood in front of the mirror.

"I was right," Julia said. The lopsided sweatshirt looked ridiculous. "We'll never pass for twins."

"I like the difference," he said.

Still striving for nonchalance, she retorted, "You'd make a homely woman."

"Then it's a good thing that I'm a man." His arm, inside the sweatshirt, embraced her. When he turned to her, his other arm encircled her. They were wrapped together in a strange cocoon. "Julia, I want to make love to you."

Though she hadn't expected to hear him speak those words, the sound was particularly gratifying. His baritone voice was a gentle, persuasive caress.

Of course, she should refuse. A lifetime of sensible living taught her that a woman should never tumble into bed with a man she'd only just met. Yet she heard herself whisper, "Yes."

Tangled in the sweatshirt, they kissed. And there was a sense of rightness, almost of perfection.

Spencer fought free from the encumbering costume and led her to his bedroom. He tore back the covers. Most skillfully, he undressed her, covering her skin with light, teasing kisses.

Julia glided beneath the handmade quilt on his bed. A wanton spirit possessed her, and she craved his touch. Though she was usually a behind-closed-doors, in-the-dark undresser, she stared as he removed his shirt and Levi's. His body was magnificent—firm and strong with wide, masculine shoulders. She threw back the quilt and welcomed him to her.

They made love in the waning afternoon of Halloween. They were two strangers who had become suddenly intimate. Julia didn't know why this had happened, and she didn't want to question too deeply. Instead, she gave herself over to the exquisite pleasure of the moment.

Lying beside him, gradually returning to earth, she sighed.

"Wonderful," she murmured. Snuggling against his warm flesh, she was close in his arms. "This has been the most remarkable day. I don't know what came over me."

"I'd call it magic," he said.

"Can't be. I don't believe in magic."

"It exists. Magic exists. You could call it serendipity or coincidence, but there are moments in history that cannot be explained. The discovery of the Rosetta Stone, the Dead Sea Scrolls, finding gold in Colorado." He smiled at her, stroked the hair off her forehead. "Sometimes you find the best things in life when you aren't even looking for them."

"And you call that magic?"

"Why not?"

She had never felt so content. If he wanted to call this moment magic, Julia would accept that explanation.

She lay quietly for a moment, allowing her mind to begin functioning. "Spencer, do you think I'm doing the right thing?"

"Right this minute? Yes."

"Actually, I was talking about starting my own business with Karen. I mean, you don't know me very well, but . . ."

He cupped her breast. "I know you."

"But we don't have a history together. And you don't know if I do my job well or not. And you haven't even met Karen."

He nodded.

Somehow, his opinion was extremely important to her. She needed him to believe in her. "Do you think I can do it? Start my own business?"

He thought for a moment, then leaned over and kissed the tip of her nose. "I know one thing, Julia."

"What's that?"

"You'll never know if you can succeed unless you try."

That was exactly what she wanted to hear. She wrapped her arms around him and hugged tightly, wishing this day would never end.

Julia had no idea what the future might bring. She wasn't even sure she and Spencer would be compatible for more than a few hours. But she was willing to try.

As it turned out, Spencer was also willing. They dated through November and December, belatedly discovering that they were good friends as well as lovers.

They balanced each other nicely, she thought. He was spontaneous. She was prepared. And they'd each moved a little closer toward the center. Though Julia continued to wear conservative suits for work, she'd added color and a couple of miniskirts.

In January, they discussed living together and decided against it because Julia's new business was taking an inordinate amount of her time and energy.

Sometimes she felt she was neglecting him, but Spencer never complained. He was the most understanding of lovers, always supportive. Even when she felt overwhelmed and unable to meet the demands of her clients, Spencer believed in her.

The worst time for an accounting business was, of course, from the middle of March to the April 15 deadline for filing IRS income tax forms. Julia was totally preoccupied, her brain filled with myriad details, rules, and regulations. If she didn't plug every loophole, if she didn't catch every discrepancy, she'd be letting her clients down. Now, more than any other time in her life, she needed to prove her competence to the people who trusted her.

At a few moments before midnight on April 15, Spencer drove her to the all-night postal drop-off and stood beside her as she watched a clerk hand-cancel the last of the tax returns.

Julia collapsed in the passenger side of his Volkswagen. "It's done. I'm finished."

"Congratulations, darling. I'm proud of you."

Her eyelids drooped. The tension begin to ebb and exhaustion set in. There was a soft tickling at her ear, then down her chin and throat. She opened her eyes and found that Spencer had placed a single red rose in her lap.

It was a perfect gesture. Simple and sweet. She held the rosebud to her lips, feeling the velvet softness of the petals and inhaling the fragrance. "Thank you, Spencer."

"Now, I'm going to take you home with me," he said. "I'm going to tuck you under the covers and let you sleep until you're ready to wake up."

"That sounds like heaven." She was almost too

tired to smile. "And what are we having for breakfast?"

"You know, honey, sometimes I think the only reason you keep me around is because you like my cooking."

"That's not true. I *love* your cooking."

She closed her eyes again.

Julia wasn't sure how she got to his house and into his bed. She wasn't even aware of how much time had passed until she rolled over and saw sunlight creeping around the edges of the window shades. A glance at his bedside clock told her that it was eleven o'clock. In the morning?

She bolted upright, then remembered. Today she had the day off. No work. No phones. And no more deadline. This was pure luxury. She lay back on the sheet and closed her eyes.

A few minutes later, she heard the door to the bedroom open. Though Spencer moved quietly, every step was audible. The bedsprings creaked when he sat on the edge of the bed.

Gently, he adjusted the covers. He touched her cheek.

"My darling," he whispered, "I'll miss you so much. How the hell am I going to live without you?"

Her eyelids snapped open. "What?"

"You're awake?" He looked startled, like a kid with his hand caught in the cookie jar. "Well, great. I'll get the coffee."

She grasped his hand. "What did you mean just now when you said you'd miss me?" There was something in his eyes that frightened her. "Oh my God, you're breaking up with me."

"No, I'm—"

"I don't blame you." She swallowed hard, choking back the lump that suddenly formed in her throat. "I've been terrible for the past month. Always working, and nasty when I wasn't. But that's over. I can make up for lost time."

"There's nothing wrong with you, Julia."

"It's because I'm too staid and practical, isn't it? You're bored with me."

"Calm down." He stood and stepped away from the bed. "I'll bring you a cup of coffee, and we can discuss this like a couple of rational human beings."

"Discuss what?" she wailed.

But he was already out the door. Julia felt the temperature in the room drop by several degrees. She was cold inside. Cold and empty. While she'd been busy with her career, she'd ignored him. And now she would lose him.

When he returned with coffee, Spencer was direct. "Drink this and listen to me. Don't interrupt."

She bobbed her head. Her fingers, grasping the ceramic blue mug, were trembling.

"I didn't want to tell you about this when you were in the middle of your deadline," he explained. "You had enough to worry about, and it was my decision anyway. We didn't need to discuss it."

"Discuss what?"

"Quiet, Julia." He took a deep breath. "I had a job offer, a guest professorship at a college near San Diego. They want me to do an in-depth seminar on the history of the Old West."

"Have you accepted?"

"Yes. I'll be there for a semester."

"I'll miss you," she said. But she could man-

age a few months without him. It wouldn't be
fun, but she'd make it.

"There's more," he said. "This seminar is only
for the summer, but there's a strong possibility
that the college will offer me a full-time position.
I really can't refuse. The only way I can further
my career at Wellington is if the department
head retires, and she's only forty."

"You're moving to California? Forever?"

He took her hand. "I wanted to tell you before,
but there was never a good time."

"I guess I should congratulate you." But it
would be too damned insincere. Her heart was
breaking.

"Maybe," he said, "you could come with me."

"You know I can't leave," she said. "I have my
business here."

"You could start up again. In California."

"With no contacts? With a whole new set of
state tax laws to learn? And I can't desert
Karen." She shook her head. "No."

"Give it a chance, Julia. It might be magic."

"Magic? Hah!"

He raised her hand to his lips and lightly
kissed her fingertips. "You don't have to work.
I'll support you."

She snatched back her hand.

Sudden outrage crashed around her like an av-
alanche. *He'd support her? No way!* If there was
one thing she'd been taught as the eldest daughter of a struggling single mother, it was never to
trust a man when he said he'd support you. Such
promises were fickle.

A modern woman needed to make her own
way on her own terms. "At least you're not pro-

posing marriage," she said. "Thank goodness for that."

In her mind, wedded bliss was the ultimate fairy tale, the glitter that turned to dust when a man changed his mind about what constituted happily ever after. The only relationship she could tolerate was an equal partnership with respect on both sides. That was what she'd thought she had with Spencer. "I was so wrong about you."

"Come on, Julia. Don't make this more than it is. I'm making a career move. Just like you did when you decided to start your own business."

"It's not the same," she shouted. "I wasn't planning to move to Timbuktu."

"San Diego," he corrected. "There are airplanes that go back and forth."

"You want a long-distance relationship?" She could feel the anger and frustration building to the point of explosion. "Well, I can't do that. I can't go flitting back and forth across half the continent. It's too expensive. And I have a business to run."

"Hell, yes. Let's not forget the business. Come off it, Julia. You're only an accountant. It's not as if you're saving the world."

She jumped out of the bed and began looking for her clothes. A ridiculous black satin blouse with an embroidered Indian jacket.

"Julia, would you please calm down?"

"Why? Because I'm being hysterical?"

"Yes!"

She buttoned her blouse and pulled on her Levi's. Digging around under the edge of the bed, she tried to find her shoes. "How could you,

Spencer? You made up your mind. Without one
word of my input." Hurt and angry, she glared
at him. "I talked over every part of my business
with you. I shared everything."

"I wasn't keeping this a secret."

"Yes, you were. Take me home."

"Not until we work this out."

"Fine." She spied his car keys on the dresser
and grabbed them. "I'll take myself home."

Before she could change her mind, Julia flung
open the bedroom door and ran down the stairs.
She was blinded by tears. She probably shouldn't
be driving, but she couldn't stay here for one second longer. Behind the wheel of his Volkswagen,
she glanced back and saw Spencer standing on
the veranda. He held up her Reeboks. "You forgot your shoes."

"Keep them," she snapped. "As a souvenir of
our former relationship."

Their former love.

3

Last April was history, Julia thought. The
showdown between her and Spencer had
left their relationship as dead as Custer at Little
Big Horn. Spencer had flown to sandier pastures
in southern California, and she had continued to
achieve modest success with Buchanan and Gallegos, Accountants. It did no good whatsoever
to wish that things might be different.

But there were always possibilities, moments for spontaneous decision making. *Like buying those wild platform heels.*

Julia flicked the turn signal for the Honda and retraced her route, returning to the shabby little boutique on Colfax Avenue.

The parking spot was still there. She hopped out, locked the car door, and went around the corner to the secondhand store named Cagim's Bazaar. The shoes were waiting.

They were gloriously gaudy, easily putting the other pumps and sandals to shame. Her first impression had been correct; Spencer would have loved these flashy shoes. But her life wasn't about Spencer Kendall. Not anymore.

The important thing was that the iridescent green and blue shoes were perfect for the gown she'd just purchased at one of the more conservative secondhand shops. The floor-length skirt was a sophisticated black crepe, but the strapless bodice was made of peacock green and blue sequins—similar to these shoes.

Could she afford them? Julia swiftly calculated the remaining balance in her shopping budget. Forty-seven dollars.

Pushing open the door to the shop, Julia entered a bazaar of gaudy preworn finery. She approached the clerk, a pixielike creature with spiky purple hair who was tunelessly humming along with a commercial on the television mounted behind the antique cash register.

"Excuse me," Julia said. "The blue and green platform shoes in the window. What size are they?"

"Too big for me," the clerk said. Her saucer-sized blue eyes seemed older than the rest of her as she surveyed Julia from head to toe. "I've never seen you here before."

"I don't dress up often," Julia said. She didn't need to add that this wasn't the sort of place where she usually shopped. Her simple beige business suit and her plain, blunt-cut brown hair eloquently illustrated her conservative style.

"Why now?" the clerk asked.

Julia explained, "I'm going to a ball on Friday night."

"Like Cinderella."

"Possibly. But I'm not looking for Prince Charming to sweep me off my feet." She had decided to attend the gala Unsinkable Molly Brown Ball, sponsored by the Denver Historical Preservation Society, in order to make contacts with upscale business people and philanthropists who could use the services of Julia's fledgling accounting firm.

"For a ball," the clerk said, "you really ought to have glass slippers."

"I'll settle for the shoes in the window."

The clerk stuck out her hand. "I'm Wendy, like in *Peter Pan*."

At least she wasn't Tinker Bell. Julia completed the handshake. "I'm Julia. May I try on the shoes?"

"Sure thing."

Julia sat on a gold brocade chaise and waited while Wendy plucked the shoes from the window. On the TV above the cash register, the local five o'clock news commentators chatted about the start of the Denver Broncos football season.

When Wendy placed the shoes in Julia's hands, the blue and green shimmered like moonlight on the surface of a neon river. The ankle strap curled invitingly. With the platform, the heel was five inches high.

"Before you put them on," Wendy said, "I should tell you that those shoes are magic. Everything in here is magic."

"How so? If I rub the instep, will a jinni pop out and grant me three wishes?"

"You don't need three." The slender young woman, as ethereal as a purple-haired flame, rested her hand on Julia's shoulder. "There's only one thing you're wishing for."

"Wealth," Julia said definitively. She was, after all, an accountant. Dollars and cents were her life.

"Not money. Your wish is for love."

"I think not." She hadn't even dated since Spencer had gone to California. Why would she ever wish for anything as painful and as dangerous as . . .

"Love," Wendy whispered so softly that the word might have been a sigh.

Julia slipped her right foot into the shoe and fastened the delicate strap. Then the left foot. A perfect fit! When she stood, the platforms balanced comfortably. She felt as if she were walking on a cloud.

On the television, Julia heard a familiar baritone voice. ". . . history can be caught and held in the bricks of a building or the red stone of the Molly Brown House . . ."

She looked up and gasped. It was Spencer's image on the television screen. His piercing blue eyes seemed to gaze directly into hers. He was California tanned. His hair was streaked with sunlight. Though his smile was easy, there was a sense of authority in his manner as he spoke about the Unsinkable Molly Brown House and the gala ball given by the Historical Preservation Society. "Our goals in preserving important landmark buildings aren't frivolous," he said.

The television commentator questioned, "Some local officials have accused the preservation society of spending too much money on buildings. Wouldn't it be better to invest in people?"

"Absolutely," Spencer said. "In Denver, we've established a precedent of creatively using the restored buildings for shelters and special schools. A structure isn't really alive unless it's lived in."

The television screen flashed an image of the stone lions outside the Molly Brown House, and the newsperson continued, "But the debate continues. Should the city of Denver spend money on renovation? Or use your tax dollars for new construction?"

Julia blinked. Had she really seen Spencer on television?

The pixie-sized Wendy stood at her elbow. "Do you want the shoes?"

"I think so." Julia pulled her gaze away from the television screen. "Yes, I want the shoes. How much?"

"Exactly forty-seven dollars." She smiled wisely. "Good luck at the ball, Cinderella."

An hour later, Julia met Karen at a café on Seventeenth Avenue. They sat on the outdoor patio, sipping iced cappuccino and watching the last of the rush hour traffic, while Julia recounted her shopping travails.

Karen listened with rapt attention as Julia concluded, "Then I put on the shoes—"

"The magic shoes?"

"They're not magic," Julia said sternly. "No matter what that strange clerk said, there is no such thing as magic slippers. Life is not a fairy tale. And these are just shoes."

"Okay." Karen nodded, and her curly black hair bounced. "Then what happened?"

"They fit perfectly. The arch matches mine. And there's just enough room for my toes. No pinching whatsoever, but my foot doesn't slide around. It's like wearing a pillow, but with support. Know what I mean?"

"You bet I do." Karen's ebony eyes were dreamy. "I had a pair of shoes like that once. Low-heeled pumps in taupe."

They shared a moment of silent reverence in tribute to good shoes. Only another woman could understand, Julia thought. Let the men quest about in search of the Holy Grail. Most women would be satisfied to find a really great pair of shoes.

Julia pulled the bag out from under the table. "Want to see them?"

"Very much."

"Don't look until I've put them on. I want you to get the full effect."

She fastened the straps and stood. In the high platform heels, she was almost statuesque. Julia struck a pose. "What do you think?"

She never heard Karen's reply. Directly in Julia's line of vision, she saw the sun-streaked hair of a tall man leaving the café. At the corner of Seventeenth Avenue, he turned and she saw his profile. Though it was only a faraway glimpse, she recognized him instantly. "Spencer."

Without considering the consequences, Julia raced to the low railing circling the outdoor portion of the café, hiked up her skirt, and hoisted her leg over it. Was that really Spencer? Was she dreaming? She had to catch up with him and find out.

Charging along the sidewalk, she rounded the street corner. Though the shoes were comfortable, they were not designed for sprinting. Julia squatted down and undid the straps. Barefoot, she dashed to the parking lot behind the restaurant in time to see a white convertible pulling away from the opposite exit.

"Spencer," she called out. "Spencer, wait!"

But he didn't hear her. The car merged into traffic and he was gone.

Her hand rose, reaching toward him. Then she realized what she was doing and her outstretched fingers became a fist. This was so typical! The very sight of Spencer had transformed her from a responsible accountant into an impulsive fool. Here she was, standing in a parking lot—like an idiot—in her bare feet. She had vaulted the railing at the café. What had come over her?

Karen darted up beside her. "Julia, what are you doing? Are you crazy?"

"I saw Spencer Kendall."

"Where?" Karen's expression brightened. "I thought he was at that college in California."

"He was here. In the café." Julia's heart clattered like an adding machine toting up quarterly revenues. "He's in town for the Molly Brown Ball."

"The event you're going to? Oh, that's wonderful! Did he call you?"

"No, I saw him on the TV news." In the back of her mind, there was a click as she made a very bizarre connection. "Right after I put on the shoes for the first time, I looked up and saw him on the television screen."

"And now you put on the shoes, and there he was." Karen clapped her hands, delighted. "I love this, Julia. It's the best kind of magic."

"Just coincidence."

"That's hard to believe. Figure the odds. How long has it been since you've seen Spencer?"

"One hundred and thirty-one days."

"So now you see him twice in one day? I'd say that's two hundred and sixty-two to one."

"Honestly, Karen. You can't figure odds like that."

"Then call it fate," Karen crowed. "You and Spencer are destined to be together. You were so happy when you were with him. And confident, too. If it hadn't been for Spencer, I don't think you would have found the nerve to quit at Morton and start up the business with me. Face it, Julia, you were the perfect couple."

"A perfect couple doesn't break up."

So why had her entire body stung with anticipation when she saw him? Though she'd told herself a million times that their relationship was over, she couldn't get him out of her system. It was just a residual attraction, she told herself. Wanting to see him was like the irresistible urge to poke at a sore tooth with her tongue. "Let's drop this, Karen. I have no desire to be with Spencer."

"Is that why you hurdled the railing and raced over here?"

Feigning nonchalance, Julia strolled back to

where she'd discarded the shoes in the grass.
They sparkled festively in the late afternoon sunlight. The shoes were ready for a party. Or a
clandestine meeting. She hooked her thumbs
through the straps and picked them up.

Contacting Spencer again was the worst thing
Julia could do. But she couldn't help wanting it.

That evening, she paced the floor in her apartment, pausing occasionally to stare at the telephone. If he wanted to see her, he'd call. He had
her phone number.

Maybe she should take the initiative and call
him.

But how could she? Julia didn't know where
he was staying. He'd rented his house to another
professor who was in town for the summer.

She couldn't call him. She didn't have his
number.

Nervously, she paced up and down the floor.

But she could find him. All it would take was
contacting one or two of his friends or maybe his
Aunt Ginny. They'd tell her where to find him.
Or maybe she could telephone around to hotels
and ask if he had a reservation.

And then what? Humiliate herself by asking
to meet him? Or maybe she could hang around
in the lobby until she "accidentally" bumped
into him.

"No," she said out loud. "Think about something else."

The Unsinkable Molly Brown Ball. It was only
two days away, on Friday. Tomorrow she had
an appointment at Armando's to have her
straight brown hair trimmed and rinsed with

henna to bring out the auburn highlights. Then she'd be ready.

Julia laid out her new gown on the pastel bedspread. Beside it, she placed the shoes.

Magic shoes? If she put them on right now, would Spencer materialize at the foot of the bed?

Though Julia wanted to be cool and cynical, she felt a twinkle of hope, such as when seeing the first star at dusk. That purple-haired clerk in the secondhand store might have been a fairy godmother pixie. As Karen had pointed out, seeing Spencer twice when she put on the shoes was more than a coincidence. Was it destiny? Magic?

Julia said, "No. There is no such thing as magic."

To prove her point, Julia slipped into the shoes. She would go outside the apartment building and walk around the block. It was just an experiment. If she didn't see Spencer, she'd know that the other two incidents were nothing more than freak random occurrences.

Though she felt ridiculous wearing the fancy shoes with her shorts and tank top, she fastened the straps, grabbed her keys, and, before she could change her mind, left the apartment, carefully locking the dead bolt.

Halfway down the hallway to the elevator, she sensed rather than heard her telephone ringing. Oh my God! What if it was Spencer calling?

She darted back, pressed her ear to the door, and listened to the ringing. Her answering machine picked up. Damn! Julia fumbled in her pocket for her keys. Frantically, she unfastened the dead bolt and the regular lock.

She ripped open the door in time to hear the

beep signaling the end of a message.

Without even closing the door, she hit the play button on the recording machine.

It was Spencer's voice.

"Hi, Julia. I guess I don't have any right to call, but I'm in town and I was thinking about you. You know, I still have your Reeboks. Maybe we should get together so I can return them."

"Yes!" she exclaimed. "Yes, Spencer. When?"

"I'll try to reach you again tomorrow," he said on the tape. "Julia, I . . . I've missed you."

A loud beep concluded his message.

"I miss you, too." She glared at the answering machine. "Dammit, Spencer. Why didn't you tell me where you were staying? Why didn't you leave a number?"

It was so typical of his absentminded behavior. He could misplace his car and forget to pay the electric bill. He was always running out of gas; he never balanced his checkbook. "Oh, Spencer, why couldn't you have left a number?"

She stormed across her apartment and slammed the door. She could have called him tonight and talked to him and found out . . . what? That she still cared about him?

Julia flopped down on the sofa and propped her feet on the coffee table. The incandescent shoes twinkled enchantingly.

Tomorrow. He said he would try to reach her tomorrow. At work? At home? At the beauty salon?

Her eyes narrowed. Maybe he'd purposely avoided leaving a number. Maybe he was planning a surprise for her.

If that was the case, why would he call and alert her?

Second-guessing had never been her strong suit, and Julia didn't pretend to understand how Spencer's mind worked.

As far as she could figure, only one thing was certain. When she finally came face-to-face with Spencer, she would be wearing the shoes.

4

In the morning, around ten o'clock, Spencer stood outside Julia Buchanan's blond brick office building on the outskirts of upper downtown Denver. In his hand, he held her Reeboks. The white leather sneakers were looking ragged, far worse than the April 15 night when he'd gently unlaced them and stripped them from her feet so she could sleep. These shoes, his souvenir from Julia, had been through a lot.

The worst abuse had occurred one day when he'd gone straight to the beach after his last class and had accidentally taken her shoes in his gym bag instead of his own. He'd been angry. Angry at himself. Angry at Julia because she wasn't there in California to organize his clothes and make sure he took the right stuff.

He'd tried to tell himself that he was better off without her. California was beautiful; the women were incredible. But all he could think about was a stubborn accountant back in Denver. God, how he missed her!

That day on the beach, he'd dug a hole in the

sand and buried her shoes in an attempt to rid himself of her memory. After he'd driven all the way back to his lonely, sparsely furnished bachelor apartment, he'd decided that it was childish to trash her shoes. He'd gone back to the beach and spent half the night probing the sands with a spade until he found them.

It had been a lot of work for a pair of sneakers. He probably ought to have them bronzed as a permanent memorial to the only woman who had ever branded her name indelibly on his soul: Julia Buchanan, the most hard-hearted, practical female on earth.

And now he was only a few strides and an elevator ride away from her. He hesitated. There was always the possibility that she still hadn't forgiven him. What if he returned her shoes, and she thanked him and said a cold, final good-bye?

Unwilling to take that risk, Spencer stashed the shoes back in his white convertible rental car. He wasn't ready to part with them yet. As long as he had the shoes, there was a reason to see her.

But he needed something else to entice Julia, something magical, something intriguing, something she couldn't resist.

Julia sat at her desk making the world's longest chain of paper clips. Though she had a stack of paperwork and would be taking off at noon to have her hair done, she couldn't concentrate.

When Karen popped over to her desk, Julia picked up her pencil and tapped the eraser, trying to give the appearance of someone who was, at least, mentally present in the office.

"I'm leaving now," Karen said. "I have to

drop off these payroll records, but I'll be back in less than an hour. In plenty of time to cover while you go to your hair appointment."

"Okay."

Karen touched her arm. "Worried about Spencer?"

"Not at all," she lied. "I'm over him."

With a forced smile, she watched Karen leave. *Over him?* Not by a long shot. After his phone message last night, Julia hadn't been able to sleep. Nor could she eat. Her stomach churned like a hamster on a wheel. When she saw Spencer again, what would she say? What would she do?

She'd been up since dawn, pawing through her wardrobe, which was something like taking a trip down memory lane. The front and center clothes were her neat business suits. To the rear was a conservative array of sweaters, slacks, blouses, and skirts. None of them seemed right.

She ventured into her second bedroom and yanked open the closet door. A riot of color and style flashed before her eyes. There were miniskirts and maxiskirts and a floor-length fake fur. Many of these, Julia realized, were clothes she'd bought long before she met Spencer. Maybe that was why he'd been able to transform her so easily.

All along, hiding inside her conservative suits and blouses, was a wilder, zanier Julia Buchanan. A woman who had flourished when Spencer took the time to nurture her.

But what should she wear today? What was appropriate attire for meeting an ex-lover? She pulled out a bright yellow sleeveless sundress with a flirty handkerchief hem. Very sexy. If she wore this, she'd be making the statement, "Look what you've been missing."

She had stuck the dress back in the closet. Julia was not nearly so self-assured.

In her meeting with Spencer, there was the whole issue of who should apologize. If she was giving the apology, she ought to drape herself in sackcloth and ashes. If she was on the receiving end, she should wear something regal, a Queen Victoria, we-are-not-amused outfit.

After much agonizing, she opted for her usual—a gray linen suit, a white silk blouse, and matching pumps. She had, however, brought the wild platform shoes, tucked into a canvas satchel beside her desk. Now she glanced at the bag, and a voice in the back of her head told her, *Put them on. Why not?* She was alone in the office. Nobody would have to know that she was crazy enough to believe in magic slippers.

As soon as she'd fastened the straps on the sparkly shoes, she heard the door to her office open. "Spencer?"

But no one was there.

"Hello?" Julia heard a skittering noise on the carpet and looked down at her feet. A puppy?

"Oh, sweetheart, what are you doing here?" It was a little basset hound with the longest ears and the saddest eyes she'd ever seen. "You're so droopy."

She picked up the puppy and held him on her lap. "How did you get into this building?"

A low male voice said, "He's with me."

She looked up and saw Spencer.

He was even more handsome than she'd remembered. She'd always liked the fit of that navy blue blazer and the way his Levi's stretched

snugly across his thighs. His blue eyes shone
with a penetrating glow. If a heart could really
have cockles, hers would be warm.

"So, Spencer, is this another runaway dog?"

"He's mine. I just bought him." He sat in the
chair opposite her desk. "I call him Icebreaker."

The puppy squirmed on her lap, and Julia
scratched behind his velvety, dangling ears. He
gave a long, low, ecstatic sounding moan. "Spencer, I hope you're not telling me that you bought
this animal just to make an entrance."

"I would never tell you that."

But it was exactly what he had done.

She frowned. He hadn't changed a bit. He was
still acting first and thinking later. Being spontaneous, no matter who or what got hurt.

"It's good to see you," he said.

"You, too."

"Were your eyes always so green?" he asked.

"Muddy brown." she corrected. "That's what
my mother always said. Muddy brown eyes with
a hint of algae at the edges."

"Your eyes are beautiful, Julia."

And her mouth was dry. Though she was trying to stay cool, she'd been four months without
him, and her emotions were on overload. His
nearness made her dizzy. With excitement? With
regret?

She wanted to make him understand about the
past, to know that he couldn't romp through life
without considering the consequences. And she
wanted to chastise him about buying a dog on a
whim. But her mind was as blank as her computer screen before she booted up.

The dog was wiggling, and she set him down
next to her fancy shoes. Instead of a deep pro-

nouncement about their relationship or lack thereof, she said, "If your puppy has an accident in here, I'll kill you."

"The guy at the pet shop told me the dog has been fully trained. Maybe that's why he looks so sad."

"You are aware that this is a business, aren't you? We generally don't cater to furry, four-legged mammals."

"Oh, I wouldn't forget that you have a career." His voice was sharp. "I remember your business. But I was going to suggest that we take a walk with Icy the basset. Even an entrepreneur like you is entitled to an occasional break."

"I'd really like to," she said, "but I—"

"Please don't tell me you have too much work to do."

Their old argument was about to resurface, and a bullheaded stubbornness rose within her. She bit her tongue to keep from snapping a response. Calmly, she said, "It's not work that I'm worried about. I have an appointment at Armando's beauty salon."

"Getting ready for a special occasion?"

"You know I am." It was annoying to be so predictable. "I would never pay Armando's prices for an everyday haircut. I haven't changed, Spencer."

"I never wanted you to."

She had missed him so desperately. With his tousled blond hair and steady grin, he looked like a mischievous boy. But his six-foot, two-inch frame was definitely the body of a full grown, very virile man.

"Sorry, Spencer. I can't play hooky from the

hairdresser. It's murder to get an appointment."
Still, she needed to make a concession, to show
him that she was willing to talk, maybe to work
things out. "Let's get together tonight."

"I don't want to wait, Julia."

"Now, Spencer, you know that deferred grat-
ification, which is the sign of an adult, is always
sweeter."

"And marinated flank steak is more tender,
but I still don't want to wait until tonight."

The office door swung open and Karen
stepped inside. With a whoop, she leapt into
Spencer's arms and gave him a huge, friendly
embrace. "It's great to see you! Spencer, you're
so tan you look like a beach bum."

He hugged her back and spun her around.

Julia would have been jealous of their easy camaraderie if she hadn't been panicked about being caught by Karen wearing the magic shoes.
The last thing she needed was Karen and Spencer together, yakking about enchanted slippers.
Under her desk, Julia hurriedly unfastened the
straps. After slipping into her white pumps, she
came around her desk.

"I'm so glad you came back to Denver," Karen
said to Spencer. "Julia has been miserable without you."

"I have not," Julia protested.

"Of course, she'd never admit—"

"Stop it," Julia said. "I hate when you talk
about me as if I'm not in the room."

"You're right." Karen beamed at both of them.
"Why don't you two take off? I'm sure you have
a lot to catch up on."

"I have to go to my hair appointment."

"Well, of course you do. But Spencer can escort you out the door." Karen glanced down and noticed Icy. "What's this?"

"Spencer's new friend," Julia said, waiting for the explosion. For the past several months, Karen had been waging an ongoing battle with her kids about getting a dog.

"Cute," she said tersely.

"Maybe you'd like to take him home to visit your family," Julia suggested.

"I wouldn't deprive Spencer of his little buddy." She went to her desk, sat behind it, and gave Julia a broad wink. "Good luck."

Good grief! What was she expecting? Karen probably would have been thrilled if Julia had thrown Spencer across a desk top and molested him right there. If anybody else had waltzed through the door with a dog, Karen would have ripped his face off.

Spencer tucked the puppy under his arm, bade Karen farewell, and held the door for Julia.

She headed down the corridor to the elevators and punched the down button.

Standing beside Spencer, with nothing separating them but thin air, she was tense. This was worse than talking to a total stranger, worse than facing the principal in grade school. She should have rehearsed, memorized a couple of succinct comments. It seemed as if volumes of words were stuck in her throat, and the pressure was building.

Her only consolation was that Spencer seemed equally ill at ease. "If I can't spend the day with you," he said, "I'll see you tonight. I'm staying at the Brown Palace."

"I wondered if you'd stay there."

"Yeah. I love the Brown. Do you remember—"

"Yes, I do." Of course she remembered. That night had begun with a carriage ride through downtown, segued into a candlelit dinner, and ended with roses at the Brown. It should have been the most perfectly romantic night of her life, but Spencer had forgotten to make reservations, and the hotel was full.

The elevator came and they boarded.

"When I was out in California," he said, "I missed you."

That was hard to believe. "With all those blond beach girls? Those carefree, spontaneous, bikini-wearing women?"

"They have no substance. They're like air and light. You're solid and real. I know I used to tease you about being too responsible, but substance needs weight."

"Are you saying I'm fat?"

"What I'm saying," he said, "is that you pay attention and you respond. Granted, you disagree with every other word, but—"

"I do not."

He smiled. "That proves my point."

"No, it doesn't."

"Proved again," he said.

"You always have to be right, don't you?"

The elevator doors opened on the ground floor, and they walked out together.

On the street, Spencer clipped a leash onto Icy's collar and put him down on the sidewalk. "Listen, Julia, I'm not always right. And I'm willing to admit when I've made a mistake."

"April sixteenth." She hadn't meant to bring up that painful topic, but there it was. The words had jumped out of her mouth. "I don't want to argue, Spencer, but we need to clear the air. I want to know your plans."

"For today? For next week?"

"For forever," she said.

"You're not going to let go of this, are you? You're so stubborn."

"You're so impossible to pin down."

"How about this, Julia. For today, one day only, let yourself relax. Bend a little. Let's just have fun."

"Spontaneous fun?"

"Right."

The old outrage built up inside her. Fun, fun, fun. It was so easy to say, easy as presto, easy as abracadabra. But, dammit, she didn't want to be angry.

A realization was growing inside her. She wanted him back. No matter what the cost, she wanted her old relationship with Spencer. But how was that going to happen? *The shoes. She needed to put on the shoes.* "Maybe you're right. Maybe we shouldn't talk about this now."

"I'm willing to forgive and forget," he offered. "Without apologies. Give me a chance, Julia."

"We'll have time, won't we? Your guest professorship should be over soon. And you'll be back here." Looking up at him, her irritation dissolved. His azure eyes seemed to reflect the Colorado sky, and she thought he was the most perfect man in the world. "Oh, Spencer. We can work this out. When are you going to move back to Denver for good?"

His gaze slipped away from her face.

"Spencer? When?"

"I don't want to spring this on you. I know you need time for discussion and—"

"What is it?"

"The college in California offered me a permanent position."

She was stunned. He was leaving her again. Why had he even bothered to return to Denver? "Then there's no chance for us."

"I haven't accepted their offer." Icy tugged at the leash, and Spencer picked up the puppy again. "I wanted to talk to you about it. The way I should have talked to you about the guest professorship."

"Turn it down," she said.

"It's a very lucrative offer. And prestigious. I have to consider it."

Through tight lips, she said, "We'll talk."

"Good. I'll see you tonight."

As she watched him leave, strolling along the sidewalk with Icy on a leash, everything seemed to move in slow motion. Her hopes for the future wavered. How could he be thinking about leaving when she wanted him so badly to stay?

Even though he was open to discussion, she didn't trust him to make the right decision, the decision to stay in Denver with her, unless he had a compelling reason. And that meant she needed to convince him.

To seduce him?

A plan of action began to form in her mind. She would entice him, enchant him. She'd weave a web so tightly around him that he would never want to be apart from her.

Fortunately, she was on her way to Armando's, and Julia figured she'd need more than a trim and a blow-dry to convince Spencer that his place was in Denver. The only place he needed to be was with her.

At Armando's, Julia sat in the barber's chair, regarding her plain, bland reflection in the mirror. She said, "I want the whole makeover, including a manicure and a facial."

Armando nodded. "We'll work you in. And the hair?"

"Curly and red. More red than the auburn henna."

"Body perm?"

"You bet."

"You'll look spectacular," he predicted. "You won't believe it, Julia. It'll be like magic."

She groaned. "Please don't say that word."

Halfway through the process, she was beginning to regret her decision, especially when the facial muck was applied. Particular attention was paid to the tired circles under her eyes with two cucumber slices and a wrap to hold them in place. She was led blindly to a a seat beneath a diffusing drier that would sink the conditioning potion into the fibers of her hair. What torture! What price beauty?

She was seated in a corner of the salon, out of view, she hoped, of passing humanity. The slight whir of soft air shut out other sounds.

Her face tingled under the mask. The technician had explained that she was opening the pores and cleansing them, which made Julia think of a million tiny holes being sluiced by astringent. She really couldn't stand much more pampering.

When someone lifted the drier from her head, she jumped. "Am I done already?"

"Hush," came a whisper. "Don't talk."

She felt a hand grasping hers. The touch was familiar and gentle. "Spencer?"

There was the slight pressure of his lips against hers, touching the only place on her face that was not covered in greenish gook. For the moment she was held in thrall, trembling. Was she dreaming? Blindly, she groped for him, catching nothing but an empty handful of air.

Julia tore at the wrap that held the cucumber slices in place over her eyes. The goopy facial mask slathered her fingers. When she finally removed the blindfold, she was sitting alone.

On her lap was a note. Squinting through the facial goo, she read, "I'll pick you up here in an hour. Spencer."

And this was his idea of discussion?

She glanced down at her lap and saw that he'd also left a single red rose. At one time, she would have considered this a sweet, caring gesture.

Now she suspected manipulation. He was trying to throw her off guard, to make her see things from his point of view.

She twirled the long stem between her fingers. Two could play at that game.

5

This time, Julia would take a clear direction on the path that seemed to lead toward inevitable intimacy with Spencer. This time, she wouldn't wander blindly, convinced by him to be spontaneous. She would chart a course, doing what she did best: making plans.

The first step was seduction. Only after she had convinced him that she was the perfect woman for him would she proceed to step two: talk him into staying in Denver.

There was probably a simpler way. Julia was quite sure that if she sat down with him and reviewed the relative costs and finances, she could show him that living in Denver at a lower salary was still more responsible than California dreaming. But Spencer had never been susceptible to logic.

Armando had just finished with her hair when Julia caught a glimpse of Spencer in the beauty shop mirrors. He sat in the waiting area and picked up a magazine. He was so innocent, she thought, so unsuspecting. That wouldn't stop her from coming after him with both barrels loaded.

"Voilà!" said Armando. "I am *finis!*"

"I like it," Julia said, touching the springy new curls that bounced around her head. A very new look for her. "What do you call this color?"

"Tawny. Not too red. Not too brown." He pinched her cheek. "Should I have someone do your makeup?"

"Just a little bit of eyeliner, mascara, and blush. After that facial, I don't want to put anything else on my pores."

"A wise decision." He snapped his fingers, summoning a young woman with a pallette of colors that reminded Julia of a face-painting kit.

In minutes, she was finished, with a subtle shading that made Julia's eyes look huge and liquid.

She retired to the back room to take off her pink smock. Underneath she was clad in the outfit she'd planned to wear home after her beauty appointment—jean shorts and a tank top. Too casual?

She sat on the bench in the changing room and dug into her canvas satchel. The shoes lurked in the shadow of the bag, glimmering, enticing. Did she dare to go out in public wearing jean shorts and gaudy platform heels?

Staring at her reflection in the mirror, she tossed her reddish curls. "If this doesn't seduce him, nothing will."

Determinedly, Julia fastened the blue and green platforms onto her feet. Then, she stood. In the heels, wearing shorts, her legs looked about two miles long. She prayed she wouldn't run into any of her clients on the street.

"Here goes."

Her hips were swinging to a natural rhythm when she sashayed out of the changing room into the beauty parlor. She paid her astronomical bill and marched right up to Spencer, who was still reading the magazine.

"I'm ready," she said.

He glanced up. "Julia?"

"What do you think?"

"I'm astonished and amazed. But in a good way." His gaze went to the shoes. "Those are incredible."

Giddy with the sensation she was creating, Julia said, "They're magic."

"How so?"

"I'm not sure yet, but there's something magic about them. The pixie in the boutique promised—"

"The pixie?"

"A little purple-haired thing who advised me to wear glass slippers to a ball. The way I figure, she must have been from another world."

"Must have been."

He rose to his feet, and she took his arm. Julia had never felt so fanciful and carefree. A freshness swept through her, like a clean breeze from the mountains, but she didn't lose sight of her purpose. "What we're going to do this afternoon is to find something I can wear with these shoes. Then we're going dancing."

"Dancing?" Spencer questioned. "I haven't been dancing since the death of disco. Are you sure about this?"

"What's the matter? No sense of adventure? No spontaneity?"

He drew himself up. "If it's dancing you want, then it's dancing you'll have."

Spencer had never seen Julia like this. As they stepped out into the afternoon sunshine and headed toward lower downtown, known as LoDo, he watched her surreptitiously from the corners of his eyes. Her newly styled hair was a flattering shade of red. Instead of her usual neat bob, a mass of lively curls shimmered in the late summer breeze. And she wore those crazy shoes—magic slippers—with her jeans shorts and a snug turquoise T-shirt with a pod of humpback whales swimming across her breasts.

He was a little disconcerted, but he would never admit it to her.

A street vendor on the Sixteenth Street Mall waved to her. "Hey, lady! Earrings to match your shirt."

She bought them. Whales and stars and a dangling moon jangled against her newly red hair. She looked funky and wild and sexy. Talking and laughing, she generously displayed the sense of fun that he'd only glimpsed before.

She was enchanting.

Their first stop was a lingerie boutique where Julia took great delight in showing him the skimpy teddies and silky black panties, firing his imagination and encouraging what was rapidly becoming a permanent state of arousal.

In the underwear shop, Spencer felt distinctly out of place. Men weren't supposed to be in these places. Men weren't even supposed to see this kind of stuff, except in the privacy of a bedroom. "Can we go?" he suggested.

"I need to buy black hose," she said.

He tried not to show too much interest in the feminine frills, but everywhere he looked there was another vision of mind-numbing sensuality. While staring at the fishnet panty hose, he backed into a mannequin wearing a lacy robe.

"Excuse me," he said to the plastic figure.

"Spencer?" Julia dangled a black garter belt from her manicured fingertips. "What do you think?"

"Just get it, and let's leave."

She stretched the lacy garment and stared at it thoughtfully. "I've never worn one before. Always had panty hose. You remember, don't you? The first day we met."

"The panty hose," he said. He would never forget that Halloween when they'd chased the dog, bought the panty-hose, and made love in the afternoon.

She snapped the garter belt. "Do you think it will be comfortable?"

"How would I know?" He threw up his hands. "Julia, I'll wait for you on the street."

"I'm almost done." She held out the garter belt toward him. Her eyes taunted him. "Feel the lace. Do you think it would itch?"

"I'm not touching that thing, okay?" Too easily he imagined the black lace stretched above the swell of her lily white buttocks. "Just get it."

She purchased the garter belt and two pairs of black silk hose.

They were back on the street, heading toward Larimer Square, when Julia reverted to her usual personality. "I can't believe I spent so much on undergarments. A totally impractical investment. I mean, nobody sees it."

"I might," he said, hopefully.

"Judging from past history," she said with a smug female grin, "you aren't the kind of guy who pays much attention to undies."

"Not your undies," he volleyed back. "It's tough to get real excited about white cotton."

"Oh? And whose lingerie excites you?"

"Remember Rita Hayworth? That woman could really fill out a slip."

"A movie star can afford to pay a fortune. I

can't." She came to an abrupt halt. "Maybe I should return this stuff."

"No," Spencer said decisively. Not only was he unwilling to return to the lingerie shop, but he also wanted her to accept the magic of her transformation. "Did buying that garter belt make you happy?"

"Happiness can't be bought," she said. "Believe me. In my own small way, I've tried."

"Have you?"

"When I was growing up, I was miserable about the cheap, unfashionable clothes my mother bought for me. The first thing I did when I had a regular paycheck was to spend every penny."

"And that didn't make you happy?"

"Made me crazy," she said. "Then I discovered secondhand stores. I hardly ever shop anywhere else."

"I didn't know that about you. All those business suits?"

"They're classic designer labels. Some other fool paid full price for them." She considered her shopping forays to be treasure hunts, digging among racks of cast offs for the one perfect outfit. It wasn't the price that made her feel good. Her pleasure came from finding exactly the right outfit or accessory. Like her magical shoes.

"Today," Spencer said, "let me be the fool."

"Your wish is granted. Spencer, you're a fool." She started walking again, taking long strides in her platform shoes. "Now what does that mean?"

"Let me buy you something new. I'm paying. And you're not allowed to check the price tag."

"I couldn't," she immediately objected. "I'm

just looking for a dancing dress that I'll probably wear only a couple of times. It's irresponsible to pay full price."

"My treat," he repeated firmly. "Whatever you want. Be spontaneous."

"Adventurous?"

"Magical and wild." He laid down the challenge. "Can you do that?"

"Watch me."

She steered him toward a shop called Bromley's. Julia had often admired the displays in its windows, but she'd never ventured inside. As she swept across the hardwood floor, her heels made a syncopated *clunkity-clunk*. This was fun! She was shopping for retail and looking as flashy as the taillights on a new model Jag.

The clerk, a cool blonde, approached her warily. "May I help you?"

"Yes, you can." Julia tipped her sunglasses down on the end of her nose. Never in her life had she felt less like an accountant. "I need a dress to wear to a dance tonight."

The problem was that in this mid-season, near the end of August, the summery clothes were gone. All the colors were muted and autumnal. The fabrics were heavy.

"I'm sorry," the clerk said, "but we're already into fall."

"Look in the back," Spencer suggested. "Maybe there's something that's not on display."

"Well, we don't have a lot of storage. And we've already had our clearances." She eyed Julia curiously. "Don't I know you from somewhere?"

"Probably not," Julia said. She kicked her leg up, resting her flashy shoe on the edge of a display platform. "The dress needs to match these."

"You're famous, aren't you?" said the clerk.

"That's right. I'm Rita Hayworth."

Spencer rolled his eyes and groaned.

The clerk gasped. "Oh, Miss Hayworth, I'm so sorry, but we don't have anything except fall clothes."

"It's okay." Julia patted her cheek. "Maybe another time."

They repeated this performance—without the Rita Hayworth reference—at two other snooty boutiques before Julia had a clear idea of what they should do. "Let's get your white convertible rental car. I know exactly where we should go."

Spencer followed her directions until they pulled up outside the tawdry secondhand shop on Colfax where Julia had found the shoes. He parked. "Here? You want to shop here?"

"Now, Spencer," she said, "don't be a snob. I know it looks seedy, but—"

"It's great." His lips spread wide in a grin as he read the sign above the door. "Cagim's Bazaar?"

"Maybe a little flamboyant," she said.

"Cagim is magic spelled backward." He came around to her door and opened it. "I like it."

The petite purple-haired clerk looked away from her MTV television show when they entered. Her small mouth pursed in a bow and her wise eyes shuttered like a camera when she regarded Julia, then Spencer, then Julia again.

Julia introduced them. "Wendy, this is Spencer."

"Hi."

"You were right," Julia said. "When you talked about my wishes, you knew what I was looking for."

"I'm always right. It's really kind of a drag." She pointed toward the gold brocade chaise. "Wait there. I've got some really great outfits for you. They're in the back."

"Something to wear tonight," Julia called after her. "Not fall clothes."

Confused, Wendy squinted toward the window. "It's not autumn, is it?"

"Not yet," Julia said.

"Oh, good. I thought I'd missed a season." She disappeared behind a beaded curtain.

Spencer sat beside Julia on the chaise. His bedazzled gaze drifted around the room. The racks and shelves were packed with a rainbow of colors and flashing sparkles. The air seemed to glow with a rose-colored light. He had a sense of rightness about being here, a sense of homecoming . . . not that his childhood home in Glenwood Canyon near Aspen had ever been like this, like a wizard's cave full of tricks and artifice and magic.

In the Kendall family, everyone worked hard and steadily, almost in a plodding fashion, toward sensible goals. Spencer and his brother were fourth generation Colorado natives, which was one of the reasons why moving to California had seemed so exciting.

"You have a dreamy look," Julia said. "What are you thinking?"

"This place reminds me of home. Or maybe I should say it reminds me of what I wanted home to be. In the mountains, there's a lot of time for dreaming."

"Did you ever think you'd grow up to be a professor?"

"My father did. He predicted I'd be the head of a department by the time I was forty. Which gives me only eight years."

"And is that what you want?"

"Sometimes."

Wendy emerged from the back room, carrying a silvery dress. "Here's something I conjured up. I'm not sure it's right, but try it."

Julia slipped behind a Chinese screen to change, quickly shed her shorts and T-shirt, and cinched herself into the silver dress, which was cut low in front, low in back, and high on the thigh. There was a futuristic look to the dress. But mainly it was revealing, as blatant as gift wrapping her naked body and saying: *Take me!*

She stuck out her tongue at her reflection in the old-fashioned full-length mirror. *Talk about trying to be something you're not!* She'd never aspired to be a sexpot, never sunk so low as to use her body to gain her desires. Even if her plan was to seduce Spencer so he wouldn't go to California, overbearing sexuality wasn't her style.

Stepping out from behind the screen, she held her arms wide. "This isn't it," she said. "It's not me."

"Not unless you've transformed into a cross between the Happy Hooker and Judy Jetson," Spencer commented.

The music blaring from MTV was an oldies video. The song was "Pretty Woman."

Julia glanced over at Wendy, who merely shrugged. "Try walking around in it."

Julia hobbled. Her wide strides were hampered by the tight skirt. Though her shoes were still comfortable, the silver dress pulled in all the wrong places. "The only thing this dress is good for," Julia said, "is jumping out of a birthday cake at a Shriners convention."

Wendy had a second offering. This outfit was complex and required help to assemble.

"It's kind of retro," said the pixie as she buttoned the lacy white sleeves that fit tight at the wrist. "Personally, I love the look. But it might not be for you."

"Why not?"

"You have to make your own magic. Clothes and makeovers can only do so much."

"And what does that mean?"

"What do you want to look like? Who do you want to be?"

"Myself."

Julia slid her arms into a blue velvet bolero vest, covered in squiggly sequins. The skirt was made of cloth daisies, stitched together, very short. A matching straw hat had a huge daisy in the middle. Wendy completed the outfit by draping half a dozen chains and beaded necklaces around Julia's throat.

This time, her reflection in the mirror was cute. Too cute. It was hard to imagine having an adult conversation in this outfit. Julia felt as if she ought to be chewing gum and ditching classes in high school.

This time, the MTV music was Madonna singing "Material Girl."

As she strutted out from behind the screen, Spencer grinned. "They're playing your song, Julia."

"I'm practical, not material." She held on to her hat and swirled in a circle. "And I'm definitely not a girl."

"Then that outfit isn't for you."

"Right."

Behind the screen, the purple-haired Wendy was waiting. As she helped Julia out of the clothes, she asked, "Have you told him?"

"Told him what?"

"How you feel about him. You've got to tell him that you love him."

"Just like that, huh? And what if he doesn't love me back?"

Love was so complicated. And so risky. Confessing to love was like placing your whole being in the hands of another person, who then had the power to crush and destroy all your hopes and dreams.

"You've got to do it."

"But I'm scared. These emotions are so non-specific." Julia longed for a mathematical formula to explain being in love. "How does anybody know for certain if they're really in love?"

"Trust."

"In what?"

"Yourself. And the other person."

That seemed reasonable. "But doesn't love mean that you'd do anything for the other person, that you'd sacrifice anything?"

"Sometimes," said the clerk.

So if she really loved Spencer, she'd give up her job and move to California with him. Then, Julia knew, she'd resent every moment. She'd live in fear of the time when he was tired of her and wanted to end their commitment.

But wasn't that similar to what she wanted him to do? Give up California and stay with her?

Wendy helped her slide into a simple dress

that had no buttons or snaps or zippers or hooks. Very simple. A cotton knit in deep forest green. Sleeveless with a scoop neck, the dress's clingy material fell from her shoulders to mid-calf, outlining every curve. The outfit was completed by a long scarf in iridescent greens and blues that flowed gracefully to her thighs. Matching gold bracelets encircled her arms above the elbow.

"This is the one," she said. Her eyes in the mirror looked deep green and mysterious. Her hair was a bright crown. She was beautiful, womanly, confident. And somehow powerful. Could love be empowering?

She emerged from behind the screen. The music was "Imagine." And Spencer's expression was everything she'd ever hoped for.

When he pulled her into his arms, she glided. "Let's see how it dances," he said.

The song played again and again. In his arms, transported to a perfect world, she danced. The word love, though unspoken, echoed in every beat.

"We'll take it," Spencer said. "The whole outfit, exactly the way it is."

"Cool," Wendy said. "I'll have to total it up."

"Cost doesn't matter. The sky's the limit."

"The sky?" She glanced heavenward, as if calculating cost from the phases of the moon. "Well then, this might be expensive, and before you pull out your gold card, I have something for you, Spencer."

"Not for me." Spencer backpedaled at ninety miles per hour. "I like your store a lot, but I'm not a fancy dresser. I can barely keep track of my neckties."

She went straight to a rack of men's clothing

and plucked out a tan corduroy jacket with leather patches at the elbow. "Here you go. Just the outfit for a writer."

"A writer?" Julia questioned. "Spencer, is there something you'd like to tell me?"

6

"**A** writer?" Spencer said. "Not really."

But he had that evasive look in his eye. Julia turned to Wendy. "Is he a writer or not?"

"Looks like one," she said vaguely.

"I'm a history professor." He tossed the corduroy sports coat on the countertop. "I'll take it."

"Ah ha!" Julia pounced. "You bought the writer's jacket."

"Okay, I've been thinking about writing a book. There are some moments in teaching that are extremely satisfying, especially at the advanced level, but I miss doing research. It's fun to dig around in the past, discovering those nuggets of magic. While I was out in California, it occurred to me that my research could translate into a book."

"On the history of the American West?"

"That's a big canvas," he said. "The geography itself is fascinating. Then there are all the people of the Old West. The cavalry and Indians. Ranchers and settlers. Traders, trappers, shopkeepers, saloon owners."

"Gypsies and healers," Wendy added.

"That's a pretty comprehensive listing," Julia said.

"Barely scratches the surface."

Though he'd talked to her before about his interest in the West, his discussions had been more like anecdotes. "I can tell, Spencer. You've really been thinking about this. Those topics sound like chapter headings."

"They're lecture titles in the seminar I've been teaching in California. If I wrote a book, I'd probably specialize in miners and madams."

"Why?"

"I have reason to believe there were examples of both in my heritage. And I'm pretty sure there was a horse thief swinging from one of the branches of ye olde Kendall family tree."

"Really? You've got to tell me more about this."

Wendy presented Spencer with a total and rang up her sale. Then, almost immediately, she returned to watching the television set above the cash register.

" 'Bye," Julia called out as they left. "I'll be seeing you."

"You can return the shoes when you're done with them."

Why would Julia want to do that? She needed all the magic she could get, and the shoes seemed to work remarkably well. She'd certainly undergone a transformation. She'd had her hair done. And she was wearing clothes that a respectable accountant shouldn't be caught dead in. Oh no, she'd keep the shoes. If it meant getting Spencer, she'd wear these platform heels for the rest of her life.

After they left the shop and headed back toward downtown, Julia had the premonition that her afternoon with him was progressing a bit too well. She felt gorgeous in her new forest green dress. Nor could she complain about Spencer's behavior. He'd been attentive, even gallant. They hadn't argued since this morning, when he dropped the bombshell about moving permanently to California.

She tilted back her head in the convertible, allowing the last rays of sunset to warm her cheeks. Even the weather was clear and sunny. So why was she scanning the skies for rain clouds?

Why not accept her good fortune? Maybe she and Spencer were on their way to happily ever after. Maybe, after tonight's planned seduction, he would move back to Denver and they would share a lifetime.

Maybe. She frowned. *You can't take maybe to the bank.* If prior experience held true, disaster usually struck at the very moment when everything seemed perfect. Like last April sixteenth, when she'd completed her tax returns.

All this compatibility had to be an illusion. How could the city air smell clean? Why would traffic noise sound like a melody to her ears?

"I can't decide," Spencer said. "You look so beautiful, I want to show you off. At the same time, I want to keep you all to myself and not share you with anyone else. Should I take you out for dinner or carry you off to my room at the Brown and call room service?"

"Here's a radical concept," she said. "Ask me what I'd like to do."

"Right," he said. "Julia? What would you like

to do this evening? Dinner? Do you still want to go dancing? Or maybe a ride in the mountains?"

"I don't know." She held the shimmering material of her scarf between her fingers, studying the flowing pattern of blue and green and silver like the ripple of sun on a distant sea.

"No plans?" he asked.

"Not a single one."

"That's my favorite kind of date. Let's just let things happen, let the night unfold." He pulled to a halt at a stoplight and turned toward her. His blue eyes teased. "Should we eat dinner here?"

"Why not?"

He parked in front of a Seventeenth Avenue restaurant. Through the wide front window, Julia could see white tablecloths, candlelight, and the dull gleam of heavy silver. An expensive choice, she thought. Spencer must be making good money in California.

After perusing the menu, she decided that it was only fair to offer to pay her own part, even though she had far exceeded her budget with the makeover and the fancy underwear.

Spencer wouldn't hear of it. "This is my treat."

"But—"

"The proper response, my dear accountant, when someone offers to pay is, thank you."

"Thank you."

But she couldn't stop herself from thinking about finances. That was what she did. If Spencer moved back here to write a book, he would probably take a cut in pay. Could he afford it? In her mind, this was a significant issue, but she knew he would never talk about money. Whenever she brought up the topic of finance, he claimed ignorance. And he probably wasn't being evasive. She had, after all, seen his checkbook, and it was a disaster.

But she needed to know. In good conscience, Julia couldn't seduce him into staying in Denver if it meant financial devastation for him. Slyly, she offered, "Tell you what, Spencer. In exchange for dinner and this dress, I'll do your taxes."

"The dress is really more my treat than yours," he said. "It's lovely."

"It's beautiful," she agreed wholeheartedly. "I don't really do justice—"

"You're lovely, Julia. And the proper response is?"

"Thank you."

He lifted his wineglass in a toast. "I'd love to have you do my taxes. Matter of fact, I can't think of anyone I'd rather have handling my assets."

The rim of her crystal glass clinked with his. "You won't be disappointed."

"Tomorrow," he said, "I'll have my papers transferred to Buchanan and Gallegos."

"Who's your accountant now?"

"Thurston Heath."

"Interesting," she said. "Thurston Heath is the Tiffany of local accounting firms. They only handle the wealthy."

"Or the people who have lived in Colorado for generations, like my family."

She eyed him suspiciously. "Spencer? Are you rich?"

"I've never really thought about it."

"Really? That's incredible."

"Why is that hard to believe?"

"I tend to identify people by their cash flow. I could more easily tell you my clients' bank balances than their names." She leaned across the table, pursuing this unlikely topic for candlelight musings. "Give me a hint. What's your tax bracket?"

He shrugged. "I really don't know."

"So your move to California wasn't based on financial considerations?"

"Absolutely not. It was a move to a prestigious school with an interesting assignment."

"You're so vague," she said.

"And you're so precise."

"But we do have something in common," she said. "We're both ambitious. You're going after prestige and knowledge. I'm after money. We're two sides of the same coin."

"Fine," he said. "I'll be heads. You be tails."

"I want to be heads," she objected. "Besides, you have a very nice tail."

"I have a *what*?"

She grinned innocently. "The proper response is . . ."

"Thank you."

"So, Spencer, tell me about the miners and the madams in the Kendall family."

As they talked, they ate their way through salads and entrées. Julia had selected trout almondine and asparagus for the main course, and she drank her share of a half liter of chardonnay.

By the end of the meal, her need for conversation had waned. She felt warm but not lazy, not blissfully contented. An inner heat prickled within her. Her plot to seduce him had, perhaps, backfired. In enticing Spencer, she'd started a fire in herself, and she really wanted to make love to him. Her mind filled with sensual images. Her body tightened, needing his caress.

"Do you still want to go dancing?" he asked.

Softly, she replied, "I want you to hold me. There should be music. I want to feel your heart beating against mine."

He took her to his suite at the Brown Palace.

A suite, Julia mused. This was posh! It was fully furnished in good imitation antiques with two small but elegant chandeliers. "This has got to be costing a bundle, Spencer."

"I'm not paying," he said. "I was offered this room by the Historical Preservation Society."

"Why?"

"There's been a flap about their use of funding. I guess my job is to lend some authenticity to their work."

"So that's why you came back to Denver."

"Maybe," he said.

"And what are you supposed to do for the society?"

"There was an interview on television, and I'm going around to sites with them on Monday after the ball."

"Nice work if you can get it. For this you get a suite?"

"There aren't many perks to being a professor. Don't begrudge me this one."

She glanced around the room. "And what have you done with the dog?"

"Icy? He's staying with Aunt Ginny."

"You're so irresponsible."

"And you love it," he said. Spencer turned on the radio, searching until he found the slow, jazzy music he preferred. He dimmed the lights in the room, pushed aside the coffee table in

front of the Queen Anne–style sofa, and plucked
a single blood red rose from the Waterford vase
on a display table.

With a formal bow, he offered her the rose.

"For you." He took her in his arms. Holding
Julia gave him a sense of completeness, fulfillment, harmony. "To be absolutely truthful—"

"That's a stretch for you."

"There's only one real reason I came back to
Denver. For you, Julia. I missed you so much
when we were apart."

"Tell me."

"I missed having someone who would remind
me when I needed to change the oil in the car
and to keep track of where I'd left my dry cleaning."

"How romantic!"

"I can't manage without you. I lost half my
socks. I was constantly late to class until I set my
clocks a half hour ahead. I missed the way you
keep me organized."

Wryly, she said, "You're really turning me on,
Spencer."

"I'm getting to that part."

"Hurry," she whispered.

"Most of all, I missed this. Touching you.
Holding you. Feeling your body against mine.
You have the softest skin."

When she leaned against him, her breasts
pressed against his chest. Perfect breasts, he
thought. Her hips snuggled against his. He
rubbed his cheek through the silken texture of
her hair. She was an absolute marvel. No other
woman could be so perfect for him.

When she tilted back her head, offering her

lips, he tasted them gently. Although a blast furnace of passion raged within him, urging haste to quench the flames, he wanted to go slowly, to stretch this pleasure into eternity.

Yet Julia tightened her arms around him. Her embrace was hard, insistent. Her mouth opened. Her tongue . . .

Spencer kissed her, full and fierce. This was the dance he'd been waiting for.

And Julia was a brilliant partner. Gracefully, she stepped away from his embrace. Weaving rhythmically to the music, she untied the scarf at her throat. The silky material slithered down her body.

His desire was full-blown, and he had to fight for control. He had to think about something else, something rote, something dull. Mentally, he began to recite the U.S. presidents in order. *George Washington, John Adams, Thomas Jefferson, James*—

Her hazel eyes were smoky as she continued her dance, lifting her arms, swaying her hips.

James Madison, James Monroe, John Quincy—

Slinking toward him, she lightly stroked his cheek and stretched her arms to encompass his shoulders. "Should I give you a massage?"

"Are you seducing me?"

"That's correct."

"I like that." *John Quincy Adams, Andrew Jackson*—

By the time she'd unbuttoned his shirt and unfastened the top button on his jeans, Spencer was up to Warren G. Harding. He couldn't hold back any longer.

Scooping her into his arms, he carried her into

the bedroom. With driving haste, he unfastened the straps on her shoes and removed them. He pulled her long dress over her head.

"White cotton panties," he said.

"I could change into that slinky garter belt."

He couldn't wait that long. "Don't."

"But it might be—"

He couldn't endure another moment of teasing. He wanted her naked body next to his own. He peeled off her underwear and bra. "You're perfect."

"Nobody's perfect."

Her voice sounded a slightly discordant note, and she frowned. Of course, she wanted this moment when they made love again to be exactly right, good for both of them.

"Are you okay?" he asked.

"A little nervous." What if she disappointed him? What if they'd both been waiting so long, imagining such marvels, that they discovered they weren't all that spectacular together anymore? What if they'd lost the magic?

"Don't ask me to wait," he said. "I've only got a handful of presidents left."

He pulled off his jeans.

Magnificent, she thought. His body. His strength.

But this wasn't going the way she'd planned. They should have talked about commitment, about how he would never leave her again. Panic twisted her stomach into knots. Things were going too fast. If she made love to him now without extracting promises, he might leave tomorrow, never to be seen again. Oh, why was she having these doubts? Why couldn't she allow the magic to happen? "My shoes."

"What?"

"Spencer, my dearest, I have to wear my shoes."

He closed his eyes and lowered his head. *Reagan, Bush, Clinton.* "Why?"

She scuttled down to the end of the bed, dragging the quilt with her, and searched the floor until she saw the shimmer of iridescent green and blue. She fastened the shoes on her feet and sighed. Now there could be magic.

Spencer lay flat on his back. "What's going on, Julia? Why are you—"

"Nothing. Really."

"You're wearing your shoes to bed. What is this? Some kind of mojo?"

"What's a mojo?"

"A good luck charm."

"Exactly." She dove back onto the bed and pulled the covers up to her chin. "Now we need to talk."

"You talk." He dug under the covers and pulled out her left leg. Holding her foot by the sole of her shoe, he extended her leg. Lightly, he traced a quivering line from her heel all the way up to her buttocks.

Julia watched in rapt fascination as he did the same with the other leg. When he kissed the back of her knees, she groaned with pleasure.

Slowly, he spread her legs and leaned over her.

His mouth claimed hers, and she responded with an unquenchable hunger. She couldn't get enough of him. Couldn't get enough of his kissing, his touching. She clung to him, breathless. With her last shred of willpower, she said,

"You've got to promise that you'll never leave me again."

"I promise."

The fierce passion of his kiss left her weak and breathless. His fingers stroked and teased the delicate flesh of her breasts. Her nipples ached with need for him.

She was beyond words, yet she said, "You've got to mean it."

"Anything you say."

His hands went lower, stealing across her belly, and he caressed her most intimate flesh.

"Oh God, Spencer."

She couldn't ask for more. His touch drove her mad. She held herself perfectly still while waves of desire crashed around her. When he held her close, his strength and her softness melted together in an almost perfect expression of passion.

Two sides of a coin. Joined.

Her mind went blank. Willingly, she submitted to the pure, unadulterated pleasure of the moment.

His touch was so skillful, so tantalizing, so right. He knew when to apply friction and when to hold back until she was begging for more. She needed him. For long months she had craved this passion more than she'd known.

When finally he thrust himself into her, her gasp of pleasure mingled with his own. Hard and fast, he stroked. Then slower. She writhed beneath him, yearning for fulfillment.

Higher and higher. She was panting. Her body was slick. She cried out. In one exact instant, she reached orgasm simultaneously with him. Together they formed the perfect arc of passion.

Her body quaked and trembled in the aftermath. *Oh my God.*

A gentle silence surrounded them.

She slept in his arms, nestled against him. For once her doubts were silent. Her dreams were magical.

7

The next morning, he was gone. Julia discovered his absence when she groped across the pillows and stabbed her fingers on the prickly thorns of a blood red rose.

"Ow!" She grabbed the note he'd written on Brown Palace stationery and placed beneath the rose—a romantic gesture, though somewhat lacking in practicality.

My dearest Julia. It seems the Historical Preservation Society actually has some work they expect me to do. We'll talk later. Spencer. There was a postscript. *Last night was the single most perfect experience of my entire life. Your proper response is?*

"Thank you," she said aloud. "Me, too."

Bedazzled with morning-after contentment, she meandered around the suite. She was humming—no, not humming. She was purring like a cat with a bowl full of heavy cream. Her usual tension, the drive to get things done, was absent. She felt almost irresponsible.

In the bathroom, she found a plush terry cloth

robe and slipped into it. The countertop was littered with Spencer's shaving equipment, and she inhaled the masculine fragrance of his aftershave until it tickled her nostrils.

Finally, she located her purse and checked her wristwatch. Nine-thirty? It was nine-thirty on a weekday and she'd just crawled out of bed?

How decadent! She wasn't at work, hadn't even called in to let Karen know where she was, and—astonishingly—the world hadn't ended.

Julia patted herself on the back. There was something to be said for not taking herself too seriously.

Lazily, she sprawled in one of the suite's antique Queen Anne–style chairs, called room service, and ordered coffee.

This was a fine life.

But it really wasn't Julia's life.

No matter how relaxed she was, she couldn't keep her busy little brain from making plans. Thus far, she'd successfully completed her first goal: seduction.

She had even gotten Spencer to vow never to leave her. Though a contract made in the heat of passion probably wasn't binding, it was a promise after all. Now what?

She picked up his note and studied his scribbled handwriting, looking for clues about what to do next.

The ball! Obviously, since Spencer had been brought here by the Historical Preservation Society, he would be required to attend the Unsinkable Molly Brown Ball. But he didn't know she had an invitation! A gala event like the ball would be the last place he'd expect to see a small-time accountant like herself.

Julia chuckled.

Carefully, she worded a note: *My darling Spencer, thank you for last night. Pure pleasure is so irresponsible, and so very glorious. Something has come up. I'll be busy today but will contact you tomorrow.*

How should she sign it?

She hesitated only an instant before writing with bold, sure strokes: *All my love, Julia.*

He'd be shocked when she showed up at the ball like a modern day Cinderella in flashy platform shoes. Spencer was always the one who popped up with surprises. But tonight, the trick would be on him.

At eleven o'clock, she strolled into the offices of Buchanan and Gallegos, still wearing her sleeveless dress and scarf from the night before. Her quandary about what to tell Karen was solved when her partner confronted her with a scowl.

"Julia, we have to talk about Spencer."

"What about Spencer?" A nasty prickle of apprehension went through her. Julia didn't want bad news. She went to the office coffeepot and filled her mug. "What has he done?"

"His accounting files were delivered here this morning by a messenger from Thurston Heath." She gestured to four cardboard packing boxes the size of orange crates. "Apparently, Thurston Heath has been taking care of our boy Spencer since birth, and they've kept his so-called records exactly as he delivered them. I've never seen such chaos."

"And what's the bad news?" Julia waited for the other shoe to drop. The whole reason she'd wanted his files was to snoop into his life, and she felt a bit sleazy about it. "Is he destitute? Is he in debt up to his eyebrows?"

"From what I can tell, he's okay. Not rich. Not poor. Average. But he could have been a millionaire."

"What do you mean?"

"I've only flipped through a couple of files, but I've found a pattern of long, detailed letters from the Thurston Heath financial advisers regarding possible investments. Spencer's response is usually a no-brainer sentence, saying yes or no."

That seemed typical of him to Julia. "I still don't see the problem. That sounds exactly like Spencer."

"He turned down an opportunity to invest—during the early days—in what is now a multi-billion dollar computer company. And do you want to know why? Because he had an opportunity to go to Tibet."

A smile twitched at the corners of Julia's mouth.

Karen continued, "However, Spencer chose to throw away thousands of dollars on a llama farm that one of his friends established. All the llamas escaped during mating season."

Julia laughed.

"Not funny," Karen said. "Not only has his portfolio been managed sloppily, but it's going to take a month of Sundays to clean this up."

"With any luck, I'll have that long."

Karen's eyebrows formed a quizzical arch. "I'm surprised at you. This kind of inefficiency usually drives you right up the wall."

"Not anymore." Julia perched on the edge of her desk. In her relationship with Spencer, this understanding was something of an epiphany.

There should have been a spotlight and a drum-roll. Instead, her office looked the same as it did on the other 364 days of the year. "Spencer's not going to change. He's not going to remember to tell me everything. He'll lose important papers and never send in a warranty. He's always going to make decisions from his heart instead of his head. And I like him exactly the way he is."

"My goodness, Julia. It sounds like you're in love."

"I am not discounting that possibility at the present time."

Julia bounced to her feet and circled the crates that contained the financial history of Spencer Kendall's life. "Is there anything in there that I should know about? Seven ex-wives? Twenty children? A criminal record?"

"Probably not, but how could I tell?" Karen muttered. "I hope you're charging him plenty for this work."

"My, my, just yesterday you were singing his praises."

"You've always said he was disorganized, but I never realized what a complete absentminded mess he was."

"Don't worry about it, Karen. Spencer will be my own personal reclamation project. There was really only one thing I wanted to know from his financial files. I wanted to know that he wasn't dead broke, that he doesn't need to keep the job in California to pay his bills."

"Not as far as I can tell."

Julia set down her coffee mug and allowed her gaze to wander around their offices, taking inventory of the sleek file cabinets and tidy desks and state-of-the-art computer equipment. "You know, partner, I'm really happy with this business we've established here. I think we're going to make it."

"You bet we will."

"And I don't feel guilty at all about taking the rest of the day off so I can get ready for the ball. I promise to come back with dozens of new clients." She scanned her office again. "You know what we need in here?"

"What?"

"Some plants. Maybe an aspen tree. And artwork. Something big and splashy. Something red."

"Splashy?"

She strode toward the door. "By the way, if Spencer happens to call, don't mention that I'm going to the ball."

"Julia?"

"What?"

"I love your new hairdo. The color is really attractive."

"Yeah, sure. Ronald McDonald wasn't using it this week and—" She stopped herself. *The proper response was . . .* "Thank you, Karen. I like it, too."

"I hope everything works out between you and Spencer. But, whatever you do, don't suggest merging assets."

"I hope we can find something more interesting to merge."

After a full day away from the office with the home answering machine picking up her calls, Julia felt rested, and her contentment showed. Her outfit and hair had turned out beautifully. The strapless green and blue sequined bodice of her gown fit well, and the straight black crepe skirt flowed easily when she walked, displaying just the right amount of leg in the slit. She'd managed an upsweep with tendrils for her hair. Even her lipstick was on straight.

But she still felt a shiver of nervousness when she parked downtown and made her way toward Currigan Hall, where the Unsinkable Molly Brown Ball was being held.

As she joined the glittering throng, Julia was very much aware that she was wearing a secondhand dress and crazy, already worn shoes. She didn't belong here. Julia hadn't been raised as a debutante. She wasn't accustomed to attending fancy, upper crust affairs.

Searching within herself for the confidence she'd had in abundance only hours ago, she tried to take a positive outlook based on the namesake of this event, Molly Brown, who was a trashy nouveau riche miner's wife when she moved to Denver. Molly was promptly rejected by the elite of society, who were, Julia thought, probably some of Spencer's ancestors.

Just as Molly had refused to be snubbed and would not apologize for her roots, Julia would not succumb to feeling sorry for her upbringing. Wearing her magic shoes, she would hold her head up high. Molly Brown had been undefeated, an unsinkable passenger when the *Titanic* went down. And Julia vowed to be the same way. She'd be cool, calm, and collected, pretending that she belonged here.

At the entrance, a doorman dressed in livery took her invitation. Was she supposed to smile at him, tip him, or ignore him?

"Thanks," she said when he returned the engraved card.

"You are most welcome, madam."

Madam? Nobody had ever called her madam. Julia wished her mother could see her now, hanging around with the rich folks, just as if she belonged here.

Spectacular decorations and effective lighting had transformed the cavernous hall into a turn-of-the-century ballroom. The chandeliers, oak wainscoting, and antique furniture were probably all real. What kind of insurance did they have on this stuff?

Waiters in white vests circulated with trays full of exotic savories and sweet tidbits. Others offered Champagne. A twelve-piece band played a wide range of dance music, something for everyone.

For a few minutes, Julia stood and watched the elegant men and gorgeous women as they danced. A cha-cha. A tango.

Then, across the room, she spied Spencer. In his classic black tuxedo and starched white shirt, he was dashing and sophisticated. The respected college professor. A gentleman from his head to his toes. He looked like a million bucks.

Slowly, Julia walked toward him. It was probably her imagination, but it seemed as if the crowd parted to let her through. She was only a few yards from him when he turned and saw her.

The instant of surprise in his gaze was worth her small subterfuge. His eyes widened. He gasped, and then he welcomed her with all his heart. His smile was dazzling white. His blue eyes sparkled with a tender intimacy.

As she returned his gaze, the rest of the glamour faded into a glittery background. Without saying a word, he offered his arm and escorted her to the dance floor as the band played a tango.

Under her breath, she whispered, "I don't know how to dance to this music."

"Neither does anyone else."

"So what do we do?"

"Fake it."

He held her tightly. They lunged and dipped gracefully—if erratically—and Julia was laughing by the time the music changed.

After a few minutes of the next dance, she decided that the jitterbug was easy, a cross between the Charleston and the twist. And she loved the waltzes that followed. In Spencer's arms she felt brilliant and beautiful. When he twirled her and her skirt flared, Julia finally knew the meaning of magic.

During pauses in the dancing, he introduced her to the wealthy people she'd come here to meet. Philanthropists. Investors. Lots of people who needed an accounting service. Everybody was polite, congenial, and pleasant.

Well, why wouldn't they be? They were all rich. Or maybe not. Maybe, like her, they were faking.

She leaned close to Spencer. "Aren't you surprised that I'm here?"

"Yes."

"Admit it, Spencer. I gotcha."

"You did. I knew, because of your new hairdo, that you were going someplace special. But I didn't know it was here."

"I guess it wouldn't be ladylike to gloat."

"I guess not. And I have a surprise for you later on."

"Tell me now."

"Then it won't be a surprise."

He took her arm and introduced her to Jason Thurston, the half owner of Thurston Heath and a very big man in Denver's financial district.

"This is the lady who's going to be handling my money from now on," Spencer said.

Though there should have been an uncomfortable, competitive coolness between the two accountants firms, Thurston pumped her outstretched hand with great enthusiasm. "I can't tell you how happy I am to meet you. Spencer's a great guy, but he's driven several of our accountants to nervous breakdowns."

"I'll try to take good care of him," she replied.

"Tell me about your firm," he said. "You're new, aren't you?"

In quick order, their conversation turned to investments and the new tax legislation. Julia was well aware that she was now in the big leagues. She'd just stepped up to the plate, and the elderly Thurston seemed delighted to welcome her onto his playing field.

More importantly, Julia thought, Spencer had a surprise for her. What could it be? Did it have something to do with another long, marvelous night of lovemaking in his Brown Palace suite? She hoped so. That would make the perfect ending for a beautiful night.

Julia was so proud of herself. Of Spencer, too. He was so classy and handsome as he jumped from one conversation to another.

She watched him as he conversed with all these other fascinating people—professors, property owners, antique dealers. Spencer fit right in, and so did she. Julia couldn't have been happier.

While Thurston treated her to a detailed analysis of the current legislation, she allowed her attention to wander. From the melange of voices, she easily picked out Spencer's baritone.

"That's right," he was saying. "I've been offered the job, and I've accepted."

A shiver raced down Julia's spine. *What job? Was he talking about the school in California?*

"They've agreed to give me time to work on my book," he said. "It's a great opportunity. And I'll be doing my own seminar on the history of the Old West."

The seminar! He was talking about California.

He continued. "Starting right away. Of course, it will take a while to get all my things packed up."

He was leaving her. Again.

So that was his surprise! Julia felt like screaming. Betrayed! He had broken his promise! Once again, Spencer had plunged a dagger straight into her heart just when she thought she was safe. Suddenly, her pulse was throbbing. She could hardly force herself to breathe. She had to get away from here, to find someplace where she could cry or yell or throw things. Somehow she had to release this horrible, gut-churning pain.

Politely, she excused herself from her conversation with Thurston. They exchanged cards. He promised to call. They would do lunch.

I've got to get out of here.

Without calling attention to herself, Julia sidled through the crowd, gaining speed as she moved toward escape. By the time she reached the door, she was almost running. She paused.

A grandfather clock beside the door showed that it was one minute until midnight. How damned appropriate! Here she was—Cinderella at the ball—and Spencer's betrayal was about to pitch her back to the ashes.

She raced out onto Fourteenth Street. The glare of headlights smacked her into harsh reality. Julia groaned. A sob caught in the back of her throat. This was the best night of her life. And the worst.

Where had she parked her car? She had to get away from here. Now! Right now!

"Julia! Julia, wait!"

It was Spencer. He had actually followed her. Was he crazy? Didn't he know that she wanted to kill him?

She whirled. "You bastard!"

"What did I do?"

"Oh, don't you dare play innocent with me. When were you going to tell me? How were you planning to break this little surprise to me? Maybe you'd just leave while I was sleeping and I'd wake up and find you gone to California."

"What the hell are you talking about?"

"I overheard your conversation. You were telling somebody how you had accepted the job in California and they would let you have time off to write and you were departing just as soon as you got packed."

"That's right," he said. "As soon as I get packed."

"Damn you, Spencer. We could have had something wonderful!"

"I'm leaving California."

"You idiot! Don't you understand? I love you!" She blinked. *What had he just said?* "You're leaving California?"

"I accepted a job offer. At Wellington Women's College, here in Denver. I'm not the head of the department, and I'm not earning a fortune, but they are going to allow me to make up my own schedule so I'll have time to work on my book." His eyebrows lifted. In a very gentle voice, he said, "And I love you, too."

"You're coming back?" Her anger subsided like a swiftly ebbing surf, gathering strength for a crashing tidal wave of inexpressible, gratifying happiness. Finally, she could dare to hope, to dream, to believe in magic. "You love me?"

"I can't live without you. When I saw you running away from the ball, like Cinderella at midnight, I knew that I would pursue you to the ends of the earth."

"Like Cinderella?"

"Yes, Julia."

"And you're my handsome prince?"

He went down on one knee before her. In his tuxedo, he looked like a old-fashioned gentleman. "My beautiful, wild Julia, I'm not a prince, not a rich man. I'm just an absentminded history professor who loves you and wants to spend the rest of his life with you."

"Oh, Spencer. I love you, too. I have for such a terribly long time. But—"

"What is it? My darling, what's wrong?"

"It's the shoes."

His expression turned guarded. "What about the shoes? You don't have some sort of weird ritual with the shoes in mind, do you? I mean, we are on a public street and—"

"The shoes are magical, and I want to make sure you're not under some kind of enchanted spell. I want this moment to be real."

"Whatever you want, Julia." He leaned over and unfastened the straps. "What we have here is Cinderella in reverse. Instead of finding the princess and fitting the glass slipper to her foot, I'm taking off your shoes."

He removed the glittering platform heels and stood before her.

"Now," she said, "ask me again."

"I adore you, Julia. Please, my dearest, consent to be my wife."

"Yes." This was real and true. As she glided into his welcoming embrace, she went up on her tiptoes for a barefoot kiss. "I love you with all my heart and both my soles."

Cassie Miles

CASSIE MILES is a woman who likes to keep both feet on the ground. When she moved to Colorado, she learned to downhill ski, cross-country ski, and water-ski. Basically, she participated in any activity that required fastening boards to her feet. Now, many years later, she spends most of her spare time reading, watching movies, attending theater and ballet performances, and keeping track of her two teenage daughters. Her idea of the perfect afternoon is a long walk to a small café where she can order a latte and sip slowly while the sun slides down behind the mountains. Travel is definitely on the agenda for her future, as long as she can get from point A to point B without boarding an aircraft.

The midlife crisis of Cassie Miles was not a pretty sight. Though she became a writer full time, and that was a very good thing, she lost a husband, a house, and a ton of security. However, after this descent into the bleakest of bleak despair, she found the most wonderful man. He's tall and skinny and still has all his hair. He makes her laugh when her two daughters threaten to destroy her sense of humor. Finding romance the second time around has been the most amazing surprise. This story and all the others are dedicated to Rick, who taught a jaded romance writer how to love again.

Discover Contemporary Romances
at Their Sizzling Hot Best
from Avon Books

THE LOVES OF
RUBY DEE
by Curtiss Ann Matlock

78106-9/$5.99 US/$7.99 Can

JONATHAN'S WIFE
by Dee Holmes

78368-1/$5.99 US/$7.99 Can

DANIEL'S GIFT
by Barbara Freethy

78189-1/$5.99 US/$7.99 Can

FAIRYTALE
by Maggie Shayne

78300-2/$5.99 US/$7.99 Can

Coming Soon

WISHES COME TRUE
by Patti Berg

78338-X/$5.99 US/$7.99 Can

Avon Romantic Treasures

Unforgettable, enthralling love stories,
sparkling with passion and adventure
from Romance's bestselling authors

LADY OF SUMMER *by Emma Merritt*
77984-6/$5.50 US/$7.50 Can

HEARTS RUN WILD *by Shelly Thacker*
78119-0/$5.99 US/$7.99 Can

JUST ONE KISS *by Samantha James*
77549-2/$5.99 US/$7.99 Can

SUNDANCER'S WOMAN *by Judith E. French*
77706-1/$5.99 US/$7.99 Can

RED SKY WARRIOR *by Genell Dellin*
77526-3/ $5.50 US/ $7.50 Can

KISSED *by Tanya Anne Crosby*
77681-2/$5.50 US/$7.50 Can

MY RUNAWAY HEART *by Miriam Minger*
78301-0/ $5.50 US/ $7.50 Can

RUNAWAY TIME *by Deborah Gordon*
77759-2/ $5.50 US/ $7.50 Can